Nightfall
Book Two of the Chronicles of Arden

First Edition

Shiriluna Nott & SaJa H.

For Dave. Thanks for sticking with me through this crazy adventure.
—Shiriluna Nott

Chhaya keep vigil, for one of your children comes. My heart is heavy
as my sister crosses the veil today. In loving memory of Amy Barrett.
Without you, sister, I may have never found my voice.
—SaJa H.

If you would like to receive notifications regarding upcoming releases in the *Chronicles of Arden* series, please sign up for Shiriluna Nott's mailing list here; http://www.shirilunanott.com/mailinglist.html
We only send updates when a new book is released.

Links to other books in the *Chronicles of Arden* series:

A CALL TO ARMS: BOOK ONE
http://www.amazon.com/dp/B00OK3HUSI

TABLE OF CONTENTS

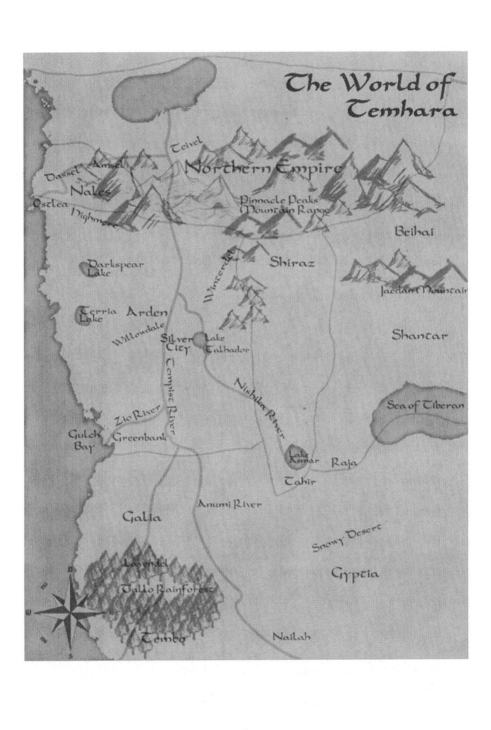

PROLOGUE

Deep below ground, not a single trace of light penetrated the thick walls of the passage. Constructed from marble and brick and devoid of any windows, the corridor was darker than a moonless night. The sound of water trickling through crevasses in the damp stone wall and the stench of rotted moss and dirt were the only indications the corridor was anything more than a hollow void.

A shrouded figure made his way through the encompassing gloom, features hidden beneath a cloak of linen. The man moved with deft silence, his footfalls assured despite the lack of light. Above him, cobwebs spanned the ceiling like tents of yellowed silk. Spiderlings skittered along the webbing, seeking out their next meal, but the sight caused the shrouded man no distress. Such horrors were commonplace here.

The passage seemed to stretch into infinity, but at last the man came to an archway where a door stood ajar. Faint light glimmered beyond the threshold, beckoning him forward. He slipped through the entrance, glancing only once over his shoulder to ensure no one followed.

Once inside the chamber, he pressed white hands to the ancient oaken wood, and the squeal of protesting hinges resonated through the darkness. The door slid shut, locking the room from the outside world.

Soft words fell from the shrouded man's mouth as he uttered an incantation. Almost instantly, a swirl of hazy-blue mist illuminated the door frame as the man's warding spell settled into place. No prying eyes or ears would infiltrate the meeting tonight.

He turned from the door, facing the interior of the room. The space was small, a former torture chamber or prison cell, perhaps, and certainly no place for civilized company to assemble. The quarters were cramped and the lack of comfort offensive, but given the earnestness of the message he'd received, the shrouded man hoped he'd be rewarded for suffering such inconveniences.

A table sat in the center of the room, and a lone mage orb hovered above, bathing the chamber in eerie false light and bringing attention to the two men who sat waiting. The shrouded man took the last remaining seat.

"I'd begun to think you'd taken it upon yourself not to show," said the first man, his voice a hiss from the far side of the table.

Distrust lingered in his words, and the shrouded man held back the urge to smirk. Trust was a frivolity reserved for the weak and foolish. The two men gathered at the table were neither of those things, which made them all the more dangerous.

The shrouded man responded without hesitation. He knew better than to show even the slightest trace of frailty. To do so would be to seal his fate. In this land, the ruthless prevailed and the feeble were plucked from power like weeds. "Never fear. My loyalty is true and steadfast. I had to ensure I was alone before coming."

The third and final man leaned closer to the mage orb, clasping pale, boney hands together. "Now that we're all accounted for, shall we begin?"

The shrouded man could feel shrewd eyes watching him. He set his jaw in a defiant gesture and returned the stare. Their menacing scowls sought to undo him, but he remained undisturbed. He had prior experience dealing with cutthroat and power-hungry politicians. Attempts to rattle his confidence almost always failed.

"We've been watching you for some time now."

He'd known, of course. He welcomed the scrutiny. If they'd been observing him, they surely knew how committed he was to their cause.

"Do you know why you've been summoned?"

The shrouded man inclined his head. "You wish to take control of the gem in the south and require my assistance."

Icy blue eyes penetrated his flesh like shards of glass. "The gem has been in trouble for some time now."

The shrouded man issued a dark chuckle. "I'd wager placing agents inside its borders has finally begun to pay off."

"Yes, but not quickly enough. We grow increasingly discontent with the sluggish progress being made."

Again, the shrouded man nodded. "The betrayer hinders our work. The gem shines far less brightly for its imperfection."

The thud of a fist slamming the table resonated off the stone walls. "Our agents have been attempting to dismantle the betrayer for years, but despite our best efforts, he continues to cling to his undeserved pedestal, perverting the ideals of the Giver of All Power and making a mockery of the order we established there centuries ago!"

"The arrogant worm has proven clever," replied the shrouded man after a bout of tense silence. "But he's not indestructible. Two years ago, one of our agents came close to wiping the imperfection clean. The betrayer's time is limited."

"It's time for this *imperfection* to be dealt with once and for all. It's time to reclaim what is ours by right."

A villainous smile crept over the shrouded man's mouth. "If you give me the means to take care of the problem, I vow to see the task through.

I assure you my spine is thicker than those you already employ. Many of them lack the conviction to be entrusted with a mission of such importance. But not I." Licking dry lips, he planned his next words with caution. "Of course, I hope my loyalty won't fall upon blind eyes."

"I can ensure you'll be rewarded accordingly, should you please us. Our favor isn't easily won, but those who succeed are bestowed power beyond their comprehension." The pale-handed man's voice dropped to a guttural snarl. "However, if you should fail—"

"I will not fail."

The silence following the bold assertion should have unnerved the shrouded man, but he'd lost his sense of fear years ago.

"Very well," said the sinister voice.

In the encroaching darkness, a trinket was pushed across the table toward him. The light of the mage orb reflected off the polished face of a small, turquoise gemstone. To any common fool, it would have seemed nothing more than a beautiful jewel, but he knew better. Even before he touched it, he could sense the disconcerting magic emanating from within.

Exhilaration flooded his veins as he took the stone, rolling the polished gem in the palm of his hand. "Is this part of the new plan?"

"The plan has already been set into motion. We need only an agent cunning enough to deliver the final blow—the blow that will destroy the betrayer and reinstate our ultimate rule over the gem in the south." The shadowed man raised one hand, blotting out the light of the mage orb. He leaned across the table, eyes glistening like eerie globules. "Are you ready to claim your place of power?"

A shrewd smile broke across the shrouded man's face. He clasped the turquoise stone, holding it tightly against his chest. "What need I do?"

CHAPTER ONE

Gibben Nemesio set a hand on his brother's shoulder. "Are you ready to meet Dean Marc?"

Calisto, the youngest of the Nemesio children, looked up at Gib and nodded eagerly. "Yes! I've been ready for the last two years."

It was a week until Harvest, the beginning of a new year and the start of Gib's last semester at Academy. The beautiful cherry trees lining the courtyard had already turned from pink to orange, and the nights were cold enough to warrant extra fire at the hearth. The streets of Silver City bustled in preparation for the imminent festivities. The autumn crop had been bountiful—surely a sign of good fortune from the Goddesses, Chhaya and Daya. If luck were on their side, a mild winter would follow. Despite the tension on Arden's northern and eastern borders, the mood around Silver was jovial.

Gib knew better than to be deceived by the illusion of safety, however. As the understudy of Seneschal Koal Adelwijn, right hand of the King, Gib saw daily the political power struggle which plagued the High Council of Arden. Radically different viewpoints threatened to boil over into a war that had nothing to do with their eastern neighbor, Shiraz. The real conflict had more to do with how Arden was being ruled, and with so much at stake, Gib found himself losing a fair amount of sleep.

Calisto all but skipped down the hallway to Dean Marc Arrio's office, the sound of his boots echoing off the smooth limestone walls. Having just celebrated his thirteenth Naming Day, Cal remained blissfully unaware of the raging political battles Gib witnessed every day, and the whispers of war were but a distant rumor to the young boy.

And I plan on keeping it that way as long as I can, Gib thought. *Daya knows I had to grow up too young. Tayver too. I want Cal to enjoy his childhood for as long as possible.*

Now a young man of sixteen, Gib's life was a stark contrast to how it had been when he was drafted three wheelturns prior. Gone was the gangling boy who had been plucked from his farm outside Willowdale and released into the middle of Silver City. He'd met highborns, councilors, royalty—the King of Arden himself. He'd trained with a prince, attended a grand ball at the palace, fallen in love, and even thwarted an assassination attempt. The story was so incredulous that Gib often found himself wondering if he were living a dream. Would he wake up any moment to find himself on the cold straw floor of his farmhouse, dressed in rags and worrying about his aching stomach? At times that seemed more plausible than the path fate had set him on.

"I'm glad there's no waiting line," Gib noted as they drew closer to the familiar polished door. "I have to eat lunch and be at the palace before the midday bell rings. Seneschal Koal told me he expected this afternoon's council session to be long."

Calisto's mouth curled downward. "You didn't have to come. If you're busy—"

"No, no. Liza brought me here on my first day. I can't very well break tradition now. Besides, I need to make sure my own classes are in order." Gib winked, earning a quiet titter from Calisto, and raised a fist to tap the door.

The two students waited only a brief moment before the door swung open, and the Dean of Academy himself came to greet them. Tall and slim, with dark hair that showed only the slightest grey flecking, Marc would have seemed intimidating if not for the twinkle in his dark eyes and the wide grin taking up the entirety of his face.

"Gib!" Marc exclaimed, smiling broadly as he reached down to give Gib a pat on the shoulder. "What are you doing here? I thought you'd already be on your way to the palace by now."

Gib returned the smile. Marc had an infectious personality and had always been kind to his students. His words of encouragement had helped Gib adjust to life at Academy when he'd first come to Silver City.

Setting a hand on Calisto's back, Gib gave the youngster a nudge forward. "I'll be on my way to the council meeting shortly. Dean Marc, this is Calisto. He's my—"

"Oh! This must be your little brother." Marc bent low and held out his hand for a shake. "*Daya*, you two could be twins!"

Calisto snickered as he shook the dean's large hand. "No, sir. I'm three years younger than Gib and already just as tall—and I'm definitely the more handsome of the two."

Gib's brown eyes danced. "Hey now! Be nice. I am understudy of Seneschal Koal, remember? You're supposed to treat me with respect." He ruffled Cal's curly mop of hair.

Cal beamed. "Understudy or not, in another few moonturns, *you'll* be looking up at *me*."

Gib's attempt to stifle a groan was in vain. It was true. Tayver, their middle brother, was already taller, and Cal threatened to close the gap any day now. *And I'm not even going to think about my friends. The last time I didn't have to look down at Nage was two years ago. Tarquin is a whole head taller than I, and he's still growing. It seems I'm destined to be surrounded by giants.*

Marc laughed at the banter as he stood back to his full height and motioned for the two brothers to come into the office. He shut the grand oak door behind them and gestured toward a pair of chairs meant for guests. "Please, have a seat. I take it you're here to get Calisto signed up for classes?"

"Yes," Gib replied. "He's going into the sentinel training program."

"I want to be in the cavalry unit someday," Cal added.

Marc slid into the chair behind his desk and pulled out a fresh sheet of parchment. "Cavalry, eh? Do you know anything about horses, Calisto?"

Cal nodded enthusiastically. "Yes, sir. I've been a stable hand for the last two years over at the Broken Arrow Inn. I love horses. Gib warned me that it's really hard to get into the Royal Cavalry unit, but I figured if I work hard enough, I've got as good of a shot as anyone else."

Gib looked down at his feet to hide a grimace. *Hard* was the word he'd used when speaking to Cal about it, but what that really meant was the cavalry program was terribly *expensive*. He wasn't sure how he would ever pay for it, but he didn't want to crush his brother's dream so soon. Liza, their only sister and eldest sibling, had already expressed her desire to help pay for the extra schooling. Even Lady Mrifa, Koal's wife, had all but insisted the Adelwijn family sponsor Cal—assistance which Gib had politely declined. *I feel guilty enough having my schooling paid for by the Crown. I'll find another way to pay for Cal's tuition.*

As a true testament to Marc's benevolent character, the dean offered only encouragement. "It sounds like you've had some excellent experience, Calisto. I'm sure it will give you an advantage should you choose to pursue your dream." He dabbed a quill into an inkwell and scribbled onto the blank parchment. "For now though, weaponry class, Ardenian Law—how are your writing and reading skills?"

"Better than mine were when I first arrived." Gib chuckled.

Cal nodded in agreement. "I can read and write pretty good—err, *well*. I can do both well. Gib and Tay taught me."

Gib's heart throbbed in his chest as he recalled Joel Adelwijn's gentle corrections as Gib himself had been learning to read. The mage trainee never once lost his patience, despite Gib's many blunders. It all seemed so long ago now. *I can't believe it's been six moonturns since I saw him.*

Snow had been clinging to the ground the last time Gib had laid eyes on his companion. Upon graduation from Academy, Joel had been sent to the kingdom of Shantar as an understudy ambassador to complete his internship and become a fully trained mage. Saying goodbye had been difficult. Gib had grown accustomed to Joel being a constant, so not having him close was a hard adjustment to make.

Gib's stomach fluttered. *Surely he'll return any day now. The internship is bound to be over soon. It won't be long before we're together again.* He did his best to push thoughts of Joel Adelwijn aside. Neither time nor distance could ever break their bond. Soon Joel would be back, and life would return to the way it had been.

"All right, Calisto," Marc replied, never glancing up from his writing. "I'll put you in Ardenian History instead. Best to get *that* class out of the way as quickly as possible." The dean rolled his eyes inconspicuously. "I was hoping that damn fool Anders Malin-Rai would retire this year, but I suppose none of us can be so lucky."

Gib fought the grin which threatened to overtake his stoic features. "At least Diedrick Lyle resigned from the Instructions Master position. Your office must be peaceful now."

"Thank The Two," snorted Marc. "If only he'd resign from the High Council as well. Diedrick and Anders both. Neither would be missed, and surely their empty seats would be filled by someone less foul." The dean glanced up, knitting his eyebrows. "Sorry. I shouldn't be discussing this right now—and not in the presence of students."

Gib gave a stiff nod, recalling heated arguments between the members of the High Council. As Seneschal Koal's understudy, Gib was allowed to observe the meetings, and lately the debates had been brutal. King Rishi had only recently managed to raise the draft age from thirteen to sixteen, preventing young boys—children—from being whisked away from their families as Gib had been. While the ruling was immensely popular among the citizens, many of the councilors were disgruntled. The conflict with Shiraz was but one border skirmish away from being a real war and the recent buildup of forces on the Nales border was also a cause for concern. Despite the King's best effort to keep Arden from marching, King Rishi was losing his battle to the will of the High Council.

People like Diedrick Lyle and Anders Malin-Rai don't care if they're sending children into war, and as long as there are bodies to throw at the enemy, they'll never stop pushing for the law to be reversed. Gib stole a glance at his younger brother and was immediately reminded why it was such an important fight to win. *Daya, send me to war, but keep Cal and Tay safe.*

Marc cleared his throat. "All right, Calisto. Your classes are set. Now I just need to find you a roommate. Actually—" The dean leafed through a heap of paperwork stacked haphazardly near the edge of his desk. "Gib, aren't you good friends with Kezra Malin-Rai?"

"Yes. She's on active sentinel duty in the city now, but we stay in touch." Gib smiled, thinking of Kezra. She'd been the only woman trainee he'd known his first year and had always been the fiercest soldier he knew.

"Perfect," Marc replied. "Her younger brother is in the same year as Calisto. I'm going to go ahead and room them together."

After Calisto's paperwork was finalized and Gib checked to be sure his own academic schedule was set, the two students bade farewell to the dean and headed out the door. Gib's head pounded as he tried to get his thoughts to form coherently. *Show Cal the dining hall. Scarf down midday meal. Go to the council meeting. In that order. Quickly.*

He set a hand on Cal's back. "Okay, I'm going to show you where the dining hall is. We can take our meal there before I have to leave."

Marc waved from the doorway as the two boys departed. "Don't be late for the meeting, Nemesio!"

Gib's stomach had begun to rumble by the time they reached the dining hall. Scores of students, ranging from first years to those in their final semester, poured into the chamber, eager smiles on their faces and voices boisterous as they prepared to eat their midday meals. Many of the long wooden benches were already occupied as Gib directed his brother into the room.

The aroma of hearty soup and freshly baked rolls invaded Gib's nostrils. "Come on, Cal. Let's find a seat."

Cal hesitated in the arched doorway. "What if people don't like me?"

Gib went back to his younger brother and placed a firm hand on his back. "Why wouldn't people like you?"

"Cause I'm poor. What if I don't fit in? They'll all think I'm a waif." Cal wrung his hands together, a nervous habit shared by all the Nemesio siblings.

Gib snorted. "I was poor and still made friends. Hell, I showed up to Academy in rags. Look at you! You have a nice, clean outfit. Isn't that one of the tunics Tay made for you?" He motioned toward his brother's outfit—a simple but well-crafted linen tunic embroidered with green lace. "No one will think you're a waif in that, Cal." Gib squeezed the younger boy's shoulder. *I need to remember to thank Tayver for Cal's new clothing when I see him next. I would have given Cal my old trainee uniforms, but they're starting to tatter. Thank The Two for Tay.*

At Lady Mrifa's recommendation, Tayver had landed a job as Joran Nireefa's apprentice in Silver City's finest tailoring guild. Tayver's natural ability to design and construct clothing had come as a surprise to everyone, and after only two years of shadowing, Tayver was turning an eye-opening profit for the guild. Every highborn in Silver knew of Master Joran's star protégé and the fantastical masterpieces he created.

Gib smiled wistfully. *Tayver was meant for city life. I've never seen him happier. Now if I can manage to get Cal and myself through Academy, I'd say I've done pretty well for us. Ma and Pa would be proud.*

A sigh escaped Gib's lips as he scanned the dining hall. "Come on. Let's get our meal. It'll be a long time until dinner."

The youngster nodded eagerly, and the two of them fell in line.

14

Though not as new to the city as Gib had been on his first day, Calisto took his time to ogle over the wide assortment of foods. He chose many different things, even taking a moment to gush over the potatoes and gravy.

Gib set a hand on the back of his brother's neck. "Let's find a seat."

As Calisto gazed at all the tables before them, his smile slipped away. "Where are you gonna sit? Where should I sit?"

"I'm going to sit with Tarquin. Over there." Gib pointed toward his regular seat, a table near the farthest corner of the dining hall which Gib and his friends had long since claimed as their own. "You can come with me, but the conversation is going to be boring and I won't be staying long. I have to report to the council room soon."

Cal nodded as his dark eyes scanned a different table, where students closer to his own age were eating and chatting amongst themselves. "What if I sit with them? Do you think they'll like me?"

"You know I do."

"I don't know any of them."

"Not yet, but look—" Gib pointed to a boy and girl, both with onyx hair, fair features, and dark eyes. "Those two there are Inez and Inan Adelwijn. They're Joel's cousins. I've met them before, and they've always been friendly." Giving Cal's shoulder another gentle squeeze, Gib continued. "And the boy next to them, he must be your roommate, Scipio Malin-Rai."

Cal still didn't offer to move. "He's Kezra's brother? How do you know?"

"The bindi gives it away."

"Bind–bindi?"

"The red diamond painted above his brow. All the children in the Malin-Rai family have one. So does their mother. She came from Shantar, and the bindi is one of the traditions of her native land."

Calisto shuffled one foot across the marble floor. "Can I sit with you if none of them like me?"

"Yes, of course." Gib laughed.

Calisto needed no more encouragement. His walk was a bit stiff as he approached the other children and spoke shyly to them. Gib couldn't make out the words, but he watched as the young students greeted his brother. The smiles on each of their faces suggested Cal would be welcome at their bench, and sure enough, a moment later they scooted down to make room for him. Gib breathed a sigh of relief. *Is this what it feels like to be a worried parent?* He shook his head and turned to join his own friend.

At the table where Gib and his friends had sat on their very first day, Tarquin Aldino looked up with a grin. His white blond hair and unnaturally ashen skin still stood out in the crowd. The wide brim of his hat served to cover his odd-colored eyes, but he was forced to squint when he looked into the light. "Gibben Nemesio! Where have you been? You're never this late to a meal."

Dropping his tray to the table, Gib sat down and chuckled. "I'd have to agree there. Today is different. I had to take my little brother to meet Dean Marc and get signed up for classes."

Tarquin nodded. "That's right. I forgot Cal was old enough for Academy this year."

Tipping up his cup, Gib took a drink and began to scarf down his meal. He wasn't trying to be rude but knew his time had to be growing short. At this rate, he would have to run all the way to the palace if he wanted any chance of being on time.

"Don't choke." Tarquin snorted a laugh as he eyed Gib's deplorable behavior. "I'm not going to save you if you do."

"Sorry," Gib apologized between mouthfuls of potatoes. "I'm late for the council meeting—"

"Oh, right. I guess I'd forgotten that, too. I suppose this means a friendly sparring match later is out of the question, eh?"

Gib nodded solemnly and let out a defeated sigh. "Koal warned that the meeting might go on all afternoon."

"Nothing bad I hope. My father didn't seem worried when I saw him earlier today." Tarquin drummed his fingers on the table. "Though he tends not to worry about much of anything of substance."

"The usual, I'm sure," Gib replied, stabbing his fork into a slice of meat. "Privileged, old men attempting to make decisions for those who are allowed no opinion or voice on the matters most concerning to them."

Tarquin barked a laugh. "You sound just like the seneschal."

Gib couldn't help but smile, forced as it may be. "I know. I guess that's what happens when I've spent an entire year shadowing him." He took a gluttonous bite, sure that he must look like some kind of starving animal. "All right. I really have to go. Pick up my tray for me?"

Tarquin waved Gib away. "Yeah, yeah. You're welcome. Have fun at the meeting. Try not to get yourself into trouble, okay?"

"Thanks, Quin. I'll do my best."

As he crossed the dining hall once more, Gib risked a glance toward Cal. His younger brother was engaging the other students, and judging by the boisterous laughter rising from the table, it seemed they were getting along. Gib made the decision not to disturb them and left the room without drawing any attention to himself. He hoped the councilors would be in as high of spirits as the children but knew that was likely wishful thinking.

Gib ushered himself silently to his seat. Most of the other understudies were present already, but Gib was relieved to see he wasn't the last to arrive. Nevertheless, Hasain Radek, eldest son and understudy of the King, turned to give Gib a wry smile. His dark eyes danced as he stuck his nose in the air. "Oh, there you are. We were beginning to think you'd lost yourself somewhere."

"We?" Gib grunted as he sat down, making sure he could see out over the rail of the balcony. "Who's we? Did you manage to make a friend?"

"No. Hasain is terrible at making friends. Being family, I have no choice but to endure his company."

Gib leaned so far from his seat he nearly tumbled, but it was worth it to see another familiar face. "Diddy! What are you doing here?"

Prince Didier Adelwijn, who sat on the far side of Hasain, broke into a gushing smile. "Father has finally convinced Mother that I'm old enough to sit in on the meetings." He stiffened in his seat and lowered his already hushed voice. "It was high time. Being sixteen and having never attended a council meeting was simply embarrassing."

Gib chuckled. It was true. He and Diddy were the same age. As a prince, Diddy should have had many more responsibilities than he'd been afforded thus far. His mother, Queen Dahlia Adelwijn, hesitated due to the scare two years ago when an assassin had attempted to kill King Rishi. Diddy had been whisked out of his classes and away from public events along with his younger siblings. While it was understandable for a mother to want to protect her children, it had become somewhat of a running joke through the palace halls that the next generation of Radek rulers was going to be coddled forever.

Hasain gave them each a pointed look. "Lower your voices. The councilors keep looking up here."

Gib rolled his eyes. He'd noticed but was disinclined to give the men below the satisfaction of cowering in his seat. Just a few short years ago, he'd have recoiled and begged pardon, but those days were long gone. Gib wasn't as fresh as he'd been when he'd arrived in Silver and, with his better understanding of who some of these men were, he found he cared very little what they thought of him.

It was always the same councilors who gave them dirty looks—the ones in favor of promoting intolerance and stamping their feet each time King Rishi tried to pass any law not directly benefiting the highborns. Their approval would never befall misfits such as bastard children—royal or not—or commoners like Gib.

They were the ones who dug their heels in and made progress so difficult. They would keep women, lowborns, and other undesirables in the depths of Arden's underbelly. If these men were allowed to make the laws, no one would ever be able to better themselves despite how hard

17

they might work. A heavy feeling settled in the pit of Gib's stomach when he thought about how different his life would have been if not for the *good* men on the council.

As if to accentuate his thoughts and lift the weight in his gut, sunlight flooded the room below. On the ground floor, two men were working tirelessly to spread the light—throwing back curtains and opening windows. The sun was strong that day and cast off even the shadows which tended to linger in the balcony where Gib and the other understudies sat.

King Rishi Radek and Seneschal Koal Adelwijn worked from opposite sides of the curtain, never sharing a word as they toiled. Their efforts were met with mixed reviews—as was typical of the council—as some men balked and others reveled in the sudden illumination.

"Of course they're opening the curtains today."

The sour hiss made Gib's hair stand on end. He didn't have to turn to know who was complaining. Liro Adelwijn, Joel's brother and Seneschal Koal's eldest son, was also an understudy and always at the top of his game—making everyone around him miserable.

"It's as if they know I already have a headache."

Gib shook his head and noticed Hasain doing the same. Liro would make a fine politician one day. He already had his complaining down to an art. A secret and wry smile curled Gib's mouth as he indulged in the thought of Liro becoming lost and never finding his way back to Silver. Arden needed no more politicians like him.

Below, the councilors shuffled and grumbled as they found their places around the great table. Gib had begun to worry about one of the empty chairs but, to his relief, Dean Marc burst through the doors not a moment later and claimed his place.

King Rishi stormed to his seat and sprawled while he waited for the meeting to proceed. A moment later, the seat to the King's immediate right was taken by Seneschal Koal, who cleared his throat pointedly. The other councilors turned expectant looks upon their king and seneschal.

Neetra Adelwijn, High Councilor of Arden and younger brother of Koal, stood briefly to call them all to order. His shrill voice rose over them and caused Gib to grit his teeth. Neetra called the names of all the councilors, and in turn, each responded to confirm their presence. From one corner, the sound of a quill scratching parchment carried despite the distance. Diedrick Lyle, the former Instructions Master, took notes of everything said. The man looked just as glowering and miserable as he had the first time Gib had met him.

As soon as attendance was confirmed, the King waved a dismissive hand and raised his voice before Neetra could even sit down. "Tell me again why we were all called here so hastily?"

The High Councilor stiffened. "Your Highness is well aware of the threat of war from our borders—"

18

King Rishi nodded and rolled his hand as if to hurry the explanation but didn't wait for Neetra to finish. "Everyone here is well aware, as is the entire country. It would seem you've done an excellent job of keeping the peace and not spreading any unnecessary fear, High Councilor."

The clip in the King's voice made Gib wince, and even from the distance he could see Neetra's face go red.

"The people of Arden have the right to know when they are in danger!"

King Rishi skewered the High Councilor with a withering glare. "I would agree, were they actually *in* danger."

A cry from several men at once made Gib jump, but Koal was already on his feet, hands waving. The seneschal's voice carried the heavy resignation of one who'd dealt with too many of these petty arguments. "All right, calm down, all of you. Councilors, my King—" Koal shot an intimidating look of his own at King Rishi, who may have smirked in response. "I suggest we proceed without throwing accusations. For the sake of the country—and our own sanity—let's all pretend to be adults here." He sat down heavily and silence followed. When it became apparent no one intended to speak up after that, Koal groaned. "First order of business?"

Neetra's shoulders were drawn tight as he pushed a piece of parchment toward his superiors. "Our numbers for the draft. I would have you both review them. Perhaps you'll have words of comfort despite the sharp decline in our recruit numbers."

Koal extended a hand, but King Rishi leaned forward and swiped the note for himself. Holding it at arm's length, he squinted and took a moment to study it. After a long, pregnant pause, a wolfish smile tore over his face, and he tossed the parchment to Koal. The King reclined once more. "Yes, High Councilor, I see a dramatic drop in the number of *children* being forced into our military."

A caustic pause filled the room. Neetra glared at King Rishi but motioned toward a man sitting across the table. "Perhaps Arden's General would like to discuss the matter further."

The man Neetra had indicated, General Morathi Adeben, lifted a cold gaze. From Gib's seat, he couldn't see the general's face but had met him enough times to remember the severe expression permanently frozen onto the hard features.

"Highness." Morathi spoke clearly and without hesitation. "High Councilor Neetra means to question the lack of fresh recruits. Where and how are we going to make up these numbers to ensure Arden's safety?"

The King tilted his head to one side but took his time responding, and when he did, he spoke directly to Neetra. "Why are you forcing the general to speak on your behalf, High Councilor? I have listened to your whining long enough to know that surely you have a mind of your own.

What was *your* concern?"

Neetra leapt from his seat so fast Gib worried the man might try to rush the ruler. It would have been an utterly ridiculous move, but Neetra wasn't above being unreasonable.

The High Councilor pointed at the King with savage intent and hissed shrilly, "Have you no care for the size of your army?"

King Rishi flashed a smug smile. "I've never preoccupied myself with size as you seem to."

Gib winced.

"I do, however, pay mind to important issues, such as the *quality* of our troops."

Neetra was so red he looked like he might burst. The High Councilor sputtered as he responded. "Surely Your Highness must see the benefit of a formidable army in times of war! Beyond tactics and training, battle is a numbers game. We need to have the greater number."

"Again, I say your worries for compensation are ill founded. And what, exactly, are you trying to compensate for? What are these times of war you speak of? Despite all of your worry and dread, we've yet to see any real threat from either border."

Councilor Anders Malin-Rai, a known sympathizer of Neetra, slammed his fist on the table. "There have been multiple skirmishes along the Shiraz border! And every day, more troops from Nales come to man the wall above Port Ostlea to the north!"

King Rishi threw his hands in the air, but Koal snarled a response before the ruler could. "No one has mentioned how these conflicts have only sprouted up since we reinforced our borders. Intimidation is ugly and breaks men down, reducing them to their most base selves."

Gib watched in silence as the argument went back and forth. Neetra and Anders continued to argue that the protection of Arden's borders was essential. King Rishi and Koal countered, questioning the reason for reinforcing a border that had previously lain silent. General Morathi remained enigmatically quiet throughout the exchange, though Gib was sure it wasn't from lack of nerve. Morathi was typically a collected man, not given to shouting. His silence was more troubling than Neetra's shrill whine.

Anders' voice rose above the others. "It's not too late to overturn this new law, councilors! What say you? It's within our power to correct this oversight now. Young men have always been called to defend their country. It's a way of life." Anders fixed a cold glare on the King. "Grievous as it may be."

Hasain flinched, and Diddy took in a sharp breath. Gib froze as well. The subject of child soldiers was a sensitive one. It had nearly divided the council in half. Only recently had numbers shifted enough to favor the King's new law, which commanded no man may be drafted against his will until his sixteenth Naming Day. Before this change, boys were considered men by their thirteenth year and could be drafted from then on.

With the ink still wet on this new law, King Rishi was more defensive than ever. The soft, silken whisper of his voice betrayed his wrath. "Grievous? Tell me, Councilor Anders, how many grievances has *your* family suffered? How many uncles, brothers, nephews, or sons have you lost to the draft? How many thirteen-year-old boys—men according to law—have you looked upon for the last time as they picked up a sword they didn't know how to use and a shield too heavy for them to carry? How many aunts or sisters have you comforted while they wept for their lost sons who were too young to own the family farm but old enough to die on the battlefield and did just that?"

Tense quiet blanketed the room, but Gib was certain he heard Liro huff.

Anders stiffened. "The lineage of lords is rarely called upon for war. It is a privilege passed on to us from those who came before—those who fought bravely." The councilor locked his jaw as he finished speaking.

King Rishi leaned farther back in his chair. Despite the low tone, his voice seemed to fill every corner of the room. "Ah, yes, unearned privilege. It must come as a comfort to know your ancestors were brave and risked life and limb in order for you to declare others—not so privileged as yourself—must be willing to die for the country."

Neetra scoffed. "This is hardly Anders' war, Highness. No one gets to choose their destined path, but we all must comply with the hand we are dealt—"

"Easy enough to say from your safe and comfortable chair, High Councilor. Would your dedication be so steadfast had your son been called to war this year?"

"Enough of this!" Neetra looked around the table at the gathered men. "Councilors, should we take a vote on overturning this law?"

Gib clenched his fists. His eyes darted from one face to another, and desperation flooded his veins. This law was so important to people like him. Countless children along the countryside would be sucked into this potential war if Neetra and Anders got their way.

Even the King, who was typically so well spoken, had fallen silent, his face a crimson mask of rage.

The sound of a throat being cleared broke the tense quiet. Joaquin Aldino, Tarquin's father, called attention to himself and made a point to avoid prolonged eye contact with any one person. "Councilors, was it not agreed that by allowing women to join the military, we reduced the need for such young soldiers?"

Several men threw their hands in the air at once. Women joining the army was yet another issue firmly dividing the council. Groans and sharp cries of protest clashed against fervent praise.

Seneschal Koal cut through the clamor to voice his opinion. "For all of the complaining endured here, Weapons Master Roland Korbin has informed me the number of our female recruits has only increased each year. Young women are pouring in from all across the country to join our forces—"

"Women are smaller and weaker than men!"

"They can't be relied upon to make rational decisions in the heat of battle!"

"They require special accommodations! Women need supplies male soldiers don't!"

"What if they become pregnant out there? What help are they then?"

Gib could barely keep up with the questions being fired. Hasain grunted and leaned closer to the rail, the young lord's brows knitted. Below, King Rishi had had enough.

"Again, with the complaining! You argue women are weaker than men, yet I've never seen a man suffer through childbirth. Rational decisions in the heat of battle are difficult for anyone, yet the late Queen Jorja Viran was one of this country's finest tactical minds. And as far as women soldiers becoming pregnant on the battlefield—" The King paused long enough to shake his head, features drawn into a sour frown. "Councilors, I assume you all understand how pregnancies happen, correct? I'm not sure when you think these soldiers are going to have the time, energy, or desire to create these pregnancies. However, I suppose if and when they do, at the very least, you can stop fretting about the need to send menstruation supplies into war camps!"

Diddy pressed his knuckles to his lips, and Gib's face burned with uncomfortable heat. Hasain stiffened and sat back quickly, a horrified frown pulling down on his mouth. Behind them, Liro made a sound of disgust, and when Gib looked back, the understudy curled his nose.

Below, Dean Marc snorted a laugh, earning a savage look from Koal as he stood once again. The seneschal's voice was level, despite his own crimson face. "Gentlemen of the council, I think we can all agree to disagree on this issue. The draft law doesn't appear to be up for recall, and the issue of women soldiers is still too new to dismiss yet. Shall we move on to the next topic?" He dropped back into his chair.

Gib smiled to himself and stole a glance toward Diddy. Had they been anywhere else, the two of them would have shared a good laugh, but now was not the time. Papers were shuffling at the table below, and Neetra's voice rose again.

"The next matter of discussion is exiled slaves." Neetra looked at the King and seneschal for a moment and, seeing no resistance, pushed on. "We're all familiar with the problem of Gyptia's slaves crossing our southern border in a claim for freedom. However, these people come here with next to no knowledge of how our government works, little valuable work experience, and often do not speak our language. They're extra mouths to feed and have become a source of hardship for some of our southern provinces."

The King twiddled his thumbs and offered nothing.

Koal frowned but replied in a measured tone, "There has been some discussion among the King, Dean Marc, and myself about how best to go about educating the Gyptian exiles so they may become a useful asset to our workforce."

Neetra huffed. "Education? Why is it Arden's responsibility to educate these slaves? They're the ones who left their own country. It's been suggested to me that perhaps we should put these people directly to work. There are menial tasks which they would be able to perform, even with their shortcomings."

Marc, who had been mostly quiet until now, leaned forward in his seat. "Some of these foreigners have exceptional skills. They've served construction masters their entire lives, or healers, or scholars. Some of them have a wealth of knowledge. We only need to bridge the communication gap, and they could be great assets to Arden—"

General Morathi lifted his frigid voice once more. "Well, I suppose they should have stayed where their talents could be used then, shouldn't they? It isn't Arden's responsibility to teach them our language, and in the meantime, there are jobs to be done. They don't have to speak Ardenian to swing a pickaxe or dig with a shovel."

"I agree," Neetra said with a curt nod. "If these slaves are going to stroll into our country and demand our protection then the least they could do is provide Arden with service."

The King shrugged. "I've never said Gyptia's refugees aren't eligible for work here, but if they're going to become citizens of our country then they should be entitled to the same opportunities as anyone else. I feel Marc makes a valid point. Why should a scholar work in the mines? Their potential would be wasted."

The high councilor waved a dismissive hand. "What care have I of their talents? They chose to leave their country and become a drain on ours. Therefore, it's suggested the exiles be put to work under Ardenian law for no less than five years without pay. Their meals and lodgings will be provided, and they will be given the opportunity to work off their debt to our country."

King Rishi squinted toward Neetra and took a breath. He held it for a brief moment before posing much the same question Gib was thinking. "Let me be sure I understand you, High Councilor. These people have risked life and limb to escape enslavement, braved the harsh desert—a fatal trek for most—and plunged themselves into an entirely foreign culture, all on the slim hope they will be able to obtain some scrap of dignity in their newfound freedom. Now you want to greet them with a sentence of indentured servitude?" The King turned up his empty palms, confusion still etched across his features. "Why would a slave leave their home country only to be a slave somewhere else?"

General Morathi smiled triumphantly. "Precisely, Highness. They won't be our problem anymore."

"It's never been Ardenian law to punish the innocent."

Not to be outdone, the general gestured about the room. "Are any of you gentleman aware of an Ardenian law which mandates our country feed and house refugees?" Murmurs made their way around the table, and although the King, Koal, and Marc all had scowls on their faces, none of them seemed to be able to think of a counterargument.

Gib shifted in his seat. He didn't know much about escaped slaves. Indeed, such issues had never once crossed his mind while he'd been growing up on the farm. He'd always been too focused on staying alive to worry about the wellbeing of strangers. However, his heart told him of the inherent injustice it would be to abuse anyone, especially someone who had nothing.

Joaquin spoke again. "Actually, General, there's no law I know of, but it's a common practice amongst the various temples throughout Arden to house the persecuted and feed the poor. Would not these people qualify for such help?"

Neetra waved a dismissive hand. "Well, *that's* another topic for debate entirely. We all know not everyone here is in favor of providing for those who refuse to provide for themselves—"

The councilors erupted into fierce debate yet again, and Gib groaned. He didn't know how any of these politicians put up with this every day. They never made any progress. The same things were argued over for ages, and rarely was anything accomplished.

Hasain nodded as if he understood Gib's thoughts. The Radek lord's voice was a low whisper, barely audible over the din below. "I don't envy Deegan for his throne."

Gib thought to respond, to offer some well wishes for the young Crowned Prince, but Liro's boot tapping the back of the chair reminded Gib to grit his teeth and keep silent. He might very well lose his mind if ever he were to become a politician and have to sit across from Liro Adelwijn each day.

The general's voice had risen once more to claim dominance over the gathered men. "Highness, you must understand in times such as these, Arden cannot be compromised in any way. Feeding all these extra mouths takes away from our troops—"

King Rishi's strained voice suggested he'd about had his fill of politics for one day. "General Morathi, there will be no *need* for troops if our peasants starve to death!"

"There will be no peasants if our lands are overtaken by the enemy!"

Neetra's shrill voice carried all too well in such confined quarters.

"The imagined enemy? From which border?" Koal didn't typically rely on sarcasm, but his use of it now effectively shut his younger brother's mouth.

The King and seneschal shared a smug smirk but couldn't hope to go uncontested.

Morathi stood, his tall form looming above the table. "Highness, I must implore you to consider these suggestions carefully. With the threat of war on both our eastern and northern borders, and a call for help from our allies in Gyptia, we are stretched thin."

Marc nodded. "Gyptia is a powerful ally. We need to be sensitive to their needs during their own time of war."

Neetra stuck his nose in the air. "Gyptia is a large country. I say their war is their own. It's their own questionable practices which have brought about civil unrest. Their peasants have been allowed too many luxuries. They forget their place."

Koal shook his head, a grim look on his face. "Mass revolt is a complicated situation, but I agree we need to be available to Sovereign Khalfani. He has treated with us and vowed to come to our aid, should we need it."

The general and High Councilor shared a dark look.

"It's not Arden's responsibility to hold Gyptia together." Morathi's voice commanded absolute attention.

Neetra nodded. "Agreed! What business is it of ours if their ungrateful peasants revolt?"

King Rishi groaned. "Ungrateful! What an idea, councilors. Imagine—the slaves don't like being slaves! Perhaps a lesson can be learned here before we ourselves condemn innocents to slavery and starvation. We may even prevent a civil war of our own!"

The council room burst into another bout of angry debate. Gib clenched his jaw. Their arguments were enough to wear on even him, and he didn't even have a voice on the matter. He looked out the window, realizing with dismay that nearly no time had passed since the meeting commenced. Marks of this petty debating still lay ahead! How could he ever hope to make a difference when his time came to speak on the council? Was all of this just a waste of his time and Koal's resources to sit in this seat and learn skills for a job Gib grew to despise more with each passing day?

He thought back to his first day in Silver, when he'd been a terrified boy of thirteen, drafted into the military and taken away from his home and family. No choice had been given to him. Neetra and other men like the High Councilor did not care that Gib had two younger brothers to feed and care for. They had no care if his story hadn't been a rarity. Other families just like his—broken and trying to keep their heads above water—

had also been torn apart to suit the needs of the army.

Gib sighed. He had to stay here. He didn't pursue this career in hope of title and wealth in his old age. He stayed the course in hope that real change was possible. Too many innocent people in Arden could only pray for change while he'd been lucky to fall into a place of potential power, and despite his dislike for the political world, he had a responsibility to uphold.

Gib stayed for the remainder of the meeting—another two marks of stifling arguments. He even forced himself to remain present and consider what was being said, to form his own opinion and think of questions to ask Koal later.

He was grateful when the session was called to an end. The moment King Rishi approved the dismissal, Gib was on his feet. Hasain and Diddy were quick to follow, both stretching their stiff muscles. Gib didn't wait for them. He made for the stairs, hoping he could reach the ground floor before he was forced to wait for the councilors to clear the hall. He also didn't want to share the tight stairway with Liro if it could be avoided.

"Well, I suppose that was enlightening," Diddy said, scurrying to catch up. "I see now why Father warned me about entering politics."

Hasain stayed a step behind as they made their way down the stone stairs. "That wasn't even the worst of it. There have been times when I thought there would be physical blows."

Gib nodded in agreement. "It's true. You'll see as much, if you decide to come back."

The council room doors burst open at that moment, and the politicians began to pour out. They rushed with such speed that the three friends were forced to wait on the stairs to avoid being trampled. Morathi and Diedrick swept away together, speaking among themselves while Koal, Marc, and the King stood inside the door and waited for the stampede to recede.

"Well, isn't this cozy?"

Gib tensed. Liro had caught up with them after all. The surge of bodies in the hall below showed little sign of dissipating. Gib had to force himself not to jump and hope for the best. Being trampled might be preferable to being stuck here with someone as foul as Liro Adelwijn.

Ever civil, Diddy took it upon himself to make small talk. "Hopefully the crowd will clear soon."

Liro's sigh was audible over the crowd. "I have an appointment with the healers to get to. Let me through!"

Gib locked his jaw, but before he could even part his lips, Hasain answered.

"Do you think we're standing here for sport? You'll have to wait your turn like everyone else."

Tension rippled around them, and Gib chose to look across the hall in a desperate attempt to ignore Liro. Koal, Marc, and King Rishi hadn't dared move yet either, though they'd been joined by the King's personal bodyguard, Aodan Galloway of Derry. The four were talking among themselves just to the side of the doorway, and Gib wished like hell he could make his way to his mentor. He'd willingly stand in silence while the older men vented if it meant he wouldn't have to feel the scrutiny of Joel's elder brother. Liro had never approved of Gib or his relationship with Joel.

"Does the King's bastard son know how to wait his turn?" Liro's voice dripped venom. "You have been given so many privileges already I fear you may never know your place."

Hasain's voice was as cold as ice. "The manner of my birth holds no bearing on the man I choose to be. You would do well to heed this same lesson."

Liro chuckled, a dry sound entirely void of mirth. "Your head has been filled with the fanciful misgivings of your sire, I see. All the better you will never rule."

Diddy gasped, and Gib whirled around on his heel. He'd wanted to stay out of this but couldn't just stand by and allow—

Hasain narrowed his eyes into dangerous slits. "My brother will be your king one day, and then you will have to bow to him. I assure you my father has taught Prince Deegan as well as he taught me. Perhaps it is *your* education that is lacking."

Liro's cruel mouth opened to strike again, but a sudden call caused the lord to glance beyond the gathered understudies. Gib turned as well, a familiar voice catching his ears. His spirit jumped. *Could it be?*

Across the hall, Koal, Marc, and King Rishi gazed in the same direction. The seneschal's face broke into a smile, and he held his hand up, waving over the crowd. Gib leaned as far from the stairs as he could without compromising his balance. There, beyond the doorway, he could make out two figures as they made their way through the corridor. One was Ambassador Cenric Leal, Arden's most accomplished envoy. The other was his current understudy, Joel Adelwijn.

CHAPTER TWO

Joel glanced over his shoulder. The light from the portal fizzled behind him as the rip between spaces collapsed on itself. For a moment, he could still see the dark forms of the Shantarian priests powering the opposite side of the rift, but then the passageway connecting the two realms dissipated completely as the priests released their grip on the magic and allowed the portal to fade into nothingness.

A moment before, he'd been standing in a crowded, humid palace in Shantar; Joel now found himself inside a familiar courtyard—the royal gardens of Silver City. It seemed impossible, but here he was. Frost-bitten vines crawled along beautiful marbled columns lining the garden, and the scent of leather and hay hung on the light breeze blowing from the stables. He breathed a deep sigh. He was home.

Joel turned toward his mentor and friend, Ambassador Cenric Leal. "Well, here we are at last. We're home."

Smoothing down a wrinkle in his embroidered jerkin, the envoy issued a chuckle. "And we made the journey intact."

"You were worried we wouldn't?"

Cenric smiled wryly, his hazel eyes twinkling. He brushed a strand of short, peppered brown hair away from his face and retorted, "Considering they had two mage *trainees* assisting with the portal, yes, I'll admit I was slightly concerned for our welfare. Trainees have no business with portal working. One mishap or loss of control and we could have died—"

"I worked with Devi and Mahinder often enough. Both of them are extremely gifted, especially considering their young age."

"Nonetheless, they are trainees."

"Shall I remind you that *I'm* technically still a trainee? I seem to recall you willingly putting your life in *my* hands a time or two these past six moonturns."

Cenric raised an eyebrow. "Not all trainees are as exceptionally skilled as you." He reached back, giving Joel a firm pat on the shoulder. "Besides, I hardly consider you a trainee anymore. In fact, as soon as you get your internship paperwork signed, you won't be."

"About time," Joel remarked, stark blue eyes sparkling with mischief. "Four years of schooling and an apprenticeship with *you* was nearly too much to bear."

The ambassador scoffed. "The feeling's mutual, don't worry."

A quartet of white-robed mages swept up to greet them. Portal guardians, they were assigned to hold vigil in the courtyard to ensure no malicious attempts to utilize the rift were carried through. Night and day, they wove protective wards around the portal so no enemies were able to infiltrate the heart of Silver City. It was an important job, being a portal guardian—one Joel had considered taking himself once he graduated. That was before his internship. Shantar had left him longing to do more.

The lead portal guardian inclined his head in greeting. "Good day, Ambassador Leal. I hope you fared well on your travels."

"Thank you," Cenric replied, smiling. "We go now to report to the King."

The mages bowed and went on their way.

Cenric looked over his shoulder at Joel. "We'll brief King Rishi and Seneschal Koal—and then I can finally be rid of you."

They shared a laugh. Still grinning, Joel turned toward the cobbled path which led to the palace. Light trickled through white clouds above, casting rays of gold across the stonework and illuminating his way. Judging by the low angle of the sun, the day was close to spent. Soon the moon would peek over the eastern horizon, and quick to follow, a cloak of darkness would wrap Arden in a veil of shadow and cold.

Joel fell in behind Cenric, eager to leave the courtyard behind in favor of the warmth the palace was sure to provide. "I only just grew accustomed to the humidity in Shantar," he joked. "And now I'll be ridiculed by my family if I complain the air feels cold here in Arden."

"Aye. It doesn't take long for the blood to thin in the south." Cenric rubbed his own shoulders as he walked. "But you'll readjust quickly enough."

"I hope so. I feel as though I've been gone half my life, not half a year."

Six moonturns was a long time to be gone, and while Joel had enjoyed his internship, a sense of relief flooded him to once again behold the familiar landscape of Arden.

Shantar, a country nestled between the arid wastelands of Shiraz and the powdery sands of Gyptia, was a place like no other. The city of Raja played home to lush foliage and exotic creatures Joel had never before witnessed. Giant red cats with black stripes and sentient, lizard-like Otherfolk called naga prowled the jungle just beyond the city gates. Birds of every color and size perched on rooftops and branches, their songs echoing across the city. They'd long since lost their shy nature—indeed it was possible to put a bit of seed in one's hand and watch the birds eat from it without fear. *I wish I could have shown them to everyone here at home.*

A twinge of anxiety caused Joel's stomach to roll. Six moonturns was a long time to be away from his loved ones, too—his father and mother, Koal and Mrifa Adelwijn, sisters Heidi and Carmen, brother Liro, and most especially, Gibben Nemesio. Joel swallowed hard.

Gods, I've missed him. I've missed our playful banter and philosophical pillow talks. No one knows me as well as Gib. I can tell him anything and know he won't judge me. Joel smiled as he reminisced about times spent with Gib, the young man who'd come to Silver City three years prior—the boy who'd managed to, in his first year, not only save the King of Arden, but also save Joel from the isolation he'd created for himself. *If it wasn't for Gib, I'd never have been able to pull myself from the darkness.*

When he'd first been offered the internship, Joel had hesitated to accept. His relationship with Gib had been flourishing, but their strength came from facing opposition *together*. They'd confronted the scandal and, at times, ugly rumors, created by the highborns of Silver City as partners. Any respect gained had been hard earned, yet *still* Joel heard the hushed whispers and saw the sideways glances among the courtiers. The greatest comfort had been knowing he wasn't alone—and looking back now, Joel wasn't sure he would have been able to get through it without Gib.

When Joel made the decision to go to Shantar, his companion took the news as well as could be expected. Stoic as always, Gib had nodded and wished Joel well, promising the distance would only strengthen their bond. Surely Gib meant it at the time, but Joel couldn't help but fret about it after all these moonturns apart. Change—good or bad—was inevitable. *How much has changed since I last was home? Have Gib's feelings remained the same? Have mine?*

He pushed the thoughts aside, choosing instead to take in the splendid scenery the royal palace offered. The grand building was barren at this time, save for scores of royal guardsmen patrolling the corridors. Clad in polished armor and equipped with longswords sheathed in gilded leather, the sentinels watched Cenric and Joel in silence as the pair moved through the stucco-covered halls, still as statues but only a strike away from ending the life of anyone foolish enough to threaten the royal family.

Every so often, a servant or groomsman would pass by. Each bowed cordially to the pair before continuing on their way, and Joel found himself frowning. The rules of etiquette in the Shantarian courts were so less rigid than those in Arden. He'd nearly forgotten the mannerisms to which he was expected to adhere now that he was home.

Lost in contemplations concerning his recent travels, Joel followed wordlessly behind his mentor until Cenric stopped to inquire of a royal guardsman as to the whereabouts of Seneschal Koal. The sentinel raised a hand and pointed down the hall leading to the council chamber. "The High Council has been in session all afternoon, Ambassador. They're due for recess at any time."

Cenric thanked the man and started down the corridor. With growing apprehension, Joel followed on his mentor's heels. If Koal was at the meeting, it was probable Gib would also be in attendance. What would it feel like to lay eyes upon him after so many moonturns apart? Would Gib be as excited to see Joel as the mage was to see Gib?

The sound of a door flying open drew Joel's attention to the end of the long hallway. He looked up, heart racing in his chest, as men began to pour from within the arched frame leading to the council chamber. It appeared that he and Cenric had arrived just in time. Peering down the hall, Joel hoped to catch a glimpse of familiar faces within the crowd.

Unfortunately, it was the face of Joel's uncle, High Councilor Neetra Adelwijn, which first came into view. With his lips pulled back in a scowl and dark eyes glinting, Neetra conversed with another councilor, snide voice traveling down the corridor, and despite knowing it would be considered impolite not to greet him, Joel stepped back and kept his head lowered so he'd go unnoticed by the High Councilor.

Joel didn't dare look up again until his uncle had already stormed past. *Good. It appears Neetra didn't notice me—or didn't care to stop and say hello.* Breathing a sigh of relief, a smile crossed his lips when he next looked down the hall. There, by the open door, his father stood between King Rishi and Marc Arrio.

"Father!" Joel called, mage robe billowing around his body as he swept toward the men.

Koal Adelwijn must have heard him, for the seneschal's head shot up. His blue orbs darted across the crowded hall before settling on Joel, eyes lighting up at the sight of his son.

Small creases formed around the corners of Koal's mouth as he smiled and raised a hand in greeting. As Joel drew nearer, he hesitated. *Should I—will it be all right to hug him here in front of everyone?*

He wasn't left fretting for long as Koal took the step forward to put his arms around his son. "Welcome home. Do you feel old yet?"

"Older perhaps, but none the wiser." Joel laughed and took the briefest moment to enjoy his father's affection.

As the embrace came to an end, Joel noticed Cenric bowing and quickly followed suit. *You imbecile. Way to be respectful.* Joel wasn't sure how he'd managed to forget the King was standing right there.

King Rishi flicked a wrist, motioning for the pair to stand. With a smirk, he turned to Koal. "Fantastic. Your *good* son has returned."

Aodan Galloway, the King's personal bodyguard, snorted from behind the King, and even Koal's mouth twitched as though he wanted to laugh.

A chuckle tickled the back of Joel's throat, but he knew it would be best to keep quiet. Straightening his back, he rose to his full height just in time to see Koal tense.

"Brother."

Joel stiffened when Liro's cold voice cut through the room like brittle ice. The older Adelwijn brother stood at the base of the gallery staircase but made no move to come closer. As always, his blue eyes were hard and critical. Joel's heart pained as he recalled a time when Liro hadn't looked upon his brother with such condemnation. They'd been friends once.

"Hello, Liro," Joel whispered in as civil a tone as he could muster. "I'm glad to see you're well."

"Likewise." The words held not a trace of warmth.

"We shall have to catch up sometime soon," Joel risked, hoping *maybe* Liro had had a change of heart while Joel had been away.

Liro locked his jaw. "I have an appointment at the Healer's Pavilion. I must take my leave." He gave their father a curt nod and reserved a bow for King Rishi. "Father, Highness." Turning on his heels, Liro departed without another word.

When did our relationship become so broken? Joel swallowed his despair and turned toward Marc Arrio next, who gave Joel a hearty clasp on his shoulder. Dean of Academy and longtime friend of the Adelwijn family, Marc had been one of the first people to accept Joel when the mage trainee, then fourteen, admitted to the rest of the world his preference of liking men. Even when the majority of the court turned their backs on Joel, Marc remained a loyal and steadfast ally. He'd even been the one to unwittingly bring Gib and Joel together when they'd been assigned as roommates—an act Joel felt he would never be able to repay.

"Welcome home!" Marc greeted Joel with a warm tone, perhaps an attempt to cover the chill left in Liro's wake. "You've been missed."

Joel flicked a modest smile. "Thank you. It's good to be back. Congratulations, by the way. While in Shantar, I received word that you and Lady Beatrice are expecting a child."

The corner of Marc's mouth quirked upward. "Who told you?"

Joel pointedly made an effort not to glance in his father's direction, earning barked laughter from the dean.

"It was your father, wasn't it?"

"Perhaps," Joel admitted, hiding a blush behind a strand of dark hair that had fallen into his face. "He may have mentioned it in a letter."

"He's horrible at keeping secrets."

Koal groaned and muttered under his breath. "Secret? It wasn't like you hadn't already told all of Silver."

"Hey," Marc joked. "It's worth boasting when a man of *my* age is still able to perform well enough to make a baby."

King Rishi's thin lips curled slyly. "It's no boasting matter when it takes a man this long to figure out how the hell to *make* a baby!"

Koal rolled his eyes at both men. "Be sure to inform me how well you're able to keep up with the little one once he begins to run rampant through your home."

32

"I'll manage!" countered Marc. "And the child only stands to benefit from the wealth of knowledge I've acquired over the years."

Koal snorted. "Yes. All forty-something of them."

As Marc and Koal continued to banter, Joel's attention shifted to the understudies still standing on the gallery steps. Liro had stormed from the chamber, but three young men remained—his cousins, Didier Adelwijn and Hasain Radek, and, standing beside them, Gibben Nemesio. Joel's heart hammered in his chest.

Six moonturns had done little to change Gib's appearance. Modest of stature but never lacking in bravery, Gib regarded Joel with devout attention, and the smile playing on Gib's lips suggested he was excited to see the other man. Gib's hair was longer than Joel remembered—soft mousy curls that just barely grazed his shoulders—and as always, Gib's rich, sun-kissed skin beckoned for touch. How long had it been since they'd held one another in an embrace? *Too long.*

Joel trembled as he studied his companion through heavy lashes but found feet and mind frozen, unable to move or even call out a greeting. It was a good thing Diddy had the clarity to step forward and break the awkward lull, or Joel might have been destined to stand there the remainder of the day.

"I'm so glad you've returned," Diddy exclaimed. Sweeping up beside Joel, the prince didn't hesitate to hug his cousin.

Joel gave Diddy a gentle pat on the back. "Were you worried I wouldn't?"

"I've read of the lavish parties and vibrant scenery in Raja," Diddy replied, a twinkle in his dark eyes. "I wouldn't have been surprised if you'd chosen to take up permanent residence there."

Hasain chuckled. "With so much of *interest* here in Arden?" He flashed a smug smile in Gib's direction before turning to face Joel. "I'm shocked Joel was gone as long as he was." Hasain offered his hand for a shake. "Welcome back."

Joel felt his face grow warm at the insinuation but brushed it off as Hasain's best attempt at humor. "Lord Hasain, I do recall you yourself sending letters home, agonizing of a homesick heart, while on your internship only one wheelturn ago. Or have you already forgotten?"

Hasain's face pinched, but for once, he seemed to be at a loss for words.

Joel clasped his cousin's hand and smiled. "Regardless, thank you for the warm welcome, cousin."

The young Radek lord grunted in response, but Joel had already turned his attention toward the last remaining understudy still to be greeted. Gib stepped down from the gallery staircase, wringing his hands together. He seemed unable to maintain eye contact, which was just as well, because Joel was having an exceptionally hard time meeting the other man's gaze. Joel's stomach and throat felt heavy, as though a giant rock sat at the base of each and prevented him from moving or speaking, and despite the cool air pouring through the window, the room seemed unbearably warm.

Joel sucked in a breath of air when he realized Gib was standing directly ahead. *Say something!* Joel opened his mouth but found himself unable to form words.

And then Gib's soft voice rose above the buzzing in Joel's ears, and the silence came crashing down. "Hello."

The single word was enough to break the ice, and Joel found his own voice just as he'd begun to doubt he ever would. "Hello, Gib."

"I'm glad you're home." A shy, handsome smile crossed Gib's face. "I–I've missed you."

"I missed you, too."

Joel resisted the urge to kiss Gib, instead, offering a hand for a simple shake. Gib took hold of it without hesitation, squeezing Joel's fingertips. Joel caressed the other man's palm for a brief moment before releasing the hand and dropping his own arm back into place at his side. They would have time later for a proper reunion—when their affections weren't being aired for all to see. As it stood right now, Joel could feel the eyes of the other gathered men upon him.

Gib seemed to understand and went back to wringing his hands together. "When did you get in?"

Joel cleared his throat. "Just now. Ambassador Cenric and I were on our way to brief the King and Seneschal Koal." He cast a glance over his shoulder, in the direction of his mentor. *I hope this briefing doesn't take all night. I'd love nothing more than to go home and spend time with Gib.*

Cenric Leal possessed no magic, but in that moment, it was as though the ambassador could read Joel's thoughts. "I'll deal with all the paperwork. Why don't you go catch up with your friends?" He winked at Joel.

"Thank you." Joel bowed his head to hide his pink cheeks. Now if only Gib wasn't on duty.

Koal exchanged a silent, knowing glance with Cenric, and then he dismissed his own understudy. "Gibben, we'll go over the notes from the council session later. Enjoy the rest of your evening."

Gib opened his mouth to respond, but his words fell upon deaf ears as Koal, Cenric, King Rishi, and the rest of their entourage had already turned and were talking amongst themselves as they departed.

Joel rubbed the back of his neck. "I suppose I should go see Mother and the girls. Would you like to accompany me?"

"Did you even have to ask?" Gib replied, laughing.

A mark later found Joel and Gib standing in the grand entranceway of the Adelwijn estate. The family servant, a wiry man with greying hair named Otos, let them inside, and almost immediately, Joel's mother and sisters flocked into the room in a flurry of exuberant screams and cheers.

Lady Mrifa threw both arms around her son's neck. "Oh, by the Light of Daya!" she squealed. "You're home!"

Nearly toppling from the force of the embrace, Joel managed to laugh before his face was covered by kisses. He sighed but tolerated the fawning for the time being. Mrifa kissed his forehead and each of his cheeks, her vice-like grip around his neck nearly enough to choke him.

"Oh, Joel. I feared you would *never* return!" Mrifa wailed against his chest.

Behind him, Heidi's voice sounded exasperated. "Mother, stop being so *embarrassing.*"

Mrifa wiped a tear from her eye as she finally relinquished her hold. She whipped around to regard her daughter, pursing plump, cherry lips. "Heidi Adelwijn, when you have children, you'll understand the worry a mother goes through when her babies go off seeking danger—"

"Danger?" Joel chuckled. "I was in Shantar, Mother, perhaps one of the most peaceful nations this side of the sea—"

"Even so! A thousand things could have gone wrong," Mrifa fretted. She paused, toying with a strand of blonde hair. "A lady at court told me of all the venomous snakes in Shantar. What if you'd been bitten by one, Joel? You might have *died!*"

Joel pressed his lips together to contain the ridiculous smile threatening to spread across his face. "The people of Shantar have been dealing with snake bites for centuries. Their healers are as well trained as ours in Arden. Had it happened—which it didn't—I would have been fine."

Mrifa rested one of her small hands against the side of his face. "Promise you won't worry me again, Joel."

Now it was Carmen's turn to snicker. The youngest of Joel's siblings crossed her arms over her bosom. "Chhaya's bane, Mother! What do you plan to do? Lock him inside the estate for the rest of his life?"

"Don't give her any ideas," Heidi groaned.

Joel managed to escape Mrifa's grasp and went to greet his sisters, giving each a hug. He held the younger of the two at arm's length after the embrace had ended. "I think you've gotten taller."

"I have." Carmen beamed.

"She's blossomed into a beautiful young woman." Mrifa gave her daughter a hard look. "Not that anyone can see her beauty beneath all those boy's clothes she chooses to wear."

Carmen stuck out her tongue. "I'm going to be a royal guardswoman one day."

"It wouldn't pain you to wear a dress once in a while—"

"Mother, I don't *like* dresses! Just because Heidi enjoys dolling herself up like a princess doesn't mean I do!"

Joel looked down so Mrifa wouldn't catch his smile. As the young lady bested her mother with a sharp tongue and wit, Carmen sounded very much like Gib's friend, Kezra Malin-Rai. In fact, since that first year when Gib and Kezra had shared weaponry class together, scores of young girls had made the decision to join the military—Carmen included. The trend to forgo basket-weaving and cooking classes in favor of physical training and politics seemed to be growing in popularity among the young women of Arden.

"Are you hungry, Joel? Gib?" Mrifa asked, face still pinched. "Tabitha is cooking us a lovely stew for dinner."

Joel nodded even as his stomach gurgled.

Likewise, Gib's eyes lit up at the mention of food. "That sounds wonderful, Lady."

Taking hold of her heavy velvet and lace skirt, Mrifa marched toward the kitchen, stopping long enough to give Gib's cheek an affectionate pinch as she passed. It seemed as though her jubilant demeanor had once again returned. "I'll inform Tabitha to set two extra plates at the table."

After bellies were full and he'd told his mother and sisters every detail of his journey, Joel excused himself from the table. Tabitha had taken it upon herself to draw him a warm bath, for which the mage was grateful. The day's excitement had begun to take its toll, and by the time Joel finished climbing the marble staircase and stripped his clothing, nothing in the world sounded more wonderful than a bath.

A sigh escaped Joel's mouth as he slid into the tub. The water verged on scorching hot, and it turned his fair skin a lovely shade of pink within moments. He settled into the water and quickly found his weary muscles relaxing.

As the steam danced across the top of the water and dampened his raven hair, Joel's eyelids fluttered closed. The aromatic oils Tabitha had placed in the water seeped into his skin, bathing him in drowsy heat. The spicy, floral scents reminded Joel of those in Shantar, and despite his excitement to be home, he found himself missing the city of Raja and its colorful culture. Thinking back on his time there, it seemed to have passed by so fast.

Yet he'd been there long enough for a seed to be planted in his soul. Observing Cenric work magic—the magic of words—had a profound impact on Joel. He'd watched in amazement as his mentor bridged the gap between differing cultures and political viewpoints, creating harmonious treaties that would benefit not only one country, but all. With no threats given or shouts exchanged, wielding only words and compassion, Cenric accomplished more in six moonturns than the High Council of Arden had accomplished in the past six years.

The idea of changing the world through peaceful negotiation struck a deep chord in Joel's heart, and he found himself dreaming of a time when he could do the same. He wanted to do what Cenric did. Joel wanted to not only see the world, but enlighten it. Perhaps he would even have opportunities to make peace with Shiraz. The High Council seemed to think war was the only solution, but what if it didn't have to come to that? What if peace were possible?

The truth was that his experience in Shantar had left Joel yearning for more. The well-trodden path he'd been walking had seemed so clear before he'd left on his internship. He would graduate and take a job at the palace, perhaps as a portal guardian or mage trainer. He'd live out his years in Silver City, and yes, his contributions to Arden would be valuable—but what if he could do more?

Joel's eyes popped open at the sound of a throat being cleared. Joel's gaze came to rest on his companion, standing in the doorway, and a smile passed over Joel's face as all thoughts of travel were cast aside.

"A message arrived just a moment ago," Gib said, lingering beneath the wooden frame that separated the bathing area from the bedchamber. The young man had changed out of his understudy uniform and now wore a simple white tunic and leather breeches.

Joel sat up a little straighter in the tub, regarding the other man from beneath heavy lashes. "Oh?"

"Hasain has invited us to the Rose Bouquet tonight. Everyone will be there, and they'll want to see you. But we can stay in if you'd like. I know you must be tired—"

"No, no," Joel replied. "I'd love to see everyone. Let's go."

"You're sure?"

"I'm sure." Joel reached for his companion, a silent invitation.

Gib crossed the room and knelt beside the tub, taking Joel's hand into his own. Joel caressed the backside of Gib's hand for a moment before lifting a free palm to the young man's face. Joel's chest tightened. "I've missed you so much."

Gib leaned into the touch as Joel began to run fingers through the brown curls crowning Gib's head. "I've missed you more than words can tell."

Joel made some kind of undignified noise as droplets welled in the corner of each of his eyes.

Gib wiped away each tear with tender care. "I love you."

Silence descended upon the pair as Gib leaned closer, stroking Joel's damp hair and cradling the base of his skull with calloused fingers. The understudy's large, brown eyes scanned Joel's—searching, pondering, seeking an answer to some question far too profound to ask—and then Gib drew their faces together until no space remained between them and their mouths were touching.

Joel trembled when their lips met, the kiss timid and soft after so many moonturns apart. It felt new again, as innocent and pure as the first time. Joel moved slowly, reacquainting himself with every dip and curve of the other man's mouth, and Gib seemed more than content to allow it.

And then, after several more moments, Gib pressed deeper still, and Joel's head swam with fuzzy euphoria as the kiss became less tame and more driven by desire. He latched onto his companion, swearing silently never to let go again. How could Joel ever say goodbye a second time? How could he forsake all that he had right here and now?

The need for air finally forced them apart, and Joel pulled back, panting and overcome by boundless emotion. "When are our friends expecting us at the Rose?"

Gib smiled coyly. "Not for another couple of marks."

"Perfect," Joel chuckled into his companion's ear.

"Are you sure you don't mind us tagging along?"

Gib smiled and looked back at his companion. Joel's cheeks were flushed with either the cool night air or the pleasantries of good company, perhaps both. Gib couldn't be sure.

Hasain had kept a step ahead of the pair but turned back long enough to reply. "You know everyone wants to see you, Joel. Stop being so modest."

Joel put a hand over his heart. "I've missed all of you terribly. It'll be so good to see everyone."

"Even if you have to come to the Rose Bouquet to see them?" Gib had to lift his voice over the merry music pouring into the street.

They shared a laugh as they followed Hasain to the steps of the tavern. The Rose Bouquet was the largest and possibly the best known tavern in all of Silver City. The three story building had once been a warehouse, but when a wealthy family of merchants purchased it years before, they had repurposed it into the establishment it was today. Gib had seen no finer place where one might get a warm meal, strong drink, a room for the night, and even someone to share a bed with—all for the right price, of course—and despite the clientele one might expect to find here, the crowd was always an assortment of mixed company. The Rose Bouquet was a place where lords and ladies could be found mingling with waifs, soldiers, and beggars.

Hasain led the way through the open door. Music, light, and laughter enveloped them, and Gib lifted his nose to the smell of stew even as Joel made a sound of appreciation. Of course, the entire dwelling was packed. No booth, table, or chair lay empty.

Gib called over the din to Hasain. "Do you know where everyone is?"

Already on his way to the bar, Hasain barely glanced back. "How would I know? Are you too spoiled to look for yourself?"

Gib let out a huff but smiled when he felt Joel's fingertips brush his own. Their eyes met and instantly, heat pooled on Gib's face. "We could just head back to the estate. They don't even know we're here yet."

"Are you trying to bribe me?" Joel quirked one brow and laughed.

Gib's face burned like someone held a torch close by. "No—I mean—oh hell, there's always tomorrow to come see everyone."

Blue eyes twinkling, Joel opened his mouth to respond, only to be stopped short by a boisterous voice shouting over the crowd. "Oh, hey! Joel *is* back! Gib Nemesio and Joel Adelwijn, over here!"

Gib grimaced. They'd been caught after all.

In a booth in the far corner, a familiar figure waved his hands at them. Nage Nessuno was wearing his sentinel uniform, but judging from his good cheer and nearly empty flagon, Gib was willing to bet his duties had ended for the day. An orphan from birth, Nage had been drafted alongside Gib. Counted among the poorest students that year, he and Nage had forged a bond as a defense against the "aloof highborns." It all seemed laughable now, seeing as they'd befriended Diddy a moment after only to find out he was a prince.

"I guess we'd be missed now," Joel whispered. "Perhaps we'll only stay for one drink?"

Gib nodded as he waved back to Nage. "Fair enough—but no more touching me. My face is already blazing."

They made their way to the booth without another word, but Joel made heavy eye contact the whole way. Gib's head didn't feel any less fuzzy by the time they got there.

Tarquin had arrived before them and was squeezed between Nage and the wall. His pale face went red. "Oh, thank The Two. I was beginning to think I'd have to put up with him by myself all night."

Rolling laughter gave rise to a hiccup before Nage cuffed his friend's arm. "Tarquin's no fun. Wouldn't even get a mead 'til he knew you two were gonna show."

Tarquin straightened the laces on his tunic absently and glanced around. "Someone had to babysit you. You're lucky that girl didn't take you seriously earlier. I would have been mortified to decline her."

Nage laughed. "The two of you should have seen it." He gasped for air. "I thought to buy him a pretty Red Rose, you see an—"

Joel hid his face behind his hands and Tarquin nearly slipped under the table. Gib couldn't help but laugh. The workers at the Rose Bouquet each wore a simple rose as part of their attire. The various colors—white, yellow, and red—showed what type of service the person offered. White and yellow roses indicated a worker was there to be seen and offer help, but it was common knowledge they weren't to be touched. Red roses, on the other hand, were reserved for the prostitutes. Gib could scarcely imagine what Tarquin would do if he found himself the subject of a Red Rose's desire.

Hasain found his way to their table. "Did I miss something?"

Joel scooted into the booth and motioned for Gib to follow. "We were discussing the events of the evening—"

"Nothing of importance!" balked Tarquin.

Gib nearly choked for trying to stop his laughing fit. "Are you going to sit down or not?"

Hasain remained standing with his drink in hand. He cast a shrewd gaze around the room and heaved a sigh. "Does anyone know if Kezra has arrived yet?"

The giddy laughter fell away as Gib and Tarquin shared a somber look. Tensions had been growing recently between some of Gib's friends—Kezra, Nawaz Arrio, and Hasain. Kezra was every bit the warrior she had trained to be, but she was also a woman, and in recent moonturns, both Nawaz and Hasain had grown fond of her undeniable strength and fiery spirit. Whether she'd asked for it or not, Kezra had won the affections of both men, putting the group of friends in an awkward position.

At first, Kezra had laughed them both off, but Gib knew she'd always favored Nawaz a little. He suspected it to be because Nawaz would spar with her and talk as though she were his equal. Hasain's flattery and charm worked with the ladies of the court, but not on Kezra.

"Yeah," Nage replied. "She and Nawaz went to get drinks a bit ago. I don't know where they are now." He tipped his flagon up and took a long pull. "Should one of us go look for 'em?"

Hasain's face pinched as he sat beside Gib. "No. They'll find their way back—if they mean to."

Silence rolled off Hasain like icy waves, and try as Gib might, he could think of nothing to say.

After a brief moment, Joel cleared his throat. Blue eyes scanned their company and his words were smooth, calm, every bit like that of an envoy. "Nage, how goes your new assignment? Though, I suppose it's not new anymore, is it?"

"It was when you left." Nage pushed his drink away and pressed out a quiet belch. "Eh, it's fine. I like bein' inside Silver better than on the outer wall."

"Really? Weren't you posted near the mine where you used to work?"

A sly smile split his face. "Exactly. Too many old 'pals' out there. I'm better off in here where no one knows me. I can meet some better—"

Tarquin perked up at that. "That's right! Now that Joel and Cenric Leal are back, you'll have to meet your lady friend's father!"

"Lady friend?" Gib asked. "What's this then? I didn't know you were courting."

Nage sank down in his seat, covering his face with one hand. "We're *not* courting."

"Not *yet*," Tarquin clarified. "But now that Nia's father is back, you'll be able to ask permission."

Joel's eyes went wide. "*Cenric's* daughter? Nage, you scoundrel, how did you manage that?"

When Nage only blushed deeper and shrugged, Joel reached across the table to give his shoulder a friendly pat. "Cenric really is a very nice man. You needn't worry about meeting him—"

"Ambassador Cenric Leal? Arden's prized envoy?" Hasain questioned coldly. "Gentry Leal and his family are of noble rank. What makes you think he's going to allow a Nessuno to court his daughter?"

Nage winced, and Joel whipped around to give Hasain a poisonous look. "Perhaps you've already forgotten Cenric's kind heart and open mind. It was only last year when *you* went on your internship with him, Hasain Radek!"

"I'm merely stating the truth," Hasain spat back. "You shouldn't give your friend false hope. A Nessuno with no name and nothing to offer shouldn't waste his time pursuing a lady of noble standing." Dark, critical eyes fell onto Nage, who was having a difficult time looking back. "You'll likely find yourself with empty hands and a broken heart."

With a half-hearted nod, Nage sank a bit farther in the booth. Gib couldn't watch in silence any longer. He opened his mouth, intent on telling Hasain to shut up, but Joel beat Gib to it.

"Titles are fickle things, Hasain Radek. You and I were both born lords without doing a thing to earn the right. Others have to work for all they have. Cenric Leal knows this, and I would encourage you to remember it as well." Joel turned back to Nage, the ghost of some uncertainty in his misty eyes. "Love should be nurtured, lest we take it for granted. And it should be prized so it may never be lost."

Hasain opened his mouth to retort, his face an angry red and looking every bit like his father in the council room. Gib stretched out his arms in a desperate attempt to create space between his companion and friend. "Enough of this. We came here to have a good time."

Joel let out a long sigh. "Gib's right. The wheel has made half a turn since I've seen any of you. This outing should be about us catching up and making light." He chose to smile, not as gloriously as was typical, but better than naught. "I suppose congratulations are in order. I see the council has been unsuccessful in overturning King Rishi's new law."

Gib and Hasain exhaled as one and, for the moment, the air became breathable again.

Tarquin jumped to fill the space so no more awkward silences could arise. "Yes, but not for lack of trying. My father has said there are those who still oppose the draft age being raised." He glanced around and lowered his voice a pitch. "Not the least of whom being General Morathi himself."

Gib inclined his head. "The general has his opinions, but for now the King still has the majority."

"Ah. Good news then," Joel said, eyes slowly warming back up.

"Hope the King's majority holds out for the sake of war, too," Nage grunted. Long fingers toyed with his flagon absently.

Hasain set his own mug down with a clunk. "My father is smarter than most of those idiot council members combined. He'd rather die than see us go to war over something as petty as a land dispute. When I take my place on the council, my first order of business will be to see someone more level-headed take the position of High Councilor."

Gib bit the inside of his cheek as he watched Joel nod in agreement. Despite family ties, Neetra Adelwijn had no supporters at this table. Even still, Gib had no desire to be stuck in the middle of a new "debate" and fished for something to change the subject. He nudged Joel. "Oh! Diddy has finally been allowed to go to council!"

Joel laughed. "I remember, dear heart. I saw him in the hall this afternoon. But good for him. I'd heard rumors Aunt Dahlia was never going to allow him out of her sight. I'd begun to worry!"

Laughter rippled around the booth. Had Diddy been present, he most likely would have scolded them for enjoying his misfortune.

"There you all are!" a familiar voice boomed.

"Oh wonderful," Tarquin chuckled. "Here comes more trouble."

Nawaz Arrio, nephew of Dean Marc and newly graduated Healer, advanced on them with Kezra at his side. They both had rosy cheeks, full smiles, and half-empty mugs. Nawaz's bright eyes danced when they landed on his step-cousin. "Joel! The rumors of your return are true! How was your trip?"

Kezra climbed into the booth beside Nage, elbowing him out of her way. "Move over, you drunk. Take your keg with you."

He snorted and swiped at her but complied. Nawaz slid into the seat as well, giving Hasain a quick grin before turning his attention back to Joel. Gib wondered if Nawaz failed to notice the sour look Hasain gave in return.

"Shantar was lovely," Joel gushed. "A bit humid, but lovely. The people were friendly and their customs vibrant—" He turned to look at Kezra. "Your mother must miss her homeland."

Kezra shrugged. "She's said she doesn't miss the snakes or heat."

Joel laughed. "Point taken, but the colors and culture were so dynamic." The mage gave her a sly look. "I thought to buy you a lovely new sari while I was there—a souvenir from my travels."

"Better you save your money, Adelwijn." Kezra gestured down toward her drab tunic and leggings. "I could have taken it to Gib's brother and asked for curtains, I suppose."

Joel tipped his head back and cackled. Gib snorted a retort about how Tayver would never dream of "wasting" such fine fabric, and Kezra then made a vague allusion to using the worthless dress as a cleaning rag.

Hasain had kept quiet since their arrival, but Gib noticed the man's dark mood resurfacing as Nawaz and Kezra bantered playfully with one another.

At last, the young Radek lord appeared unable to hold his tongue any longer. "Where were the two of you just now? I didn't see you when I arrived."

Always the clown, Nawaz wagged his eyebrows and leaned across the table. "Maybe we were hidin'."

Gib had the distinct impression Nawaz shouldn't perhaps get so close to his longtime friend. Hasain looked like a hissing snake, poised for a strike, but Nawaz seemed oblivious.

Kezra, however, seemed to pick up on his foul mood. She leveled Hasain with a heavy, unapologetic stare. "We were outside, getting some air on the porch."

Hasain sneered. "I thought the porch was reserved for prostitutes and those too poor to buy a room for their services."

Nawaz's vibrant eyes went cold as he turned a scowl onto Hasain. "Watch your mouth."

Hasain lowered his face but continued to mutter indiscernible insults under his breath.

Gib winced. He hadn't caught the words, but the intent was clear.

Across the table, Kezra's wild hair flew out in all directions as she took to her feet, glowering above Hasain. "If you have something to say then say it so we may hear—none of this slithering on your belly and hissing through poison fangs. You're not a politician *yet*, Hasain."

The booth went silent. Joel's hand was squeezing Gib's knee beneath the table. Shooting his companion a glance, Gib wished he could think of something to say or do. If someone didn't end the argument now, Kezra was likely to dive over the table and throw a punch.

Hasain's face went a terrible crimson, but he didn't rush to counter

43

her. When he did finally find his voice, it was stifled and low. "Apologies. It seems I can't speak tonight without causing offense."

Nawaz opened his mouth, but Hasain was already sliding out of the booth and standing.

He gave a curt bow. "I take my leave. Goodnight."

"Hasain—"

Nawaz started after his friend, but Hasain was too quick. Waving Nawaz off, Hasain turned on his heel, making no stops on his way out the door. Nawaz slouched back in his seat, disgust and disappointment etched across his typically lighthearted features.

"Sorry guys. Things are, uh, a little rough right now."

Joel leaned across the table and laid a hand over his cousin's. "You know you have my support, as you supported me not so long ago. Truth be told, Hasain wasn't in much mood for merriment even before you arrived. Don't take his disposition to heart."

Kezra gave Nawaz a thump on the shoulder. "He'll come around. He's just feeling pinched right now."

The past year had seen a lot of changes for the gang of friends. Coming into adulthood was no small step. Gib gripped Joel's hand, hoping the two of them wouldn't encounter any such troubles. They'd already had to fight so hard for what they had. Daya, would they have to fight any more? He looked at Joel. Those misty blue eyes with their supernatural wisdom always comforted Gib—only now, Joel was looking at the floor, perhaps even willfully avoiding Gib's eyes.

CHAPTER THREE

Gib drifted into consciousness. Bathed in warmth, he was slow to open his eyes, taking a moment to revel in the security of knowing he wasn't waking up to an aching stomach or drafty farmhouse. No, those days were long past. This morning, he was awakening in the safest, most loving place he could ever imagine. Joel's prone form beside him was proof enough of that.

Sunlight flooded the room, casting rays of gold across Gib's pillow and quilted bedspread. Taking a moment to yawn and stretch his limbs, he blinked the sleepiness from his eyes and turned a fond gaze onto his companion.

Joel looked lovely. Flecks of light hit his soft, onyx hair and fair skin, showering him in an aura that seemed almost magical. A telltale curl played at his lips while he slept, causing Gib to want to smile, too. Absently, he brushed a wave of Joel's hair away from his eyes. *It's still hard to believe he's home.*

One sennight had passed since Joel's return from Shantar, and Gib found himself spending more time at the Adelwijn estate in the past seven days than he had in the past seven moonturns combined. Tarquin spared no mercy. He'd teased Gib in class on more than one occasion, asking coyly if he ever planned to inform his roommate that Gib had moved out of their shared dormitory room. Gib had huffed and blushed, but he couldn't exactly defend himself. He *had* been spending every waking moment—and night—with Joel. *But can anyone really fault me for wanting to be with him? We've been apart for six moonturns!*

Joel rolled onto his side as he began to stir from slumber, and Gib couldn't resist the urge to lean forward and place a light kiss on his companion's mouth. Joel's eyes fluttered open, his crystal orbs impossibly blue and bottomless.

"Good morning," Gib whispered. Modest heat rose to his cheeks when he realized he'd been caught gaping at the other man.

Joel put a hand to his mouth as he yawned. "I slept in."

"No, the eighth bell hasn't even tolled yet."

A soft chuckle made its way through Joel's parted lips. "That *is* sleeping in for me! In Shantar, Cenric demanded I be awake and dressed

45

before the sun rose."

"It's Harvest festival," Gib replied gently, sliding closer to his companion. "We can sleep as long as we want."

Joel arched an eyebrow. "Sleep? Is that what you had in mind?"

Gib *did* blush now. He fumbled over his next words. "You know what I meant."

Slender arms went around Gib's shoulders, pulling him closer. "I missed you."

"I missed you, too."

Silence fell across the room as they shared a prolonged kiss, leaving Gib breathless and lightheaded. *Daya, how did I ever get through all those moonturns without him?*

He relinquished Joel's mouth only when they both were sputtering for air. Tracing a finger along the ridge of Joel's jaw, Gib could feel the slightest trace of stubble where the well-shaven hair had begun to grow back. His hand finally came to rest against Joel's cheek. "I'm so glad you're back. Things can return to the way they were. We can pick up right where we left off."

A twinge of uncertainty flashed behind Joel's eyes. If Gib hadn't been looking, he wouldn't have even caught it. But he did. His pulse quickened. Was something wrong?

A moment later, however, Joel smiled and his placid demeanor returned. "I'm glad to be home."

Joel's pleasant tone was genuine. Nothing suggested he felt otherwise. Gib relaxed his tense shoulders. Surely he'd just been imagining things. *Way to be paranoid, you fool.*

"I suppose I should get dressed," Gib murmured. "Tay and Cal are supposed to stop by this morning. We're gonna write to Liza."

Joel propped himself up by his elbows. "Any word from her lately?"

Gib shook his head. "Nope. But no news is good news, I guess."

"I'm sure she's fine," Joel replied, squeezing Gib's hand. "My father says the northern border hasn't seen anything more than the occasional skirmish. Hopefully, the High Council will realize how foolish they're being and send the soldiers stationed in Port Ostlea home."

Gib stared down at his hands. Liza was more than capable of taking care of herself, but that didn't stop him from worrying about his elder sister. She'd been on active duty in the north ever since the High Council deemed it necessary to build up forces there, in case the tiny nation of Nales made a move against Arden's northernmost city, Port Ostlea. Seneschal Koal and King Rishi adamantly voted against the measure, but the decree had passed anyway. *It's ridiculous,* Gib lamented. *One person starts a rumor that Nales is holding secret meetings with Shiraz and suddenly we're verging on war with two countries instead of one!*

Joel cleared his throat as he climbed from the bed. "I'm going to draw hot water for a bath. I have to go see Cenric after our morning meal."

"Oh?" Gib quirked a brow. "During the festival?"

Joel didn't glance up as he slipped into a cotton bathrobe. "Internship papers. I have to get them signed."

"Oh, good. So you'll *officially* be a free man."

"Indeed," Joel replied, grinning handsomely.

Joel went to bathe, leaving Gib to dress in private. He could smell the aroma of fresh bread rising from the kitchen, and his stomach gurgled in anticipation of the delicious meal Tabitha had undoubtedly prepared. Running fingers through his curls, Gib slipped from the bedchamber and made his way downstairs.

He was surprised to find Calisto already waiting for him. The young student sat at the dining room table and chatted with Tabitha as she set out plates. When Gib came through the door, Cal's eyes brightened. "There you are! What took you so long?"

Gib scratched his head as he took a seat beside his brother. "What do you mean? I was sleeping."

"*Sleeping?*" Cal chided. "The sun's been up for two marks already. I would know. I was up at dawn!"

"Well, why did you get up so early?" Gib asked, ruffling the younger boy's mop of hair. "You don't have classes today. The festival is going on."

Cal sighed like an impatient child. "Classes, no. But I had morning chores."

"Ah, yes. I remember those." Gib held back laughter. He wasn't made to do chores anymore—another perk of being Koal's understudy.

Tabitha smiled as she filled their goblets with milk. "Would you like bread with your eggs this morning, Gibben?"

Gib nodded. "That sounds delicious. Thank you, Tabitha."

The servant girl turned to Cal next. "How about you, Calisto? Are you hungry?"

"Yes, please!" Cal chirped.

Gib waited until Tabitha had left the room to tease his brother. "Don't they feed you morning meal at Academy anymore?"

Cal grinned. "Of course they do. But I worked up an appetite during my chores. And besides, the food is better here. Tabitha always makes me something special."

Sure enough, Tabitha returned with a loaf of steaming bread and scrambled eggs—and an apple fritter for Calisto. Gib chuckled as he watched the youngster devour the treat in three hearty bites. "Careful you don't spoil him too awfully much, Tabitha."

A little while later, Joel joined them. His damp hair was combed back, and he'd donned a fresh set of mage robes. As he sat down, Gib caught the faint scent of lavender soap wafting from Joel's polished, ivory skin. Tabitha served him eggs, and Gib offered half of his loaf. Joel thanked them both graciously.

"How do you like your classes, Cal?" Joel asked as they dined.

"Good," Cal replied, pausing to take a drink. "I like them all—well, except Ardenian History. I think I'd like the class better if I had a different teacher. Professor Anders Malin-Rai doesn't really seem to like his job or care about how the students do."

"Shocking revelation," Joel remarked tersely.

Gib rolled his eyes. "No doubt." He had nothing good to say about Councilor Anders. The man might be Kezra's sire, but the father and daughter were as different as night was to day. Gib heard a soft knock at the door just then. "That must be Tayver." He started to get up, but Tabitha flew by to answer the call.

Tayver strutted into the room in a flurry of golden buttons and elaborate silk tassels. He wore his hair longer than the other two brothers, choosing to tame his unruly curls by binding them into a ponytail at the nape of his neck. Tabitha took his cloak, and he thanked the servant by planting a light kiss on the backside of her hand. Her cheeks went a rosy pink.

Gib tried not to snort. "Hello, Tay."

"Glad to see you all had the courtesy to wait for me." Tayver sat down heavily between his brothers.

"Would you like some breakfast?" Joel asked, leaning forward in his chair.

Tayver waved a hand. "No, no. I took my meal with Master Joran before I left. Would you imagine he roused me an entire mark before dawn to start our new work order?"

"I'm sorry," Joel replied. "That sounds dreadful."

"Oh no, I love it!" Tayver chuckled. "We've been commissioned to create a wedding gown for Lady Rosalin Elsey. She's marrying some disgustingly rich lord from Greenbank and wants the entire garment crafted from sea silk. *Sea silk*! Do you know how expensive that is? One foot of fabric is, like, a hundred gold coins!" He laughed as though it was the most absurd thing in the world. "Anyway, Master Joran trusts only me to assist him with such a monumental task, so I'm going to be a very busy man for the next few sennights."

"I'm sure your fellow understudies are *so* jealous," Gib teased him.

"Oh, undoubtedly."

Tabitha returned with a mug of tea, which Tayver accepted. He sipped at the simmering liquid for a moment before setting it down. "So, are we going to write Liza? Who brought the quill and parchment?"

Gib thumped the rucksack sitting in his lap. "Right here." He pulled a quill and inkwell from within and a piece of parchment a moment later.

Joel cleared his throat as he took one final sip from his chalice. "I'm going to excuse myself. I have to go to the palace to visit my mentor." He held out a tentative hand to Gib. "See you this evening?"

"Yes. I'm going to meet Tarquin at the festival, but I'll be back afterwards." Gib squeezed the offered hand and leaned up to press a gentle kiss to Joel's mouth. Tayver and Calisto didn't even bat an eyelash at the sight. He'd told them about Joel around the time they sold the farm, and both boys had been completely supportive. Liza, likewise, had expressed acceptance, even outright glee. It was good to know his family approved of the relationship.

Gib watched his companion depart. *I'm truly the luckiest person in Arden. My brothers are safe, my sister is alive, I'm the understudy of Seneschal Koal, and Joel is home and here to stay. I'm on top of a blissful pedestal, and I couldn't be any happier.*

As he laid out the parchment and began to write, an unexplainable lump manifested in his chest. The only downside to sitting at the crest of a pedestal was that it was so very easy to be knocked down.

Joel sucked in a sharp breath as he set both hands against the closed door leading to Ambassador Cenric's suite. His stomach was in knots and his knees felt as though they might give out, but despite that, he raised a fist to tap the wooden door.

"Come in," came Cenric's immediate response from inside.

Joel bit his lip and pushed through the threshold. He still wasn't exactly sure what he hoped to accomplish by visiting Cenric. He'd told Gib earlier that he was going to get his internship paperwork signed, but even now, standing in the doorway of the envoy's suite, Joel wasn't sure if he actually planned to sign anything. *All I know is I had about a million questions to ask Cenric and now that I'm here, I can think of none of them.*

Cenric lounged upon a cushioned bench, and he wasn't alone. A young woman around Joel's age sat beside him. Given the fact that she and Cenric shared the same hazel eyes, round faces, and cropped brown hair, Joel found it safe to assume this was one of Cenric's daughters. In fact, Joel was pretty sure he'd met her in passing at some court function or another but couldn't recall her name.

"Ah, Joel," the ambassador greeted. A mix of confusion and courteousness passed across his face. "I didn't expect to see you today. Did I manage to forget about a scheduled meeting—"

"*Oh*, no, no," Joel corrected, feeling his ears beginning to burn. "I just—my internship papers—it's nothing important. I can stop by another time if you're entertaining company."

Cenric waved a hand in the air. "Oh, stop with the modesty. Come in, come in. Have a seat!"

As Joel turned to close the door, the young woman sitting beside

Cenric let out a snort. "Seneschal Koal's son is your understudy, Da? Why didn't you tell me?"

Cenric groaned. "Gara, meet Joel Adelwijn. Joel, this is my elder daughter, Gara Leal."

"Hello." Joel moved closer and offered his hand for a shake.

Gara stared at his hand but didn't take hold of it. Amusement flashed behind her green eyes. "You don't remember me, do you?"

Joel swallowed. *Should I?* "Uh, I—"

It must have been painfully obvious he had no idea what she was going on about because a moment later, Gara grinned and elaborated further. "Many years ago, at a particularly boring Aithne ball, you and I got into some trouble together. We stashed firecrackers in the tinder pile before the King set it on fire—"

Joel's jaw dropped. Suddenly he remembered *everything*. "And the entire pyre exploded into a ball of blue flame, and everyone standing watch nearly died of fright!"

Gara threw her head back and laughed, nearly in hysterics. "Yes! It was so funny!"

"My father didn't think so."

"Yeah, mine either." Gara glanced at Cenric, who was sporting a most-displeased frown. "In fact, I think King Rishi was the only person who found any humor in our little prank."

Cenric crossed his arms over his chest. "One guess as to who Gara stole those firecrackers from. Let's just say I never brought any more trinkets from Beihai back with me on subsequent trips to the country."

Joel covered his red face. "For the record, it was all her idea, Cenric. I was young and easily impressionable." *In fact, that was pretty much the exact line I used to justify the incident to Father. Not that he believed me. I was still sentenced to house arrest for a solid moonturn afterward.*

"I don't doubt it," Cenric replied. "Gara's always been a bit of a hell-raiser."

The young woman beamed. "I learned from the best, Da." She leapt from the bench and took a playful bow, and it was then Joel realized she was clad in a lengthy tunic and trousers. It was no wonder Joel hadn't recognized her. The girl he remembered from the Aithne ball had been wearing a beautiful dress and had long, flowing hair—a far cry from the boyish haircut and clothing style Gara now donned.

"Well, it's been grand, but I'm afraid I have to go," Gara said. She leaned down and planted a peck on her father's forehead. "Try to come home at a reasonable time tonight, Da. Contrary to what you might believe, Ma, Nia, and I miss you—not to mention you're supposed to be relaxing before you're assigned a new mission, remember?"

"Yes, yes." Cenric shooed her away. "I'll come home right after I finish making copies of these documents I brought back from Shantar.

You'd think the Crown could afford to send me a scribe to do such things, but what do I know? Now off with you. And stay out of trouble, all right?"

Laughter echoed off the walls as Gara departed.

Joel turned to give his mentor an incredulous stare. "She seems like a handful."

Cenric went to his writing desk and sat down. "Mmm, yes. The Blessed Son gifted me two beautiful daughters. Both are—spirited. Nia's got her mother's disposition. Soft and gentle until someone angers her and then—" He chuckled to himself. "Well, let's just say I feel bad for the young man who's recently begun to court her. Gara, on the other hand, marches to her own beat. She's an adventurer like me, though I doubt she'll ever be an ambassador. She's much too apt to speak her mind and cause entire alliances to come crashing down."

"Some would call that courage," Joel reflected. "There aren't many people left in this world who are brave enough to say what they're feeling."

Cenric turned to look over his shoulder. "Oh, I'm not disagreeing with you. But an abrasive personality has no place in the heart of an envoy, don't you think?" He took up a quill and dabbed the end into an inkwell sitting beside him. "I've learned over the years that patience most certainly *is* a virtue—as well as a quick wit and the ability to compromise. You know, Joel, *you'd* make a fantastic envoy, should you ever decide it's the career path you want to take. I don't think I've ever mentored a more level-headed youngster."

Joel cleared his throat. "That's actually what I came here to discuss."

For several moments longer, the scribble of Cenric's quill was the only sound to be heard, and Joel politely remained quiet while the ambassador worked. Joel gazed around the suite while he waited, taking time to gawk at just how many *things* were crammed into the small space.

Various trinkets and oddities littered the room. A tapestry made from fine silk and dyed with bright pigments hung from one wall, while an odd-looking stringed instrument—some kind of crude guitar perhaps—was propped upright in the corner of the room beneath a medallion constructed of beads and feathers. Oil paintings, too numerous to count, took up any remaining space on the wall—and the canvases were also stacked in hazardous piles around the suite. Even Cenric's writing desk was a jumble. A tall vase filled with dried blossoms sat precariously close to the edge, pushed aside by a stack of parchment paper and books, some of which were covered in so much dust Joel couldn't even read the titles. On the other side of the table lay a strange wooden board. It had checkered squares painted onto it and small figurines that could be moved around.

"Senet," Cenric grunted, and Joel realized the ambassador had set the quill down and turned around on his stool. "A game from Gyptia. All about strategy and wit. Games can take marks, even days, to complete. I brought it back from Gyptia after my last excursion, though I don't know why I bothered. All the damn thing does is take up space, and I don't have enough spare time to even play a full game."

Joel cast his gaze around the room again. "Are all of these items souvenirs from your travels?"

"Yes, mostly. I try to bring back something from every land I visit."

"Well, I guess it's safe to assume you've seen the entire world then."

Cenric chuckled. "Most of it. I've been as far south as Gyptia and all the way into the mountainous Northern Empire in the far north."

"Have you ever been to Shiraz?" Joel asked, thinking of the conflict on the eastern border.

"No, not Shiraz." Cenric's voice was flat. "The last Ardenian envoy sent into Shiraz was our late Queen Jorja—and well, we all know how *that* ended."

Joel winced. Many years ago, Queen Jorja had gone into Shiraz in the hope of avoiding war, to promote peace—only to be betrayed. They'd slaughtered her entire party and thrown Jorja's body across the border as a message that there'd be no further talking between the nations. Arden had mourned the loss of their Queen, known for her tactical mind and firm justice. Joel had been too young to remember the incident, though the Ardenian history books all praised Jorja's final act as valiant.

Cenric cleared his throat and changed the subject. "What questions did you have to ask me?"

Joel suddenly found it hard to meet the envoy's gaze, so he opted to stare at the various paintings on the walls instead. "Do you remember the warning you gave me right before we left for Shantar? About becoming entranced by the idea of changing the world?"

The older man nodded. "I do."

"Well, I've been giving it some thought since we returned home, and I think—" Joel paused, wringing his hands. "If you have no other trainees lined up yet, I think perhaps I'd like to remain your understudy for the time being. You're the best at the job, and I know there's a wealth of knowledge to be learned from your wisdom."

"Are you saying you want to be an ambassador?"

"I–I think so. I mean, I'm not completely sure, but I can't get the idea out of my head."

Cenric leaned back, resting his elbows on the writing desk behind him. "You know there's more to ambassadorial work than admiring the pretty scenery, don't you?"

"Of course I do." Joel played with the sleeve of his pristine mage robe. "I want to do something meaningful, Cenric. If I possess these qualities you speak of, I want to put them to good use. I can go into these foreign countries with an open mind and not only share my ideas with them but also be willing to *hear* what they have to say. I can listen, truly *listen*. And be willing to make changes for the betterment of Arden. I love my country, but our allegiances are few and far between during these times of war—mostly because people on both sides of the conflict are too stubborn to sit and hear what the other side has to say. If only one person stands up and suggests compromise, surely others will follow. I want to be that person, the one who takes a stand."

"I admire all you've said, Joel. You have wisdom beyond your age, and as I said before, I whole-heartedly believe you have the necessary qualities to be an outstanding envoy," Cenric replied, keeping his voice carefully neutral. "But it's not a decision to make lightly. You have so much going for you here in Silver—a father and mother who love you, siblings, friends—and someone dear to your heart. You're a powerful mage. You could rise in the ranks, even sit on the council one day, all without having to leave the people you love."

Joel bit his bottom lip. "Why are you trying to talk me out of it?"

"I'm not," the envoy replied, shaking his head. "I just want you to be aware of the reality of the situation. The life of an ambassador is one of solitude. It's hard to maintain friends and family while constantly on the move."

"You've been able to. You have children. You're happily married—"

Skeptical laughter burst from Cenric's mouth. "My wife has the heart of a saint. She's about the only woman in Arden who would deal with having an ambassador for a husband. Alas, our marriage has never been without its struggles. How could it be? I was absent from the start. When I left on my first mission, my wife was with child. I returned from the Northern Empire to a little girl almost a full wheelturn old who had no idea who I was. Do you know how many Naming Day celebrations I missed? How many memories I'll never be able to replicate or replace? I was stationed in Galia the year Gara entered Academy, and in Gyptia when Nia discovered she had the Healing gift. I wasn't there when they needed me most—and even if my family forgives my absence over the years, it doesn't mean I can. I'm Arden's most coveted envoy but the worst kind of father and husband." Cenric's eyes were distant as he met Joel's uneasy gaze. "So what you have to ask yourself, Joel, is whether or not you're willing to make such sacrifices. I've done great things for Arden. I've helped to create treaties and trade agreements. I've been the negotiator when both sides wanted to resort to violence and instead walked away from the table as allies. And yes, I've seen places most people only dream of—but all of it was at a cost. *All of it.*"

Joel swallowed even as his stomach twisted into uncomfortable knots. He'd already known that by becoming an envoy his relationship with Gib would be strained—but the thought of losing Gib altogether had never crossed his mind. *It would be selfish to ask Gib to put his life on hold if I decide to make a career as an envoy. Daya, I'm not sure I can leave him again. We've been through so much together. I don't know if I could ever find happiness without him*

53

by my side.

Joel blinked in contemplation. "You've given me much to ponder."

Cenric turned and fished through the pile of parchment paper on his desk. At last, he pulled a couple of documents from within the clutter. "These are your internship papers."

Joel took note of the blank space at the bottom of the page.

"Why don't we just leave them unsigned for the time being?"

Joel forced a smile. "Thank you. My head's feeling a bit full. I'll go home and—think things over now, if that's all right?"

"Of course." Cenric gave him a gentle pat on the forearm. "Take your time. I'm in no rush to get rid of you just yet, understudy."

Mustering another smile, Joel stood to take his leave. *I'm going back to the estate and talking to Gib about this. I'm done with secrets. He deserves to know what's going on—and I need his insight. If he doesn't want me to go then—*

As Joel reached for the handle, someone pounded the door from the outside. The loud bang surprised him enough to take a step backward.

"Oh, *now* what?" Cenric groaned from behind Joel. "Never a moment's peace! Well, go on. Let the fiend inside!"

Following his mentor's command, Joel pulled the door open and was surprised to see a pair of royal guardsmen waiting outside.

"Is Ambassador Cenric Leal here?" one of the sentinels demanded.

Joel looked over his shoulder in time to see Cenric rise from his stool. The envoy came to the door and peered out. His joyful demeanor hardened at the sight of the guards. "Gentlemen, what can I do for you?"

"Ambassador Cenric Leal, by order of King Rishi Radek, you've been summoned to the council room."

"*Now?*"

The guardsman's voice remained flat. "I insist you follow us immediately, Ambassador."

A horrible chill found its way up Joel's spine. *What is this about? Why the urgency?*

Cenric's mouth pulled back into a grave frown as he glanced at Joel. "Well, understudy, it looks like you aren't going home quite yet. Come, let us see what's so important that the King has requested my company."

Cool winds gusted, blowing Gib's hair all about his rosy cheeks.

Tarquin laughed and gave his friend a pat on the back. "Should have brought a bonnet. Your fair curls are looking a mess."

"Ha-ha, very funny." Gib pulled his cloak tighter. "Let's find a cider stand and buy a drink."

Tarquin followed close on Gib's heels as the two friends wove their way through the crowded streets of Trader's Row. The annual Harvest Festival was in full swing, and vendors had their carts lined up to sell their wares. Gib never had a lot of pocket money, but he had enough for a warm drink and some food.

"I can only stay out for a little while. Cal asked me to come help him with his reading later," Gib said as they walked.

"How has his first sennight of Academy treated him? Does he like his classes?"

As tall and gangly as Gib was short and stout, Tarquin fumbled along while trying not to bump into anyone. Honestly, Gib had no idea how someone who'd completed two years of sentinel training could be so clumsy on his feet. He supposed it had to do with how quickly his friend was growing *up* but not *out*. Tarquin was currently all knees and elbows. *I just wish I'd grow upwards first. I'd even take the knocking knees.*

They stopped at a stand and purchased two mugs of steaming cider. "Oh, well enough. He's making friends with his roommate." Gib accepted and paid for his drink and then waited while Tarquin did the same. "He helped me write to Liza just this morning."

Tarquin blew air on his drink before tasting it. "Any word from her yet?"

Gib shook his head, and silence stole across them as they drank. Being a soldier posted on an active border was no task for the faint of heart, and Gib knew he could receive word of Liza's death just as easily as a letter from her hand. Calisto and Tayver knew too but, thus far, neither of them had said as much.

"No news is good news." Tarquin's voice was hushed as he spoke. "Asher's been out there a time or two for reinforcements. He said the Nales border is more stable than Shiraz's." He was trying to be helpful— his earnest tone said as much—but Gib couldn't help the churning in his stomach.

"That's what I keep telling Cal. Liza's better off in the north than to the east." Gib tried to comfort himself with the knowledge that Asher Aldino, Tarquin's older brother, had gone to Nales and made a safe return. But Asher was a politician and rarely saw the front line of any skirmishes. *Liza is fine. Until I have that letter in my hand, she's fine.*

They finished their drinks without another word and handed the mugs back to the vendor. Blood warmed, Gib and Tarquin ventured back out into the busy street toward the Rose Bouquet. The music and entertainment there never failed to attract a large crowd. As they drew closer, the first upbeat notes tickled their ears. A smile passed between them, and silently the friends agreed not to discuss Liza or the borders anymore.

Tarquin gave a sly smile and asked, "Is Joel going to meet up with us?"

"I don't know. He had to go visit Ambassador Cenric this morning. I barely got a chance to see him."

"Really? It seems you've had all the time in the world to see him. Since his return, I don't think you've spent a single night in our dorm room."

Gib's face burst hot, and he pounced on Tarquin rather than try to force coherent words from a stuttering mouth. The two friends laughed and staggered through the street as the music became louder with each passing step. Longer limbs eventually won the struggle despite Tarquin's lack of grace, and Gib was forced to walk with his head under his friend's armpit for several paces. When they reached the Rose Bouquet, however, Tarquin showed mercy and turned Gib loose.

As always, the owners knew how to throw a party. The music was festive and loud, amplified by the mages who worked for the tavern. Joel had mentioned before that while magery wasn't an incredibly rare gift, it had varying levels of strength, so it only stood to reason the weaker mages might find themselves looking for less strenuous careers. Gib supposed if he'd been born with the ability, amplifying music wouldn't be the worst job he could think of.

Tarquin had already begun to clap along with the rhythm. From under the wide brim of his hat, his pale eyes squinted toward the stage. "I like the singer. I heard she wrote most of the band's songs herself."

Gib had to stand on his tiptoes to be able to make out the performance platform. He could barely see the lead female performer dancing and singing on the stage. "I like this song. It's the one about child soldiers. It created a stir last summer, didn't it? I thought Neetra was going to have a fit. He wanted to arrest the entire troupe, but the King shot him down."

Tarquin leaned in and lowered his voice. "Do you think he's out here somewhere? The King, I mean. Do you suppose he's listening, too?"

Gib laughed. "What? Hidden under a cloak and driving Koal insane by 'not behaving like royalty'? Maybe in his younger days, but I doubt it now." The smile left him, and he lost the tune of the song. "The council is so cross with him most days he doesn't go anywhere without his personal bodyguard and an entourage of royal sentinels. He's not even allowed to walk alone through the palace."

"Father has told me as much." Tarquin stopped clapping and shook his head. "He says he remembers when the King would openly defy the court and say things most unbecoming for royalty. He'd behave in ways Father wouldn't fully discuss." A small laugh escaped him. "Apparently there was always a strong distaste for the rules—"

"Sounds like a scoundrel. Anyone I know?"

Gib jumped in place when the new voice rose just behind. Hasain smiled down, looking for all the world like his father—from the wild glint in his eye to the dimples in his cheeks. He stood with a regal rigidity all his own, however—a reminder of his true nature.

Gib frowned at Hasain. "It would seem you have your own healthy disrespect for protocol. Shouldn't you have a guard of some sort?"

Hasain opened his mouth but was cut off by rambunctious laughter. A moment later, Nawaz Arrio pushed his way through the crowd to join the group. He was red faced and smiling like a fiend. "Oh, you three better run! When she gets here she's gonna—"

"*Nawaz Arrio! You miserable horse's arse! Get back here!*"

Kezra's onyx hair bristled and fanned in every direction, and her sentinel uniform and face were soaked as she tromped up to the group. At some point she must have wiped her forehead and smudged her bindi. The crimson diamond now looked like a terrible scratch across her brow.

Gib raised an eyebrow and attempted not to laugh. "What happened to you, Kezra? You look like a drowned rat!" He lost his battle then and snickered with Nawaz, who also appreciated the joke.

While they were enjoying a good laugh at her expense, Tarquin had already whisked the cloak from his shoulders and offered it to her. His face was cherry red as he held it at arm's length. "H–here, Kezra. You'll catch your death in those wet clothes."

Kezra halted in her attempt to catch the troublemaker who'd wronged her. Looking down at herself and then back to Tarquin, who couldn't hold her gaze, she seemed like she would decline his generous offering. But then her face softened just a little, and she nodded graciously. "Thanks. But now you're going to freeze." Kezra whipped around to snarl at Nawaz. "You could do with some common sense and manners like Tarquin!"

Blue eyes danced as Nawaz peeked out from behind a sour looking Hasain. "You looked bored. I came over to say hello."

"And to dump a damned *rain barrel* over my head!"

"That was an accident—"

"The hell it was!"

Just as she was preparing to throw Tarquin's cloak over her shoulders, Hasain sighed and stepped forward. "Enough of this. If you put that on, it'll get wet, too." He snatched the garment from her and tossed it back to Tarquin—who was still staring at the cobblestones—before pulling off gloves and muttering an incantation. As if it were no trouble at all, Hasain gestured toward her tunic, and Gib watched as the heavy fabric dried before his eyes.

"And to think I didn't even know you were a mage for the longest time," Gib laughed, staring incredulously at Hasain. "You wear your white robes so sparingly I guess I never noticed."

Hasain was as smug as a cat with a feather on its lip. "Anyone born with the gift can become a mage. Extra training is required to be a politician. I choose to make the most of myself." He gestured toward Kezra's dry uniform. "Simple. Problem solved."

If Hasain was waiting for thanks, he was surely disappointed when Kezra stepped around him and pointed at Nawaz. "I could arrest you, you know!"

Nawaz turned a devilish grin on her. "Empty threats, dear. You can shackle me if you want though. Just go gentle at first."

"Ugh," Gib groaned, falling back a step.

Tarquin had his back to them already, his crimson face reminding Gib of a pyre. Hasain made some strangled sound of discontent, and Kezra, of all people, laughed like a fiend.

Her mirth effectively covered the sounds of another man as he approached. Tall and slender, he swept through the crowd with precision and authority. His white mage robes billowed out behind him and his sour, haughty frown made people jump out of the way faster. Gib didn't notice him until the man was an arm's length away.

"Kezra! What the hell happened back there? Did you catch the guy who—oh, it's *him*." The man narrowed his emerald eyes and gave Nawaz a shrewd look. "I suppose this means he won't be getting arrested."

Nawaz ducked behind Kezra. "Sorry, Zandi. I didn't see how close you were standin' to her. I didn't mean for you to get wet, too!" He chuckled and ruined any credibility he might have hoped to build.

"Well, that makes it all better then, doesn't it?" The newcomer crossed thin arms over his chest.

Gib only then noticed how out of sorts the man looked with his mussed hair and wet uniform.

Zandi Malin-Rai was Kezra's elder brother, and though they shared the same dark skin and green eyes, that was about where their similarities ended. He definitely took after their father for build and features as well as his cold disposition—though despite his icy words and detached nature, he wasn't unhandsome.

Kezra waved off her brother's concerns. "If you'd been doing your job and not bothering me then you wouldn't have been in the line of fire."

"That hardly makes his behavior excusable!" Zandi rubbed his hands together briskly before repeating the same magic trick Hasain had performed just moments before. Zandi muttered under his breath the entire time, still giving Nawaz death glares.

Gib shook his head. "You mages and your magic. I suppose I'll never understand it."

Zandi's green eyes flew wide, and his cheeks went a shade darker. His hands came up to fidget with his long onyx hair as he avoided eye contact with Gib. Cutting his sister a vicious glare, he muttered, "You didn't mention your friends were here. You should introduce us properly."

It seemed a funny request. Gib had met Zandi before and was sure everyone else here had, too. With the exception of Gib, all those present were of noble birth and had fathers or step-fathers on the High Council. More than once they'd all crossed paths at formal events and holidays. Gib owed his good fortune of being Koal's understudy as his means of attending these same gatherings.

Kezra didn't even try to be discreet about her brother's odd inquiry. In fact, true to the nature of any sibling, she had a smug look in her eye as she ridiculed him in public. "You know damned well who he is! Gib, this is Zandi. Zandi, that's Gib—not that you didn't know. You need me to remind you who Tarquin is? How about Hasain? Or Nawaz?"

Zandi openly fumed, and Gib took it upon himself to laugh them out of the awkward situation. After all, it had happened to him more than once while trying to remember the names of everyone at court. He offered his hand for a shake. "I'm Gibben, but please call me Gib. And don't worry, I wouldn't remember my name either if I were you."

Zandi's grip was tentative as the mage took hold of his hand. "I remember your name, Gibben Nemesio of Willowdale, understudy to Seneschal Koal Adelwijn."

Gib was at an utter loss for words. If Zandi remembered his name then what were the reintroductions for?

Confusion must have shown on his face, and the mage withdrew his hand with a small smile. An awkward lump rose in Gib's throat. Had he missed something? Why did he feel like everyone was grinning at him?

"All right. I've had enough of this. I'm going back to work." Kezra snorted and pushed past her brother, grabbing his arm on her way through. "*We* have to go back to work."

At last, Zandi's emerald eyes fell away from Gib. The mage gave a curt nod and followed at Kezra's heels. "Fine, yes. And let me fix your bindi. You look terrible." Just before they slipped back into the crowd, Zandi looked back one last time. "It was good to see you again, Gib."

Gib waved, still confounded by the entire meeting. When he turned back to the others, Tarquin and Nawaz were both watching him. While Tarquin tried not to smile too broadly, Nawaz's grin was nothing short of lewd.

Gib's eyes went wide. "What? What's everyone staring at?"

Nawaz clapped him so firmly on the shoulder Gib nearly tumbled. "So tell me, friend, where is Joel today?"

"He had to see his mentor, why?"

Without knowing Nawaz so well, Gib would have been intimidated by their height difference and the lord's manner. Nawaz bore down on Gib with a wicked beam. "I just have to wonder if Zandi's greeting would have been so warm had Joel been at your side."

Tarquin tittered, and Gib could feel his guts twist. *Oh*. He hadn't realized. "I don't think that's what—" His voice faltered. Actually, maybe it sort of made sense. A strange warmth fluttered in his chest like soft butterfly wings tickling him from the inside. Zandi was taken with him? The warmth spread to Gib's face. He'd never been the object of anyone's desire before. Well, Joel hardly counted seeing as Gib had longed for the other man first. *Joel.* "Well, I'm flattered then, but he'll have to look elsewhere."

Nawaz wagged his eyebrows. "For now anyway." When Gib shook his head, Nawaz tsked. "You're no fun. There's no harm in lookin'. Speaking of which, I'm going to get closer to the stage so I can watch the dancin'."

"Dancing? Today? It's too cold for that out here." Tarquin gasped and glanced toward the raised platform.

Nawaz laughed and slung an arm over Tarquin's shoulders, leading him into the crowd. "Boy, you worry too much. The cold air is a *good* thing. It makes them blush and keeps things perky."

A horrified look crossed Tarquin's white face, and Gib found himself giggling at his friend's expense.

"We can't go up there. This is indecent!" Tarquin floundered and looked back at Gib. "Gib! Come with me!"

"Hell no," Gib laughed. "You two enjoy yourselves. I have a little brother to help with his reading."

The pair slipped farther into the crowd, and Gib had just turned to make a hasty retreat when he noticed Hasain was still standing nearby, scowling at Nawaz's back. "Nawaz better watch himself or he may find marrying Heidi his only option."

Not this again. Gib sidestepped and tried to excuse himself. "Kezra knows her own mind well enough, and for now, she chooses him."

"For now, perhaps. He'll slip up sooner or later, and she'll see how useless he is."

Gib didn't want to become involved in this, but he was about done listening to Hasain's accusations. "Or you could simply wish them well and be their friend, as they would do for you. Joel and I are as opposite as night and day and so far we're—"

"Deluded?" Hasain's words were sharp as a bee sting.

Gib never knew how to take the Radek lord. One moment he was arguing on behalf of the poor and underprivileged, while in the next breath he was belittling anyone who crossed him.

"Where is Joel, anyway?"

Reeling from the fresh insult, Gib considered not answering. His voice was strained when he managed to find it. "He went to see Ambassador Cenric, to sign off on his internship. Why?"

Hasain frowned. "Interesting. No matter, I suppose. But speaking of Ambassador Leal, before I left the palace today, Father was in a fierce mood. When I tried to ask him about it, he shooed me away and was yelling something about 'sending Cenric or no one.'"

A chill swept up Gib's spine. He tried to ignore it. "A shame. Cenric only just returned."

"A good thing for Joel that he's signing off then."

Gib nodded and thought to head to the Adelwijn estate. Surely Cal would be waiting by then. Gib hesitated where he stood though, lingering just a moment longer. "King Rishi was visibly upset? You don't—you don't know where he was sending Cenric, do you?"

"If I knew, I would have said as much."

The cold seeped into Gib's core, bone deep. "You don't think he'd send Cenric to Shiraz, right? I mean—after Queen Jorja and all."

Hasain sighed, and some of his rigidity slipped away. "I don't know. I hope not. He hates—it kills him a little to send others into known doom."

"It can't always be avoided. And I suppose it's better to risk the life of one rather than many in a war."

"Tell that to the one who is sent. Tell that to their family."

Joel trailed Cenric as they arrived outside the council room doors. Joel's nerves had been on edge since their hasty summons, and he belatedly realized he'd been wringing his hands the entire way there. Cenric had asked again what the urgency was, but their royal guardsmen escorts could only apologize and lead them onward.

The heavy door swung open before Cenric could knock, and inside, King Rishi's strange Blessed Mages watched them with eerie violet eyes. Joel began to nod in greeting, but he was pushed along too fast to have a chance.

As the pair of sentinels who'd escorted Cenric and Joel took post outside the door, Koal Adelwijn's stern voice called out. "Ah, Cenric, sorry to pull you back in here so soon—" The seneschal's hard gaze fell onto his son and the stilted words made Joel cringe. "What is he doing here? This isn't a meeting for children."

Joel frowned. "I'm not a child."

Before Joel managed to get himself into any more trouble, Cenric stepped in. "Apologies, Seneschal Koal. I tried to ask what this meeting was about, but the guardsmen were vowed to silence. It is common practice for a master to bring his understudy while still on duty."

He bowed and motioned for Joel to do the same. The look in Cenric's eye suggested he was in no mood for an unruly student, so Joel complied, biting back any harsh words he'd had for his father. *Right now, he is the seneschal of Arden and I am an envoy trainee. Behave as such.*

Koal's sharp gaze was heavy, but Joel met those eyes with as much determination as he could muster, a task made more difficult by their current company. Beyond the strange Blessed Mages and the seneschal, the King and his personal bodyguard were also present. Joel couldn't help but feel he was in way over his head. He clasped clammy hands behind his back to keep them from shaking and took a deep breath. If his father was ever going to see Joel as anything more than a child, now was the time to prove himself.

"Enough of this. There's no time for arguments." King Rishi looked haggard, face pale and eyes swollen. He stood tensely by the head of the council table. "There's been a summons from the Northern Empire, Leal. I have no intention of sending anyone, but Neetra will be here any moment and he's demanding—"

"He's nearly here." The female Blessed Mage, Natori, kept her voice low, but everyone paused to listen to her words. "Hurry."

The King nodded and an odd look crossed his face, something Joel had never seen before. King Rishi appeared to be—frightened. His voice didn't shake, but his hands trembled. "You know full well why I can't send anyone in there, Leal, but the council will demand action if that idiot stirs up enough trouble."

Koal sighed. "And if he whips Anders and Morathi into some sort of frenzy, who knows what their demands will be. Malin-Rai used to be an envoy before he got caught with his pants around his ankles in Shantar. We don't need his sort representing Arden."

Cenric only nodded. "The Empire has stayed quiet almost since the start of your rule, Highness. Why would they reach out now?"

"They've expressed a desire to treat with us," Koal replied. "They've invited the King himself."

Cenric laughed absurdly. "They can't be serious!"

"It's a trap." King Rishi began to pace. "It must be. No one welcomes a traitor back into their midst."

"Neetra is in the hall," NezReth, the male Blessed Mage, rasped. His eyes were unfocused, consciousness elsewhere—in the hall perhaps.

Joel felt himself shying away from the strange otherworldly pair of mages despite knowing the King and his father both trusted them, perhaps more than anyone else in the kingdom.

"The King's right," Koal agreed. "There must be something more than peace on their minds. The last time they reached out to Arden was to offer a husband for Jorja in an attempt to merge us into their realm."

"I remember," Cenric said, a clever smile crossing his lips which was clearly directed at King Rishi. "And it didn't work out quite the way they'd hoped. Seems an arrogant young prince accepted the marriage proposal but refused the merger."

King Rishi winced. "I never said my actions weren't foolish. Now we have to figure out how to spare Arden from my arrogance—and Neetra's

62

idiocy."

The stark change in the King's demeanor gave Joel chills, and when the doors opened an instant later, he almost jumped out of his skin. His uncle, High Councilor Neetra Adelwijn, strode in with all the authority granted the King himself. At his heels was Joel's brother, Liro.

Koal balked for a second time. "What is *he* doing here?"

Before Neetra could respond, King Rishi demanded the door be shut and, surprisingly, Liro complied with a cordial nod. He swung the heavy door closed with a bang, and Joel blinked. Where had the Blessed Mages gone? He glanced around, and when he still could not locate them, Joel opened his mouth to ask—a single dark eye met his, and King Rishi's bodyguard, Aodan, gave a stern shake of his head. *Neetra despises the Mages. I suppose it's better he doesn't know they're here. Or were here. Or whatever.*

"Had I known *everyone* was going to be bringing their apprentices I'd have dragged mine along, too!" Koal pointed at Liro. "He shouldn't be here, Neetra."

Neetra's cold dark eyes narrowed. "Liro is hardly that bedraggled, illiterate waif you pride yourself on 'saving.' Liro is knowledgeable and well versed in many customs of the Northern Empire. His expertise could prove invaluable here."

Joel felt like he'd taken a physical blow. Koal's voice boomed in the confined space. "*My* understudy is none of your concern—and Liro's knowledge is secondhand from books and scrolls. Cenric has *actually been* to the Empire. So much for this being a restricted meeting. I suppose the security of Arden is a small matter!"

Liro drew himself to his full height but kept his voice carefully neutral. He'd even mirrored Joel and put his hands behind his back. Fixing an unreadable look on the seneschal, Liro replied, "What's the matter, Father? Do you not trust me with the security of Arden?" He flicked his eyes to Joel. "And what title does your *favorite* son hold that his presence was requested above mine?"

Koal's face went an ugly red, and Joel found himself reeling for a second time. He wanted to talk back, to yell and demand apologies from both his uncle and brother, but now was not the time. *You are an envoy, and this is a political talk. Prove to them you can do this.*

The King had apparently had enough of the family dispute as well. King Rishi looked down on Liro with a sneer. "Joel knows when to keep his mouth shut. You could learn well from his example, but I fear your uncle has had too much access to you for that to happen."

Neetra made an undignified grunt, and Liro pressed his lips together. Koal stormed over to his designated seat at the council table and motioned for everyone else to follow. Joel trailed Cenric and was careful to choose a chair beside him. Joel breathed a sigh of relief when Neetra and Liro sat across from him. At least he had the table as a barrier. It was a shame, though, that he'd have to endure Liro's scowl.

The King dropped into his chair, wearing a mask of indifference. It was typical for him to remain aloof and condescending in the presence of his council—Joel had seen it many times—but now, his rigid shoulders and tired face whispered of his lie. He wasn't quite as confident as he wanted them all to believe.

King Rishi glared at Neetra. "I suppose you have something to say about all of this."

"Highness, you must know the futility of ignoring the Northern Empire." Neetra's high whine rang off the vaulted ceiling. "They are too powerful and could take us by force if they chose—"

"Let's see 'em get through the mountains first!" Aodan growled, breaking his typical silence. The bodyguard stood by the window, his eyepatch shifting as he raised a brow, one good eye glinting dangerously.

Neetra curled a lip. "Their army is far superior to ours, Highness. There's no point in lying to ourselves. If we offend them we can't hope to defend ourselves should they take action against us. But could you imagine if they were an ally?" Neetra huffed a laugh. "Who would stand against us? Not even Gyptia would dare act lightly."

"Gyptia isn't a concern," King Rishi replied. "The Northern Empire has never once offered an alliance since I took the throne. Does their sudden interest not raise any suspicions for you?"

Neetra scoffed. "Perhaps they grow as tired of Shiraz as we."

"Or they are ready to dethrone their 'traitor.'"

"You have reigned for twenty-eight years. Do you not think they would have acted sooner if they intended to exact revenge?"

The King rubbed his shoulder absently, and Joel had to blink away memories of the assassin's arrow pierced through the very same place, two years prior. "Maybe they have only failed to remove me sooner."

Neetra clenched his jaw and offered nothing more.

The silence was suffocating until Cenric cleared his throat. "It has been my experience that peace talks are not often sought out by the Northern Empire because of their lofty position. I might also be suspicious of such an offer."

"With all due respect, Ambassador Leal." Liro's voice was crisp and detached. "Your last mission to the Northern Empire was how many years ago?"

Cenric met the uncouth question head on. "Thirty now, Lord Adelwijn, and may I remind you it was the last mission *any* Ardenian envoy made to the Empire? I was an understudy myself, and when my mentor and I returned we were forcibly provided 'company.'" He glanced at King Rishi and the ruler waved Cenric on, allowing him to finish the story. "Despite the niceties of what your school texts may report, I assure you, Arden was hard pressed to deny the Empire's 'friendly' offer of a suitor for Princess Jorja. Their intent then was to merge our countries, for Arden to come under Imperial rule—"

Neetra's shrill voice spiked. "We cannot know that for sure! There have been suggestions of a cultural misunderstanding—"

The King moved like a cat, slamming his fist on the table so quickly everyone present jumped. "*Lies!* I was there, High Councilor! You can sprinkle as much sugar on that poison dart as you want, but it remains lethal!"

"All right, keep calm," said Koal. He waved the King into submission and took a deep breath, perhaps to calm his own nerves. "We can go in circles forever discussing the intent of this offer, but the fact remains that there *has been* an offer, and we need to respond."

King Rishi shook his head. "No one's going. It's a trap."

"We cannot ignore this offer!" Neetra leaned across the table. "Send someone else if you will not go, Highness, but we must respond."

"Who? Who do I send to die, High Councilor? Perhaps you'd like to go on behalf of Arden?"

"I'll gladly take this honor. Arden can only stand to suffer if we ignore such a powerful potential ally—"

Koal sat up straight. "The hell we're sending you! You can't keep the councilors civil. How can we trust you not to make rash decisions in a foreign country?"

Neetra fired back about the council deserving representation on this envoy mission, and Joel pressed his hands to his temples. Too many opinions were being thrown around. He was confused and beginning to regret coming along. How did Gib put up with these kinds of meetings day in and day out?

Joel glanced over to the drawn curtains, wishing for even a small breeze, when he noticed Aodan's curious stance. Despite the cool outside, the bodyguard had chosen to sit in the sill, most likely to remain out of the way. However, now something seemed to have caught his attention, and he was staring upward. A chill swept up Joel's spine. He glanced toward the balcony as well. *Stop worrying. There's no assassin up there.*

What had the bodyguard noticed then? How in the two worlds could he see anything with only one eye in this gloomy room? Joel could feel his pulse quicken and reminded himself to breathe. The argument continued around them. Did no one else see Aodan? Did no one else care?

"I'll go before we send Neetra!" Koal fought his way to the top of the debate, and Joel's heart iced over. *Not Father. It's too dangerous!* Koal wasn't a young man anymore, and he was no envoy. "It stands to reason— if we don't send our king then we should send his Right Hand, not some random politician."

Neetra snarled like a stray dog. "I will have you know, *brother*, I am the High Councilor of all Arden. I believe I have as much authority as you—"

"With all due respect, gentlemen, the Empire would likely find more favor in the status of the seneschal." Cenric was the voice of reason, as all his years in the field had taught him. "If they're not going to treat with the King then surely his Right Hand would be their next preference—that is, short of a crowned prince."

The King's face contorted into a fearsome scowl, and he pointed directly at the ambassador. "*No!* Deegan is not old enough, and I would sooner *die* than send him over that border!"

Joel's heart pounded in his chest. His father couldn't go. His mother would be distraught! The King needed Koal. Surely he would stop all of this nonsense—and what was Aodan doing now? The bodyguard had slunk behind them all on his way to the stairs. Joel glanced at the balcony again.

Koal and the King shared a look so brief Joel wasn't sure he'd seen it at all, but then they each laid a discreet hand atop their sword hilts and he knew they were onto whatever Aodan was investigating. Neetra babbled on, entirely oblivious, while Liro looked up only when Aodan's lean form shot up the balcony steps. The bodyguard was so stealthy Joel didn't hear a single footfall. And then—

"Aodan, *stop!* It's me!"

The indignant cry of their apparent spy stopped even Neetra mid-sentence. Koal and King Rishi were on their feet with their blades pulled in an instant. The commotion upstairs came to a crescendo with what sounded like a body crashing to the floor, and an instant later, someone was gasping for mercy and fumbling to crawl down the stairs. "Stop! *Stop!* I'm sorry!"

Hasain Radek scrabbled at the stone steps, his white mage robes tangled hopelessly about his legs, dark hair in utter disarray. Aodan was hot on his trail, crimson face pulled into a fierce snarl. As the young lord struggled to gain his feet, Aodan planted one foot firmly on Hasain's prone backside and shoved him the rest of the way down the flight. "You get down there or I'll kick yer arse so hard you'll have ta loosen yer collar to shit!"

Joel bit the inside of his cheek while Koal and King Rishi both threw their free hands into the air and sheathed their swords. Hasain tried to babble some form of apology, but his father was on him so quickly he had no time. The King grabbed the front of Hasain's robe and hoisted him to his feet as though he were still a young child.

Hasain cowered. "I'm sorry, Father. I just—I wanted to know what had you so worried this morning."

King Rishi shook him like a rag doll. "Have you forgotten what sort of capital offense it is to spy on the King? Hasain, you know better!"

"I'm sorry! I meant no offense. I only wanted to be sure you were safe—"

"Not your concern!"

Aodan paced behind them, still agitated. "Yer lucky I didn't slice yer throat an' think to ask questions later. How'd ya even get up there?"

The room went silent. The only sound to be heard was Hasain's ragged breathing. "I snuck in. There was no council meeting scheduled for today, so I knew the back door wouldn't be guarded."

Koal glared up at the balcony. "But it damned well better have been locked."

"It was!" Hasain waved his hands. "The soldiers made sure of it. I just—" He glared down, unable to meet anyone's eyes. "I unlocked it."

King Rishi reeled. "You have a key?"

"N–no. It wasn't a difficult spell—" Hasain took a deep breath. "I'm sorry! I didn't mean to cause so much trouble. Father, I swear—"

"*King*. In this council room, I am your *king*!" King Rishi shoved Hasain into an empty chair so hard the wood creaked. "Now you shut your mouth and sit there. You already know more than you should. I'll think of a punishment fitting to your crime later."

Koal and the King took their seats while Neetra raised a brow and spoke down his nose to them. "A crime indeed. What does the old law say about spies?"

"They're to be hung." Liro's response was automatic and uncaring.

Hasain flinched.

King Rishi glared from his seat at the head of the table. "What does the old law say about those who threaten the royal family?"

"Their tongues are to be cut out *before* they're hung." Koal met his eldest son's eyes with the same severity King Rishi had treated Hasain to.

Liro scowled but said nothing more.

Cenric cleared his throat, and all eyes turned toward the ambassador. "Highness, have you chosen who will go on this envoy mission? Are we going forward at all? What is your plan of action?"

King Rishi took a deep breath and held it. Joel tried not to look directly in the King's face but had never known him to be so conflicted. He suddenly looked his age. The thin lines around his mouth and eyes paid him no favor when he wasn't smiling. King Rishi shook his head, but a bitter resignation was about him. "The Northern Empire has called for treaty talks with Arden—and Arden will answer."

The clamor rose like a high wind, and Joel had to brace himself. Koal and Neetra were each demanding the other stay behind while Cenric offered suggestions and informed the King he would need to familiarize himself with Imperial etiquette. Liro pressed about his own wealth of knowledge concerning the Northern Empire.

Joel's mouth went dry. Should he go with Cenric? Or was it a foolish child's dream of becoming an envoy? If he declined this mission, essentially he would be refusing his first difficult task. To do so would as much as admit defeat.

"Neetra doesn't hold high enough rank to go, and why send one of our councilors anyway? The High Council should trust their seneschal to report back to them and the King honestly. *I'm* going to head this mission." Koal's stone cold voice made Joel shudder. His father couldn't go. Surely the King would decline him.

"I will not have you ride to your death," replied King Rishi. "Send Neetra."

Neetra puffed up like a peacock before the full implication of the King's words settled on him. "These worries of death and disaster are ill-founded, Highness!"

"Quite the contrary." Cenric fought to have his voice heard. "My King, I have to speak truthfully here. From what I remember of the Northern Empire, they are very concerned with titles. To send your High Councilor may be misinterpreted as disrespectful. I believe Arden's best hope lies in sending your highest official if you will not be going yourself."

Koal locked eyes with the King, and Joel knew they were sharing some unspoken agreement. They had worked together for nearly thirty years. They didn't need to speak to understand one another. Joel's heart pounded. *Not my father. He's too old for this. Mother cannot lose him.*

King Rishi sighed at long last. "Fine. If you are so determined, Koal. Go."

"Highness, please!" Joel bleated. "My father can't be sent into such danger!"

Joel didn't know what had gotten into him. He knew better than to speak against the decree of the King, but he seemed to have no control over his own mouth. All eyes were on him, and he felt his face burst with uncomfortable heat. Koal's shrewd look wasn't angry—indeed, anger would have been preferable to the disappointment looming in his eyes.

Joel swallowed and looked down at the table. "I'm sorry to speak out of place. But, Highness, you yourself have said nothing good can come from sending our people across the border."

Neetra scoffed. "Koal, you would do well to teach your son how to behave in the presence of grown men."

Liro laughed. It sounded like a dry cough. The room began to spin out of control, and all Joel could do was focus on getting his ragged breathing back under control.

It seemed no one was going to say another word until the King, of all people, responded. His laugh was broken. "Joel is the only one speaking any sense. But seeing as I am clearly out-voted, I suppose his and my unpopular opinion will have to remain just that."

Joel dared look up but froze when he realized the King's dark eyes were focused on him.

"Seneschal Koal has spoken. He will go because I have yet to find a force to reckon with his will."

King Rishi was sorry. Joel could see it in the King's eyes. He couldn't say it here, but he was apologizing. Joel nodded stiffly, but the seed of a new idea had already taken root in his heart. As the others continued to speak, it took bloom.

"Who else will be going then?" Neetra asked. The High Councilor looked like he'd been slapped in the face. "Liro has an excellent wealth of knowledge, and he is all but ready to step onto the High Council. He would make a useful addition to the team."

Koal narrowed his eyes. "No! There's no reason to send young men into this potentially dangerous situation—"

"Highness," Cenric cut in before any argument between Koal and Liro could explode. "I think it would also be expected that *some* member of the royal family attend—"

King Rishi and Hasain responded at once. The King adamantly declined even as Hasain shot up from his chair. "I could go! I'm a Radek, but not a crowned prince! Arden wouldn't have to risk their royalty."

"*None* of my children will cross that border!"

Hasain was just as sharp in his retort. "Very well. Anger the Northern Empire and seal our fates." The King whipped around to glare at him, and Joel thought it almost comical how much they looked alike in their anger. If not for the King's long braid and thin mustache, or Hasain's youth, they could have been brothers with their matching golden skin and defiant almond eyes.

Neetra jumped back into the fray. "If I will not be going then at least take my understudy! The High Council will demand one of our own be on the inside."

"I am fully confident in my capability," Liro agreed.

Joel closed his eyes against the whirlwind of voices and opinions. It was too much. How could anyone glean anything from this pandemonium?

"*Enough!*" King Rishi leapt from his seat and paced the length of the room. "Koal is seneschal and can make decisions on my behalf. He will have to go."

Joel stiffened in his seat. "Da, please!"

Koal's eyes narrowed into dangerous slits. "Not here, Joel. Not now."

Face unbearably hot, Joel opened his mouth to object, but the King spoke over him. "Cenric, you are the only one with past experience. You will have to go."

Cenric gave a modest bow from his seat. "Of course, my King."

"Then I must go as well!" Joel exclaimed. There, he'd said it. Heart hammering, the young mage continued. "I am still Cenric's understudy. I must follow where he goes."

Koal was on his feet in an instant and bearing down on his son. Joel couldn't remember a time he'd been more intimidated by his father. "This mission will be too dangerous for an understudy. There is no way you're going. That's the end of it!"

"This is how envoys are trained! If I don't go to this mission I may as well admit I'm a coward and stay in Silver City for the rest of my life—"

Koal whirled to face the King. "Tell him he can't go. This is no place for an understudy."

"This is no place for any of us!" King Rishi continued his long strides back and forth, face drawn into a grim frown. His eyes flicked to Joel, who for a moment feared the worst, but then the King's attention refocused onto Cenric. "Must royalty go? Jorja's family is distant. I have none save my children, and they are either too young or not in line for the throne."

Cenric glanced sideways at Hasain and kept his voice low. "It could perhaps be a son not in line for the throne, Highness."

The King grew silent and stopped in his tracks, his back to the other men. The air was stagnant and palpable, yet the quiet was utterly deceptive. This was the calm before the storm. Back straight and rigid, King Rishi issued a growl so low and feral it barely sounded human at all. "I will sooner go to war than send any of my children across the border."

Hasain flew to his feet. "This is nonsense! You are impeding our progress, and you know it!"

The King spun around, grabbed a chair, and threw it across the room. His voice was a terrible shriek, like some wounded animal. "I am your *king*! I said no! *You are not going!*"

Joel found himself pulling back, trying to distance himself from them as much as possible. Hasain, on the other hand, dove straight into the line of fire. "You can't do this. You can't condemn an entire country to preserve one life!"

"I am the King. I can do whatever the hell I want! I can even arrest you if you dare defy me!"

Hasain shook his head, eyes visibly wet, even in the low light. "No."

"No?"

"No." Hasain didn't back down. "It's a crime to defy the *king* but you aren't being my king. Right now you're letting your emotions cloud your judgment. Right now you're being my father."

Joel couldn't breathe. Between his own father's heavy glare and the King's deafening silence, no air was left in the room. No one moved or dared say a word until at long last King Rishi turned on one heel and made for the door. "Fine. Go. Take any who will go with you. Meet your doom and go to hell!"

Aodan was on the King's trail even as he flung the door open. Koal stretched out one hand in protest. "Rishi, wait! Damn it!" He took chase as well, pausing in the doorway long enough to dismiss the rest of the gathered men. "Get out of here, all of you. I'll let you know when I have the final list of who's going." Then he turned and flew down the corridor, his red cape billowing behind him.

CHAPTER FOUR

"*At the beginning of all, the Two Goddesses, Daya and Chhaya, created the Otherealm, a world of magic, and ruled in peace. But there came a time when They grew lonely. Their love for one another was all-encompassing and with that love and Their magic They forged Children for themselves. One thousand immortal Children were created to populate the world with them, and They were happy.*

"*However, even immortals grasp the passage of time and eventually some of the Children became filled by corruption. Powerful and greedy, they were disobedient to their Mothers, and The Two were hurt and unhappy. They decided to try again, to make a more obedient race of children.*

"*So Daya and Chhaya created the mortal world, Temhara, and filled it with humanity. Though the humans lived short lives, they knew their creators and respected them. Humans didn't live long enough to become greedy as the Children in the Otherealm had, and they wielded no magic, for back in the beginning, magic did not exist in the mortal realm.*

"*The creation of the mortal world and the humans caused the one thousand Children to despair. How could their Mothers betray them and choose to love another race? So their eldest and favorite Child, the Blessed Son of Light, decided to go to war against the humans and the mortal world. He rallied as many Children together as would follow and set to destroy those who had stolen the love of The Two.*

"*The Blessed Son of Light was the first Child created by The Two and was one of Their favorites. However, another Child who had been forged much later was also a favorite, and he felt compassion for the human race. This pale Child was known for his kind heart and gentle spirit, so much that the other half of the original one thousand Children gladly followed him into battle against the Son of Light.*

"*The Great War tore the mortal world asunder, and for a time there was worry humanity would die out. The Blessed Son of Light and pale Child fought ruthlessly against one another. Their battle was so fierce it created cracks deep enough so that the magic from the Otherealm leaked through. The brothers fought until their great love for one another withered away and was lost.*

"*Hurt by the apparent betrayal of his Mothers and the loss of his brother's love, the Blessed Son of Light struck one last time in desperation to rid the realms of humanity. But what the Son did not know was that his brother had fallen in love with a human woman, and when his final blow fell, the woman was killed. The pale Child's grief was so great that the Son became remorseful and finally abandoned the Great War.*

"The pale Child went to The Two and begged for his love to be raised from death so they might be together, at least for the short length of her mortal lifetime. The Two mourned for their Child's broken heart but would not raise her. Shattered beyond repair, the pale Child fled his Mothers and Their love to grow bitter. His anger and resentment eventually caused him to hate humanity. This pale Child became known as the Love-Lost Child.

"As a result of the Great War, the Blessed Son of Light became a beacon of hope for humanity, vowing to never try to wipe them from existence again. He instead took them under his guidance and, even now, gives gifts to those he deems worthy. He shows favor to humans until the Love-Lost Child returns to take his place as the one who loved them first. He always hopes his brother will return to him and to the ways of good."

Calisto stopped to take a drink after reading the entire passage. He cradled the book, *Tales of Fae*, as if it were a small child or something equally precious. One of the texts from the Adelwijn's personal library, it was the favorite of many and had been one of the first books Gib had cut his teeth on.

Gib nodded with a smile, encouraging his brother to continue. Already, at only thirteen years of age, Calisto could read as well, if not better, than Gib. Earlier in his life, Gib might have been embarrassed by this, but now he couldn't help but swell with pride. Cal would do well for himself at this rate. He wished their parents could be here to see.

Calisto frowned down at the text for a moment. "So why do people worship The Two? Because they created everything?"

"Mmm-hmm." Gib peered out the study window, searching the courtyard of the Adelwijn estate below and wondering when Joel would return. It was already well past midday meal and he was still nowhere to be seen. "The temple in Willowdale pays homage to The Two."

Calisto's brows knitted high on his forehead. "But the temple in the palace doesn't? Didn't you say that one was for someone else?"

"The royal temple worships the Blessed Son." Gib turned his back to the window. Watching it wasn't going to make Joel arrive any faster. "You see, back before Arden was its own country, the people used to worship the Son of Light instead."

"Why?"

"Because the Son realized he was doing wrong by humanity and decided to fight for us instead of against us. When Arden pulled away from the Northern Empire, there weren't laws to tell the people who to worship anymore. So people from different lands brought religions from their countries here. That's why some temples worship the two goddesses, Chhaya and Daya, and some worship the Son."

"Well, which one's right?"

"What do you mean?"

"Which temple is right? Who should people worship?"

Gib rubbed the back of his neck. Hell, he'd never thought of that before. Back when they'd had the farm, there hadn't been time to worship anyone. "I don't think it matters so much *who* you worship so long as you're doing your best to be a good person." When he was met with a dubious look, Gib chuckled and went on. "I mean, if you listen to the story, it was really about not harming one another. The Children of The Two became jealous and tried to hurt humanity. But the Love-Lost Child decided not to hurt others and eventually the Blessed Son of Light changed his mind as well."

Calisto cocked his head to one side and pondered. "So that's why the law protects the different temples? So people can worship whoever they want?" He didn't wait long enough for Gib to answer. "We were taught in class today that some places even worship other Children of The Two. Not just the Son."

"That's right. Gyptia and Shantar worship many different Children and have temples for them all." The sound of the front door opening and closing didn't go unnoticed, and Gib had to force himself not to peek out into the hall. Had he missed Joel's approach? "Some countries even allow Otherfolk access to their temples."

Stars shone in the youngster's eyes. "Otherfolk? Like the people who aren't human?"

The sound of approaching footsteps in the hallway flitted into the room, but Gib tried to remain focused on the conversation. "Yeah. Like the goblins, demharlins, and—" He searched back in his memory but couldn't recall the word he was looking for. "The snake Folk. I can't remember their right name."

"Naga."

Both Nemesio brothers turned to look at Joel, who stood beneath the arched doorframe. The mage's fair face was drawn, and his guarded eyes concealed some unknown emotion Gib couldn't readily place. Gib wanted to go to him but something in Joel's stance suggested he wasn't ready to be approached. Despite any apparent discomfort, he was lovely, and Gib longed to touch him.

"The naga," Joel continued in a neutral tone, "are indigenous to the jungles of Shantar and Beihai."

"Indige—what?" Calisto blinked, looking from his brother to Joel and back again.

When Gib shrugged, offering only a sheepish smile, Joel favored them with a smile of his own and went on. He came fully into the room and sat on the window sill. "Indigenous. It means that's where they live, where they come from. The naga are believed to be the children of Jahara, one of the Children of The Two. They help protect the jungles of Shantar and Beihai, and in return, the people do not persecute them."

"Why would anyone want to hurt them?" Calisto asked. He closed the *Tales of Fae* and smiled in a dreamy sort of way. "It would be a great adventure to go out into the unknown and meet all the different kinds of Otherfolk. Why do the laws here keep humans and Otherfolk separate?"

Gib was still at a loss. This was something else he'd never had time to think about. Apart from the tall tales he'd heard in the market in Willowdale, he'd never paid any mind to the Otherfolk.

Joel sighed. "Well, the law which prohibits humans from interacting with the Otherfolk is an old one and could perhaps be done away with, but unfortunately it rarely comes up as a topic of interest. Folk do not naturally inhabit the land near Silver, where the majority of Arden's laws are made and unmade. If there is no one to bring interest to an old law, it can't be contested, can it?"

"I suppose not." Calisto scuffed a foot across the floor. "It seems unfair. Folk can't help being born Folk any more than Gib and I could help being born poor. And why keep humans and Otherfolk separate anyway?"

"Many people think the Otherfolk are violent. We've been told from a young age to be wary of any who are different from us. There are stories of children being lost in the mountains and woods, so people assume the Folk must be the ones to blame."

"Are they really dangerous?"

Joel shook his head. "I wouldn't know. I've never known any in person, and I wouldn't presume to judge."

Calisto stuck out his bottom lip. Gib knew that look anywhere. Surely the youth was thinking up more questions even now, but instead of asking them, he delved back into the book.

Joel cleared his throat. "Gib? Could I see you for a moment?"

Something is wrong. Gib tried not to frown. "Uh, sure. Here? Or—"

A moment's hesitation didn't go unnoticed. Calisto lifted his face from reading and rolled his eyes. "Go ahead. Go be *alone.*"

Gib wanted to be able to laugh, but Joel's demeanor made him think twice. With a small nod to his brother, Gib crossed the room. Joel didn't wait for Gib to close the gap. Before he could reach out and touch his companion, Joel turned on his heels and made for the door. If Calisto noticed, he didn't say anything. Gib wished he could be so lucky.

Joel led the way into the sitting room. Otos must have recently stoked the fire. The heat emitted from the flames engulfed the entire room, yet Gib couldn't seem to find any warmth. Joel's cold disposition sapped it all.

They went to the couch and sat down, side by side. Gib stole a worried glance at his companion. "Joel, what's wrong?"

The mage didn't immediately answer. He turned his face to the hearth, staring at the roaring fire. The flames danced, reflecting off his endless blue eyes. "My father is going to the Northern Empire."

Gib blinked, momentarily unable to comprehend the other man's words. *The Northern Empire? The same country Arden fought so hard to free itself from all those generations ago?* "I don't—what? Why? How did this happen?"

Joel kept his voice neutral, as though he'd been training to deliver the news for years. "It appears the Northern Empire wants to meet with Arden to discuss a peace treaty. They asked the King himself to go, but Father and King Rishi agreed it was too dangerous, given the King's past dealings with the Empire." Deep despair crossed Joel's fair features. "I tried to talk Father out of going, but he wouldn't hear it."

"Why Koal? Surely someone else could go. The seneschal is needed here!"

"Father is the Right Hand of King Rishi. He can make executive decisions on behalf of our country." Joel sighed. "Truth be told, I believe he made the decision to go because the next choice was to send Neetra."

Gib winced. "Neetra can't be trusted with such an immense task."

"Exactly."

Head still spinning, Gib reached out and took Joel's hands. *No wonder he's sad. He's worried for his father. Hell, I'm worried! But I need to be here for Joel, now more than ever. Stay calm. Breathe.* "When does Koal leave?"

"On the morn."

"So soon?"

Joel nodded. "Yes."

Gib scooted closer to Joel, lifting one hand to stroke the side of his face. "I'm here for you. Whatever you need—"

"Father isn't the only person going."

A spike of dread shot from Gib's stomach to his throat. "O–oh? W–who else?" He had to force the words from his mouth.

Joel stared hard at the floor.

Why won't he look at me?

"Ambassador Cenric is the only living envoy in all of Arden who's been to the Northern Empire. He's familiar with the culture and the differences in language."

"Cenric is going?"

"Yes." Joel took a deep breath and grasped Gib's hands. They trembled together, and Joel could barely meet Gib's eyes. "Gib, I'm going, too."

Joel watched from the shadowed enclave as the two young men trained. Light poured through the rafters above them onto the bare floor of the arena, illuminating the golden tiles as Didier and Gibben sparred. Equipped with practice swords made from thick maple, they danced across the area in a fury of angry grunts and sighs as each tried to best the other.

Diddy, taller and broader, would have seemed the likely victor, but though smaller and half a head shorter, Gib's agility couldn't be overlooked. More than once, he rushed the prince, and Diddy was barely able to sidestep his friend and avoid a nasty jab to the ribcage.

Joel waited until they stopped for a reprieve before making his presence known. Clearing his throat, he stepped away from the marbled archway and onto the arena floor. Gib refused to look Joel in the eye, though Diddy flashed a weak smile in the man's direction.

Sweat covered the prince's forehead and dripped down the length of his pointed nose. "Cousin, hello," he greeted. "The arena is perhaps the last place I'd expect to see you."

"Well, these *are* strange times we find ourselves thrown into," Joel replied, clasping his hands together in front of his body.

Diddy nodded solemnly. "Strange indeed." He turned long enough to replace his weapon on the rack stationed against the far wall, and his personal servant, Gideon, scampered over to help the prince remove his wrist and leg armor. Diddy's next words were tentative and hushed. "I'm sorry to hear you're leaving again. You've only just returned."

Gib's shoulders stiffened as he busied himself with gathering training equipment that had been strewn across the arena. Joel grimaced when his companion still refused to meet his gaze. *He's upset.* "Someone has to go. Cenric was brave enough to volunteer, and as his understudy, I have a duty to follow."

"I'm sure everything will be all right." The enthusiasm in Diddy's voice was forced, and the way the prince wrung his hands together betrayed his nerves. "Cenric is the best envoy Father could ever send, not to mention Uncle—*Seneschal* Koal will be there to assure Arden isn't taken advantage of during negotiations."

Hoping Diddy was right, Joel couldn't help the feeling of dread seeping into his heart. Doing his best to maintain his composure, he mustered a smile and replied, "Indeed. I'm sure the journey will be quite dull. Mostly politics and mountains of paperwork—"

They heard a deafening crash as Gib slammed a helmet onto the weaponry rack. The sound echoed off the palace walls, and both Diddy and Joel went still. The tension in the air was so thick Joel found it hard to breathe.

Diddy's face was drawn when he next spoke. "I'm going to take my leave." The prince gripped Joel's shoulder in passing. "Promise me you'll come see Mother and the others before you leave."

"Of course I will."

Diddy nodded his head once, stiffly, and departed without another word. Gideon followed only a pace behind, as silent and steadfast as a shadow. Within moments, Joel and Gib were the only two remaining in the arena.

"Might we talk?" Joel asked, taking a tentative step forward.

Horrible silence followed the question. Gib seemed determined not to respond, choosing instead to rearrange the weapon rack while keeping his back to Joel. He wanted so desperately to go to Gib but forced himself to wait. *He has every right to be angry, to be scared.*

At long last, just when Joel thought he might go mad from the ugly quiet, Gib uttered a sigh and said, "How did you know I'd be here?"

"We've been together almost three years, Gibben. You think I don't know your habits?" The mage smiled wistfully. "It was either here or the dining hall—"

"I'm glad you find this funny."

Joel winced. "I know you're mad. What can I do to fix this?" He extended a hand, offering it to Gib. "Please—"

Gib swung around to face Joel, features contorted in a mask of pain. "You can't fix it now! You're *leaving* tomorrow! You're going to the Northern Empire. I'm no fool, Joel Adelwijn. Don't try to convince me there's no peril! We both know *damned* well how dangerous it will be!"

"Please, Gib, let me explain."

Gib's brown eyes, normally so full of optimism and hope, speared Joel, cutting through flesh and bone, down to his very core. "*Why?*" Gib croaked. "Why do you have to go?"

Joel approached his companion, keeping both hands in the air. "It's complicated, but I promise to answer your questions. Just—just calm down, all right?"

Gib crossed his arms over his chest and glared at the floor.

Joel motioned toward the stairwell which led outside. "Why don't we go onto the balcony? We can talk there, and the fresh air will do us both some good." He reached a tentative hand forward, resting it on Gib's arm. "Please?"

Gib's shoulders lost some of their rigidity at the touch. "All right. Fine." He turned on his heels without another word, and Joel had to trot to keep up.

Golden sunlight poured through the doorway as they passed through. Below, the palace courtyard sprawled across the ground like a blanket. Wilted shrubs and browning trees lined the edge of the lawn, rising up to collide with the horizon and spreading shadows across the tufts of grass still clinging to life. The sky above was cloudless, an endless sea of deep blues and reds stretching as far as the eye could see. A light breeze cut through the air, blowing leaves around the courtyard below. Joel wrapped his arms around his shoulders to ward off the frigid autumn wind. The waning sun was doing little to warm the deep-seated chill in his bones.

Gib went to the edge of the balcony and leaned over it, resting his forearms on the white stone railing that encased the balcony.

Joel set a hand on the rail as he came to stand beside Gib. The breeze whipped hair about Joel's face as he collected his thoughts. "I know I only just returned," he finally began. "I didn't plan on leaving again, but when Cenric was called upon by King Rishi to act as chief envoy on this mission, as his understudy, it was my duty to go."

"*Horseshit!*" Gib spat. "Your internship papers were signed! You said yourself you were going to see Cenric this morning to get them signed. Cenric can't make you go if you're no longer his understudy!"

"The papers were never signed."

Deep despair crossed Gib's face, and Joel wanted so badly to reach for it but stayed his hand. He stared forward, gazing at the setting sun, because looking at Gib was causing Joel's heart to ache too terribly to bear.

"I had the chance to sign them. They were right in front of me."

Gib shook his head, confusion etched across his features.

Oh Goddesses, give me strength. "I couldn't." Joel swallowed, still unable to meet his companion's eyes. "I wouldn't."

"I don't—I don't understand," Gib whispered. "What do you mean, 'you wouldn't'?"

A deep, somber silence fell over them, but the pounding in Joel's ears was deafening. He wanted to run and hide. He wanted to fade into the shadows and disappear rather than stay here and admit the way he felt to Gib. *No. I have to tell him. He has a right to know.* Joel closed his eyes and let out a breath of air. *It's time.*

The words tumbled from his mouth in a rush. "Something overcame me while I was in Shantar—a feeling, a responsibility to Arden. A duty. Surely you know of what I speak?" Joel dared to look at the other man now, searching his endless brown eyes for some kind of understanding. All Joel found was hurt. "Our country needs people like you and me, Gib. So many people aren't given a voice, and we are lucky enough to be in a position to change the world. One day, you will sit on the High Council. You'll bring the change Arden so desperately needs. And I will be an envoy, traveling afar to promote peace between Arden and our neighbors. If I can do anything to prevent warfare—to prevent lives on both sides of the border from being lost—I have to try. We *can* change the world, Gib, I know it."

"I was under the impression we were going to change the world together, side by side." Gib's voice shook, though Joel could see Gib was trying to remain stoic. "You leaving wasn't part of the plan."

The mage took hold of Gib's hands. "I love you. I cherish every single moment we've spent together, and I wouldn't change any of it for the world."

"Then *why* are you leaving? If you cherish what we have, why are you leaving again? You were gone for six moonturns, Joel. *Six!* And now you're going again—possibly never to return! I've tried to be as supportive as I can, but *dammit* Joel, I can't—it isn't fair!" Gib threw his hands into the air.

"There, I said it. If that makes me a selfish person, fine, I don't care anymore. I'm not okay with you going to the Northern Empire! I'm not okay with living in fear that you might not return! I don't support this decision."

Joel grabbed for his companion's hands, but Gib tore away from Joel completely and took a step back.

"Gib, please—just listen to me!"

Gib turned and stormed toward the door, and Joel was certain Gib was about to leave, but instead, he put his back to one of the great pillars that supported the roof and slid to the floor. He pulled his knees to his chest and wrapped his arms around them. "Nothing you can say will fix this."

"Gib—" Joel sat beside him. "I promise I'll come back."

"You can't promise *anything*! You have no idea what you're getting into."

"I have to go. My father is old. He needs me. Cenric needs me. I'm a mage. I can offer both of them protection, if ever the need arises."

Gib gave Joel a sharp look. "And what of the *army* of mages the Northern Empire is rumored to wield? You're only *one* mage, Joel. What will you do should the Empire betray you? You can't defend yourself against an entire army if they choose to attack."

"What if they don't want to attack us, Gib? What if they *actually* want to peacefully treat with us? What if by going I help open a trade agreement between our nation and theirs? Or create a way for the exchange of knowledge? I'm sure there are things we can teach each other, if only minds are open to the idea. We only stand to benefit from going! And I will learn invaluable lessons from my mentor. Cenric is the most respected ambassador in Arden, and I'd be crazy not to follow him while I have the chance."

"Even if all these wonderful dreams of yours come to pass—even *if* you come back from the Northern Empire, then what? You'll come home just to be sent somewhere else?"

"As an envoy, I'd go wherever I'm needed next—wherever assistance is called for."

Gib took fistfuls of his own hair with both hands, shaking his head. "I don't know how we're supposed to have a life together if you're always gone."

Joel leaned his head against the marble pillar behind him and slammed his eyes shut. *I know. You're right. It's not fair for you. I can't expect you to put your life on hold for me.* Cenric's warning suddenly flew to the forefront of Joel's mind. The ambassador had said sacrifices would need to be made, should Joel choose to be an envoy. *The life of an envoy is one of solitude.* He dared to look at his companion, and the agony in Gib's eyes was unbearable, heart-wrenching. *You'd wait for me. I know you would, but I can't put you through that. I can't be selfish. I have to let you go. No matter how much I love you.* "I don't think this is going to work."

"What?"

"If I'm to be an envoy, I'll be gone more than I'm not. It would be selfish to ask you to live in such a way—putting your life on hold each and every time I go." Joel sucked in an agonizing breath, his lungs feeling raw. "I can't ask that of you. You deserve better."

Gib wiped at his wet eyes. "So that's it? You're leaving and we're through?"

Joel blinked away tears of his own. *I love you. I love you more than anyone else in the world. But I can't have you worrying about me. You deserve someone who will be there for you. You deserve to be happy. I have to let you go.* He nodded once. "It's best this way. You may not agree now, but you will someday."

"You're right. I don't agree." Gib's voice was hollow as he stood. "But you've made your decision, and I will respect it." He turned and walked away without another word.

Joel listened to the other man's receding footsteps until the sound faded out completely and only silence remained. Gasping wetly, Joel raised his eyes to the setting sun. Brilliant rays of gold lit up the sky, dusting the world below with warmth—only he felt none of it. He felt nothing but sharp, bitter cold imprisoning his heart in a tomb of ice. *Oh Goddesses. I've broken him. I've broken his heart.* The mage buried his face in his hands and wept.

Gib's heart ached as he wandered aimlessly through the streets of Silver. He barely noticed darkness had already blanketed the city or how cold he was—he'd forgotten his cloak back at the arena. His body and mind were numb, and all he could do was trod onward.

The events of the day were a jumbled blur in his head, and try as he might, Gib couldn't make sense of any of it. *I don't understand. I woke up this morning wrapped in Joel's embrace. He smiled at me, kissed me, and we spoke of our love to one another—and now, just like that, I may never see him again. I didn't even know anything was wrong.*

Everything had happened so fast—the news of the mission to the Northern Empire, Joel's announcement that he wanted to be an envoy, the ending of their relationship. In the blink of an eye, Gib's world had been shattered. He didn't even know how to pick up the crumbled ruins of his life.

Sudden light illuminated his path as a man moved along the opposite side of the street, setting fire to each of the lamps lining the cobblestone path. The man gave a polite nod, but Gib couldn't find it within himself to return the gesture. Indeed, he felt as though he'd never smile or be merry again.

Laughter and music filtered through the alleyways, and Gib finally had the awareness to realize he'd found his way to Traders Row. Close by, patrons on the steps of the Rose Bouquet drank and danced. None of them seemed to notice Gib as he hurried by. He didn't want to hear laughter or music or risk running into any of his friends. He just wanted to be alone.

Gib's feet moved of their own accord, and he soon found himself standing in front of the Adelwijn estate. He approached the wrought iron gate, setting his hands against the cold metal as he peered into the dark courtyard beyond. So much of Gib's life had taken place within these stone walls. *And now there's nothing for me. Just a house brimming with forsaken memories.* He blinked back tears.

Actually, that wasn't true. Gib had belongings here. Clothing, books, and several other personal items. He glanced over his shoulder, wondering if Joel had made his way home yet. *Should I go inside and get my things?* Gib debated in silence. Surely Joel wouldn't appreciate Gib's belongings taking up space. They'd serve to be nothing but a bitter reminder of their failed romance.

I'll just go in and quietly collect my things and be gone before anyone even knows I'm there. Not allowing himself time to second guess his decision, Gib slipped through the gate. He hoped to go unnoticed, though the servants and Lady Mrifa were used to Gib coming and leaving. *Goddesses, don't let Joel be here yet. I won't be able to hold myself together if I have to look upon his face again.*

He saw no sign of Joel or any of the other Adelwijn family members inside, though faint candlelight could be seen beneath the door leading to the servant quarters. Gib whisked past the closed door, hoping to draw neither Tabitha's nor Otos' attention, and headed for the stairwell.

Joel's room—the same room Gib had shared for the past three years—lay abandoned. Indeed, things were as they had been when the companions had left together that morning. Gib touched shaking fingertips to the quilted bedspread as he passed by. How was it possible they'd left the room laughing and joking earlier and now Gib was here to pack his bags?

Gib wiped a tear from his eye and rustled through a pile of clothing until he found his rucksack. Losing the battle to despair, he began to fling things into it. Clothing, books, a pair of boots—Gib paused when his hands landed on *Tales of Fae*. *No. This is Joel's. It stays here.* He set the book aside and continued to collect his things until, at last, he could find nothing more. *There. It's done. Now there's nothing more to remind Joel of me.* Gib hoisted the bag onto his shoulder. *Time to leave.* He turned and left the room without a further glance, knowing it would have done him in.

The rucksack was lighter on his shoulder than he would have expected. Did he really have so little at the estate? It seemed like he'd spent so much of his life here, and he could hardly comprehend how easily he was able to remove himself—though he'd have to come back for formal goodbyes to the girls and Lady Mrifa. Even Otos and Tabitha had grown friendly with him over the past three years. It was going to be like saying goodbye to family. Fresh tears threatened to pour from his eyes. *Don't do this now. Not here. No more tears tonight.*

Steeling himself for the journey back to the dormitory, Gib hoped to get out the door without catching anyone's attention. And he sure as hell hoped to put some distance between himself and the estate before Joel showed up. Gib didn't want to make this messy. Enough feelings had been hurt already.

The front door was in sight, and fortunately, no one else was. He could perhaps get out of here unnoticed after all—

"Why *you*? Why must it always be you to risk your life?" Lady Mrifa's voice came from the dining room. It was a higher pitch than Gib was used to hearing, and she sounded like she'd been crying. "You even said King Rishi wanted you to stay. Why are you doing this?"

Gib debated leaving. He had no place listening to this, but if he passed by they would see him. If he turned around and went to the back door, Otos and Tabitha were sure to hear him. He had no clear means of escape.

Koal's strained voice came next. "Neetra can't be trusted to go, Mrifa. If I don't go then he is next in line. The Northern Empire is too powerful and dangerous to entrust to him."

"But the King *wanted* him to go—"

"No. Rishi is an idiot—and also desperate. If he were thinking clearly he wouldn't even entertain the idea of sending Neetra."

"He's desperate because his son is going as well. He knows how dangerous this is!"

Koal sighed, and it took a while for him to respond. "I know. He has every reason to worry for his son. Hasain will likely be viewed as the product of a traitor and could fall victim to some imbecile still holding a grudge. That's why it's my responsibility to go and—"

Something slammed, perhaps her hand on the dining table. "You have responsibilities here, too! Life doesn't stand still in this house just because you're gone so often!"

Gib winced. Was this what was in store for him should he join the High Council? "What of your daughter and her heart? How long will you keep Heidi waiting for an answer?"

"Not this right now. I have important things to worry over! Promising Heidi to a suitor is the least of my concerns—"

"*Three years*! You have kept her waiting for three years. She is seventeen. Her friends are courting or engaged. One of them is already married. She wants to be able to have a family, but she also wants your permission to do this properly."

"There are more pressing matters!"

"There are always more pressing matters!"

Gib rested his forehead against the wall and closed his eyes. He'd never heard Lady Mrifa yell before, and it tore him up inside.

"This is your *family*, or what's left of it with both our sons going—" Her gasp was wet, and Gib had to fight back his own tears.

Light footsteps sounded, and the rustling of fabric followed. Koal's voice was low, too quiet for Gib to pick up the words, but he caught their meaning. Hushed sounds of comfort and tender promises were made. There may have even been a kiss. Gib seriously considered heading for the back door and ignoring Otos or Tabitha if they saw him.

The lady seemed to pull herself together though. "There is no choice? They must go?"

"I've tried to deny them. I've also tried to talk them out of it, but they're both stubborn."

Lady Mrifa sniffled. "I know. They're so different from one another, but they both have your stubborn streak." She took a ragged breath. "And Heidi—she needs an answer."

Koal sighed. "I know. Look, when I return, *if* Nawaz wants to marry Heidi, I will allow it. If no one else has made an offer, Nawaz will be given full permission to pursue her."

"Other offers? You know she has her heart set on him."

"He's never once asked me for her hand, Mrifa. He's never offered to court her. You can't force affection."

Gib thought of Kezra. She and Nawaz seemed well suited to one another, better than he and Heidi—

Mrifa lowered her voice. "If Nawaz doesn't marry her, I don't know that she'll marry at all." A poignant silence fell over the entire house.

Is this unrequited love? Heidi and I may not be so different. If I can't have Joel, I don't know if I can love anyone else.

Koal offered more words of comfort, and the husband and wife slipped away toward the sitting room. Gib waited for them to be well out of earshot before he made for the door. He'd just reached for the handle when another sound caught his attention. More sniffling.

He turned, just as Heidi crept away from the shadowed place by the stairs. Her footfalls were ghostly silent, and she passed him with barely a second glance. The hollowed despair in her eyes resonated deep in Gib's soul. Tonight their sorrows were mutual.

CHAPTER FIVE

The climbing sun had yet to breech Silver's eastern horizon, its vibrant rose and violet tendrils only just beginning to lighten the heavens. The sunrise would have been beautiful if not for the dark storm clouds in the western sky and the promise of impending rain. Gib pulled his cloak tighter and bustled across the palace courtyard at Koal's heels.

Forsaking the early mark, more people were present than Gib would have thought. Dean Marc—of all people—had somehow beaten them there and stood with the royal family and families of the other envoys. They had formed a farewell party on the open terrace facing the courtyard.

Joel seemed determined to stay three careful steps ahead of Gib. He never looked back, and the two young men hadn't shared a single word since they'd met up at the palace gate. Joel's white mage robes flowed behind him, hindered only slightly by his rucksack. It looked like he was travelling light, but perhaps that was normal for an envoy. Gib wouldn't know, and he supposed he'd never have reason to ask now. He locked his jaw, forcing himself to look away. *He'll be fine. They'll all be fine.*

As they approached, Queen Dahlia came forward to hug her brother. "Mrifa and the girls?"

Koal's voice was a trained calm as he embraced her. "At home. They saw us off."

Gib closed his eyes, trying not to imagine the haunted, lost look Lady Mrifa's eyes must have held as she said her goodbyes. *The poor lady. She stands to lose her husband and both sons.*

"Of course." Queen Dahlia nodded. Her voice held a broken quality, and Gib was sure she'd been crying.

Gib stayed back as Joel hugged Diddy and the rest of his cousins. Joel's beautiful smile seemed forced as they all wished him well. Gib's heart clenched. It wouldn't always be like this, would it? Surely this devastating pain would eventually subside.

Gib raised his head just as Marc slapped Koal on the back. The dean wore the biggest smile of anyone there. "Clean knickers every day and wash behind your ears."

Koal shoved Marc aside and dropped his pack to the ground with a light thud. "Maybe we should take you. I reckon the Northern Empire could use a new court jester."

Marc laughed so loudly it earned a couple of looks from the others. "I'll pass. Now, you're sure you want to leave Gib under my watch? Am I allowed to make him miserable?" He stole a devilish look across the yard, and Gib found himself smiling faintly in return.

"Run. It's your only chance." King Rishi approached so quietly Gib hadn't heard his footfalls at all. He began to bow, but the King waved a flippant hand. "Don't do that here. There's no one to impress."

Any apology Gib could think of died on his lips as he was pushed aside by the others as they followed the King. Aodan's ever-watchful dark eye glinted in the sunlight, and the strange Blessed Mages, NezReth and Natori, walked so lightly it almost seemed as though they were floating across the dew-covered grass.

The King wasted no time going to Koal, and a moment later, Cenric Leal joined them. A girl about Gib's age followed on the envoy's heels. She was carrying a large roll of parchment and, at the King's command, she unfurled it to reveal a weathered map. Curiosity overtook Gib's troubled mind, and he wandered closer, though he made sure to stay out of their way.

Cenric's helper held one end of the large map while Koal took hold of the other. This left King Rishi and Cenric to point to various places and discuss methods of escape. Gib's gut clenched again. Why were they going to the Northern Empire if it was so dangerous? Would this really be the last time he would see either his mentor or his love? The cold bite of reason clamped down on his heart. *Joel isn't mine anymore.*

Gib shifted his attention back to Joel, watching as the mage spoke quietly to his cousins. Hasain stood with them, one arm around his weeping mother. Gib recognized her from working in the royal kitchen. Rya was her name, he vaguely remembered Hasain mentioning. She'd never looked as frail as she did in this moment, saying what may be her final goodbyes to her son. Gib ached for her and for his own broken heart.

Cenric's voice lifted over the hum in Gib's ears. "This is all fine and well, Highness, but we must hope for the best. Should we have to flee Teivel, we all know how slim our chances will be."

The King's mouth slanted into a fine line. "I am well aware of the direness of the situation, Ambassador. However, I feel it advantageous to discuss your best possible escape routes now, if in the unlikely event any of you walk out of there alive."

Gib sucked in a sharp breath, and the girl holding the map did the same.

Koal cleared his throat, fixing sharp eyes on the King. "Enough of this. Let's not collect the fee for our tombs just yet. We're alive and well now."

"Agreed," Cenric insisted. "And we may just be standing on the

86

precipice of history. Who knows what good fortune this venture may bring." He clapped the girl on her shoulder and gave her a smile, but something in Cenric's voice suggested even he wasn't convinced.

Gib looked over to Joel once more and caught the mage's devastated blue eyes. Why was he doing this? One as young as he had no good reason to go. Hasain had the misfortune of representing the royal family, and Liro apparently insisted on going, but Joel was only a freshly graduated mage. He had *one* envoy mission under his belt. He wasn't a politician and stood to gain nothing from this mission except near certain death. The hollow ache in Gib's chest made him want to heave.

The sound of the map being rerolled brought him back to the present. The girl cradled the parchment as if it were a child, and she stood so close to Cenric she could have been holding his hand. Gib wiped a hand across his eyes and refused to look back to Joel.

Koal was complaining about his eldest son under his breath. "Where is Liro? If he's not here when the portal opens then we'll have to leave him behind."

"That'd be a shame," Aodan muttered, never looking away from the stone archway. Gib only now realized the King's bodyguard bore a blade on his left hip and bracers on each arm. Gib frowned. The Blessed Mages were also behaving peculiarly, or rather, more peculiarly than normal. They had swept across the yard and seemed to be examining the stone archway where the portal would form. The King watched them narrowly.

None of this did anything to help settle Gib's already frayed nerves. *Are they worried about an attack? Should I have a weapon too?*

His hands rested uneasily on his hips as he watched the Blessed Mages continue to circle and examine the arch. The longer they took, the more certain Gib was that he didn't want Joel to go. Something shook inside him—a terrible rage he would rather ignore than acknowledge he was capable of. Would Joel still go if Gib demanded the mage stay? And if not, was there a way for Gib to rush the portal as well and go with them? He may not have a sword in hand, but he could damned well get between Joel and an oncoming attack.

Gib's thoughts were derailed by a heavy sigh. He looked over in time to catch the King staring at Koal. All of the ruler's vigor seemed to have withered away, leaving him to suddenly look old and frail.

Koal must have felt the heavy look on his back, for he turned to face the King. "What? Do I have something on my face?"

King Rishi shook his head. "No. You're going to die—and there's nothing I can do to stop it."

Koal cast a look toward the family members gathered close by. "Keep your voice down. And, in case you didn't know, I have no intention of dying. I'm no fool. I'll keep my guard up while I'm there—"

"Take Aodan with you. He has sworn to go and watch over you all."

"No. Who'd be left to watch over you? I won't be here. You'll need him all the more."

"This is ludicrous!" King Rishi balked. "A fine king in a grand kingdom. I can't stop my seneschal from meeting his death or send my bodyguard to protect him for fear of being stabbed in my back! I can't even protect my own son—or yours."

King Rishi glanced over toward where Hasain and Joel stood on the terrace with the royal family, and Gib couldn't help but look, too. Hasain deliberately avoided eye contact, and Joel busied himself by talking to the youngest of the royal children, Crowned Prince Deegan and Princess Gudrin. If the mage felt their eyes at his back, he didn't indicate it.

Koal dropped his voice so low Gib had to strain to hear it. "Rishi, I—I swear to you, I will protect Hasain—with my own life if need be. He and Joel will be under my constant watch." He took a shuddering breath and gazed across the courtyard, his eyes focusing on nothing in particular. "However, in the event I don't return—"

"Mrifa and the girls will be looked after. They are of little consequence to those who seek to undo you or me. I promise they will be cared for." The King glared into the same distance.

A creeping sensation that time was no longer on his side made Gib realize he should perhaps try to say a goodbye to Joel. Who knew when Gib would see Joel again—or even *if* he'd see him again.

Gib refused to cry as he wandered toward the others. Hasain still held his mother under one arm, but she appeared to have collected herself for the moment. Another young man stood with them. Gib recognized him as Hasain's younger brother, Tular. He nodded in their general direction, and Hasain returned the gesture.

Joel's back was an arm's length away. Gib could have touched the pristine white robe if he'd had the courage to. Instead, Gib stood against the palace wall and hugged his arms around himself. Thunder rumbled in the vast distance, and the bleak clouds rolled across what would have been a breathtaking sunrise.

"You're going to watch after your sister and mother, aren't you?" Cenric's voice was a careful calm.

Cenric's assistant wiped one of her hazel eyes and nodded. "Come back to us, Da. Nia will never forgive you if she decides to marry this fella of hers and you're not there." Her face and neck were mottled red as she fought for control over her trembling lip.

"You know I'll be back," Cenric murmured, stroking her hair. "Only death could keep me from you girls."

Da? So this was one of Cenric's daughters? Gib frowned. The ambassador was leaving behind two daughters and a wife. What if he didn't come back? Then what? Would Cenric not be present to witness Nage and his daughter married? Gib couldn't bring himself to look directly at the pair but caught their embrace from the corner of his eye. He swallowed against the bile in his throat. None of this seemed fair. None of these people should be forced to leave their families.

Joel's misty blue eyes turned onto Gib, and he froze. It wasn't worth the heartache of never saying goodbye, was it? Gib's feet moved without his instruction toward the other man and, to his relief, Joel didn't turn his back again.

Gib stood before Joel for what felt like an eternity. His mind whirled, but any thought of what to say slipped from his grasp. He kept his arms around himself, unsure if he was allowed to touch his former companion or not. Joel, for his part, didn't offer to close the gap either. What was this wall between them? Would it always be there?

"I–I don't know what to say," Gib confessed. "But I don't want you to go without saying anything."

Joel's rigid posture relaxed slightly, and he sighed. "Same. I don't know how to say goodbye to you again." He tugged at one sleeve absently, glaring at the stone ground.

"Goodbye is too final. Like maybe we'll never see each other again." Gib fought to keep from trembling. "We will, won't we? When you come back? I will at least see you again?"

Joel was biting his lip so hard that a red line marred his skin. "Of course. Gib, I—" Unknowable thoughts and emotions played behind his devastated eyes, and he reached out with one hand, only to drop it down by his side the next instant. The wall was still there. "When I return, I would hope to see you well and happy." His voice was flat and there might have been more to what had been said than simple words, but Gib was too tired and hurt to try to decipher it.

How would he have me be happy without him? Gib looked away. The sky grew darker by the moment, and the winds had begun to blow cold air through the courtyard. They were running out of time. Gib swallowed. "Promise you'll be careful. Promise you're not—going to your death." He could barely say the words.

Joel flinched as if he'd been burned. "I will be careful, but I won't make a vow I may not be able to keep. I have no intention of making this my final journey, but only a fool would refuse to see the inherent danger of this mission."

So, father and son were the same. They knew full well the risk they were taking and still refused to stay behind. Gib's stomach twisted so hard he nearly doubled over. He fought to meet Joel's gaze. "I would have gone with you. I would have offered my sword to protect you and Koal. Neither of you even asked."

"I know. And he knows. The fewer men King Rishi sends, the fewer who are in direct danger. Neither my father nor I would risk you needlessly." Joel blinked and tipped his head back. He may have stopped the tears from spilling over, but Gib wasn't blind. He saw them glistening in Joel's misty eyes.

"Strength doesn't mean you have to act on your own." Gib took a step forward. "You don't have to be so vulnerable."

Joel shook his head. "No. I go to protect my father so he will not be alone. You stay to finish your training. Live fully." He slammed his eyes shut and, somehow, the tears still did not fall.

Perhaps his heart isn't so torn as mine, Gib thought. *Maybe his is already healing.*

"A cup can be full of shadow. Full and empty at once. And so my life shall be without you. But I won't force you to stay." Gib backed away. If Joel's mind was set then no force in the two worlds could change it. Gib could give him nothing more than his freedom.

The devastation on Joel's face almost beckoned an apology. Almost—but no. Gib was too hurt to say anything more. He turned on one heel and returned to Koal's side. Perhaps the seneschal would have some need of him before he too rushed to meet his fate.

As Gib drew closer to his mentor, approaching footfalls sounded from across the courtyard. As if the bitter taste in Gib's mouth wasn't enough on its own, Liro Adelwijn made his entrance.

Koal's narrow eyes conveyed his sentiment. "Where were you? You're nearly late—"

Liro's face remained cold as he approached his father. "I saw no reason to be early. Surely none of these well wishes or farewells are for me."

"Your mother and sisters would have liked to say their goodbyes."

"Goodbye or good riddance?"

"I would say both apply," King Rishi muttered under his breath.

Liro turned to look straight at the King. "No reason to whisper your distaste, Highness. You needn't spare my feelings."

King Rishi glared dangerously, and Aodan turned his dark eye on Liro, shrewd and calculating. The air felt static, and some darkness inside Gib beckoned the older men on, wishing they would put Liro in his place once and for all.

Koal responded first, his guttural threat akin to an animalistic growl. "Get your arse over there and keep that mouth shut or you'll find yourself staying in Arden after all."

A tight smile pulled at Liro's mouth as he inclined his head—a mockery of a bow to the King—before turning to take his place by the palace wall. Seeing him standing side by side with his younger brother, Gib wondered how the same features that made Joel beautiful could be so warped to make Liro ugly.

The Blessed Mages returned to King Rishi's side. "The arch is secured," Natori announced.

"You're sure?"

She looked directly at the King, stoic features showing no trace of doubt or worry. "Yes. If the Empire's spell is malicious, we *will* know."

King Rishi nodded and glanced up at the sky. "It must be nearly time. The envoys should assemble. The rift will open as soon as the sun clears the horizon."

Gib didn't know how the King could tell where the sun was. The pink and violet hues from earlier were gone, smudged out by sinister storm clouds.

"Envoys!" Koal announced. "It's time to gather."

All around, Gib watched as final goodbyes were exchanged. Cenric's daughter held her emotions well, not even a single tear slipping through. Rya gave Hasain a final hug. As she relinquished her son, Queen Dahlia took hold of Rya's hand, and the two mothers wept silently together.

Marc stepped closer and gave Koal another hearty clap on the shoulder. His smile was wide and lively, but a shadow in his eyes made Gib unsure about its sincerity. "Now remember what I said about those clean knickers. They're important, should you get caught with your pants down."

Koal smiled and put a hand on Marc's shoulder. "Take care of Beatrice and that baby."

Hasain approached, managing to keep up stoic pretenses until he stood before his father.

King Rishi had gone pale. His courageous mask was showing its wear. Eyes damp, he reached for his son, putting a hand on either side of the young lord's face. "You don't have to do this."

Hasain grasped his father's forearms. "I would show you my quality. I only ask that you believe in me."

"I know your quality. I have never doubted it, and you need to do the same." King Rishi took a deep breath before pressing a kiss to Hasain's forehead. "Be safe. Come back to your family. We love you."

Gib felt a hand on his shoulder. He looked into his mentor's eyes, and Koal smiled down at him. "You'll have to take care of Marc for me, I'm afraid. I hate to leave you in such a predicament, but you have to understand, no one else wanted him."

A hollow laugh escaped Gib's throat. "I'll try my best to keep him out of trouble."

Koal chuckled and turned next toward King Rishi. He held out his right hand, earning a sneer from the ruler. Even so, the King clasped the offered hand anyway.

"Don't make any stupid decisions there," King Rishi warned.

"Don't let Neetra go to war with Shiraz while I'm gone," the seneschal replied.

"Without you to separate us in the council room, going to war should be the least of your concerns. If the little rat is dead upon your return, know I only acted on the impulse you've squashed for years." A wolfish grin stole over his face. "And should *you* die, take comfort, Koal. I'll be sure to have your tomb engraved with fine praise for the King's favorite servant."

Koal rolled his eyes as he reached down for his rucksack but stopped short when NezReth, of all people, snatched it up for him.

The Blessed Mage bowed. "Allow me. It will get in the way of your cape."

Koal turned to glare at the King. "What's this?"

"Don't try to stop me," King Rishi replied. "He's going with you."

"And you'll just sit in the palace and hope no one makes an attack on you?"

"I gave you the choice to take Aodan, and you refused. NezReth is not a choice. Natori will be here with me. We both know she's more formidable than him anyway."

If NezReth was offended, it didn't show on his placid face. In fact, the Blessed Mage didn't seem to be paying attention to their conversation at all. Pale, lavender eyes flashed in the direction of the archway before he made his way to where the envoys stood waiting. Liro, Joel, and Hasain all appeared to do a double take as the Blessed Mage approached. Cenric was the only one who didn't seem surprised, although it could merely have been his training showing through.

Koal locked eyes with the King. "Damn you and your pride! This isn't safe!"

"There's no time to argue. And you're not going to win anyway. Just go."

"Fine. But don't think this conversation is over. When I come back, I'm giving you hell for this."

King Rishi smirked. "I suppose I can rest assured you *will* come back then."

Silence settled over the courtyard like a heavy blanket. Joel faced the archway, but as Gib watched, Joel lifted a sleeve and wiped at his eyes. Gib's heart tore in two. *I should be going with him—or be stopping him from going at all! I should be doing something besides standing here, dammit!*

Koal strode across the courtyard. No sooner had he taken his place beside Cenric did the sky open above and rain begin to fall. Gib clutched the terrace rail and watched. Somewhere in the back of his foggy mind, he was aware of rain droplets sinking into his hair and making his scalp cold.

Joel, I love you. I should have said it. I should have told you.

A large hand rested atop his shoulder. He twisted his head around to look at Marc. He didn't return Gib's gaze or say one word, but tears tracked down both sides of the dean's face. Gib wiped his own eyes, only now aware that he'd been crying, too.

As he stole one final glance toward Joel, the hairs on the back of his neck stood on end and a shiver raced from the tips of his toes to his crown of curls. Gib shuddered as the rain fell in violent pellets against his skin. Something was about to happen. He could feel it.

As if The Two wept with them, heavy, cold rain began to fall from the clouds. Joel raised his eyes to the darkened sky, thankful the rain helped disguise the tears streaming down his fair cheeks. Refusing to look back, knowing that even a glance at Gib would reduce him to horrible, uncontrolled sobbing, Joel fixed his eyes on the stone arch, the place where the portal would appear.

At the sound of a throat clearing, Joel turned to meet Hasain's somber gaze. The young lord's face was drawn and sullen, and his complexion looked unnaturally blanched, as though the stark white of his mage robes had somehow bled through the fabric and onto his skin. *He's nervous, too.*

"Be sure to keep your thoughts cloaked at all times," Hasain warned, speaking in a low, hushed tone. "We'll find no friends where we go, and there are those who would attempt to read your mind if given the opportunity."

Joel swallowed the frigid spike in his throat. "I've heard of such magery. I'll keep myself and our party warded always."

Hasain gave a curt nod. "As will I." A firm hand closed around Joel's forearm as Hasain leveled another warning glance. "Don't ever let your guard down. And trust *no one.*"

"I understand," Joel replied, holding back a shudder.

Hasain released the grip on Joel's arm and motioned for him to move closer to the stone arch. "Come. It's almost time. When the portal opens, we must be ready to pass through."

Feeling lightheaded, Joel did as directed and trailed silently behind Hasain. The pair of men came to stand beside the other members of their party—Seneschal Koal, Ambassador Cenric, Liro, and the Blessed Mage, NezReth. *His* presence had come as a surprise to Joel. No one had mentioned NezReth would be accompanying them to the Northern Empire until moments before, when King Rishi had all but demanded Koal accept the mage into the party.

Joel stole a sideways glance at the enigmatic figure, hidden beneath a white cloak and layered robe made from wool. NezReth's strange violet eyes were focused on the stone archway as though it were the most important thing in the world.

Koal readjusted the red cape cascading down his left shoulder. The cape covered a fitted overcoat embroidered with blue and golden thread, with the image of the rising phoenix sewn onto the fabric. He was dressed elaborately—more so than Joel was used to seeing—though he supposed if what everyone said about the Northern Empire was true, his father wanted to make a good first impression.

Cenric, too, was dressed to impress. The ambassador wore a blue jerkin similar to those worn by the Healers—though this one, with its brass buttons and laced sleeves, was more ornamental than anything a Healer would wear in the field.

Joel shifted the weight of his pack from one shoulder to the other. Standing among these grown men in their fine clothing did nothing but remind him how young and unexperienced he truly was. *What am I doing here? I don't belong in such company.* A desperate feeling made its way to his throat, and with it, the urge to turn and look back at Gib returned. *No. Don't. If I change my mind now, I'll be seen as a coward.*

"What's taking so long?" Liro asked, pulling his cloak tighter as the cold drizzle intensified into steady rainfall.

Joel would have laughed at his elder brother's discomfort if he wasn't feeling so demoralized himself.

"Why hasn't the portal opened?"

Koal cleared his throat pointedly. "Patience, Liro."

"There," NezReth announced a moment later in a wispy voice. He raised one slender hand to point at the archway. "Prepare yourselves."

Sucking in a deep breath, Joel shifted his eyes to look. At first, nothing seemed out of the ordinary, but as he continued to study the archway, a strange tingling sensation caused the fine hairs on the back of his neck and arms to rise, and he *knew* something was about to happen. As he watched, tendrils of blue energy began to swirl between the crevasses and cracks of the stone masonry. Like an eerie mist, the magic spread rapidly, sweeping over the entirety of the arch and the empty space inside.

Joel held his breath. He could feel the power building now—immense amounts of energy pooling in the center of the archway, tearing a hole in the Void between space and time and connecting two places separated by vast distance. Magic crackled like lightning as the energy tendrils anchored to the stones of the arch, and Joel clung to his cloak as a violent blast of wind came hurtling through the portal, lashing all who were gathered in the courtyard.

Joel squinted his eyes against the barrage of dead leaves and sand pelting his face. Through the veil of the archway, he could see tall pillars and the lush greenery of a garden. It was as though he were looking through an open window or doorway. *It is a doorway,* Joel reminded himself. *And the Northern Empire lies beyond it—*

NezReth's voice rose above the screaming wind. "The portal is open! We must go now!"

At first, no one moved. Joel's own body was frozen in place, paralyzed by fear and doubt. He'd been through portals before—he and

94

Cenric had used a portal to get to and from Shantar—but the immensity of what he was about to do gripped him in sudden terror. *I shouldn't be going. What was I thinking? This isn't peaceful Shantar. This is the Northern Empire*—

Cenric lurched forward, the first in the party to move. His short hair flew about his head, and the determined frown pulling at his lips only accentuated the age lines around his mouth and eyes. Without so much as a flinch, the ambassador stepped through the threshold.

"You next, Joel," Koal commanded. "Hurry now!"

When Joel didn't immediately respond, Hasain shoved him hard in the back. "Go!"

Joel forced his legs to move. It felt as though both appendages were as heavy as marble pillars. Taking several shuddering steps forward, he approached the crackling portal. There was no turning back now. This was it. With eyes slammed shut and breath locked deep inside his chest, Joel jumped through the swirling veil.

A blast of warm air hit him in the face, and a feeling of complete weightlessness passed over him as he traveled through the rip in the Void. Terrible thoughts of somehow becoming trapped there flew to the front of his mind, but before panic had a chance to set in, the sensation ebbed and he crossed safely to the far side.

He staggered, momentarily unable to ground his feet, but then NezReth came through and Joel felt a pair of hands on his back, steadying him. The Blessed Mage smiled, but Joel had no time to utter thanks, as the remaining members of the party still waited on the far side of the portal.

Joel darted out of the way, looking over his shoulder in time to see his father and brother pass through. Hasain brought up the rear. On the Ardenian side of the portal, Joel could still see the faces of his friends and family. King Rishi looked on, a worried frown pulling at his mouth. Beside him stood Queen Dahlia, and only a pace behind her stood Gib, shadowing Dean Marc. Joel couldn't be sure, but Gib's eyes appeared to be wet with tears. Joel wished he could now say the words he'd wanted to tell Gib earlier. *I love you. I'm so sorry.*

An instant after Hasain's feet hit the ground, the portal shuddered, and Joel could feel the magic dissipate as it collapsed in on itself. The glowing blue light vanished, and the tendrils of magic seeped back into the cracks of the stonework, disappearing from sight. Where he had seen his friends and family a moment before, stood a wall of granite.

"Damn portal," Koal muttered under his breath as he hastily readjusted his crimson cape.

Joel straightened his own frazzled hair as he looked around. They stood in the middle of a lush garden. Vines, heavy with fruit, clung to wooden trellises, and shrubs with leafy palms lay nestled among vibrant flowers of every color and size. Trees with winding, crooked bases and strange leathery leaves provided shade to the area, and smooth granite and limestone pavers created a walkway along the greenery. At the end of the path lay an open terrace, and beyond that, beautiful stone buildings with terracotta rooftops—reminiscent of the architectural style used at the palace in Silver City—rose in the distance.

The humid air was warm, which came as a surprise to Joel. Though he'd never been farther north than a few dozen leagues from Silver City, he knew from studying maps that Teivel, the capital city of the Northern Empire, sat high above the Pinnacle Peaks to Arden's northernmost border—a place known for its harsh winters and only slightly less frigid summers. Why then, did it look and feel as though he'd stepped into a tropical paradise?

Hasain tugged at his collar, peeling the heavy fabric away from his neck. "Why is it so hot?"

"Magic," Cenric replied at once. He nodded toward the sky. "The inner city of Teivel is climate controlled year-round. How else do you think such exotic flora is able to grow this far north?"

The entire city is kept warm? But how? Joel raised his eyes to study the skyline, and tentatively he reached out with his magic to inspect it. Sure enough, he could detect a strange, iridescent film far above, nearly invisible to the naked eye but easily traceable by magic. *It's a dome*, he realized. *A barrier made from magic. It must keep the cold out.*

He'd heard of such a thing, but never on such a large scale. During the coldest days of winter in Arden, the rich could hire a mage to bring warmth to a single room in a household, but such a spell was incredibly taxing on a mage's power reserves so families mostly opted to build the fire in the hearth extra tall instead of paying for such services. If a single Ardenian mage could barely keep *one* room heated, then how in the two worlds were the mages of the Northern Empire able to keep an *entire city* warm *year-round?* The amount of magical energy needed for such a feat seemed incomprehensible. Joel opened his mouth to ask about it, but the sound of approaching footfalls caught his attention.

A dozen soldiers marched onto the terrace and turned toward the Ardenian party. Each wore splendid armor and longswords on their hips. Breastplates gilded with golden powder covered black, knee-length tunics, and leather sandals with metal studs protected the soldiers' feet. Twelve sets of calculating eyes regarded the party from within feathered helms made from steel and polished to a sharp shine. Wordlessly, the patrol swept down the path, coming within several paces of Joel and the other Ardenian men, before halting. Joel waited on pins and needles to see what would happen next.

Movement finally occurred, and some of the soldiers shifted aside as one final newcomer joined the precession. A man dressed in a long golden robe made from sea silk stood out among the dark clothing of the soldiers like the sun against rain clouds. His haughty stance and elaborate clothing suggested he was of high rank, although Joel couldn't be sure what title the man held. Jewels of sapphire and ruby clung to his white fingers, and blond hair fell to graze his shoulders in perfect ringlets.

The man clasped both hands together as he regarded the party in silence, his pale blue eyes passing over each of them, studying and undoubtedly judging. Even as the man gave a curt head bow in greeting, no trace of a smile passed across his thin lips and high cheekbones. Joel tried to imagine such a face showing pleasantries and was unable to. This man reminded Joel every bit of Liro or Neetra, and without even knowing him, Joel knew the man would have been welcomed with open arms by the other highborns on the High Council.

"On behalf of His Grace, Emperor Lichas Sarpedon, Supreme Ruler of all the North and blessed by the Son of Light Himself, I extend a fair greeting and welcome your party to Teivel." The robed man's voice was as smooth as the silk he wore, and despite slight discrepancies in pronunciation, Joel was able to follow the conversation. "I am Archmage Adrian Titus, overseer of the Mage Order of Teivel. I will be your host and guide for the longevity of your stay."

Koal stepped forward, sweeping into a gracious bow. "I am Koal Adelwijn, seneschal of Arden and Right Hand of King Rishi Radek. These are Cenric Leal, Chief Ambassador of Arden, Hasain Radek, eldest son of the King, Liro Adelwijn, understudy to the High Councilor of Arden, and mages Joel Adelwijn and NezReth, of the King's inner court."

A frown crossed Adrian's fair features. "Right Hand of the King? Forgive me, but the Emperor was expecting Rishi Radek to make the journey to Teivel. The message His Grace sent specifically requested the King of Arden's presence."

Koal nodded and spoke as though he'd been expecting such a response. "As I'm sure you're already aware, Arden is in the middle of a conflict with Shiraz and Nales. Both countries threaten to take our country to war, and *King* Rishi was unable to leave his seat vacant under such dire conditions. However, the King has granted me authority to make decisions on behalf of Arden and has sent his eldest son as a gesture of good faith."

"Eldest son—but not the Crowned Prince?"

Joel knew his father well enough not to be fooled by his hardened exterior or carefully neutral tone. Koal's response was every bit that of a well-trained envoy. "Arden's Crowned Prince Deegan is but a mere boy of twelve and would be no asset to our negotiations. Lord Hasain, however, is well schooled in both politics and diplomacy."

Adrian issued a pompous chuckle. "It isn't I you need worry about assuring, but His Grace, the Emperor."

"Then let us meet him," Koal insisted, his voice spiking just enough to draw notice.

Adrian fixed a cold stare on the seneschal, and for a moment, Joel feared his father might have overstepped the fine line between civil disagreement and brash disregard of courtesy. *Not that we've been received politely either. This Adrian Titus is as haughty as "dear" Uncle Neetra.*

Adrian straightened his back and turned his nose upward. "His Grace is holding court this mark. He's expecting you. Come with me. You may leave your packs in the hands of the servants. Rest assured they will deliver your belongings to your suite unharmed."

A pair of young women dressed in simple white dresses appeared beside Adrian and waited in silence, keeping their faces lowered and hands clasped together. Joel gripped the strap slung over his shoulder. He didn't want to hand over his belongings to complete strangers. However, a moment later, Koal nodded his approval, so Joel grudgingly took the pack from his back and set it on the ground. The other members of the party did the same, and the servant girls moved forward to collect the rucksacks.

"Follow me," Adrian said.

He swung around without awaiting a response, and silently the soldiers swept up to flank both sides of the Ardenian party, giving Joel and the other men no choice but to follow behind the Archmage. Joel cast a glance at his father, but Koal's troubled eyes were focused ahead. Cenric offered a smile when Joel met the ambassador's gaze, though Liro made no move to acknowledge his presence. Hasain glared miserably at the floor and followed a pace behind the rest of the group.

They followed along onto a paved pathway much wider than the one cutting through the garden. Stone villas with colorful tiled roofs and silken curtains in lieu of shutters lined the street. Each of these homes had small gardens of their own, featuring flowering plants, leafy ferns, and shrubs brimming with fruit.

As they walked on, Joel began to see more people. Women dressed in elaborate silk dresses, wearing ornate necklaces and pearls around their wrists congregated beneath shaded terraces, while young men and women in white tunics served them wine. They all turned curious eyes toward the Ardenian envoys as they passed.

Soldiers also patrolled the streets. Joel noted how quickly people moved aside to let them pass as well as the concern etched onto their faces. He frowned in thought. Did the people here have to worry about soldier brutality? Were the citizens of Teivel afraid of the very people who were supposed to protect them? If so, what did this have to say about the Emperor himself?

Joel stopped his pondering when an enormous shadow passed across his line of vision. He turned his face skyward, realizing they were now walking along the base of a giant wall. The marble stone, stacked higher than even the tallest villas, loomed above the surrounding rooftops, and upon further inspection, Joel could see armed soldiers walking along the top of the structure. Whatever lay on the other side of the wall must have been important to be so closely guarded.

Adrian led the group to a gateway, reinforced by thick iron bars and five men in military uniforms standing guard beside it. No questions were asked nor were pleasantries exchanged as Adrian approached the soldiers. The men bowed hastily to the Archmage and called for the gate to be raised. Joel watched as a pair of soldiers on the wall hurried to crank a lever, and with a loud wail of protesting hinges, the gate rose.

"We're now entering the grounds of the Imperial palace," Adrian announced, motioning for the envoys to follow.

He led them through a lush courtyard that put the one outside the palace in Silver City to shame. Poppy flowers blanketed the ground in a sea of red, yellow, and violet, and beautiful marble statues depicting various Imperial heroes of the past overlooked a pond with crystal clear waters that shimmered in the sunlight. The water seemed to have a life of its own, and as he stared at it, Joel realized that giant colorful fish swirled and danced just below the surface. Even as he watched, a servant went to the edge of the pond and began to sprinkle grain into the water. The fish went into a feeding frenzy, weaving among one another as each tried to get its share of the food. Joel could have stared in awe for days, but all too soon, their guide led the party through the garden and beneath a great stone arch covered in ivy.

The inside of the Imperial palace was a lavish display of the Empire's finery. The entire building was constructed from shimmering white marble, the pillars intricately carved to look as though vines and ivy grew up them. Open arches allowed for the breeze from outside to freely freshen the air, and Joel could see full well why they would need the magic dome after all. The Imperial palace was not suited for cold weather.

All around them hung tapestries woven from fine silk and other glistening materials, each one depicting different legends and histories. One particularly fine curtain told the tale of the Empire fighting off the dragons which were rumored to have inhabited these lands centuries ago. The Imperial soldiers had been embroidered with brightly dyed thread while the dragons were gem encrusted. One such dragon had been speared, and tiny rubies spewed from its wound in place of blood.

They walked in near silence; the only sounds were their boots as they made their way through a grand hall. Servants stood out of the way, so still they could have been statues. Joel fought the urge to shudder. Despite the grandeur, he felt as though he were walking through a graveyard.

Ahead of them, Adrian waved one arm outward in a sweeping gesture, bringing them all to a halt. Joel didn't have to lean around his company to see the gilded door before them. As tall as a giant, it shone and sparkled as if it were a treasure on its own.

Joel couldn't guess how many gems covered the door in its intricate mosaic depiction of the Blessed Son of Light. The mighty deity wielded a great sword and shield and must have stood ten feet tall. Joel took in a breath and felt Hasain bump into his back. Joel turned to look at his cousin only to find him likewise transfixed by the door. It would have been lovely if not for the ruby blood "dripping" from the Son's sword.

Two hulking soldiers stood before the door, their eyes staring straight forward. It was almost as if they were in some sort of trance, but a moment later they stepped aside and the door drifted open as if by a breeze. Joel tentatively began to reach out with his magic, just to see if he could sense how the substantial door could open so easily. Before he could extend his awareness, however, NezReth's violet eyes were on him, clearly warning him to stop. The Blessed Mage didn't have to say a word. His fierce stare said everything. Joel hastily recalled his magic probe.

They were ushered into a grand courtroom. The white marble walls gave the impression of standing within a pearl, and the vines on these pillars were *very* real, another fantastical waste of magic. They bloomed with wild flowers unlike anything Joel had ever seen before, and their luxurious scent wafted over to him even from a distance. Adrian gave another simple wave of his arm, and both Koal and Cenric seemed to understand what he wanted. Their party came to a stop.

The sound of the door slamming shut behind them bounced off the high, vaulted ceilings. Joel winced. It was as though the deafening bang were sealing his doom, ensnaring the party of Ardenian men within the clutches of the Northern Empire. Perhaps they were destined to be trapped here—not that anything could be done about it now. *No turning back. I made the decision to come, and now I must see the mission through to whatever end fate has planned. I can't abandon Father. I have already abandoned Gib—* Hasain nudged his arm just then, disrupting Joel's unhinging thoughts. He sucked in a gasp of air and stood tall, forcing himself to stop trembling. *No weaknesses. I can't show weakness.*

Joel kept his face lowered, but he could feel all eyes in the room settle onto him and his comrades. Soft music had been playing a moment before, but he'd been unaware of it until it stopped. The eerie quiet was nearly enough to undo him.

The Archmage strolled to the front of the room, his golden robe sweeping across the bare marble floor behind him. Dozens of courtiers moved aside as he passed. In fact, within a few moments, enough people were standing between Joel and the front of the room that he couldn't see Adrian any longer. He could hear him, however.

Adrian's voice rose high and clear. "Your Grace, Supreme Ruler of all North and blessed disciple of the Son of Light, your guests from Arden have arrived."

Joel flinched. Was that how they were to refer to Emperor Lichas each time they spoke? He'd never be able to remember that. Would Koal? Joel cast a worried glance in his father's direction.

If Koal was intimidated, he was doing a damn good job of hiding it. The seneschal swept forward, red cape billowing regally, and the courtiers moved to let him through, giving Joel a view of the mighty throne at last.

Koal took to one knee. "Your Grace, Emperor Lichas Sarpedon, please accept Arden's humblest gratitude for being welcomed into your fine hall." He bowed his head, and the rest of their party followed suit, each going down onto one knee.

Joel held his breath as he dared to look at the Emperor from beneath heavy lashes. He'd heard many stories about the ruler of the North, a man who'd been sitting on the throne since the time when Joel's own father had been a child—so it came as quite a shock not to see a withered old man sitting before his gaze. Joel blinked in confusion.

The man who sat upon the throne was not old. Crystal blue eyes stared down the length of a prominent nose, and his strong, square jaw was set in a firm frown free of any age lines or wrinkles. A golden crown perched atop his head, and only the slightest amount of silver streaked his cropped blond curls. The man wore an embellished tunic with intricate gilded beadwork sewn into it, and the cape around his shoulders was designed to look like golden dragon scales.

This can't be Emperor Lichas, Joel thought even as he knelt before the man. *He was the ruler of the Empire when King Rishi was still a child. He should be close to eighty years old! He should be an old man! What is this?*

The Emperor's heavy gaze remained on them for an eternity before he finally gave a stiff nod. "Gratitude accepted. Arise and introduce your party to my court." Joel's head felt light as he stood.

"I am Seneschal Koal Adelwijn, Right Hand of King Rishi Radek. I have been sent on behalf of His Highness to make all decisions, henceforth, in regard to Arden." Koal stepped aside and motioned each of them through, one at a time.

Joel's mind wandered as his father's voice droned around him. He glanced from side to side, taking in the patrons and courtiers of the Emperor's court. Not a single smile was seen in the entire place.

His name was called, and he stepped forward. He wished he'd paid closer attention to how Cenric behaved when he'd taken his turn, but Joel's thoughts were proving to be most distracting. As soon as he was introduced, he went to stand beside his mentor.

"And this is Lord Hasain Radek, eldest son of the King and trainee of the High Council. He has accompanied us as a good faith showing from our King."

Hasain bowed, and Joel caught the sound of whispers among the gathered patrons. Hasain didn't say anything, but his red face spoke for him. He must have heard them, too.

With introductions over, the Emperor continued to stare at them for some time. His face was hard, unreadable, and his blue eyes flicked from

101

one member of their party to the next as if he were memorizing their faces. Perhaps he was. After another stifled bout of silence, he took a deep breath and turned a somber gaze onto Koal. "We are most seriously displeased to hear of the trouble your king has been having with his eastern and northern borders. It is our hope to offer enlightenment to our brethren in the south. Perhaps our counsel can prove beneficial."

Koal nodded. "Counsel is always welcomed, Your Grace. Arden would be most grateful."

"Very well then." Emperor Lichas motioned toward Adrian. "Have our guests shown to their quarters so they may change out of their wet clothes and prepare for the morning meal."

Adrian nodded. "Yes, Your Grace."

Joel's stomach was in knots as he bowed and backed away from the throne, and the look of contempt upon Emperor Lichas Sarpedon's ageless face only caused more icy unease to seep into Joel's veins.

CHAPTER SIX

Adrian led them through another set of winding corridors and open terraces. They took so many twists and turns that Joel's head was spinning by the time they arrived at the wing of the palace reserved for envoys and royal guests.

The Archmage stopped before a door covered with more intricate drawings carved into the wood. It seemed not even one door, wall, pillar, or ceiling within the palace was to be left standing bare.

Adrian turned to face the group. "Your quarters are beyond this door. You will find private bed chambers, a common room, and a shared privy. If you need anything, ring the bell and a servant will promptly assist you."

Koal gave a courteous bow. "Your hospitality is most generous."

Adrian's face remained frigid, and Joel was beginning to wonder if this man even knew *how* to smile. "A servant will be sent to fetch you as soon as the morning meal is ready, and I'll send word when the Emperor and his council are prepared to see you. In the meantime, please feel at ease to roam the halls at your leisure. The palace offers many amenities I believe will be to your liking." Adrian turned sharply on his heels and walked away before Koal could even open his mouth to reply.

As soon as they were alone, Cenric cleared his throat and smiled wryly. "Well, we're all still alive and fighting—can't ask for a better start to our mission than that." He motioned toward the door. "Shall we?"

Joel let out a sigh as he passed through the threshold. The corridor opened into a luxurious common room. Silk curtains rustled in the breeze, and the smell of fresh saffron hung in the air. One side of the room lay open to an outdoor terrace, and beyond that, Joel could see a sprawling private garden. As promised, their rucksacks and other belongings had been delivered and sat on a lounge in the middle of the space.

Koal cast a troubled look around the room. "NezReth—?"

"The suite is clear, Seneschal," the Blessed Mage replied swiftly. "We are alone."

Koal's shoulders relaxed, though his frown didn't completely fall away. "Can you make sure it stays that way, mage?"

NezReth titled his head downward, nodding once. "I will ward the quarters so no scrying magic can be used against us. However, we must use caution when speaking under scrutiny. Spies may be planted, even among the servants."

"That's right," Cenric added. "Better to trust no one. Assume any words we say in public will be reported back to the Emperor."

Koal crossed his arms over his chest. His blue eyes moved among the three youngest members of the party, and Joel couldn't help but shrink away from his father's withering glare. "You heard Cenric and NezReth. The three of you, keep your mouths shut about Arden. Leave discussions of our country's welfare to *me*. Is that understood?"

Liro rolled his eyes. "You needn't scold me as though I'm one of the *children*, Father."

Hasain swung his head around, leveling Liro with a glare. "And what qualities and experience do you possess that set you so far apart from Joel and me? If we're to be labeled children, then certainly you should be, too."

Joel cringed as his brother opened his mouth to no doubt spit acid at Hasain, but Koal stepped in to snuff out Liro's fiery words before they had a chance to manifest. "Enough. Both of you, shut up! I didn't bring you along so I could suffer listening to your attempts to best one another with snide remarks and childish insults. You don't have to like each other, but you do need to be civil. We have enough working against us as it is without worrying about fighting amongst ourselves."

Liro locked his jaw and stormed over to the lounge, fishing through the pile of rucksacks until he found his bag. Hasain glared at the back of Liro's head but smartly kept his own mouth shut.

"Everyone get their belongings and claim a bed," Koal commanded. His brow remained furrowed, even after Hasain and Liro had gone their separate ways, leading Joel to believe something deeper and darker was on his father's mind.

"Da?" he began to ask, but Koal waved him away.

"Go find a room and get settled in, Joel. Cenric, NezReth—a word with you both, please?"

Joel blinked. *He sees me as nothing but a burden. I'll always be a child in his eyes.* Hanging his head, he went to the lounge and scooped up his pack. Slinging it over one shoulder, he turned and entered the corridor Hasain and Liro had just taken. *I suppose I should check in on them to ensure no blood has been spilt between here and the sleeping quarters.*

Koal's voice flitted down the corridor, and Joel slowed his pace. He knew he shouldn't be eavesdropping, but the gravity of the words caught his attention and held him spellbound. "I'll tell you what concerns me already. Emperor Lichas—he's been reigning since I was a boy! I may not be a scholar, but I'm no fool! His youth can't be natural."

Cenric snorted. "Agreed. I actually *met* Sarpedon thirty years ago and he looks *exactly the same* as he did then. He hasn't aged a day. Can anyone explain this?"

"NezReth?" Koal demanded.

Terrible silence marred the suite until NezReth replied in a quiet, hesitant voice. "Magic is capable of such strange and, often times, perverse things, but I am afraid I have no answers to give you—only unverified speculations. I will need to delve further into this matter."

"In the meantime, we all must stay alert. Something about this situation feels very wrong," Koal whispered.

Cenric issued a lengthy sigh. "I don't like it. I don't like any of it."

"Like it or not, we're here. It's too soon to go running with our tails tucked. The least we can do is meet with the Emperor and listen to his proposal—and plan accordingly from there."

Joel forced his legs to move. If they hadn't invited him into the conversation then he shouldn't be listening. A chill crept up his spine as he slid into one of the empty bedchambers. What kind of power did the Northern Empire possess if they were not only able to control the weather, but also prolong the life of their ruler? He'd never heard of such magery. *And if NezReth isn't sure either, this must be some rare or forbidden magic indeed. Has the Emperor somehow managed to defy time? Is that why he isn't aging?*

Shaking his head, Joel turned to examine the room. Silken curtains rustled in the breeze coming through a single, oval-shaped window. Fresh morning light poured into the chamber, illuminating the white marble walls and colorful motifs on the bedspread. He could see the garden outside, and the smell of spiced food and flowers hung on the air. It was a shame he couldn't bring himself to enjoy any of the beauty the palace offered.

Joel flopped down onto the bed and stared at the decorative stucco ceiling. He exhaled slowly, feeling as though it was the first real breath he'd gotten since arriving in Teivel. *Chhaya's bane. What did I get myself into? I'm not cut out for this.* He closed his eyes, and all he could see was Gib's face. A deep, wrenching ache gripped his heart. *I'm so sorry, Gib. I shouldn't have left the way I did.*

"Joel?" Cenric called tentatively from the door.

Joel hurried to sit up, wiping his damp cheeks with a sleeve. "S–sorry. I was just resting for a moment."

"It's all right." Cenric's smile was genuine as always, which reminded Joel why he respected the ambassador so much. Cenric motioned toward the bed. "May I talk to you about something before we're called for mealtime?"

Joel scooted over to make room, doing his best to push thoughts of Gib aside. "Yes, of course." *This isn't about the Emperor, is it? Did they catch me listening to their conversation?*

Cenric sat on the edge of the bed and turned to face Joel. "I'm sure you've done your own research about the Northern Empire, but I felt it wise to warn you about something, in case it was overlooked during your own studies." His smile fell away. "Things are different here. Laws are—

more strict, and the penalties for disobedience much harsher. I'm not sure whether you're aware or not, but romanticizing with someone of the same gender—" Cenric's cheeks were turning a noticeable shade of red as he stumbled over his words. "—is forbidden in the Northern Empire."

Joel let out a horrified gasp. What, exactly, was Cenric implying? All the emotion he'd kept bottled inside manifested as bitter anger and poured out. "I'm well aware of the law— do you really think so little of me? Are you worried I might seduce some poor Imperial courtier and ruin Arden's chance at peaceful negotiation? I can't believe you would even suggest such a thing!"

Shock crossed Cenric's face, and Joel knew he'd overstepped his boundaries. He glared at his hands, which sat in his lap and trembled as he tried to contain the despair billowing inside his heart. *I should have stayed with Gib. Now I have nothing. I ripped his heart out and then didn't even tell him how sorry I was. I don't deserve to survive this mission, and I don't deserve Gib.*

"I apologize," Joel whispered. "I didn't mean to raise my voice at you. I just—I said goodbye to Gib—possibly forever—and I'm really, *really* not interested in pursuing anyone here, so you and the others needn't worry." A rebellious tear slid down one cheek.

"I wasn't suggesting you would, I swear to you." Cenric leaned in, placing a hand on Joel's shoulder. "I know you wouldn't ever compromise the mission, and I know your heart lies with Gib. I only wanted to remind you not to speak openly about your personal life. We'll find no friends here, and *any* one of us could mistakenly say something that could be used against us." Squeezing Joel's shoulder, Cenric lowered his voice even further. "I'm sorry. You shouldn't have to hide who you are from anyone. But while we're here—"

"I understand. It has to be this way."

Cenric sighed, hazel eyes sorrowful. "It's not fair. This is why I had reservations about coming to Teivel. Arden is not without her faults, but we've made remarkable progress breaking away from the influence of the Northern Empire. I just—see no good to come from this meeting between the two nations. The last time Sarpedon offered an alliance, his goal was to extend the Empire's law to encompass all of Arden beneath it. He wanted to take over the country. I can only pray that isn't the case now." Cenric's voice trailed off in an eerie wisp as he stared aimlessly across the room.

"You've been an ambassador of Arden for over half your life. Father has been seneschal for nearly as long. Between the two of you, I know the country will never be led astray or taken advantage of."

Cenric met Joel's gaze, and for the first time since their conversation had begun, the envoy's frown dissipated, replaced by a weak smile. "Share some of your confidence with this old fool, will you?" He patted Joel on the shoulder one last time before taking to his feet. "I should put on presentable clothing. I'm sure we'll be called for morning meal any time now." Cenric paused beneath the door frame. "And try not to worry about what's going on back home. From what you've told me of Gib, he seems to be a good fellow. I'm sure he understands why you chose to come. Likewise, I'm sure he'll be happy to see you upon your return."

Joel sucked in a sharp breath. "Yes. I'm sure you're right." *No. You don't know. No one knows. I ruined everything, and I have only myself to blame for it.*

Cenric departed, leaving Joel alone to wallow in his emotions for some time. Finally, he wiped his eyes dry and took a deep breath. *Pull yourself together. You're here now. There's nothing that can be done about Gib while you're in the Empire, and feeling sorry for yourself isn't going to help the mission. You came to assist Cenric and protect Father. Now how about you actually do something useful!*

He changed out of his damp clothing and into a clean robe, hoping a fresh set of clothes would help renew his spirit. By the time he meandered back into the common room, his stomach was growling as ferociously as a wild animal. *I certainly hope mealtime is sooner than later.*

Cenric smiled as Joel sat down beside him on the lounge. "Feel better?"

Joel's cheeks flushed as the other envoys turned to look at him. Unable to maintain eye contact with any of them, he opted to stare at the intricate threadwork on the lounge. "Much better now that I'm out of those wet clothes." He bit his tongue and hoped no one would notice his discomfort. *I don't need Father worrying about me—or to give Liro any excuses to remind me what a disappointment I am.*

Koal unraveled a blank sheet of parchment and waved it at Hasain. "Fetch me an inkwell and quill. I need to start my report for the King."

Hasain locked his jaw but did as he was told. Liro stood against one of the pillars toward the back of the room and smirked openly at the young lord's misfortune.

Cenric cocked his head to the side. "Already? We've barely unpacked."

Sighing, Koal sat behind the only table the suite had to offer. "I promised him weekly updates." Hasain came back a moment later, handing Koal the quill and setting the inkwell onto the table. Koal thanked him with a silent nod.

"Have you given any thought to your messages being intercepted?" Cenric asked, his brows furrowing with concern. "What then?"

Koal dipped the very tip of the feathered quill into the inkwell. "NezReth has assured me they won't be."

"They will not be," NezReth reiterated. He stood in a shadowy enclave on the far side of the suite, violet eyes ever vigilant as they scanned the garden outside.

The ambassador nodded his head, offering no further debate. "I trust your judgment, mage."

Magic, Joel concluded. *He'll ward the message with protective magic before Father sends it to King Rishi.* He'd heard of such a thing before. Mages would often enchant a message containing particularly important news so if anyone false attempted to open it, the parchment would burst into flames or the ink would bleed so the words were illegible.

A light tapping sound came from the door just then, and the conversation ground to a halt. Koal looked up from the parchment paper. "I imagine that's our call for breakfast."

When no one else made a move to answer the door, Joel sighed and slipped out of his seat. *I might as well make myself useful for something.* He trotted across the room and grasped the brass door handle, wishing he knew how to command the door to swing open with a flick of his wrist, as Adrian Titus had demonstrated was possible. He pulled the door open.

A young man stood in the hallway and jumped to attention as the door hinges squealed. He wore a plain white tunic much like any of the other servants Joel had seen, though the embroidered gold thread on his sleeves and silken belt around his waist seemed out of place for such a lowly rank. Although the color of his hair was darker than most in this land, his complexion was as fair as any of them, and a pair of inquisitive green eyes measured Joel in a not unfriendly way.

"Greetings," said the newcomer, his voice a soft tenor. He bent forward in a cordial bow. "I am Kirk Bhadrayu, mage trainee and apprentice of Archmage Adrian Titus."

Politely, Joel tipped his own head forward. "My name is Joel Adelwijn, understudy ambassador and mage of Silver City."

The young man smiled—a genuine smile, the first Joel had witnessed since arriving in Teivel. Such a show of emotion surprised him after all the scowls he'd received in the throne room.

"Well met, Joel Adelwijn," Kirk replied. "My master has sent me to see to it your party is comfortable."

His smile was infectious, and Joel found himself smiling back, despite his somber mood.

"Thank you. We are." Joel moved aside and motioned for the other man to enter the suite. "Please, come inside, if you'd like."

"O–oh, no, that's all right." Kirk looked at the floor, a faint blush coming to his cheeks, and Joel had to wonder if he'd mistakenly said something offensive.

Trying to salvage the situation, Joel cleared his throat and asked, "Might you know when breakfast will be served?"

Kirk's eyes lit up. "Your meal is awaiting you. That's actually the main reason I came to introduce myself. If you're ready, I can take your party there right now."

When Joel turned to ask the other envoys, not one of them objected.

The mage trainee, Kirk, led them to a beautiful courtyard, shaded by a canopy billowing in the light breeze. Beneath it was the most exquisite table Joel had ever seen. Carved from smooth alabaster, it was at least twenty hands in length and sparkled brighter than sunlight reflecting off a winter landscape. Even the table legs were luxurious—each carved in the shape of a dragon and made to look as though they were holding the weight of the tabletop with their talons.

Joel's stomach gurgled at the sight of all the bountiful food waiting for them. Bread so fresh it was still steaming tumbled out of wicker baskets, and platters of colorful fruit and roasted meats made his mouth water. As they took their seats around the table, a pair of servants filled their goblets with wine.

Kirk, who had been standing to the side of the table, cleared his throat as the envoys began to serve themselves. "Once you've eaten your fill, His Grace, Emperor Sarpedon, has requested your presence in the council chamber. You can ask any of the servants to lead you there. I will take my leave now, but my master has charged me with your well-being for the duration of your visit, so if you need anything, request a servant to find me immediately."

"Of course," replied Koal. "I speak for all of us when I say we are most grateful for our host's hospitality."

Kirk bowed and departed without another word.

Joel took his time filling his plate. Such a wide variety of foods were offered that he had a hard time choosing what to sample first. Passing on the roasted quail, he opted to try melon and the small, sticky purple fruits Cenric called figs. The party ate in silence for some time, and despite his growling stomach, Joel found himself pushing his food around rather than eating it.

His mind kept dwelling on the conversation he'd overheard between his father and NezReth—and it worried him deeply. Like so much else about this city, the Emperor's youth was a conundrum. Had Emperor Sarpedon somehow learned to stop the natural progression of aging and, if so, by what means? *Something is very wrong about all of this. The magically controlled weather, Sarpedon's agelessness, the complete waste of magical resources everywhere I look—where is the Northern Empire getting all the energy to maintain this way of life?*

Birds twittered above the canopy, interrupting his dark musings, and Joel raised his face to watch them. His eyes widened at what he saw. *Not birds. What in the two worlds?*

Strange little winged creatures perched along the tops of the pillars, chirping like songbirds. Indeed, their feathered wings and beaks were reminiscent of a falcon, yet the lower halves of their bodies were covered in hardened scales, and long, reptilian tails sprouted from their hindquarters. Joel had never seen such an oddity before.

He looked across the table at Cenric. "What are those things?"

"Cockatrices," the ambassador replied, turning to watch the strange creatures as they fluttered and squeaked.

Joel shook his head. "What?"

"It is rumored," NezReth explained in a quiet voice, "that the cockatrices are descendants of true dragons. Many centuries ago, before the dragons were driven to extinction, Imperial mages used magic to fuse young dragonlings with various animals. Through trial and error, they essentially created three new species—the basilisk, manticore, and of course, the cockatrice. Of the three, the cockatrice thrived."

Cenric chuckled. "Yes. The Empire did a fantastic job creating a new pest to infest the city. Though, I'll admit, they're more aesthetically pleasing than rats."

Joel scrutinized the tiny, chattering reptiles, finding it difficult to believe they were descendants of the majestic, fire-breathing dragons he'd read about in the *Tales of Fae*. Somehow they seemed but a cruel parody of their beautiful ancestors. Joel frowned. The idea of warping magic in such a way didn't sit well in his stomach. Were the Imperial mages so arrogant they believed they had the right to experiment on living creatures?

"Of course, the cockatrices' super speed makes them quite useful to the Empire," Cenric continued. "I'm sure they would have been eliminated completely if they didn't make such fine messengers."

"Super speed?" Hasain asked as he filled his plate with fresh fruit and bread.

"Yes. They can travel astonishingly fast over long distances."

A smug smile crossed Hasain's lips. "Arden's messenger pigeons can do the same."

"Ah, but the cockatrice is capable of flying so fast their form cannot be seen by the naked eye," Cenric replied, giving Hasain a wry smile of his own. "In one day, they can cover the distance a pigeon would take weeks to traverse. How else do you think we were able to get a response back to the Northern Empire so fast when they requested we come to Teivel?"

Hasain refocused his attention onto his plate. He shrugged, and Joel could tell by the faint shade of pink on Hasain's cheeks he knew he'd been bested and was having trouble admitting it to himself.

The party ate in silence after that, though the cockatrices continued to chirp above, almost as if they were serenading the envoys. A gentle breeze blew through the terrace, rustling Joel's raven hair and cooling the humid air just enough to be comfortable. Joel wondered in passing how the people outside the inner city were faring. How cold was it beyond the borders of this magical paradise? He frowned, wondering if Emperor

Sarpedon and his wealthy patricians ever thought of the unfortunate people beyond the dome. Did they even care?

All at once, the silence came crashing down as a small army of servants and courtiers made their way into the courtyard. Girls with pearls around their necks and draped in fine silk gowns giggled and chatted while servants scampered at their heels with extravagant parasols held high to keep the sun from reaching the ladies' eyes. No one in the procession paid the dining envoys any heed. Indeed, all their attention seemed to be centered on one person within the group. The courtier ladies were all but hanging from the arm of a young man.

He couldn't have been any older than Liro or Hasain, and he carried himself with the overzealous confidence of a person born into nobility. He swept onto the terrace with his entourage trailing behind his long cape. Wispy curls crowned the youth's head, and the sea silk tunic wrapped around his lean body matched his golden hair as though it had been planned that way. Two blue eyes fell upon the envoys, and Joel could detect a trace of condescension behind the boy's reserved stare.

"Ah," he called out in a crisp baritone voice. "These must be our visitors from Arden."

Joel cast a glance at Cenric, as though the mentor could silently answer all his questions. *Who is this? Should we bow to him?*

"Greetings," the man continued. "I am Prince Alerio Sarpedon, first of my name and son of His Grace, Emperor Lichas Sarpedon. It gives me great pleasure to meet you, envoys. I'll be dining with you this fine morning."

Joel blinked in shock and could see that even Cenric appeared to be surprised. *This is the prince? Why is he here? And why weren't we informed we would be dining with him?*

Koal began to rise from his cushioned seat, but the prince motioned for him to stay where he was. "Please, stay seated. No doubt you have all endured a long journey and are famished. Sit and enjoy the bounty of the Empire." With the flick of a wrist, he turned and dismissed his gaggle of courtiers. The ladies played the game flawlessly, batting flirtatious eyelashes and uttering coy words of longing as they wished their prince farewell.

Prince Alerio sat down at the head of the table, and the servants who had followed him onto the terrace rushed to make him comfortable and fill his goblet with wine. One servant even held a parasol above the prince's head to keep the sun from his eyes.

Joel watched, dumbfounded. He'd never seen anything like this before. Not one of his royal cousins back home would have sat back and allowed their servants to do so much. *But then again, King Rishi and Aunt Dahlia always encouraged them to be independent. Just because they were born into privilege didn't mean they couldn't do things for themselves.* Obviously things were different here in the Northern Empire.

Koal bowed his head instead and proceeded to introduce the Ardenian envoys. Prince Alerio nodded amiably as each member of the party was announced, although the way his eyes tended to wander around the table suggested he was already bored. As Joel sampled the delicious melon on his plate, he watched the prince out of the corner of his eye. While not as calculating as the Emperor himself, something about Prince Alerio's demeanor didn't quite sit well with Joel. *He's more than just a pampered royal. He's dangerous. I can feel it.*

"Tell me, envoys," Prince Alerio said as he popped a grape into his mouth. "What is your impression of the Imperial palace thus far?"

Cenric spoke first, giving Koal a much needed reprieve. "The palace is magnificent, Your Highness. Truly a masterpiece of art and craftsmanship. To be guests within these splendid walls is a great honor."

Alerio puffed up like a strutting peacock, and Joel had to wonder if the prince had asked the question simply to have his ego stroked. *Though judging by his entourage of courtiers, he's quite at home with both attention and flattery and needs no more of either.*

"Yes," the prince replied in a pleased voice. "My ancestors who constructed this fortress certainly had extravagant tastes. Though, of course, I'm sure the royal palace in Silver City is likewise statuesque. Arden *is*, after all, a child of our great Empire."

"A child with a voice and mind of her own," Hasain reminded him, voice as brittle as glass.

Alerio fixed his eyes onto Hasain. "I'm sure the son of a king would know all about the need to have his own voice and mind. It must be incredibly hard for you to walk in the shadow of your sire knowing you shall never overtake him. Tell me, Lord Hasain, since you aren't eligible for the throne, what plans have you made for yourself?"

Joel could see Hasain struggling to stay collected and, for a moment, feared the young Radek lord might say something uncouth and put their mission in jeopardy.

Hasain clenched his jaw tightly. "I choose to walk in my father's shadow so I may learn from his wisdom, and one day, when my brother is King of Arden, I shall be his right hand and most trusted advisor."

"A noble goal indeed." Alerio raised his goblet and took a long drink. "So, there are two princes of Arden?"

"That's right. My brothers, Crowned Prince Deegan and Prince Didier."

"And do you have sisters, Lord Hasain? Are there any princesses of Arden?"

"One. Princess Gudrin."

Alerio leaned forward in his seat. He rested his elbows on the table and clasped his hands together. "I see. Does Arden have any arrangements for her to marry?"

Joel's heartbeat quickened in his chest. *He's not suggesting what I think he is, right? He can't be serious!*

Hasain narrowed his eyes at the foreign prince. "No. Princess Gudrin is only nine years old."

Alerio met Hasain's stare abrasively, and Joel tensed his shoulders, wishing he could somehow disappear. *Please Hasain, not here. We're not in Arden. Please remember that.*

The silence stretched on as the two men stared across the table at one another, sizing each other up. It seemed neither would be the first to relent, but finally, Prince Alerio broke eye contact.

He shrugged his shoulders and went on speaking as though the tense moment had never occurred. "I have a sister, too. Claudia is twelve— plenty old enough for the Empire to begin to seek out a marital alliance on her behalf. Perhaps it's even possible this meeting between nations will conclude with the ringing of wedding bells."

Joel winced even as he watched Koal sit straighter in his seat. The seneschal cleared his throat and flashed a warning glance at Hasain, who was so red-faced he looked as though he might burst.

"With all due respect, Your Highness," Koal replied gingerly. "I don't believe we came here with the intention of discussing marriage proposals. That decision rests in the hands of the King of Arden."

Alerio's left eyebrow ticked. "Correct me if I'm mistaken, Seneschal Koal, but did you not say yourself that while you're here, your king has appointed you to make *all* decisions on his behalf?"

"The marriage of his children is something I *will not* interfere with. King Rishi would want a say in the matter."

The Imperial prince shrugged again and motioned for a servant to refill his goblet. "I suppose it matters not. There will be additional options to explore when the envoys from Nales and Shiraz arrive. Perhaps they will be more open to such discussions."

Joel reeled, nearly choking on his drink. *Envoys from Nales and Shiraz? What?*

Time seemed to stand still as everyone at the table froze. Koal and Cenric exchanged worried glances, Hasain paled, and NezReth's chest heaved as he let out a sharp breath of air. Even Liro's typical expression of indifference had been replaced by wide-eyed surprise.

None of this went unnoticed by Prince Alerio. A smirk pulled at his mouth as calculating eyes flitted around the table, passing over each of the envoys. "Oh. You didn't know? I thought His Grace would have mentioned the fact to you earlier." Joel could detect smug satisfaction in Alerio's voice and was certain it hadn't gone unnoticed by the others either.

Cenric was the first to recover from the shocking words. "Ambassadors from Shiraz and Nales are coming here, to Teivel?"

Alerio took time to chew the mouthful of roasted quail meat he'd just bitten into before replying. "Yes. They should be arriving any time now."

Joel's stomach twisted into tight knots, and his meal threatened to make a reappearance. *What does this mean? Will we have to see them? Will we have to talk to them? Shiraz has sworn Arden an enemy, and relations with Nales have been going sour for years. What will happen if we have to be in the same room as them?*

"Why weren't we informed about this sooner?" Koal demanded, sharp voice cutting through the silence like a sword.

Wisps of Alerio's curly blond hair sparkled in the sunlight as he shrugged. "That, I cannot answer for you. You shall have to ask the Emperor when you see him. Save your questions for His Grace."

Koal folded his arms across his broad chest. "That I will."

After mid-day meal, Gib was summoned to Marc's office. The bleak day had since cleared up, but Gib's mood was hardly light. Despite the meal being as fine as any Academy had to offer, he couldn't bring himself to eat.

Marc stood outside his office door, lacing up one boot. When he heard Gib approach, the dean offered a wide smile. Gib wished he could return it, but no part of him felt like smiling. As if Marc understood, he stood to his full height and put a firm hand on his underling's shoulder. "It'll get easier. I used to hate watching Koal ride off to danger and war when we were younger, but I grew to trust him over the years. I know you and Joel—" He faltered, looking for the right words. "Your relationship with him is different than mine and Koal's, but know you're not alone. Many of us are worried for them."

Gib looked up, his mouth moving but no sound coming out. His instinct was to explain that he and Joel were no longer companions, that Joel had ended it, but he couldn't bring himself to say it. Marc didn't need to know. What could the knowledge possibly do other than cause awkward apologies? Gib nodded. "I know. Joel is inexperienced, though, and Koal isn't a young man anymore."

Marc thumped Gib's shoulder and laughed. "That he's not. None of us are these days, but you must believe me, Gib. Koal is a warrior." Marc withdrew his hand and cocked his head to one side. "Have you ever heard the tales of his younger years? Did he tell you any of the stories of him, King Rishi, and Queen Jorja striking out to the different corners of Arden to strengthen the country?"

"No." Gib shook his head. He couldn't recall Koal sharing anything like that.

Marc began walking, gesturing for Gib to follow. "I'll have to think of some of my favorites. Of course, those tend to be the ones where I was there, too. But maybe we can catch King Rishi or Aodan in the right mood sometime and they'll tell other stories."

Gib tried to process this new information. It sounded plausible that the King and Koal had been formidable in the past. Hell, they were intimidating now. He imagined the both of them being terrors when they'd still had youth on their side.

He followed Marc out of the academy doors, but it wasn't until after the guard had allowed them across the bridge leading to the palace that Gib even thought to question their destination. "Is there a council meeting today?"

Marc shook his head. "No. That'll resume tomorrow. Rishi, err—the King has declared he won't be taking counsel today. Today we form our strategy."

Gib raised an eyebrow as they entered the palace. "Strategy?"

"For how we're going to keep the country afloat without our seneschal."

They promptly passed the corridors he was familiar with and went into a different wing of the palace. More soldiers were here, all of them royal palace guards with their intimidating armor and scrutinizing glares. Gib swallowed and kept close to his mentor.

"What do you mean? Can't the country run without a seneschal for a while?"

Gib looked at the walls as they passed, taking in life-sized portraits of the royal family and monarchs from the past. Several portraits depicted King Rishi—a couple even had Queen Dahlia and their children present. As they progressed, the portraits seemed to go back in time. The royal children grew younger and younger until they were gone. King Rishi stood alone in one picture, much younger and looking so similar to Hasain it was surreal. Beside it hung a full length picture of a different woman wearing the Queen's crown. She held the hand of a young girl and had one hand placed on her pregnant stomach. "Who—?"

Marc stopped, and Gib nearly bumped into him. The dean chuckled and looked at the portrait with Gib. "Queen Jorja, the King's first wife, and their daughter, Princess Nikki."

Gib stared into the fierce green gaze of Queen Jorja. Her light brown hair was pulled back into a high bun inside her crown, and she didn't wear a dress like Queen Dahlia did. The previous queen's outfit looked more apt for riding than dancing. Gib looked at the young girl, and a knot formed in his gut. He'd never heard of Princess Nikki before.

"She died before she reached your age." Marc's smile was sad, memory heavy. "The Princess barely outlived her mother."

Gib felt a heavy weight in his heart. "I didn't even know of her."

Marc shook his head. "Rishi doesn't speak about her much. Losing his wife was hard, but to then lose their daughter so quickly—" He took a breath. "It was a dark time."

He didn't want to ask, but the question burned at the back of his mind. "And the baby not yet born in the portrait?"

"Stillborn. She'd had trouble since conception, and everyone knew the baby might not make it. She demanded the portrait be made while the child still lived and no one had the heart to stop her."

"Why isn't the King in this portrait?" Once Gib said the words, he thought maybe he'd been too forward, but Marc didn't reprimand him.

"Times were different then. The King was only painted with male heirs, and the Queen with her daughters. There was less focus on royals being a family and more on the production of future kings." Marc reached out and touched the very bottom of the canvas as if he could reach back through time. His smile wasn't sad so much anymore, but sharp. "Rishi did away with that tradition when he took his new wife."

Gib nodded, looking around at the other portraits. It was true. Kings of old were depicted with sons, not daughters, and Queens stood with their girl children or alone. "It's almost sad to see."

Marc's hand was on Gib's shoulder again, steering him away. "We go to plan now, lest all of King Rishi and Koal's hard work go in vain. There are those who would still prefer the old ways."

"Will you have to help the King keep Arden from slipping backwards?"

"Someone will. Koal's boots are big. I don't know if I could fill them—but Rishi cannot be forced to carry the full weight of the country on his own. No one person should ever be left with such a task."

Gib's head was full, but he thought he understood. The immensity of what was expected of mere men was daunting to him. He'd had his work cut out for him when he had to keep a farm and two children. How could one man be expected to run an entire country? Even with the council to help, it seemed impossible. *And the council doesn't work smoothly. They bicker and halt progress for the sake of proving petty points. How is any king or queen supposed to rise above that?*

They reached a corridor where they had to stop and declare themselves to the guards. Even from the entrance of the hall, Gib could see more sentinels standing watch at the other end. Marc didn't joke with these men. He stated his full title and gestured for Gib to do the same before informing the soldiers of his purpose there. They let him pass, but the silence around them made Gib feel ill at ease.

They reached one of the only doors on the wing, and Marc knelt to take off his boots. "We carry them in with us," he told Gib. "In Beihai, people don't wear their shoes inside a home."

"Home?" Gib's stomach knotted. "Whose home is this?" He was

sure he knew but couldn't bring himself to believe it.

Marc flashed him a wicked smile. "The King has adopted many Ardenian customs, but he held onto this one from his native country."

Gib's head felt light as he bent to undress his own feet. This was the King's personal quarters? In all the time he'd shadowed Koal, he'd never been brought here. He began to tell Marc this but realized the dean wouldn't have explained about their shoes if he'd thought Gib had been here before. Head still swimming, he could barely get his mouth to work. "We just carry our boots around with us?"

"Yep. The King expects you to hold onto them the entire time." Marc snickered but grudgingly gave up the ruse at Gib's scowl. "All right. No. There's a mat to set them on inside. And slippers lined along the wall for guests to use."

"Slippers? Why take our boots off if we're just going to put on slippers?"

"In Beihai, tables have short legs and people sit on cushions on the floor. Shoes that have been worn outside are seen as dirty and are left on the front steps. The King obviously doesn't have front steps so he allows us to put them on a mat inside."

"People in Beihai sit on the floor? Even nobles?"

"Yep. He was even more afraid of chairs upon his arrival to Arden than you."

"Hey!" Gib gave the dean a narrow look, recalling his first day in Silver and being afraid to dirty the fine chair offered to him in the office.

Marc wagged his brows, and Gib lost what control he had.

They were sharing a good laugh and standing with their boots in hand when the King's door flew open. King Rishi stood there, giving them a cool look. "Are you mocking me out here? If so, at least do it where I can't hear you—like over in Shantar or down in Gyptia."

Marc grinned widely. "Not sure that's far enough. My voice carries pretty well."

King Rishi stepped aside and motioned for them to enter. "I'm aware."

Marc gave a mocking bow as he crossed the threshold, and the King groaned. Gib hesitated, looking down at his bare feet. What if they were dirty? Or smelled? Would he be reprimanded? Laughed at? It wasn't like he'd known he was going to be coming to the King's personal quarters.

King Rishi's dark eyes glimmered with what looked like laughter as he studied Gib. "Are you going to stay in the hallway, Gibben Nemesio?"

Gib blanched. "I, uh—sorry." He jumped across the threshold and was sure he heard the King's faint chuckle. *Fantastic. I'm barely in the door and already looking a fool.* "Where should I—" Flustered, he let his question die off when he noted the rug where footwear was aligned in two neat rows.

Everything from elegant court shoes to warrior boots sat together in order from large to small, adult to child. Gib smiled at the thought of the youngest prince and princess placing their shoes alongside those of their parents.

The slippers were on the opposite wall, lined just as neatly. He picked a pair he thought would fit and fumbled to put them on. They were delicate compared to anything he was used to, and he didn't want to risk ripping the fine material. Somewhere beyond him, he was vaguely aware of Marc and the King talking. He snapped to full attention at the mention of his name.

"Isn't that right, Gib?" Marc's voice was cheerful and his smile troublesome. He glanced at the King. "It's like the first time I met him. He was afraid to sit in the chair."

"Oh, so the slippers scare him? I see. By the time he gets them on, you'll have to leave for supper."

Gib gasped, mouth agape. He didn't even know what to say to that. Marc and the King both burst into laughter upon examining Gib's face. The words fell from Gib's mouth before he could think to censor them. "I see what Seneschal Koal meant about always being surrounded by children."

The King gestured for them to follow farther into his private quarters. "You'll learn all too soon, Gibben Nemesio, that youth is fleeting. Immaturity, however, can be nurtured for a lifetime." He was still laughing as he swept over to a chair by his balcony and perched as lightly as a feather upon it. Marc wasted no time in taking the seat opposite and making quick work of the pedestal between them. Gib ventured a step closer to get a better look.

It was a game of some sort, he'd wager, with a slew of small pieces for either player. Marc sorted the colors—pearl for himself and jade for King Rishi. The King, for his part, barely took notice as he was looking out the window. Gib trained his gaze in the same direction and realized King Rishi was staring down at the courtyard. Only marks before, Gib had stood out there beside Joel for what may have been the last time.

Grief wrung his heart and he looked away, still unwilling to dwell on the treacherous emotions seeking to undo him. He'd promised himself he'd find either Tarquin or Kezra later and speak to them about what he was going through, but he hadn't yet found the time. For now, he placated himself with the lovely surroundings in the royal suite.

The architecture was much the same here as it was in the other parts of the palace Gib was familiar with, only this room seemed more akin to a home, with all of the shoes, several small toys on one shelf, and what looked like a child's school things on another. The bookshelves themselves were of a more modest size and cluttered with too many books, nothing at all like the grand library near the council chamber or the one inside

Academy.

Lush, crimson curtains framed each grand window but were pulled back to allow in what sunlight the day had to offer. The furniture was primarily made of dark wood and detailed with hand paintings telling stories of legends Gib could not place. One reoccurring figure was that of a twisting crimson serpent.

"The dragon of Beihai."

Gib jumped. "What?"

King Rishi was watching from across the room. He gestured toward the serpent. "The red dragon of Beihai is the creature you keep looking at. There was a time when it was not a mere shadow of the Empire's golden dragon. In its prime, it represented peace and prosperity. Now all dragons from the north are seen as conquerors."

"I've never seen such a dragon," Gib admitted. "It almost looks like a viper to my eyes."

The King smiled, but it was a sad, tired mockery of what it should have been. "Yes. The Empire's dragon casts a long shadow. Like the country it hails from, the golden dragon blots out all others who would stand with or beside it. It does not share its glory, only absorbs those smaller than itself in its undying quest to conquer all."

Marc made the first move on the game board. His light mood from earlier seemed to have vanished. "Who are we waiting for?"

"Roland." The King's words were clipped as he made a counter move. "Aodan went for him."

Gib watched as they continued their game despite neither of them taking any pleasure from it. As their pieces moved and were lost to one another, Gib gathered it was a strategy exercise but didn't grasp what constituted a proper move and what did not. As their play wore on, he also deduced that either Marc wasn't good at strategy or the King was exceptional.

Time passed, and the only sound was the clicking of the game pieces. King Rishi told Gib he could sit in one of the window sills if he wished, so he did, just to feel less in the way. Marc and the King were nearly done with their game when a knock on the door interrupted their play. King Rishi was on his feet in an instant, and Marc breathed a sigh of relief, looking to Gib. "Just in time. He'd nearly licked me—"

"Don't lick Marc. He prob'ly tastes as bad as he smells," Aodan Galloway called from the doorway.

Marc laughed. "I'd tell you where you could lick me, Derr, but I'll keep polite in front of Gib."

The bodyguard's red hair fell in his face as he knelt to put on his slippers. Blowing a stray strand from his eye, Aodan offered only the barest of smiles—a somewhat frightening look. "Koal's underling? He's heard worse in 'is time. Council meetings an' all."

Marc shrugged but didn't get to respond before a different voice grumbled from the hallway, "Move your arse, Galloway! I'm standing out here, shoeless, like some beggar."

Gib smiled. It wasn't often he got to see Weapons Master Roland Korbin anymore. After training under him the first two years at Academy, Gib had moved on to become Koal's understudy. It was good to see his old weapons trainer again.

Roland's dark hair and sun-worn skin didn't look any worse for wear when he crossed the threshold, and Gib had to wonder if training new recruits helped keep the master young. Their eyes met briefly, and it was hard to tell what he was thinking behind his shrewd, hazel eyes.

The King didn't offer to greet his new guests, and no one bothered to pretend their visit was for pleasure. As soon as the door was closed, Roland crossed his arms over his broad chest and went for the point. "So Marc's here as well. I s'pose this isn't lucky chance."

King Rishi began pacing. Not an encouraging sign. "We need to be prepared to head Neetra off tomorrow. He's going to push me even harder now that Koal is absent."

"He's bent on going to war with Shiraz." Marc's voice was cold, uncharacteristic for his typical good nature.

Roland groaned. "Neetra's mad. He'd have us discharge our women soldiers before we even began to march. I don't know how he thinks the army can handle war and troop thinning at the same time."

King Rishi threw his hands into the air. "He'd simply lower the draft age again. Surely once a child is privy trained they can pick up a sword and shield for Arden!" His pacing grew more agitated by the moment.

"At least Neetra's down a man, too," Roland offered as he leaned against a bookcase. "He's also lost his Right Hand in this."

"Aye," Aodan agreed. "That Liro is almost as dangerous as his uncle. It's best to keep our watch on him."

Gib bit his lip. This topic was scarcely ever breeched. Even in his short years in Silver, Gib had come to know how unpopular Koal's elder son was. Despite the undying loyalty many felt for the seneschal, Liro was not extended such favor.

"Liro is still young and foolhardy, but Koal trusts him. He knows his son. We have to trust his judgment." The King sounded tired, like he might not believe the words himself.

Roland shook his head. "I trust and respect Koal as much as any of the rest of you, but we all know his sight is clouded on that boy. Ever since he was born, Koal's been skittish of 'im. He's just not a good egg, Liro. Joel is Koal's son as well, and look at the difference in them! I'd trust Joel in a position of power but Liro? No. He's a snake."

King Rishi silenced them all with the wave of a hand. "We're not here to discuss Liro. Right now, he's as far away as our seneschal. We need a plan to deal with Neetra before he manages to tip the balance in the council room."

"You're right. We'll be down a vote with Koal absent," Marc said. "This isn't a good time for him to be gone."

"There's never a good time for him to be gone!" The King stopped next to the window, looking outside. He held his hands behind his back, and his blank face did little to conceal his unease. At long last, he issued a deep sigh and turned to look at the other men in the room. "I need one of you to be the acting seneschal while Koal's gone."

Marc and Roland both froze. The air felt stiff, heavy. Gib didn't envy either man their positions. Filling the shoes of the seneschal was no light task. Both the dean and weapons master seemed fully aware of this as their eyes met.

Marc opened his mouth, but Roland beat him to it. "Well, don't look at me. It's a hell of a jump to go from training soldiers to becoming the Right Hand of the King!"

"I'm only a dean," Marc lamented. "I can tell students what classes would benefit them most. Other than that, I'm a healer. I've next to no combat experience."

"What good is combat experience in the council room? Unless I'm able to meet Neetra with a blade, I'm useless!" Roland countered.

Aodan chuckled darkly. "My vote's for Roland then."

Something dangerously like fire crossed over the King's features. "I'm serious. Someone needs to sit in for Koal. Neetra will be relentless now. I'll need someone there to support me."

Both candidates fell silent for a time. Gib looked down at his hands as he twisted them together. He could see why neither Marc nor Roland were keen on taking the job, but the King was right. Someone had to do it.

Their voices were softer when next they spoke. Marc and Roland embraced a steel-like resolve and tackled the problem with logic instead of emotion. Marc pointed out that Roland's war experience would be valuable if they had to dissuade the majority of the council from sending their troops to march on Shiraz. The King countered, expressing concern over General Morathi Adeben. Roland was only the Weapons Master—Morathi outranked him.

Gib cleared his throat, offering his own tentatively spoken input. "Morathi's also already on the council. He has seniority in the eyes of the other councilors." He wasn't sure what possessed him to speak. Surely the King would have asked for his opinion if he wanted it. "S–sorry."

Roland gestured toward Gib hastily. "See? Even an understudy knows more about the politics of the council than me! I'm not a member of the High Council. Marc, the politicians are more likely to listen to you simply because they already know you and would favor your experience."

The King rubbed his chin as he paced. "It would be in our favor to pull you in, Roland. With Koal gone and Marc taking his place, we still lose one vote. If you step in, Marc can stay in his chair with his vote and you can fill in for Koal."

Gib bit his bottom lip. He could see a flaw in this. Was he allowed to speak? They hadn't reprimanded him a moment ago—but what if he'd merely been lucky that time? Roland's shoulders slouched. With a defeated sigh, he nodded. It seemed he was going to accept the offer.

Gib swallowed, his heart hammering. "Wait—I'm sorry to speak without being asked, but do you not worry General Morathi might defame Roland? For the sake of saving votes for his own cause?" He flinched, waiting to be reprimanded.

Marc nodded. "Gib has a point. Neetra and Morathi typically favor the same vote, and they have a lot of pull over the councilors who are on the fence. Roland's inexperience may hurt us more than help."

King Rishi's face contorted as he paced, and the tension in his shoulders made the rest of his body look equally rigid.

He went for so long without saying anything that Aodan eventually broke the spell. "Rishi?"

The King came to a full stop in the center of the room. His dark eyes, typically so shrewd and in control, looked glassy, panicked. "None of these choices are good! We stand on the sword's edge yet again. Will this never get any easier?"

"Runnin' a country isn't easy," Aodan replied. "It's not fer the faint of heart. You know that." The bodyguard folded his arms across his narrow chest. "Now choose, Highness."

The King whipped around and set a fierce gaze on the other man. Aodan didn't back down—he didn't so much as flinch—and Gib had to wonder how he could be so unflappable under such a heavy look.

King Rishi finally sighed in defeat and gestured toward the "victor," Marc.

Visible relief washed over Roland, but he turned to Marc in the next instant. "You'll tell me if you need help with anything. I'll do what I can for you. Deal?"

Marc had gone pale, but he kept command of his voice. "I can't pull you away from your work. Our young troops may need you more than ever now."

"I'll announce it at council tomorrow," King Rishi said, looking at Marc. "You'll sit in Koal's seat until he returns."

If he returns. Gib's treacherous thoughts slipped away from him before he could squash them. He didn't want to think in such a way, but it was true, wasn't it? They had no guarantee any of their friends would come home. The King might lose his most trusted advisor and eldest son in one blow. Gib might lose his first love. He sniffed, refusing to let the tears overtake him. He *would* speak to Kezra or Tarquin later. It was a promise to himself.

Roland bowed to the King, only to be waved off with an irritated groan. "I should get back out to the field. My assistant is overseeing the class for me now, but I want to cover new formations with the students today."

"Yes. Especially if there's any chance we'll be going to war." King Rishi sounded exhausted, like he hadn't slept in years.

"It's been good to have enthusiastic students to work with," Roland said as he made for the door. "They learn faster when they choose to become a soldier on their own. Tell *that* to your general."

Marc and the King both offered half smiles at that, but Gib got the distinct impression Roland wasn't making conversation. General Morathi had never hidden his distaste for female soldiers and raising the draft age. A cold lump settled in Gib's stomach just thinking about the havoc Morathi and Neetra could wreak together without Koal present to be the voice of reason.

Roland took off his slippers and grabbed his boots before reaching for the door—only to have it swing open before he could touch it.

"Get in there, both of you, before I decide to tell your father how you've behaved!" A woman's voice carried from the hallway, and Gib craned his neck to see who it was.

Crowned Prince Deegan and Princess Gudrin shuffled through the door, sour looks on their dirty faces. Queen Dahlia came through an instant later, holding the hem of her dress in one hand and her delicate shoes in the other. The instant she saw everyone was watching them, her powdered cheeks turned a lovely shade of pink. "Oh, I'm sorry. I didn't realize anyone was here."

King Rishi laughed. "Rough day?"

The Queen made to bow, but Marc raised his voice as she did. "It's only us. No one important." A smile split his face in two when she glanced around and seemed to come to the same conclusion for herself.

She relaxed with a sigh. "Oh, they're being awful. Making messes in the garden, chasing each other with the tools—I only wanted to bring them inside." She plucked up a pair of slippers and tried to get out of the way as quickly as possible. When King Rishi stroked her arm in passing, she fixed him with a hard glare. "You could have told me you were going to take your meeting here. I would have taken the children elsewhere."

The King shook his head, still smiling. "We were done anyway. You couldn't have known—" His voice clipped to a halt when Princess Gudrin wrapped her arms around his waist and buried her dirty face against his fine clothing. He put a hand atop her head and gently pushed her back. "Don't try to win me over to your side. Go get cleaned up!"

Gib bit the inside of his cheek to keep from grinning. How many

123

times had Cal or Tay done the same thing to him when they were still little and their father had reprimanded them? Gudrin reacted about as well, fat tears rolling down her cheeks as she whined and ran through a door which must have led to additional wings in the royal suite. The Queen followed her, exasperation etched into her features.

Roland shook a finger at the King. "It should be a crime to break the princess's heart, Highness."

Crowned Prince Deegan stomped toward the same door. "She *was* being a brat. If she behaves like that when *I'm* king, I'll banish her!" The Weapons Master barked a laugh as King Rishi shooed his son into the other room.

Roland took his leave a moment later, closing the door behind him. As soon as he was gone, Marc sighed and turned to the King. The smile he'd displayed for the Queen and children had already vanished. "How do you think Neetra is going to handle this news?"

King Rishi sank down into his chair. He wiped at the dirt smudge his daughter had left on his clothing, but even Gib could tell it was only a distraction. "About as well as you think. He's going to make my life a living hell."

"We'll hope for Koal's swift return then."

"We'll hope for his return."

The King's forlorn voice made Gib wince. He still refused to think about it. Perhaps if he kept pushing the thoughts away, he could escape them entirely. Maybe he could wait so long Joel would return before ever having to embrace this grief.

Marc stood. "Right. Okay then, Gib. I think we can go."

Gib was on his feet and following his mentor before he knew he was doing it. They removed their slippers wordlessly and each took boots in hand. Gib turned to bow to King Rishi and, for once, the King bowed his head in return instead of waving Gib off as a troublesome nuisance. The King looked like a ghost, sitting there with hollow eyes and worried thoughts. The room suddenly felt empty, and Gib almost didn't want to leave. He opened his mouth but had no idea what to say.

"Papa!"

Princess Gudrin ran from the other room just then and jumped into the King's lap. He smiled and seemed to come back to life. Gudrin looked over and realized Gib and Marc were still standing there. She cleared her throat and lifted her chin, looking every bit a princess. "I mean—King Rishi—can Deegan and I go horseback riding?"

"I don't know, *can* you?"

King Rishi's sly smirk reassured Gib. The King was going to be all right, despite Koal's absence. He had his family to keep him grounded.

The princess groaned. "*May* we?"

Gib didn't stay to listen to their negotiations. Marc put a hand on

Gib's shoulder, and he followed behind the dean. They left the royal suite, quietly closing the door and putting on their boots in the hall. Their departure was marked by silence, only broken by their footfalls. Gib's head swam as they passed the portraits in the hall. He couldn't help but steal one more glance at the royal family and long for his own. They were his strength, even with Joel so far away.

CHAPTER SEVEN

The council chamber of the Northern Empire was dark and uninviting, with cold stone walls and no windows. Mage orbs hovering in the rafters above glowed brightly, filling the space with eerie blue false light, but the illumination did little to settle Joel's nerves as he took a seat at the enormous oval-shaped table in the center of the room. Liro sat to Joel's right, and Hasain claimed the seat to the left. NezReth scooted into the chair next to the young Radek lord, while Koal and Cenric seated themselves on the far side of Liro.

A half-dozen men dressed in Imperial silk entered the room, and leading the pack was Adrian Titus. The Archmage of Teivel swept through the chamber, his chin raised arrogantly and golden robe caressing the floor behind his sandaled feet as he walked. He sat down across from Koal, and his followers took seats beside him. Even in the dim light, Joel took notice of Adrian's fierce scowl. In fact, not even one of the Imperial councilmen smiled. They merely stared forward, faces as cold and unmoving as the stone walls and eyes devoid of emotion. All of this only served as a reminder of the grave situation the Ardenian envoys faced. Joel clasped his clammy hands together beneath the tabletop, waiting for someone to speak. No one did. Uneasy silence settled over the room, and he hated every second of it.

The door swung open, and Emperor Lichas Sarpedon marched into the chamber. The crown perched atop his blond curls glowed in the false light, and his crystal eyes were sharp and calculating. As he approached the table, those gathered around it stood and bowed to him. Joel followed along, copying the others, but his eyes were already trained on the five men who had come through the chamber door behind the Emperor. All of them were dressed in strange, exotic clothing Joel had never seen before. *Are these the—? Yes, these have to be the emissaries from Nales and Shiraz.* He stiffened as he took his seat and was thankful his trembling hands were hidden beneath the long sleeves of his mage robe.

Emperor Lichas cleared his throat, gesturing toward the strangers. "Chancellor Garron Saronul and Lord Stirling Braun, of Nales."

Two of the men stepped forward. Both were tall and lean and wore loose-fitting coats lined with fur. Thick, braided belts ensured their outerwear stayed in place, and cotton trousers dyed a deep shade of blue covered their legs. Both men bowed to Emperor Lichas, and the broader of the two replied in a jarring, heavily accented voice, "It is an honor to be here, Supreme Ruler of the North." They sat down without another word.

Emperor Lichas turned to the remaining men and introduced them as well. "Princes Kadar and Rami Dhaki, of Shiraz."

A nervous lump formed in Joel's throat as he dared look at the men from the country so many citizens in Arden feared and hated.

Two of the three men wore richly colored jackets with long, billowy sleeves made from satin. A wide waistband folded around the trunk of their bodies several times, and both men donned conical felt caps topped with stunning peacock feathers and golden embroidery. A third, more modestly dressed man stood beside them, and as the Emperor spoke, this man turned to his comrades and began speaking to them in a language Joel didn't understand.

The extravagantly dressed princes of Shiraz listened to their companion, who seemed to be an interpreter. Once he'd finished speaking, one of the princes replied in the same foreign tongue. The translator relayed his words to the Imperial king. "On behalf of the Holy Seven of Tahir and the mighty Dhaki bloodline, we accept your invitation to Teivel. Let us reach a mutual agreement so we may end the bloodshed on our western border."

They came forward to take their seats, and Joel felt his mouth go dry when he realized they meant to sit directly across from him. He met their frigid dark eyes for only a moment before having to drop his gaze to the table. *Chhaya's bane, I can't believe I am sitting across from two of the Dhaki princes!*

The Dhaki bloodline had been ruling Shiraz for the past eight generations. Known for their iron-fisted rule, they'd slain thousands of their own people to maintain command over their domain. Rebellions were pacified with swift violence, and the laws of the land were absolute and unyielding. Worst of all, the Dhaki used *fear* as their greatest weapon. Executions were highly publicized events. They *wanted* to display their so-called "justice" being delivered. They *wanted* the people to see what happened when the law was disobeyed. Joel had a sneaking suspicion that the Northern Empire used similar tactics. *If the common folk live in constant fear, if their hopes and dreams are always being squashed, it's unlikely they'll rise against their oppressors.*

Joel knew, as an ambassador, he was supposed to keep an open mind—but he couldn't help the raw anger creeping into his heart. How were they expected to negotiate peace with these oppressors? Why hadn't the Emperor told them emissaries from Shiraz and Nales would be here? Why hadn't they been given warning in advance? Was this blatant trickery or had Sarpedon been so preoccupied that he'd forgotten to inform them? How could anything be expected to be accomplished?

Joel blinked. *If we'd known they would be here, would anything have changed? Would we not have come?* He stole another glance at the foreign men sitting across the table and realized he wasn't being fair. *I'm already making assumptions, and we haven't even gotten a chance to hear what they have to say. Isn't that what being an ambassador is all about? Listening and compromise? I feel sorrow for their people, but we're here to find a way to keep our own people from dying needlessly. This could be a chance to end the conflict on our borders. We can stop this war before it even begins and save the lives of countless Ardenian soldiers. I have to remain civil— and not allow my judgment to get in the way.*

The Emperor's hardened stare passed across each of the gathered men as he took a seat beside Adrian. "Shall we begin?"

Fresh sheets of parchment paper were passed around the table. Joel took one, as did Hasain and Liro. They had previously decided that the three younger members of their party would take notes and listen, while Koal and Cenric did all of the speaking and negotiations.

Adrian addressed the table. "We call to order this meeting of our neighbors, the lands Shiraz, Nales, and Arden, pertaining to the prospect of peace across all our nations. Under the watch of His Grace, Emperor Lichas Sarpedon, may the Blessed Son of Light bless our efforts and bring His wisdom to light."

Emperor Lichas gestured toward Koal with a simple dip of his head. "What say you, representatives of Arden?"

Joel had no idea how his father was able to respond with such grace under the scrutiny of so many sets of powerful eyes. "While we of Arden were surprised to learn our neighbors Shiraz and Nales would be present today, we would like to express our gratitude for this opportunity to search out a peaceful solution to our differences."

Murmurs rose from the table as the interpreter spoke to the Dhaki princes. A moment later, one of them responded. He frowned as he spoke, as if the words tasted bitter in his mouth. The interpreter didn't wait for permission to speak. He did as his prince commanded. "We will speak of peace when our holy lands have been returned to us. The faith of our good people has been shaken."

Koal nodded in the way a parent might respond to a strong willed child. He'd clearly seen this coming. "The history of our shared border has been regrettable for some time, Prince Kadar. Arden's position on the matter, however, has not changed. The war in which Arden claimed the land took place some eighty years ago, before anyone at this table was even born."

Joel glanced at the Emperor. Was that true? Who knew how long this man had been kept unnaturally young?

"There have long since been settlements placed there. What would Arden do with our people who now inhabit the area? Where would we put them?"

128

Joel listened as the interpreter relayed the message and caught Hasain scribbling away out of the corner of his eye. The King's son kept his face carefully neutral, but the tremble in his hand gave away his true feelings.

"The land is sacred to Shiraz," came the Dhaki prince's reply. "It is there that the Great Prophet Selahattin Ata was born. It is there that he united the nomadic clans together and went on to found our glorious country. The land is holy to our people, but it means nothing to Arden. To give it back would be the most reasonable course of action—yet your king refuses."

Koal's voice was a trained calm. "Our king is in no position to renegotiate our border. This war is old news to Arden, and our council won't vote to turn over the land. King Rishi cannot act without the council's approval. His hands are tied in the matter."

"What king is unable to rule his country? Perhaps your council needs to be reminded of their place."

"Our customs have been in place since the formation of our country and aren't likely to change any time soon. For the length of Arden's proud history, our system of government has served us well."

"While your customs serve you well, they do not help our people who wish to worship as they once did!"

With a friendly, open face, Cenric leaned a little closer and cleared his throat, drawing the attention of everyone gathered. "Princes Kadar and Rami, perhaps another solution can be found. Surely the same wisdom which has helped the Dhaki bloodline rule for eight generations can find a peaceful compromise. Are there temples Arden could help to build for your people? Or would it help to open the border so that your people may visit the old land to worship?"

Hasain stiffened in his seat but kept his thoughts to himself. Joel was glad because he was certain he and Hasain shared the same sentiment. Opening the border sounded like a recipe for disaster.

Prince Kadar openly balked, his dark eyes narrowing into dangerous slits. "Our lands are precious to us. You would dangle them before us as a constant reminder of what is no longer ours? *This* is your idea of a peaceful solution?"

Cenric stayed calm despite the prince's outburst of rage. "Then perhaps your majesties may have another suggestion?"

Back and forth the negotiations went until the Dhaki princes were as agitated as Koal and even Cenric's patience seemed to be wearing thin. When even NezReth had lifted shrewd eyes to watch the encounter, Emperor Sarpedon finally waved to Adrian.

The Archmage cleared his throat. "Perhaps this conversation should be set aside for now so both parties may recollect themselves."

Joel breathed a sigh of relief. *Thank The Two.*

Liro shifted in his seat for the first time, drawing attention to himself.

And then, to Joel's utter shock, he *spoke*. "The wisdom of the Northern Empire is most appreciated. Arden could learn well from this experience, seeing as our own council meetings often descend into boorish dissention long before such a time as this."

Joel's insides felt as though they'd frozen over. The underlings weren't supposed to talk, but Liro had either forgotten, or more likely, he'd disregarded the rules all together.

Liro's words sat like a heavy rock in the middle of the room. Joel couldn't look up from his lap, but he could feel Koal's white hot glare directed at his eldest son. Liro made no indication of being uncomfortable; his posture remained relaxed as he clasped his hands loosely together on the tabletop.

When Joel was finally able to lift his eyes, he caught a heavy look being shared between his brother and the Archmage. Despair blossomed within Joel. *Liro shouldn't have said that. He's supposed to be fighting for Arden, not showing support for the Empire!*

Adrian broke eye contact with Liro and gestured toward the representatives from Nales, as though he'd already forgotten about the exchange. "Chancellor Garron, what say you to Arden?"

The chancellor frowned and looked across the table toward Koal. "We come to speak of the tension on our southern border. The build up of your military troops in Ostlea is troublesome to our people in Dalibor, the township closest to our shared border. What is the need for so many soldiers, Seneschal Koal Adelwijn?"

Koal sighed, and his voice sounded tired when he replied. "There have been rumors of Nales creating an alliance with Shiraz of late, so our council passed a vote to reinforce our northernmost border just in case. Unfortunately, with their nerves on edge already, Arden's High Council is quick to act on any possible threat of war."

Garron's reddened face twisted into an angry scowl. "If Arden is so worried, they would do well to speak *to* Nales rather than *about* Nales. Our country has no intent to join in a war that is not ours."

Koal rubbed his face and snapped his fingers in the direction of the underlings. He pointed toward their parchment, silently telling them to take note of the conversation. "Then Nales *hasn't* been meeting with Shiraz, Chancellor?"

Garron took his time responding. "I did not say that. Our meetings are our own, but if you must know, Seneschal, Nales has recently spoken to Shiraz in an attempt to open trade between our country and theirs. It does not serve your country to worry needlessly."

"I would agree. Jumping to conclusions is an often dangerous game." Koal kept his tone neutral, but Joel knew what his father couldn't say aloud. It would have been bad form to explain in front of all of these strangers how Arden's High Councilor kept the country in a state of panic.

Rumors and lies were common trade from his uncle's lips, almost as bad as Shiraz's intimidation methods. How could Arden ever hope to prosper under such conditions?

Mind and heart heavy with woe, Joel glared down at the parchment resting on the table and continued to take notes.

The meeting went long into the afternoon before Emperor Sarpedon finally declared a recess. While no end to the border dispute was yet in sight, swords remained sheathed and no blood pooled on the chamber floor. Joel supposed, in that respect, the meeting had been a small success. At least he knew it was possible for the leaders to be in the same room together.

Joel stayed quiet as they returned to the suite. Thoughts of the council meeting weighed heavily on his mind, and while the others engaged in conversation, he was too distracted to lend his own voice. Fumbling with the notes he'd written, Joel stared at the ground and wondered if reaching a peaceful agreement would ever be possible. Arden's laws were so fundamentally different from Shiraz and Nales. Would they be able to find common ground?

This is what I signed up for, Joel reminded himself. *These types of situations are what ambassadors are trained for. This is why I left my home, my family—Gib. I came here to learn how to make a difference in the world. I can't give up so easily or the sacrifices I made will all be in vain.*

"Father," Liro was saying. "I must insist on seeing a healer." The elder brother clutched his skull with both hands as he walked into the suite. His blanched face was drained of all color, and despite Liro's best attempt to hide the terrible agony, Joel could see it in his eyes.

Liro had been fighting such headaches since childhood. The healers hadn't been able to cure it—they weren't even able to give him a proper diagnosis. They could only offer temporary treatments to pacify the headaches. Sometimes herbal medicines were enough, but more often than not, magical intervention needed to be called upon to block the incredible pain.

Joel frowned, wishing he could offer words of comfort but knowing he would only be scorned for it. He remembered, back when they had still been close, he would often hold a wet cloth to Liro's forehead and sit with him until the pain subsided. Those days were long over.

Koal directed his son to sit down on the lounge. "Here, rest. I'll call a servant—"

"I can find a servant by myself."

Concern etched the seneschal's face. "Then I can help you find the healer's wing."

"I'm not a child. I can find my own way." Liro's voice was clipped as he peered out at Koal from between his fingers.

Koal gave his son a stiff nod and finally relented. "Very well. Go. And when you return, we *will* be discussing the issue of you speaking during that council meeting."

Liro departed, leaving perturbed silence in his wake. Koal was still frowning as he set to work writing his report for King Rishi. Cenric clapped him on the shoulder as he walked past, offering silent support. Joel leafed through his own notes, rebellious mind wandering again. It seemed he was destined to have no control over his thoughts while on this mission.

"Joel, why don't you take a short break before we review the notes you took during the meeting," Cenric suggested.

"All right," Joel heard himself respond numbly. Perhaps some sunshine and fresh air *would* do him good. After being locked in that chamber for the past three marks, he had begun to wonder if he'd ever see the light again.

He went onto the terrace, eyelids fluttering as harsh, blinding sunlight hit him in the face. Gazing across the garden, Joel admired all the flowers, placed in perfect little rows. The hedges had been trimmed recently, their straight edges giving Joel the impression they'd been carved from the same stone as the palace, and the still waters of the pond reflected wispy white clouds from the sky above. The view was vibrant and beautiful, like a painting years in the making. As he admired the scenery, Joel wondered with wry amusement if the people in this marvelous stone city ever found themselves jaded.

Gib had joked on more than one occasion about how the highborns in Silver City enjoyed such extravagant lives that they'd lost the ability to see the beauty surrounding them—that they'd never appreciate it unless it was suddenly gone. Joel swallowed, shaking his head. *It works the same way with people. I didn't appreciate what I had with Gib, and now he's gone.*

Sighing, he sat down on a bench beneath the shade of a tree. Peering straight up, he saw purple fruits growing among the spiny leaves. Birds, hidden from view, sang in the branches far above. Or perhaps they weren't birds at all. Maybe they were cockatrices. He supposed he couldn't really know without catching a glimpse of them.

For a time, he merely sat there, watching the grass dance in the gentle breeze. Despite the palace walls looming behind him, it was easy to feel removed, as though he were the only person left in the world. If he closed his eyes, he could almost believe he was sitting in the inner courtyard of the Adelwijn estate on a beautiful summer day, family nearby and Gib by his side. They sat together, hands intertwined, laughing over some tasteless joke they'd heard at the Rose Bouquet the night before, with not a worry in the world.

Joel couldn't help the whimper that escaped his throat. *I'll never have that again. Cenric was right. If I become an ambassador, I'll see all the beauty the world has to offer. But what good is all of that if I have no one to share it with? I don't want to be alone—*

Quiet voices beyond the hedge line caught his attention, pulling him out of his forlorn reverie. Two people were talking—or rather, one was sobbing while the other attempted to calm her.

"I can't do it anymore," cried a young girl. "I just can't!"

"Shhh. Calm down, Kenisha," replied the soft voice of a boy. "Tell me what happened."

Joel leaned a little closer to the hedge. He knew he shouldn't be eavesdropping—for a second time that day—on what was surely meant to be a private conversation, but if he got up and walked away, he'd be heard.

More sobbing ensued before the girl was able to catch her breath. "It's *him* again!"

"Has he—hurt you?"

The terrible silence left in wake of the question made Joel shudder.

"No. Not yet anyway. But I know he plans to. It'll be just like what happened to Daphne!"

"Daphne? What happened to her?"

"He—he started giving her attention. He told her she had certain obligations as a servant. He said she needed to fulfill *all* her duties."

"He hasn't the right—"

"Oh no? And who was going to take a stand and tell him so? Daphne was a lowly servant. To disobey him would have only sealed her fate sooner."

"What happened?"

The girl sniffled again. "She did as he wished. Kept her mouth shut about it, of course. But then the pregnancy began to show, and—and he dismissed her. He sent her home to her family on the outskirts, beyond the protection of the dome, just as the onslaught of winter arrived."

Another bout of miserable silence lingered in the air. Joel realized he'd been holding his breath only when fire began to burn down the back of his throat and into his lungs.

Finally, the male voice came again, just as quietly as before, but heavy with resolve. "That won't happen to you. I promise."

"You can't know that for sure! What if it does? I can't be banished like Daphne. I have no home left to go to. If I'm sent beyond the barrier—I'll die out there on my own, Kirk!"

Joel's brow furrowed. Kirk? The same Kirk who'd shown them to their meal earlier? The apprentice of the Archmage? It had to be. Joel tipped his head closer to the hedge.

"Listen to me," the boy replied, confirming Joel's suspicions. He recognized the mage trainee's soft tenor voice from their first meeting. "In two more years, I'll be done with my apprenticeship. I'll be earning my own purse, and I promise the first thing I'll do is get you out of this palace. I swear it on our mother's grave."

"*Two years?*" Her anguished voice cracked.

"I know. I *know* it's a long time, but I can't earn my title any faster." He gave a deep sigh, like wind cutting through the trees. "What if I try to get you reassigned? Perhaps my master could use another servant girl. He's not the kindest man, but at least you wouldn't have to worry about—mistreatment."

"No. He already hates being saddled with you. Asking for a favor would only make your own life more difficult. I can't ask that of you."

"You're my sister," Kirk replied. "You can ask anything of me, and you know it."

"You've done enough for me already. When the mages came to take you to the palace, you fought for me to come, too. I'd be out on the streets if it wasn't for you. I'd probably be dead—or worse, working in a brothel."

"I saved you from one horrible fate only to put you in danger here, too!"

"It's dangerous everywhere. At least here I don't have to worry about starving. Or freezing to death. You remember how it was outside the barrier, don't you? For now, I'll take my chances serving *him* rather than fighting to survive out there. But if he continues to—"

New voices carried on the wind, interrupting the siblings. Someone was approaching.

The girl's voice came again, fast and hushed. "I have to go. You're supposed to be looking in on your charges, and I'm late to the kitchen. We both stand to be reprimanded if we're caught here. Stay well, brother."

"Be careful, Kenisha."

Joel could hear the sound of hurried footsteps on stone pavers as the girl made her retreat. He stood to leave, too, feeling as though he'd already lingered longer than was strictly necessary, but froze in place as a new voice bellowed from beyond the hedge.

"*Kirk Bhadrayu!*" a brash voice called out.

Kirk sucked in a sharp breath.

"Oh, look, Brutus," snickered a second voice. "It's your *favorite* mage trainee!"

The first newcomer issued a snort. "My favorite trainee to torment, perhaps."

"Hello, Brutus. Hello, Taichi," Kirk replied after a moment, voice timid and possibly even a little frightened.

Joel listened as the other boys' footsteps drew nearer, until they were so close Joel himself took a step back. They were right on the other side of the hedge; he could have reached out and touched them.

"What are you doing out here?" the first boy demanded. "I thought Master Titus told you to go make sure our guests from Arden were pacified."

"Yeah!" said the second boy. "Why aren't you checking on the envoys?"

Kirk went silent, and Joel realized the trainee didn't have an excuse to give the other boys. Kirk's sister had warned they both stood to get into trouble if they were caught conversing. Was unfair and unnecessary justice about to be served? Would these bullies torment him if they found out the truth? Or possibly worse, would they tattle on Kirk to the Archmage? Adrian Titus didn't seem to be the type of man anyone should cross.

Joel wrung his hands together, feeling terrible for the young man. Kirk had been the only one to show any genuine kindness to the Ardenian envoys since their arrival, and now he stood to be unfairly reprimanded. *But he's done nothing wrong! He was comforting his sister! Will really get into trouble for such a petty offence?*

"I–I was." Kirk's smooth voice had gone choppy as he fumbled for an excuse.

"Oh? Then explain why you're out here. Or perhaps you'd like to explain it to Master Titus."

"No, please, I was just—"

Joel had heard enough. He wasn't sure what he planned to do, even as he slipped through a break in the hedge line. But he couldn't stand there and just let the poor boy get into trouble when it was so clearly undeserved. Joel straightened to his full height and set his nose high in the air, morphing from humble ambassador to haughty Ardenian highborn in the blink of an eye.

"He was helping me," Joel declared as he stepped into the full view of the Imperial youths. Kirk jumped and whirled around to look at him, green eyes wide. Joel smiled tightly before turning a fierce stare onto the other boys.

The two burly, square-faced boys had Kirk cornered against the shrubbery. They'd been scowling at their quarry, but when Joel announced his presence, both took a tentative step back, uncertainty etching their faces.

"Greetings," Joel called out to them. All trace of warmth had drained from his voice. "I heard angry voices through the hedge, so I came to see what the fuss was about."

"Who are you?" one of the boys asked, crossing his arms over his chest. He wore a white tunic lined with golden lace, the same as Kirk's, leading Joel to assume this youngster was also a trainee.

"My name is Joel Adelwijn, mage and ambassador of Arden. Kirk Bhadrayu was kind enough to help me retrieve a trinket I misplaced while sitting in the garden earlier," Joel replied without hesitation. He extended one hand and motioned toward his bare fingers. "You see, I lost my ring. It's been in the Adelwijn family for generations and is very important to me. Kirk was just checking to see if it had fallen into the hedges, since I spent so much time admiring them earlier." *Thank The Two I forgot that damn ring in Arden.* Joel looked Kirk straight in the face. "Isn't that right?"

Kirk's uncertain eyes flickered back and forth between his peers and the Ardenian envoy, and for a moment Joel worried the boy might not follow along with the ruse. After a tense lull, however, Kirk nodded stiffly and responded. "Yes. That's what I was doing. I was helping Lord Joel Adelwijn find his ring."

"So you see, gentlemen, no crime has been committed here." Joel's voice was cool as he leveled the two instigators.

The boys floundered. "Uh, well, I—we were just—"

"I think you were just leaving," Joel finished the sentence for them in a clipped voice, imagining that he must have sounded every bit as pretentious as his uncle. He stuck his nose farther into the air and his scowl only grew more severe. "Unless, perhaps, you'd like to get onto your hands and knees and help search for my ring, too?"

The boys exchanged wide-eyed glances with one another, and Joel might have laughed at their distress if the situation hadn't been so serious.

"We have lessons to attend," one of them managed to sputter.

"Our master would be unforgiving should we be late," said the other.

Joel nodded. "That's a shame. Surely four sets of eyes searching would have been more efficient than two—but, of course, lessons are of the utmost importance. You best be on your way so Kirk and I may resume our mission."

"Y–yes, Ambassador."

Both boys scuttled away without another word, and Joel grinned quite devilishly at the backs of their heads as they departed.

After the boys were well out of earshot, a shuddering sigh escaped Kirk's lips. He stared at the lawn, as though his attention was held there against his will. "Thank you, m'lord. You didn't have to do that."

Joel frowned, still watching the pathway to ensure they were alone. "Yes, I did. If there's one thing I cannot bring myself to do, it's turning a blind eye to injustice."

Kirk shook his head, still refusing to look up. "Sometimes it's easier just to shut your eyes and close your ears, especially in this city, where injustice is so commonplace."

"Perhaps walking away would have been easier, but I've never been one to take the easy road." A forsaken smile flitted across Joel's face as he thought about the trials and tribulations he and Gib had faced—and conquered—together. "Sometimes the path less trodden leads you to wonderful places you never expected."

Kirk did raise his eyes now, hesitantly meeting Joel's gaze. "If only all men could be courageous enough to choose such a path," the boy replied in a voice so quiet it verged on a whisper. Uncertain green eyes fixed onto Joel's blue ones. "The conversation with my sister—"

"Won't be mentioned to anyone. I promise."

Color finally returned to Kirk's white cheeks. "Thank you. If my master found out—" He stopped there, and Joel judged it wise not to push the subject further.

Joel motioned for Kirk to follow him through the hedges and back into the garden. "Come. We best get out of here before anyone else happens upon us. I'm fresh out of excuses to make."

Joel's last remark finally won a smile from the other boy. Kirk smiled as he slipped through the break in the shrubbery. "I can't argue that."

"Who were those buffoons anyway?" Joel asked as he brushed bits of dirt and broken bark from his white robe.

Kirk's cheeks flushed red anew. "Fellow apprentices. Master Titus currently has four understudies. Brutus and Taichi were the two you just had the 'honor' of meeting."

"Honor indeed," Joel laughed.

The young Imperial raised a hand to his mouth, attempting to cover the smile spreading across his face, and it yet again occurred to Joel how *little* every other person in the Northern Empire tended to show such pleasantries.

Kirk's eyes flickered around the private garden. "This garden has always been one of my favorites on the palace grounds. At times when no guests are being housed and the suite lies empty, I often come here to study without worry of being disturbed. I like the serenity. When I'm out here, it's easier to forget my hardships."

Earlier that morning, Joel would have doubted this boy, living in a vast and beautiful palace and training with one of the most powerful mages in the land, knew the meaning of true hardship. But after listening to the conversation between Kirk and his sister and witnessing the treatment of the trainee by his fellow students, Joel had no reason to doubt his proclamation. *Just because someone lives amongst kings doesn't necessarily make them royalty, too. And people who possess everything they could ever desire can still feel empty inside. It's never wise to judge someone by their outer shell, for it's often just that—a shell, a mask, a clever façade.*

"I understand," Joel replied. "Sometimes it's easier to lock yourself away from the world, rather than face it."

Kirk turned to stare at him. "Yes. Sometimes the pain of loss is too much to bear."

The pain of loss. Joel's stomach twisted into knots. He missed Gib so much in that instant it hurt. *Oh, Gib. I messed everything up. I tore our souls apart and left him to pick up the broken pieces. By the light of The Two, I hope he can forgive me—*

Cenric's voice drifted out to where they were standing just then. "Joel? Are you ready to go over the notes from the meeting?"

Joel turned his head in the direction of the suite, desperately trying to harness his wild emotions. He couldn't see his mentor from where he stood but heard quiet voices as Cenric and Hasain conversed inside the common room. They were waiting for him.

He stole a glance at Kirk, wondering if they should even be talking like this. Would Cenric or Koal be angry if they noticed Joel wasn't alone? The mage trainee seemed genuine, but he was still an Imperial and, therefore, a threat. Joel bit the inside of his mouth as he fretted. *Hasain warned me to trust no one. But it's not like I've said anything I shouldn't. Isn't it okay so long as I'm not revealing anything?* All the wisdom he possessed screamed of the others' disapproval. This interaction wouldn't be encouraged by them.

"I—should go," Kirk said, following Joel's gaze. No doubt he'd also heard the voices of the other envoys and perhaps even realized he and Joel stood to get into trouble. "Archmage Titus will be expecting me soon."

Joel managed to nod. "Yes, all right. I think that would be best."

Kirk turned to leave but looked back over his shoulder long enough to smile once more. "Again, thank you. It's rare to be treated with such kindness."

Joel bowed his head. "Farewell."

He sighed, closed his eyes to recollect his thoughts, and then returned to the suite.

The sun had sunk below the western horizon a mark earlier when Gib found his way to the Rose Bouquet. He didn't feel like drinking and dancing tonight, but he was fairly certain he'd find at least one of his friends here. He'd gone back to the dormitory, but Tarquin had been absent. Gib waited for his roommate for what felt like an eternity, but when he still didn't return, Gib sought out Kezra instead. Truthfully, she was the better option anyway. Tarquin meant well but often lacked the insight she possessed. Gib hoped Kezra could offer some sound advice.

The merry music met him on his way through the doors but did nothing to lift his spirit. Inside, he was bombarded with the usual smells of delicious food, strong drink, and perfume. Laughter and singing engulfed him, beckoning him to join in, but Gib couldn't even lift his mouth into a smile. When a bar maid made eye contact, he waved her off. He didn't feel like drinking anything. Gib peered around the tavern and despair rose up through his chest when he didn't see any familiar faces. Where was Kezra?

Gib was so intent on finding her that when a large hand clapped his shoulder, he nearly jumped through the roof.

Nawaz's crystal eyes sparkled as he followed Gib's gaze onto the dance floor. "See somethin' you like out there?"

Gib swallowed, trying to ignore the ache in his heart. "Trying to find anyone I know."

"Oh. Poor luck, that. You only managed to find me." Nawaz laughed, and Gib wished he could laugh, too. But he just couldn't. Nawaz seemed to pick up on it and lowered his voice. "Is everything all right?"

Gib's chest suddenly felt heavy. He could barely open his mouth, and his eyes burned with terrible sadness. Were his emotions really running this rampant? He took a breath and tried to speak, but no words would form.

Nawaz seemed to understand. He squeezed Gib's shoulder in a gentle way. "Kez and I are sittin' over in the corner. Nage and his girl are around, too. Why don't you come sit with us?"

"Thanks. That would be—nice."

Gib followed the young lord to an empty booth, where they took seats opposite one another. Nawaz studied Gib for a moment, and he could tell now, being face to face, that Nawaz's merry mood was something of a façade. His eyes had lost their shine in a matter of moments and his face appeared drawn.

Nawaz slumped back in his seat. "How are you?"

Gib sucked in a deep breath and held it for a moment. "Not good. I mean, how well should I be?"

"I suppose you have a point." Nawaz looked out toward the crowd and shook his head. "I said my goodbyes to Hasain and Joel yesterday. I didn't want to see them off."

"It was somber. They left just as it started raining. It was like the world wept."

Nawaz didn't look at him. "How was Joel?"

Gib slammed his eyes shut. Nawaz didn't know. No one knew. He had to tell someone before he burst, but in this moment he only wanted Kezra. Over the past three years, she'd come to his aid more than once. Rough around the edges, Kezra nevertheless was able to offer support in a way Gib's other friends typically didn't feel comfortable with. She was the only person he knew who could punch his shoulder with one arm while hugging him with the other. "Joel was—quiet."

"Probably kicking himself in the arse."

What was that supposed to mean? Gib looked Nawaz over narrowly and felt the first pang of suspicion blossoming in his chest. "What would he have to regret? He's well on his way to having everything he wants."

Nawaz leaned across the booth and met Gib's gaze head on and with such devotion that Gib almost had to look away. "Horse shit. It wasn't an easy choice for him, Gib. You gotta know that."

"To go to the Northern Empire?"

"Don't play dumb with me. Joel came to me last night and—"

A tidal wave of grief and rage floored Gib. Not only had Joel dismissed him but then he'd gone out and told others? Was nothing sacred anymore? Since when did they air their dirty laundry for everyone to see? "He did *what*?"

"Keep your voice down. He needed someone to talk to. He came to me because he couldn't think of anyone else."

Gib slammed his fist on the table and thought about getting up and leaving. "He could have spoken to *me*! He could have let me know he was going to tell everyone! He could have warned me the secret wasn't a secret!" The words poured out of his mouth before his mind could catch up. He wasn't making sense and was raving like a lunatic, but he didn't care. How could Joel hurt him like this? Didn't he care at all? Did Joel really think so little of him? Gib wiped at his eyes as tears threatened to fall.

Nawaz looked like he'd been slapped across the face. His eyes were wide, and his mouth dropped open. It took him a moment to catch up and, when he did, his fair complexion had turned a dusty crimson. "Bad form! Don't you know Joel well enough to know what you mean to him? He's a good man. He thinks the world of you. He came to me because he was hurting and needed to talk. How can you begrudge him that?"

Gib couldn't answer. When he opened his mouth, only a sob escaped. He wiped his eyes again, but it was no use. He couldn't keep up with the tears.

Nawaz's features softened. "Calm down. I'm sorry. I shouldn't have been so harsh with you. This has gotta be hell for you, too. Here." He pulled a kerchief from his pocket and slid it across the table.

Gib accepted it, wiping his wet eyes and blowing his nose. He needed to pull himself together. Kezra and Nage could come back any minute. *Kezra*. "Does Kezra already know, too?"

Nawaz twisted his ring around his finger absently. Gib watched as the Adelwijn insignia came into view and disappeared with each rotation. "She was there with me last night. I mean, Joel knew she was there. He came to talk to me, but Kez was there, too." He stopped fumbling for words and went quiet.

Gib looked down at his hands. Truthfully, he didn't begrudge Nawaz or Kezra for being involved. "I didn't mean anything by it. I was angry— I *am* angry. I know Kezra is trustworthy and Joel knows as well. It's just hard to—" He took a ragged breath. "It's hard to accept that it's real. He's really gone, and he doesn't want me anymore."

Nawaz shook his head. "Not true, not for an instant. Joel is going through a rough time right now. He's trying to find his way. The life of an envoy is difficult, and he didn't want you to be forced to wait for him if he's going to be gone so often." Blue eyes sought to make contact, and

Gib obliged only because he felt guilty for being so foul a moment before. "You have to know that letting you go is the hardest thing he's ever had to do. It's not a decision he made lightly. You do know that, don't you?"

Of course Gib knew it. Somewhere deep down, he understood this choice hadn't been an easy one for Joel but couldn't help feeling the raw hurt. "It's going to take time. I don't want to hate him—hell, I don't even know if I can get over him." Gib dabbed his nose with the kerchief again. "And I'm sorry for the way I spoke of him. You're right, it was bad form."

"You don't have to apologize to me. If I were in your shoes I'd do worse. I'd probably knock somebody's teeth out and land my arse in the stockades for my efforts." Nawaz chuckled, but it sounded hollow.

Gib sighed. He didn't know what to say to that.

They sat in silence for a time before his ears detected the sound of familiar voices approaching. Gib wiped his face one more time for good measure, winning a discreet nod from Nawaz, and took a deep breath. Gib didn't want to be a complete mess if he was going to meet Nage's lady friend.

"Well look at what the cat dragged in," Nage taunted in a chipper voice. He carried a drink in either hand and walked arm in arm with his guest.

Gib tried to smile but knew his best attempt fell flat.

Nage was preoccupied, however, and seemed to take no notice. He could barely take his eyes off the young woman by his side. "Gib, this is Nia Leal."

She was all smiles and kind eyes. Gib noted how her soft brown hair and round face looked undoubtedly like the girl who'd seen Cenric off that morning. Nia curtsied and offered a hand. "It's a pleasure to make your acquaintance, Gibben Nemesio. Nage has told me so much about you."

Gib took her hand and laid a gentle kiss upon it, playing the part as though he'd been born into the highborn world himself. "The pleasure is all mine. I hope Nage has chosen to tell you good things."

"Nope." Nage didn't elaborate further, but the glimmer in his eyes gave away his fib.

Nia laughed and allowed Nage to help her into the booth. "Of course he said all good things. It's not every day one gets to boast knowing the hero who saved the King."

Gib's cheeks burned. *Daya, are people still going on about that?* "It's really not the adventure folks make it out to be. I was in the right place at the right time. Anyone else would have done the same."

Nia's eyes were a lovely piercing green and exuded intelligence. She grinned and leaned to speak into Nage's ear—though she did so loudly enough for everyone to hear. "You're right. He's too modest."

Nage shot Gib a grin. "Told ya. If it had been me, everyone would know what I did. I'd be my own biggest fan."

141

Kezra approached the booth behind the happy couple, carrying two mugs as well. She frowned down at Nawaz upon arrival. "Oh, *there* you are. I suppose your hands are broken and you couldn't carry your own drink?"

"I wouldn't want to hinder your independence, Lady Malin-Rai." Nawaz smiled as if he'd been doing it all night and laughed like he hadn't shared heated words with Gib moments before. It occurred to Gib how much Nawaz could be likened to his uncle. Marc had played the same fool that very morning while seeing the envoys off.

Kezra wasn't buying Nawaz's charm. She arched one brow and spat at him, "I'll hinder your silver tongue when I cut it from your mouth!"

Nawaz laughed and took one of the mugs from her. "I was gonna carry my own drink, but then I found this waif and brought him back to our table." He pointed at Gib.

Kezra looked at Gib for the first time, and her features softened for just an instant. If Gib hadn't known to look, he would have never even seen it. "Finally took a night to yourself, did you?"

"Thought I'd come bother you," Gib replied, forcing a smile. "Maybe have a chat."

Her nod was almost unperceivable, but Gib knew she understood he wanted to speak privately. "A little later?"

If that was the best she could do, then he would wait. It would be awkward to get up and leave the others now. Nage would no doubt question their absence, and Nawaz would likely be hard pressed to come up with a clever lie to disguise what was really going on. Gib sighed. He wasn't ready to share the truth with everyone yet—especially Nage, who seemed to be so happy.

Their party grew in size by one more person just then as Kezra's elder brother, Zandi Malin-Rai, trotted over to the table, carrying a drink of his own. His high voice rang across the tavern, and his fierce emerald eyes were narrowed into slits. "Thanks for leaving me by myself back there, Kezra! I looked up and you were gone."

Kezra scooted closer to Nawaz, allowing her brother room to sit. "Oh, shut your mouth. If you can't find your way from the bar to the table then you have no right to be out on your own."

"Yes, mother." Zandi sat with an exasperated huff and took a drink from his mug. Looking across the table for the first time, he landed his gaze on Gib and just about choked. "Oh, h–hello."

Gib nodded with a half-smile. "Hello again."

"What's the game tonight?" Nawaz asked before awkward silence could bloom. He was already pulling a deck of cards from his pocket and counting heads. "Any suggestions?"

"No gambling," Kezra said. "We wouldn't want to give Nia the wrong impression here."

Nia smiled slyly. "Oh? I'd be willing to bet I could match you in a

142

game of wager, Lady Kezra. I happen to know my way around betting games."

Nage laughed, and Gib had to admit he hadn't expected a lady such as Nia Leal to have any interest—let alone knowledge—of such boorish games.

Kezra seemed even more surprised. Her mouth fell open, and for just a moment she appeared to be at a loss for words. Finally, she chuckled and replied, "All right then. If it'd please you, I'll gladly kick your ar—show you up in a hand or two."

Laughter made its way around the table, and the game took off. Nia proved to be a formidable match for even Kezra, and by the time their drinks were gone, Nawaz and Nage were placing bets against each other's companion. Nia remained every bit a highborn dame while Kezra was reduced to cursing most *unlike* a lady by the end of the game.

Gib breathed a sigh of relief when at last the game was over, an entire mark later. Nage and Nia excused themselves quietly. She explained how she had a curfew and Nage had promised her mother he would walk her home. Nawaz gave them a lewd smile.

Nia curtsied again. "It was so nice to meet all of you. I see now why Nage speaks highly of his friends."

Nawaz barked a laugh, and Kezra made a crude gesture. Nage shot them both a poisonous warning glare as he saw his lady to the door. There would be hell to pay later, Gib was sure of it. He almost wanted to smile.

Zandi had remained oddly reserved throughout the game, nothing at all like he'd acted at the festival the day before. When they all stood to leave, he gathered the empty mugs and excused himself. He didn't even say goodbye as he bustled toward the bar.

When Nawaz asked Kezra for a single dance before they departed, she looked across the table at Gib. What could he do? Tell her no? Demand she listen to his woes instead of enjoying her time with Nawaz? No. He wouldn't do that. Gib smiled weakly and motioned toward the door. "I'm gonna step out for some air. Meet me out there?"

"All right. I won't be long." Kezra allowed Nawaz to lead her onto the floor where patrons were dancing and clapping along with the music.

Gib didn't stay to watch. Instead, he wandered to the porch, the frigid night air cutting against his face and hands. Shuddering, he pulled his cloak closer and made his way down the tavern steps. He wasn't in the mood to listen to the sounds of people laughing and enjoying themselves. Bitterness rose like bile in his chest, and he ventured far enough to put some distance between himself and the tavern porch. He hoped Kezra wouldn't have to look too hard for him.

"Gibben Nemesio?"

Zandi Malin-Rai's melodic voice cut through the winter night.

Gib's breath caught. Not now. Why now? He didn't know if he had the reserve for more interaction tonight. The air escaped his lungs in a rush as he turned to face the other man. "Yes?"

Zandi's eyes were wide and unsure. His dark complexion helped disguise the crimson tinge on his cheeks but didn't hide it entirely. Gib wondered if it was the cold coloring them or something he wasn't prepared to deal with.

"It's frigid out here. You'll catch your death." Zandi's voice was soft, even shy.

"I suppose. I'm not going to stay long. Kezra and I are going for a walk when she comes out."

"I see." Zandi absently toyed with a tendril of his long, dark hair. The majority of his hair was tied back at the nap of his neck, but a few wisps had escaped the ribbon holding it in place. "You—you're sure you don't want to wait inside for her? I mean, she may be a few minutes."

Gib didn't want to come across as rude, but he couldn't think of anything nice to say. "I'm fine. I can handle a little bit of cold."

Zandi looked at the ground, some unpleasant emotion like dejection or hurt passing across his placid features. "Of course. Well, goodnight." He turned awkwardly to leave.

"Goodnight," Gib replied coolly.

Surely this would be the obvious end to their conversation. However, after taking only a few short steps, Zandi turned back, looking as conflicted as ever.

"I'm sorry about Joel."

His stiff words pricked Gib's skin. Sorry about what? How much did Zandi know? And how? Had Kezra or Nawaz told him, too? Irrational anger clenched at Gib's heart, and he had to fight very hard not to lash out. He'd thought he had managed to get this under control back inside the tavern.

"*Sorry?*" Even the single word dripped acid.

Zandi recoiled. "I—I don't mean to be so forward. I just—over time Kezra has mentioned you and your—Joel—in passing. I know the two of you are close." He glanced around, as if looking for an escape, and Gib had to wonder if his rage was so evident. "It must be hard for you with him so far away. I'm sure you're worried sick, but with the seneschal there, surely Joel is safe."

Joel? Safe? Then this can't be about him and me parting ways. Zandi doesn't know. Gib deflated, his rigid stance draining. He felt like a fool. Kezra and Nawaz were his friends. They wouldn't tell others about what he was going through. He shouldn't have doubted them. And he shouldn't have taken it out on Zandi, who was only trying to wish him well. "Thank you. It is hard. I do worry for him but—you're right, I'm sure."

The brief smile that crossed Zandi's face was lovely and almost made Gib feel warm. "Worry does no good, you know. Perhaps you could think

144

of what's to come in the future, when Joel returns." He took a tentative step closer.

"Right. The future." Gib caught himself before he could shake his head. *This poor fool has no idea he's rubbing salt in the wound.* "The future will undoubtedly hold many new things. Nothing ever stays the same."

"The only constant thing is change—and the world *is* slowly changing." Thinly veiled excitement buzzed in Zandi's voice. "I know your mind and heart must be heavy right now, but you should know there are others who think highly of you and Joel for what changes you're bringing."

Gib frowned. "Changes? I don't follow."

Zandi glanced around as if to be sure they were alone. "The two of you being publicly unashamed. There are others who look up to the both of you. Gibben, you're the understudy of the seneschal. If one day you sit on the High Council, there is hope for all who love unconventionally. Don't you see?"

Gib's head was too full for this. What was Zandi saying? Was it the drink talking? Or were there actually people out there who were paying attention to him? Joel had always been subjected to scrutiny—it came with the territory of being Koal's son, but Gib? Why would anyone take note of him? He was just an impoverished farmer who'd been drafted into the military.

"I'm no one to look up to. And Joel would rather not be in the public eye."

Zandi's emerald eyes dashed around once again. "Whether you would have it or not, people have taken note. There are others—others like you and Joel—who envy your openness."

Gib clenched his jaw. On a different day this would have meant something more to him. If he weren't busy mourning his loss and fretting for Joel's welfare, he might have been more receptive to this conversation. But for now he was tired, lonely, and hurt.

His voice came out as a harsh snap. "Then they would be fools. Being open about yourself is taxing. It kills you a little each time someone strikes you down—and there are many who strike us down. Tell your friends, or whoever they are, they need to look to someone else." He turned his back and hoped Zandi would get the hint.

Stifling silence claimed the night. Even the Rose Bouquet's music seemed to be leagues away. Zandi sighed at long last. "There isn't anyone else to look up to. Joel Adelwijn set a new standard when he proclaimed his preference for his own. There were so many who were against him but so many more of us who silently wished we could be so brave. And then you came along and fell in beside him without so much as batting an eye. And more than that? The seneschal has accepted you both! The King has looked the other way. Do you even know what sort of hero you are?"

Gib ground his teeth together, hating himself a little for how he was behaving but unable to listen to this anymore. "Don't you have somewhere to go?"

"Send me away." Zandi was standing right behind him now. When had he closed the gap? "But know you are a beacon of hope—whether you would have it or not."

Done. He was done. Spinning on one heel, Gib rounded to glare at the other man. "Hope? There isn't any hope left. Not with Joel gone to the Northern Empire and me left here so broken. You may mean well, but you have no idea what you're talking about. I'll ask you again, Zandi Malin-Rai, haven't you somewhere to go? *Now?*"

Zandi's face twisted in such a way that Gib could scarcely tell how handsome he was beneath the scowl. "*I* have no idea what I'm talking about? Begging your pardon, but *you* don't know what *you're* talking about. Do you think you're the only one to be different? To be not 'normal'? And on top of that, do you have any idea what it's like to be what I am and have a father like mine? Lord Anders Malin-Rai, of the High Council? Imagine how proud he must be of his soldier daughter and eldest son who refuses to marry! At least you have your hope. Joel will return to you, and you'll have your other half to share your burdens. Some of us are alone!"

"With any luck, Joel *will* return, but not to me!" Gib's chest heaved, and he felt as though the world would spin right out from under him. "We're not invincible. Our pedestal doesn't lift us as high as you imagine. The real world still jumps up to bite us in the arse once in a while. Joel and I aren't some tale of Fae. We're human and fallible. And we're *done*! There is no 'we' anymore."

Zandi's emerald eyes were wide in the moonlight, but if he was angered by Gib's harsh words, there was no way to see it through his sorrow. Gib wanted to be enraged, to continue to fuel the fire that had blazed in his soul a moment before but now guttered to dance with death. Why was Zandi, a perfect stranger, looking on Gib with so much sympathy? Zandi should have dismissed Gib as a raging lunatic! And yet, there the other man stood, openly sharing Gib's pain.

A long moment passed where they said nothing before Zandi sighed, his breath a wispy cloud on the wind. "I'm sorry. I didn't know." He wrapped his arms around himself and looked out into the distance. A devastated smile cracked his face. "And here I was, going on about how perfect the two of you were. You must think me the worst sort of fool."

Gib wrung his hands, his fingers numb from the cold he could no longer feel. "You're no fool. It's not common knowledge yet. It won't be until he returns—if he returns."

"This is why you wait for Kezra?" Zandi choked on a broken laugh, his eyes lowered to the cobblestone street beneath his boots. A shameful, terrible blush covered his face. "I should have known something was amiss. She's my pillar, too. Kezra is stronger than I've ever been."

146

"You couldn't have known. But yes. I wait for her in hopes she can offer some sort of comfort or wisdom."

"She will. She doesn't know she does it, but she does. I suppose you already know that though, being friends with her and all."

"I do."

Both men turned to look in the direction of the Rose Bouquet when the music momentarily faded away, until the silence was broken by a new song. Zandi straightened to his full height. "She'll be along shortly then. I, uh, I'll take my leave and hope you may find some way to forgive my egregious oversight."

Gib's heart hammered in his chest, and he found himself actually reaching for the other man. "Zandi, wait. This whole thing with Joel and me—"

The mage had already turned and begun to walk away. He looked back, only for the briefest of moments. "A secret, I know. I have many shortcomings, but I assure you, I'm well-schooled in keeping secrets. I'll tell no one."

"Thank you."

Zandi nodded his head once, slowly. "I wish you well, Gibben Nemesio of Willowdale. And I am sorry. Truly."

Somewhere in the distance Nawaz Arrio's whoop of laughter caught Gib's attention, and he glanced toward the tavern steps. Kezra was sure to be on her way. He turned back to Zandi a moment later, only to realize he'd already slipped away and was gone.

"I'm sorry, too," Gib whispered into the darkness. "I'm sorry for the death of your heroes."

CHAPTER EIGHT

The days passed by quickly in an endless procession of council meetings, leaving Joel feeling drained. He would have returned to the suite crawling at the end of each session had it been appropriate behavior. Somehow he did manage to drag himself to the privacy of his bedchamber, where he'd promptly collapse and spend the rest of the evening wondering why he'd ever volunteered to come here. Joel wasn't quite sure how his father and mentor managed to keep their sanity intact. Koal and Cenric were doing all the talking and negotiating—Joel only took notes and kept his mouth shut and *he* could barely remain rational.

Joel tapped the feathered end of his quill against the oak tabletop. They had just returned from one such meeting, and now he and Cenric sat at the only desk the suite offered and reviewed Joel's notes. Hasain lazed on the lounge behind them, and Joel could hear Koal's and NezReth's voices carrying in from the terrace as they talked in quiet voices to one another.

Noticeably absent was Liro. After the envoys had been dismissed from the council chamber, Liro had proclaimed he was going to the library and slipped away without awaiting a response. He'd been spending an abnormal amount of time by himself, and while it was no secret that Liro and Hasain were unable to tolerate the presence of one another, Joel had to wonder if Liro simply couldn't stomach being in the same room as him or if something deeper was going on.

*I wish he would speak to me. We used to be able to talk. We used to be open with each other. But now—*Joel's heart clenched. *Now there's a great wall between us. When I need his advice the most, he's shut me out.*

He stared at the notes before him but didn't actually see the words. They blurred together on the parchment. His mind drifted back to Gib—always to Gib. Had he moved on? Or like Joel, was he barely able to suppress his grief? *I hope he's at least talking to his friends about it. Surely they can offer comfort. I know I certainly could use someone to talk to right about now.*

But who was there, really? His father and Cenric were far too busy to pester, Liro had all but shut him out, and NezReth's uncanny silence made the Blessed Mage unapproachable. Out of all the envoys, Hasain seemed the best option. But he tended to be rude and haughty, and Joel wasn't sure he could deal with Hasain's abrasive opinions right then.

"Joel?" Cenric's voice cut through his disordered thoughts. "Did you remember to take notes on that last bit about Nales' request for full demilitarization on the northern border? Koal will need to mention it in his next report to the King."

Joel blinked. How long had his mentor been speaking to him? "What? I—I'm sorry." He winced at his own stupidity and could already feel warmth rushing to his cheeks. "I apologize. I've been distracted all day."

"No need to apologize," Cenric replied, sympathetic as always. "You've been working hard. Why don't we take a break, hmm?"

Joel breathed a sigh of relief. "That would be wonderful. My mind keeps drifting to those back home. I never imagined I'd miss my family so much."

Cenric's smile was warm, but his eyes reflected sadness of his own. "Aye. I know what you mean. I keep thinking of my two daughters. Gara's Naming Day celebration is only a sennight away. I don't suppose I'll be there to partake in the festivities with her."

Joel suppressed a frown. It disheartened him to witness his mentor in such low spirits. "I'm sure Gara understands why you can't be home. You do a great service to Arden by being here. She must know that."

"You're right. It just—at times, it gets to me." The ambassador set down his quill and leaned back in his chair. He remained quiet for a long pause, and Joel could tell something more weighed on his mind. Finally, he sighed and met Joel's gaze. "My youngest daughter Nia has also been in my thoughts. Tell me, Joel, this young man she wishes to marry, is he a good sort? You know him, don't you?"

"Nage? I know him a little. He's one of Gib's best friends. I know he was born into the most unfortunate of circumstances, but despite that, he's made a decent life for himself as a sentinel. Gib trusts him, and I trust Gib's judgment."

Cenric dipped his head in agreement. "I reckon Gib's a good judge of character—Koal wouldn't have taken him as an understudy if he wasn't—and I'm sure Nage will treat Nia with all the respect she deserves, should they be married. It's just—hard to let her go. It seems only yesterday she was an infant, and now, she wants to marry. Children grow up so fast."

Koal entered the room just then and took a seat on the lounge beside Hasain. "That they do. I don't envy the choice you must make, Cenric. As parents, it often feels it's our duty to keep our children under the protection of our wings forever."

"Ah, yes, but they'll never learn to fly that way." Cenric tilted his head to the side as he regarded Koal. "What of your own daughter, Seneschal? Joel tells me Heidi is requesting to be married herself."

Koal frowned. The creases around his mouth and eyes had never been more prominent than they were in that moment. *He's getting old*, Joel realized. *His age is finally catching up with him.* Joel had to wonder if the stress of his father's job was only hastening the aging process. Would he eventually work himself straight to the grave?

"Aye," Koal replied at length. "Heidi has turned a blind eye to every suitor to approach her. For three years, she's fixated herself on Nawaz Arrio. She's quite smitten by him."

"Really? No kidding." Cenric rubbed his chin absently. "Huh. Well I can't say I saw that match coming. Heidi's a little—" He paused, searching for the right word.

"Straight-laced?" Joel offered, trying not to chuckle.

A laugh escaped Cenric's pursed lips. "Indeed! And Nawaz Arrio is so—well, they seem to be two completely different people."

Joel kept his personal feelings on the matter to himself. The truth was, Nawaz just wasn't interested in pursuing a relationship with Heidi. Wasn't that obvious enough by the way Nawaz hung off Kezra Malin-Rai's arm at the Rose Bouquet? *Heidi needs to open her eyes and see reason. The reality is that Nawaz's heart already belongs to another.*

Koal sighed, reaching up to massage his temples. "I promised my wife I'd give Heidi a definitive answer when I came home. I know she thinks she loves Nawaz, but I have my doubts he reciprocates such feelings."

To Joel's surprise, it was Hasain who spoke next. The young Radek lord cleared his throat and turned his dark eyes onto Koal. "I believe marriage would do Nawaz well. He's young and brash, but all he really needs is a bit of structure in his life. Heidi would be a good fit for him. She could ground him, and I truly feel he'd settle down and take responsibility as her husband and a man."

Joel had to bite his tongue to remain silent. He could barely believe what he was hearing. Hasain and Nawaz were best friends. Why was Hasain pushing for Nawaz to marry Heidi when he *knew* how much his comrade liked Kezra? What game was Hasain playing?

Meeting Hasain's stare, Koal nodded once but the frown on his mouth betrayed his conflict. "I suppose you know him best. You and Nawaz have always been close friends."

"I do know Nawaz," Hasain replied. "And I would never suggest the idea if it wasn't in his best interest. Nawaz needs guidance. Having a wife to care for would surely keep him on a good path."

Joel glared openly at Hasain. Exactly *whose* best interest would it be in for Nawaz to marry Heidi? Surely neither Nawaz nor Heidi's! Why was Hasain suddenly so invested in the future of his friend? A terrible thought hit Joel like a bag of bricks. *Daya! His words aren't sincere. He doesn't care about Nawaz's future. He just wants to ensure Nawaz doesn't marry Kezra. If Nawaz marries Heidi, Hasain would be free to pursue Kezra. He wants her for himself.*

Joel had witnessed Hasain's jealousy at the Rose Bouquet firsthand.

He'd seen the way his cousin acted when Nawaz and Kezra arrived together. He'd noticed the rage in Hasain's eyes. Dread tugged at Joel's heart. Was Hasain truly putting his own selfish desires ahead of his best friend's happiness? This wasn't the Hasain that Joel had grown up with. What was Hasain thinking?

"It's certainly something to consider," Koal said. "I know Nawaz has a good head on his shoulders. I only worry his heart isn't in the right place."

The glint in Hasain's eyes was unsettling. "Give his heart time to adjust. Heidi's a good match. He'll quickly realize he was an idiot for not marrying her sooner."

A deep sigh escaped Koal's slanted mouth. "Perhaps. No matter, now isn't the time to dedicate thought to Heidi and Nawaz's potential arrangement."

It was just as well they ended the conversation when they did, for a moment later, a swift knock came from the door. Out of habit, Joel began to rise from his chair, but Koal motioned for his son to sit and crossed the room to answer the call.

Archmage Adrian Titus waited in the corridor—and Liro was with him. Standing side by side and both dressed in shimmering golden robes, the two men could have been twins, if not for the contrasting color of their hair.

Joel's heart sunk. Why was Liro with Adrian? He was supposed to be at the library. Was it possible he had lied about his whereabouts? *Stop jumping to conclusions. It's possible he crossed paths with Adrian in the hall. And even if they have been speaking, Liro knows better than to reveal anything of importance about Arden—doesn't he?*

Koal greeted the Archmage with a small bow, though he never once looked away from Liro. "Archmage Titus, to what do we owe the pleasure?"

Adrian returned the gesture, his words equally devoid of mirth. "I come with good tidings. His Grace, Emperor Sarpedon, has extended an invitation to your party."

"An invitation?"

"Father," Liro spoke, his voice a careful cool. "We've been invited to attend the match this afternoon."

Koal's brow furrowed. "Match? What match?"

A smirk crossed Liro's mouth as he stuck his nose farther into the air. "The gladiator match taking place within the amphitheater. It's the talk of the entire city. You hadn't heard?"

Koal's words were deliberate and slow. "No, I hadn't."

Adrian barely allowed Koal to finish before replying. "I can inform His Grace of your acceptance then?" It was formed as a question, though Joel was sure it was anything but.

"No," Koal said, shaking his head. "We must politely decline. Blood sport is forbidden in Arden, and I'm afraid its entertainment would be lost on us."

Liro's cold eyes narrowed into slits. Joel could see the mask of rage written across his brother's face.

The Archmage was likewise displeased. "I would reconsider your decision, Seneschal." The hostile clip in Adrian's voice couldn't be ignored. He turned frigid blue eyes onto Koal, and Joel could feel the hair on the back of his neck stand on end. "Emperor Sarpedon has requested his distinguished guests from Arden attend. He would be most displeased should you not accept the invitation."

Silence filled every corner of the suite. Joel held his breath. Out of the corner of his eye, he could see Hasain frozen on the edge of his seat, face drawn and pale. NezReth remained quiet as he watched from the shadows, and even Koal seemed to be at a loss for words.

Cenric, however, swiftly recovered. "You're correct, Archmage. We wouldn't want to displease our host. Emperor Sarpedon has been gracious to extend an invitation to us. Of course we'll attend."

Koal clamped his mouth shut. He didn't offer to speak, but his furious eyes spoke volumes.

"Good," Adrian replied, smug satisfaction dripping from his words. "I'll leave you to prepare then." The Archmage turned on one heel and departed.

As soon as they were alone, Koal slammed the door shut and whirled around to face Liro. "What in hell were you thinking, fraternizing with the enemy?"

Liro crossed his arms over his chest. "Now that's a bold accusation to make, Father."

"Don't take that tone with me!" Koal barked.

Joel flinched, wishing he could disappear into the shadows and forgo listening to his father and brother argue.

Liro's eyes glinted dangerously as he responded. "I was merely on my way back to the suite when Master Titus and I stumbled upon one another. I saw no harm in walking the rest of the way here with him. And when did we determine the Northern Empire to be our enemy? It seems to me they've been nothing if not hospitable and more than sympathetic to Arden's plight."

"Horseshit!" Koal spat so harshly that even Hasain winced away from the seneschal's words. "In case you've forgotten, it's not up to you to align our countries. At this rate, the Emperor will be expecting us to sign some sort of treaty or have our royal children marrying theirs."

"And would that be such a bad idea?" countered Liro. "Think of the sway Arden would hold over our neighboring countries if we had the power of the Northern Empire to back us. No one would dare threaten our borders ever again. No arrangements have yet been made for Deegan or Gudrin. A marital alliance for either of them would only stand to strengthen Arden."

Koal threw his hands in the air. Joel couldn't even breathe as he watched his father begin to pace. "It was a mistake to bring you. The longer you're here, the more I see it."

The silence engulfed them like a thick fog. Joel could barely raise his eyes to steal a glance at his brother and, when Joel did, the sight almost undid him. Always so stone-cold and unflinching, Liro's perfect mask shuddered and failed for the briefest moment. Hopeless anguish flashed behind his clouded eyes only to be crushed and replaced with hatred so powerful it sent a chill soaring down Joel's spine.

Liro lowered his voice to a quiet hiss. "Your true feelings never cease to amaze me, Father."

Koal may have flinched, but he covered it quickly. "Don't try to play to my sympathies. You know full well what you're doing and what sort of treachery you're promoting. The whole purpose of us coming here was a new attempt for the Northern Empire to absorb Arden. Rishi was right. Sarpedon won't rest until he has us under his thumb."

"Assumptions are dangerous things," Liro replied, raising his chin into the air and looking like Neetra for all the world. "Why should we take to heart the prejudiced opinion of one foolish, cowardly boy hoping to escape the duties he swore to his country?"

Hasain leapt to his feet, hands balled into fists at his sides. "How *dare* you! You would openly mock the King? Call him foolish? A coward?"

Liro lifted one brow but kept his face blank. "If the shoe fits, I suppose."

"My father is a good and noble king! His past is irrelevant! Look at all he's done for our country! He's brought peace and prosperity to our lands, treated with neighboring countries, raised the quality of life for everyone, not just the wealthy. Because of his rule, Arden has moved forward to embrace all of her people, not only the privileged few!"

"And when we are overrun with uneducated peasants, who will defend our country? When all our traditions have been torn apart and sent to hell, where will Arden's strength come from? The women soldiers or the illiterate farmers?"

Hasain swept forward, coming dangerously close to Liro. "You're still worried about losing your power, aren't you? You don't care for the people of Arden, only yourself and your privilege."

"That's something, coming from the king's bastard son who's still riding his father's coattails."

Hasain launched himself at the other man, but Koal stepped in before the first blow could fall. He shoved Hasain back and glared at the two young men. "Enough of this, both of you! We're in the Empire. Our focus needs to be here."

No one moved or said anything for what felt like an eternity, but finally, Cenric cleared his throat. "Agreed, and all of that aside, an invitation has been extended to us here and now. A course of action must be chosen."

"Invitation? More like an order," Hasain muttered under his breath, still glaring at Liro.

Cenric turned his hazel eyes to Koal. "What say you? Do we attend this gladiator tournament?"

A deep sigh escaped the seneschal's mouth. He stared beyond them all, looking out onto the terrace, his eyes distant and filled to the brim with worry. "What choice have we now?"

"What choice did we ever have?" Joel whispered.

Stagnant silence settled over the envoys, filling every corner of the suite, until Koal whirled around, his features hard and determined once again. "Go. Prepare yourselves. We leave in a mark. And may The Two forgive us for bearing witness to such travesty." He stormed toward his private quarters without another word.

Joel glanced up when Cenric touched his shoulder. Finding it difficult to swallow, Joel flashed his mentor a false smile. "So, this gladiator match, is it—will there be—will people—die?"

Cenric sighed, hanging his head in defeat. "Blood sport has always been an integrated part of Imperial culture."

"But how can they allow it?" Joel blurted. "How can they allow people—humans—to fight to the death? To *slaughter* one another as though they're cattle?" He wrapped his arms around himself, feeling chilled to the bone despite the humid air blowing in from the terrace.

"The Imperial people believe death by combat is one of the most honorable ways a man can die." Cenric rubbed the back of his neck absently. "Many of the gladiators who fight believe they'll find redemption in the afterlife."

"Well, they certainly won't find it in *this* life," Liro remarked in a snide tone. He turned to look at Joel, leveling him with a cruel gaze. "Don't waste time pitying them, brother. Most within the arena are convicted murderers and thieves—uncouth vagrants, unworthy of forgiveness. May the Blessed Son have mercy on their damned souls."

"It's not our place to pass judgment, young Lord Adelwijn," Cenric warned as he passed by Liro. "Now come, both of you. We're obligated to attend the tournament. Let's get it over with."

Liro scowled at the ambassador's back as Cenric departed the room. Joel found his brother's glare to be most troubling.

Gib squeezed through the crowded hall leading to Marc's office, praying time was still on his side. Although honestly, he knew he had little reason to worry. Marc was probably not even ready to leave for the meeting.

The dean was notorious for being the last to arrive for council and the first out the door when it ended. Likewise, Marc wasn't known for his insight or wisdom but, rather, as a peace keeper. It had been a gamble to have him take Koal's vacant seat, and so far, Neetra hadn't been kind. The High Councilor took every opportunity to point out any flaws or weaknesses Marc might have. It was hardly any wonder King Rishi seemed to be on a rapid decline.

Gib locked his jaw and tried not to think about it. The envoys had been gone for almost an entire moonturn now. Marc and the King just needed to hold on until their return.

As Gib reached the office door, a strange foreboding rose within him. The door was slightly ajar. Had Marc already left and accidentally forgotten to lock up? Gib knocked as he peeked inside, not wanting to seem too forward, but also a bit worried. The office was never left open.

When it became apparent no one was going to answer, he slipped past the threshold. Inside, his attention was drawn to Marc's cluttered desk and belongings. If Gib hadn't known any better, he would have reason to believe these were signs of a struggle—but time had taught him well. The dean was just a messy worker.

Gib shook his head and called out. "Marc? Are you here?"

No immediate answer came, but Gib thought he heard a sound from the closet and decided to investigate. He hesitated before opening the door. It felt too personal to be peeking around, but he soothed himself with the knowledge that he wasn't doing it to snoop. Gib pulled the heavy oak door open.

Nothing. Only crates overflowing with paperwork containing who-knew-what. Gib had to stifle a laugh. Marc really was a slob.

"I'm tellin' you, he's breathing down the back of my neck all the time. He won't leave me alone!"

Nawaz's voice carried from the hall and sounded as if it were drawing closer. Gib cursed at himself for entering the office without permission.

"He has a point, you know." Marc was with Nawaz. They were likely both on their way in. "You're not a boy anymore. At eighteen, with a fine job as a healer, you should be looking for a wife."

Gib winced. Damn it all to hell. Not only was he in a place he shouldn't be, but he was also likely to be immersed into a conversation he wanted nothing to do with. When their shadows fell across the open door, he sucked in a breath and tried to look as confident—and innocent—as possible.

"Why in hell is this open?" Gib heard the dean mutter.

155

A split second later, Marc burst inside, dark eyes on fire. Gib refused to jump, but his throat may have let forth an undignified squeak.

Marc's face relaxed when he saw Gib. "What are you doing in here? And why did you leave the door open?"

Heat blossomed on Gib's cheeks, and even though neither Marc nor Nawaz seemed to be judging him, he still felt the need to explain himself. "I didn't! I came to join you for the meeting, and the door was already open. I was concerned, so I came in to make sure everything was all right."

Marc slapped Nawaz on the shoulder. "See? I told you, this door is broken. This is the third time in as many days I've found it ajar."

Nawaz had already turned his crystal eyes to the jamb and was examining both hinges and latch. "I don't see anything wrong with it. It hasn't always slipped the bolt, has it?" He took to one knee and peered into the place where the bar was meant to catch the frame.

"No." Marc went to gather the things on his desk. He silently motioned for Gib to fetch a bag and stacked what would be needed for the council meeting into a disordered pile. "It's only been the last few days. I'll have to get a smith to look at it."

"You might want to have a mage ward it," Nawaz suggested in a low voice.

Marc stuffed his things into his pack and very deliberately didn't make eye contact with his nephew. "Why would I do that?"

Nawaz gave Gib a desperate look, and Gib knew he was being called upon for help. "Nawaz may be right. With you as the acting seneschal and this being a new problem, you can't be too careful."

"Ridiculous, both of you! What would anyone want in here anyway? School records? Healers notes? *Old* healers notes at that—"

"Uncle, please," Nawaz pleaded. "Just this once, err on the side of caution."

Silence among such loud men was most uncomfortable, and Gib wished he could hide under the desk or leave the room. Marc resisted for only a moment longer before hanging his head. "All right. I'll talk to Rishi about it—after the meeting and not in front of Neetra."

Nawaz rolled his eyes. "Right. Because he's nothing but trouble and you know it."

"You're against him because you don't want to marry."

Nawaz folded his arms over his chest. "I'm against him because he's been against me from the moment we met! Koal knows it too, as well as the King. Neetra is a snake, and he's done nothing but make trouble since Koal stepped through that portal!"

Gib's stomach flopped. It was true. The very day Koal and the other envoys departed, Neetra resumed his campaign to lower the draft age. General Morathi had also come forward to speak about his dislike for the female soldiers, who apparently were "holding back the progress and morale of the army." Each day was an endless battle in the council room. The tension was building to a crescendo. Gib could feel it, and he was sure everyone else could too.

Marc picked up his pack and swung it over a shoulder, motioning for Gib to follow him. "You're not telling me anything I wasn't already aware of. I have to go now. Rishi is probably beside himself wondering where I am." He gave his nephew a severe stare. "Remember to go check on your aunt for me. She has to rest throughout the day or her ankles swell and her back hurts so much that neither of us get any sleep."

Gib chuckled. "The baby is already causing trouble? It's not even here yet."

"Right. Our hands are going to be full when it arrives."

A small laugh rippled between them, but Gib noticed Nawaz didn't join in. The young lord seemed ill at ease as he shifted his weight from one foot to the other.

"You'll consider my offer, uncle?"

Marc's shoulders visibly tensed. "Nawaz—"

"Consider it. You know I could be useful on the Eastern border."

Marc lowered his voice. "It's a hell of a stretch for you to relocate just to avoid marriage. It's dangerous out there!"

Gib stared at his feet. He'd hoped to avoid this conversation. Even as he listened to the desperate words, he couldn't help but think of Heidi and the broken look they'd shared a moon cycle earlier. Kezra weighed equally heavily on his mind as she seemed to be well suited with Nawaz.

"I don't care if I never marry," Nawaz replied. "But if I do, I damned well want to wed the one I love."

"Have you asked her?" Marc asked. "Your Kezra? You said Neetra doesn't care who you marry, just so long as—"

Nawaz laughed brokenly. "*My* Kezra? Kezra belongs to no one, and she won't marry me." He retched on the acid truth, drawing Gib's pity. "I asked her in a roundabout way not long ago. She won't do it. She won't marry anyone, ever. I'm sure of it."

Gib didn't doubt it. Kezra was one of his dearest friends and a fine warrior, but she was also independent. She'd told Gib before that she never had any intention of marrying or having children. "I shouldn't have to," she'd said. "Why are all women expected to marry and have children? Is that all Arden thinks we're any good for? My blade is as deadly as any man's, but no one cares about that. They care only that I can bear sons."

"Then why is Heidi such a bad option?" Marc implored.

He wasn't trying to hurt Nawaz, but his nephew recoiled as though he'd been burned. "I never said Heidi was a bad choice! It's just—she's not *my* choice. She's a good girl, but I don't want her. I don't know if I could ever love her. She deserves someone who'll be good to her, someone who'll hang off of her like—"

"Like she hangs off of you?" Marc hit the nail on the head.

Nawaz's face pinched. His crystal eyes froze over in an instant, and not a trace of smile could be found. "You know what? Never mind. I'm clearly not talking to the right person about this." He stepped toward the door.

Marc floundered, reaching out with one hand. "Wait! Wait just a moment. I'm sorry. I didn't mean it like that."

"No. You go to your meeting. I'm sorry I bothered you." Nawaz turned and stormed from the room.

Marc's mouth moved without a sound, and his dark eyes followed Nawaz's back until the young lord's blue jerkin disappeared into the sea of students beyond the door. The dean dropped his arm to his side. "Damn it! I'm no good at this. Now I've hurt him, too."

Gib placed a hand on Marc's forearm and directed him away from the office. Making sure the door was latched, Gib stayed at his mentor's side as they started their trek to the palace. "He'll cool down. Nawaz has a hot temper sometimes."

Marc followed behind Gib rather than lead the way. Deep, all encompassing fear fogged Marc's normally cheerful brown eyes. "I don't know how long I can keep doing this, Gib. Koal needs to come back before Neetra breaks down Arden and Nawaz both!"

"Why does Neetra suddenly want Nawaz married anyway? Is there a reason for it? Is it about inheritances? Does Neetra not want to have to give Nawaz anything from his estate?"

Marc barked a humorless laugh. "Neetra wouldn't give anything to Nawaz if his life depended on it. He's only ever tolerated the boy, and just barely that. No, Neetra doesn't want to be tied to him any more. If he can get Nawaz married off then Neetra's legal obligations end there."

"What if Nawaz refuses?"

"Then Neetra will take his crest. He'll be stripped of his title."

Marc said it as if it was no big deal, as if it wouldn't shatter Nawaz beyond repair. Gib couldn't imagine what it would be like to have been born with authority and power only to have them both snatched away on a whim.

"He wouldn't be a lord anymore? Can Neetra even do that?"

They passed through the gate to the palace with little more than a nod to the guard. Marc sighed. "He can in this circumstance. Nawaz isn't Neetra's son. Nawaz is only a lord because Neetra 'showed him favor' and granted Nawaz the title after marrying Bahari. If he disowns Nawaz—and he will if Nawaz doesn't do as he's told—then Nawaz stands to lose everything."

Bile rose up the back of Gib's throat. Neetra was despicable. Did he really think so little of his stepson? Nawaz was loud and rough around the edges, but he wasn't a bad man. Why did Neetra continue to push Nawaz away?

"You know what I think," Marc pressed on. "I think maybe Neetra wants to make a match for Inan and can't do it until Nawaz is out of the way. I mean, I don't know for sure, but time will tell."

Gib shuddered. He supposed it was all fine and well that he hadn't been born with a title or the responsibility that went along with it. He enjoyed not having to worry about marriage or retaining a family crest.

Allowing the conversation to fizzle out, they proceeded the rest of the way in silence. The hall outside the council room stood empty, save for a small gathering of men. King Rishi waited by the high wooden door, surrounded by an entourage—Aodan, Didier, and Crowned Prince Deegan, as well as a handful of palace guards.

Marc picked up his pace as he and Gib drew closer. "Oh, hell. You didn't have to wait out here for me!"

Gib tried not to stare at King Rishi's haggard face. Dark circles had formed under the ruler's eyes, and his skin was blanched a sickly white color.

King Rishi looked down his nose at Marc. "It wouldn't do for me to enter without my acting seneschal. It's not as if we could start without you."

"I suppose, but you didn't have to wait out in the hall!"

The King hesitated, casting a wary look around. "I can't—I can't go in there alone. If I have to listen to that imbecile rant and rave one more time I may hang myself."

Gib sucked in a sharp breath, and Prince Deegan's youthful face pinched. They could have heard a pin drop for the lack of sound. No one dared say anything, though Diddy met Gib's eyes with a look of abject terror. This kind of talk was so unlike King Rishi. Was Neetra truly wearing him down so quickly?

Marc's cold laugh echoed across the empty corridor. "Come on now, it's not so bad." He smiled, but even Gib could tell it wasn't as bright as usual.

King Rishi clenched one fist and raised it to his chest. His breaths came out in ragged wisps of air, and for a moment, Gib worried for the King's well being. He wouldn't pass out, would he? Was the stress of running a country without his Right Hand too much for him to bear?

Deegan looked up at the King and pursed his lips, looking very much like Koal, the boy's uncle. Actually, Gib noted absently, the Crowned Prince favored the Adelwijn side of his family. He looked very little like his sire, though the brooding quality in his dark eyes was reminiscent of Hasain.

Diddy put a hand on the King's shoulder. "Father." He didn't say anything more, but King Rishi seemed to take strength from the small gesture.

King Rishi locked his jaw. "Koal needs to return before I go mad."

"Neetra's insufferable." Gib had voiced his opinion before he could think to censor himself. Both princes nodded in agreement, and even Aodan grunted his assent.

"Oh hell, enough of this pity party." The bodyguard's rough voice filled the empty hall. "Koal will be back when he's able. In the meantime, the two of you have ta keep that bastard in there from turnin' Arden on its head." He met the King's sulking sneer and pointed to the door. "Ya know Koal would say the same. Now get in there, both of ya."

Groaning, Marc reached for the door handle. "He's right. Waiting gives the demons time. Let's just do it."

With a heave, the door was pulled open, and Gib watched as Marc and the King marched inside. The palace sentinels began to follow, and Gib quirked a brow. That was peculiar. He couldn't recall a time the royal guards had been called *inside* the council room.

Before the last soldier could cross the threshold, Aodan grabbed the soldier's arm and snarled, "Remember, yer all to be watchin' the King. This isn't a time for a nap or screwin' around. You have the Queen's orders."

The royal guardsman bowed so low the crest of his helm nearly brushed the floor. "Yes, Master Galloway."

Aodan waved the sentinel off before turning on his heel. He narrowed his single eye at Diddy. "All right, let's go."

Diddy wordlessly climbed the stairs that would take them to the balcony. Gib hesitated. What was going on? "All due respect, Sir Aodan, but why are you coming with us?" No answer came immediately, and he could feel his ears and cheeks beginning to burn. Perhaps he wasn't meant to question these odd circumstances.

It was the youngest prince who finally responded. Crowned Prince Deegan pointed at Aodan's back. "Mother has agreed to allow me to sit in on the council meeting, but she gave express instructions for how I was to be guarded."

The curt look on the bodyguard's face suggested he wasn't entirely happy with the assignment. Aodan cut a glare back at them both but spoke directly to Deegan. "Aye, an' just remember that I'm not wipin' any noses or kissin' any scrapes. This is a meeting of men an' if ya plan on ever comin' back, ya need to behave like an adult."

Prince Deegan's face remained stoic while Aodan watched, but as soon as his back was turned, a devious smile flashed across the young royal's mouth. Gib had to hold back a grin of his own. There. Deegan looked more like his father now.

"Sit where Diddy tells ya an' keep yer mouth shut," Aodan ordered.

Diddy scooted down to his usual seat and patted the empty one beside him. He kept his voice a light whisper. "Here, Deegan. Hasain's seat."

Gib swallowed, trying to ward off the nausea rising in his guts. Was having the young Crowned Prince attend the meeting a way for King Rishi to prepare for the worst? Was he filling Hasain's seat in the event his eldest son didn't return? Gib tried desperately not to think about it too much. *They're going to come back. The envoys will be all right. Joel will be all right.*

Deegan stuck his nose in the air as the understudies of the other councilors watched his every move. As the prince took his seat with all the dignity of an overstuffed peacock, Gib could *feel* their eyes on his back, watching the Crowned Prince and his entourage. Gib had to wonder how the royal family tolerated such constant scrutiny.

As if to answer Gib's thoughts, Deegan turned a grave look onto their audience. "The show is over. You may pick your chins off the floor now." With red faces, the understudies promptly redirected their gazes.

Gib bit the inside of his cheek to keep from grinning even as Aodan swatted the back of the young prince's head. "Enough sass!"

Down below, Neetra Adelwijn's pompous voice rose above the din. "Well, it *is* about time, Highness. You could have sent word to let us know if you wanted us to meet at a later time."

Any good humor in the balcony instantly died as Gib turned his attention to the council table. King Rishi's features were set in a hard, emotionless veil, and his voice was but a sigh, tired and lacking any real fire. "Had I known you had more pressing matters to attend to, High Councilor, I would have gladly granted you permission to take leave. Even now the offer stands, if you wish to go."

Neetra snorted a haughty laugh. "I will not abandon post so easily, Highness." He made a vague gesture toward Koal's seat, currently occupied by Marc. "How is our seneschal? Have you received word from him recently?"

King Rishi's fist clenched tight on the table top, but before he could open his mouth to respond, Marc spoke up. "We have Seneschal Koal's notes from the Northern Empire here. However, we'll wait for everyone to be present." He nodded toward an empty chair near the end of the table. "Has anyone seen Diedrick Lyle? It's not like him to be late."

Gib frowned. Marc was right. That was odd. Always one of the first to arrive for council, Lyle had been punctual for as long as Gib could remember.

"Lord Lyle is typically a very responsible member of our council," Neetra huffed. "I trust he will have an excuse for his tardiness. Should we start without him?"

The councilors glanced around the table at one another, and the general opinion seemed to be receptive to the idea, but even as they chose to commence without him, the doors swung open and a harried looking Diedrick swept inside.

Red faced, he went to his seat immediately, uttering a vague and unsatisfactory excuse. "Apologies. I was held up."

Neetra's smug voice carried above the table. "Well, we're all here. Shall we proceed, Highness?"

King Rishi's face was white as he called the meeting to order. "Very well, High Councilor."

A mark hadn't yet passed when a man appeared at their door to take them to the amphitheater. Joel's stomach knotted as their guide led him and the other envoys through the palace gates and into the city. Sunlight poured through the magic veil above, but the rays felt harsh against his skin and did nothing to lighten his dark mood. No one spoke as they walked.

The streets bustled with people. In stark contrast to the envoys, most of them chattered amongst themselves as they went about their business. Joel imagined he and his comrades must have appeared as though they were going to a burial service. He grimaced. *Partially true. How many warriors will I be forced to watch die today?* Joel tried not to think about it as he followed behind Cenric.

A great fortress crafted from limestone and marble loomed ahead. Stone columns climbed so high they blotted out the sun and cast dark shadows across the city below. Great statuaries were carved into the rock, each depicting mighty Imperial warriors, dressed head to toe in armor and bearing longswords and shields. Their square, angled faces were sculpted with such fine detail they could have been real. Unblinking stone eyes stared down at the citizens of Teivel in the streets below. Joel sucked in a sharp breath of air. He knew it was ridiculous, but he felt as though those lifeless, marble eyes were reading the depths of his soul.

The uncanny sensation finally ebbed when the guide led them through a tunnel at the base of the building. Torches lined the interior of the tunnel, illuminating damp, mossy walls. The temperature inside dropped enough that Joel wished he'd brought a cloak. At the far end of the corridor, light poured through an arched gateway. Joel nearly had to sprint to keep up as they moved straight toward the light source. His stomach rolled with anxiety.

Joel's mouth hung ajar as they passed through the other end of the tunnel. A vast arena lay below. A pit of white sand served as the performance area, surrounded by three tiers of seating and a brick wall dividing the arena from the spectators. Two barred gates on opposing ends of the playing field led below ground and seemed to be the only way in or out of the arena. Joel imagined once the gates were lowered, the only method of escape would be victory in the ring—or death.

He shuddered and looked away from the pit, choosing to focus his attention on the spectator area instead. All around him, patricians dressed in clothing more aptly suited for a wedding or great feast conversed with one another. Servants bustled from one person to the next, offering wine and sweet treats from platters. Light, cheerful music drifted on the breeze, and Joel was shocked when he realized an ensemble of musicians played beneath a nearby awning.

Disgust passed across Joel's face as he looked from one courtier to the next. Didn't they know they were about to watch people *slay* each other? Why were they acting as though they were attending a party? This wasn't a time for food and music. It was a time for mourning! In a matter of minutes, people were going to *die*. How could these spectators be so nonchalant? He didn't have time to delve further as their guide motioned for them to follow him to the Emperor's box.

Emperor Lichas sat front and center on a dais above the pit. Adrian Titus lounged to the Emperor's immediate right, and beside the Archmage were the two Shiraz princes and Chancellor Garron. To the Emperor's left sat a beautiful young woman with elaborately woven blonde hair and a stunning lavender dress fit for a queen. The other members of the royal court lounged on plush, velvet cushions behind the Emperor's party. A silk canopy tented them, preventing the midday sun from touching their skin and eyes.

The guide stepped before the dais and took to one knee. "Your Grace, your distinguished guests have arrived."

Emperor Lichas lifted his chalice, and immediately a servant boy was by his side to fill it. "Be welcomed to the amphitheater, visitors from Arden. You've come to Teivel at the most opportune time. Thrice a year, our mighty gladiators battle for fame and glory within the arena, and today promises to be a match the people will talk about for years to come."

Joel bent forward, staring at the dusty marble steps as he bowed alongside the others. He could feel the Emperor's cold stare pass across the group of envoys without needing to glance up, and a sudden fear gripped his heart. What if he couldn't do this? What if he was unable to watch the match? Did he stand to get into trouble?

"As always, your hospitality is most generous, Your Grace," Koal said, rising to his full height once again.

Lichas motioned to the woman sitting beside him. "This is my wife, Cassia."

The young woman rose to her feet, extending her hand to Koal.

Koal took hold of it. His large, calloused hand dwarfed hers. "It's a pleasure to meet you, Empress. Words cannot accurately describe your beauty."

Cassia nodded regally and replied in a soft, well-rehearsed voice, "Thank you, Seneschal of Arden. I hope you've found Teivel to your liking

163

thus far."

"We have, Empress."

"It pleases me to hear that, Seneschal," she replied, her tone lukewarm. When Koal released her hand, Cassia bowed hastily and returned to her cushion. She did not once make eye contact with her husband.

The Emperor cleared his throat. "Envoys, take a seat. The match will commence shortly—" He narrowed his eyes in Joel's direction, and for a brief moment, the mage thought he'd done something to offend the ruler. But no, the Emperor was glaring *beyond* Joel, at someone else. "Ah, Alerio, there you are. Tardy, as usual."

"Your Grace," Prince Alerio greeted, locking his jaw in a most stubborn display. He'd somehow managed to approach undetected, perhaps because no flock of courtiers hung from his arm today. The sunlight reflected off his golden crown and hair as he bowed to his sire. "Please forgive my lateness."

"You are forgiven," the Emperor sighed. "Go take your seat."

Alerio's shrewd eyes flashed toward the envoys. "May I propose Lord Hasain Radek and his peers sit with my party during the match?"

Joel glanced at Hasain in time to see the young lord's shoulders tense. Koal frowned as well but said nothing. *Sit where? Is Alerio not sitting with the rest of his family?*

Emperor Lichas took a sip from his chalice, watching the envoys carefully from the corner of his eye. "If Hasain Radek and his peers desire to sit with you, they may."

Joel swallowed. The Emperor had phrased his words as though they had the option to decline, but did they really? Or was this the same as the Emperor's invitation?

"What say you, Lord Hasain?" Alerio asked. His smooth voice unsettled Joel's nerves. "The other lords and I would quite enjoy your company. You as well, Lords Liro and Joel Adelwijn."

Hasain's uncertain eyes flashed toward Koal, clearly seeking some kind of answer from the seneschal. Joel could feel his own heart racing.

I don't want to go sit with them. What if they mean to pry for information? Father told us not to discuss Arden with any of these Imperials. Can I refuse to answer questions, or will such behavior be perceived as rude? Joel stole a glance at Liro, doubting his brother would be able to contain his own personal opinions. *This is a bad idea.*

Koal gave no spoken answer, but his pale blue eyes met Hasain's dark ones, and some form of silent, mutual understanding passed between the seneschal and the young Radek. Joel thought he understood, too. This was Hasain's decision to make. He was the son of the King. To ask permission in front of these Imperial highborns would have painted him in a bad light. In this instance, he couldn't afford to show any weakness.

Hasain straightened his back, voice steady and assured despite the wariness he surely must have felt. "It would be an honor to accompany you, Prince. We accept your invitation."

Joel's pulse thudded in his ears, louder than thunder or violent deluge. So it was decided.

"Very good," Alerio replied, motioning for them to follow.

Cenric touched Joel's shoulder as he passed. "We'll find you at the end of the match." The ambassador's tepid smile and gingerly spoken words did little to settle Joel's stomach.

He followed behind Hasain, Liro, and the prince. Leaving the dais behind, they climbed to the third and highest tier of seating, where a silk awning shadowed a private viewing box. Joel cast aside his worry long enough to gawk at the scenery. From way up here, the panoramic view of the amphitheater was incredible. He began to grow dizzy staring at the gathered courtiers in the stands below and had to focus his attention elsewhere.

Two youthful, well-dressed men waited in the private box. They were as different from one another as night was from day—one stout with coarse, light brown hair, the other towering above his companion, with wispy blond hair and sharp azure eyes.

Prince Alerio gestured toward them as he moved beneath the canopy. "Lord Balios Theron, son of Councilor Theron. And my cousin, Lord Stavros Sarpedon. These are Lord Hasain Radek, son of King Rishi Radek, and Lords Liro and Joel Adelwijn—our guests from Arden." Both men nodded cordially and uttered quiet greetings, but Joel sensed no gregariousness from either lord.

Alerio tapped the limestone bench. "Have a seat." He flagged down a servant as Joel and the others seated themselves, and a moment later, wine was being poured for the party. Joel accepted a gilded chalice, if only to be polite. He grasped it between his fingers, thankful that by holding the goblet, he wouldn't be tempted to wring his hands.

Balios, who sat on the opposite side of the prince, glanced around his peer to stare at the foreign lords. "My prince has informed me this is your first visit to our grand empire. Have you found it to your liking so far?"

"Teivel is extravagant," Liro responded as he accepted a drink. "In comparison, Silver City looks like an unkempt hovel." He chuckled darkly. "Of course, Silver is brimming with vagrants, thieves, waifs, and other undesirables. They serve no purpose other than to tarnish our otherwise beautiful city. I must say, I stand impressed when I look upon Teivel. It seems you've found a way to purge your streets of such *uncouth* company."

Balios nodded, his mouth twitching as the telltale signs of a smirk flashed across his thin lips. "The scum is kept outside the dome, on the outskirts of the city."

Joel held back the urge to glower. He knew it would be unwise to state his own opinion or scold Liro for voicing his, so Joel remained silent.

"As it should be," Alerio sneered. "Even still, the peasants are an ugly smear against our white walls. If I were Emperor, I'd have half a mind to send the Imperial army outside the dome to slaughter the whole lot of them."

Joel could only think of Gib and his family. Had they all been born here, Gib would be one of those "ugly smears." Would Joel have held the same opinion as Alerio and his friends? Would he have been so cruel as to wish for Gib to be slaughtered simply because of his birth status? Joel's chest ached at the thought of it.

"It would free up space for those more deserving," Balios chuckled. "The dome could be extended once the filth was washed away."

Joel couldn't take any more. He *had* to say something. His voice sounded foreign to him. "If not for your peasants, who would service your country?" Liro's deadly glare burned into his brother, but he couldn't stop now that he'd begun. "Surely you wouldn't have your elite doing the lowly, mundane tasks required to keep your grand city afloat."

The prince's eyes speared Joel as sharply as any blade. "Our best servants have long bloodlines, Lord Adelwijn. They are more than capable of doing any job an uneducated, unrefined vagrant could do."

Tense silence grew around them, and Joel locked his jaw to keep from saying more. He glared at his boots and wished desperately for the heat in his cheeks to subside.

After a moment, Hasain cleared his throat, stepping up to make amends for Joel's folly. "Apologies, Prince Alerio. Arden's guidelines are so very different from your own. We haven't enough servants to be rid of our lower class just yet, no matter how unsavory they may be."

Joel wanted to be offended. He wanted to shout at Hasain to take it back. Gib wasn't unsavory! Nor were his family or friend Nage. Being commonborn was no crime, and it didn't make a person less desirable. He wanted to fuel his rage but knew better. Hasain had just saved Joel's neck.

Alerio waved the wine server away and turned to address Hasain directly. "How fare the council sessions between our lands? You've been meeting for a moonturn now. I would hope to hear good news."

Hasain took a delicate sip from his chalice before gracing the Imperial prince with a response. "Despite our differences, we've made progress restoring harmony between our nation and yours."

"And what of Shiraz and Nales?"

Hasain paused, his mouth pulling into a severe slant as he thought out his next words. "Old grudges die hard. But Arden is ready to cast these fears of war aside and work to make peace with both Shiraz and Nales. No one will benefit from bloodshed, but much is to be gained if we set aside our differing ideals and focus on how we can help each another instead."

Cold laughter rippled from Alerio's parted lips. "Spoken like a true politician! Perhaps you'll make an excellent advisor to your future king after all."

Joel swallowed, glaring at the ground beneath his sandaled feet. *Are they picking fun at Hasain? Is this some kind of joke? Did they invite us to sit with them just for their amusement?*

"Yes," Stavros agreed, smirking. "The son of the 'notorious traitor' shows potential!"

The Imperial youths shared a round of sinister laughter, and to Joel's dismay, Liro indulged in their mirth as well. The mage bit the inside of his cheek until he tasted blood on his tongue. *Why are they tormenting him? Why are they being so cruel? And Liro too! Stop it! Stop laughing!*

Hasain's face was drawn, his complexion washed out and pale. His typical poised, self-assured shell seemed to have crumbled, leaving behind a vulnerable and exposed child who clearly wasn't used to being scorned in such a way. Joel wanted to offer words of comfort. He wanted to defend his cousin. But Joel smartly held his tongue, knowing he was already treading thin water.

Hasain opened his mouth, but at that moment, a horn blared from far below and all eyes turned toward the arena.

"About time," Alerio groaned, taking another drink from his half-empty chalice.

The sound of grinding hinges echoed across the amphitheater as the heavy metal gates within the arena were raised. Joel shifted forward in his seat to get a better view.

Twenty men trotted through the open gates and onto the playing field. Each had donned plate armor and carried a shield and weapon. The gleam of metal blades and sharpened pikes sent a shiver careening up the length of Joel's spine.

The gladiators lifted their weapons into the air, kicking up dust in their wake as they strode along the outer edge of the arena. The crowd clapped and cheered. Joel couldn't bring himself to do either. All he could think about was how, in a matter of minutes, almost all of these warriors would be dead. He peered down, looking at the Emperor's dais, trying to catch a glimpse of his father or mentor. Neither was visible. A terrible fear gripped Joel's heart. He'd never felt so alone.

Alerio and his two cronies were discussing which of the gladiators they believed would be victorious. Pulling a money pouch free from his waistband, Balios glared at Stavros and snorted. "It's obvious you haven't any common sense. The Thief from Paion has no chance of winning!"

Stavros let out an incredulous laugh. "And what makes you so confident Nikodemos the Murderer will win?"

"I heard he took down half a dozen Imperial soldiers when they came to arrest him," Balios replied. "It took a small army to overtake and subdue him. The man's an animal."

"Ten golden coins says you're wrong."

"You're on!"

Joel couldn't believe what he was hearing. Were they really placing bets on which gladiator they thought would win? Were they really speaking about these *people* in such a degrading way? As though they were cattle or dogs?

Balios turned his eyes onto Alerio. "What say you, Prince? Who do you think will win?"

The Imperial prince stroked his clean-shaven chin. After a moment of reflection, he pointed toward a brute of a man, one so tall he towered over the rest of the warriors. "I'll bet ten gold coins on the barbarian."

Stavros quirked an eyebrow. "The savage from the mountains, eh? Not a bad choice, I suppose. He may be dumber than common livestock, but at least he's built like an ox."

"Precisely," Alerio replied, smiling most self-assuredly. "I feel brawn will prevail."

A second round of horns sounded from the arena floor, and Joel watched as the gladiators spread out now, standing within several paces of each other, but far enough away that they were out of arm's reach. Each man knelt on one knee, bowing to the Emperor.

The master of ceremonies, a wiry, grey-haired man dressed in red silk, made his way to a podium above the ring and raised both hands into the air. Silence fell across the amphitheater, and Joel waited to see what would happen next.

"Under the watchful eye of our good and gracious Emperor Lichas Sarpedon, Supreme Ruler of the North, and in the presence of the mighty Blessed Son of Light and Giver of All Power, welcome to the arena." The announcer's voice was crisp and clear, carrying well across the coliseum. "Fighters, you've entered this sacred ground as convicts, thieves, and murderers, but you will leave as champions."

The gladiators stared forward with vapid eyes, shields and weapons in hand. Their armored bodies shimmered as the midday sun cast harsh, bright light down from the heavens. They stood silent and unmoving. Waiting.

The announcer continued his speech. "In the end, most of you will be dead. But fear not. By fighting and dying valiantly, redemption shall be earned and your souls will be cleared of all wrong-doing in the eyes of our God. What say you, gladiators? Are you ready to yield yourselves to destiny? Are you ready to be redeemed?"

At once, swords and pikes were raised into the air, and the warriors voices joined together in one unified and resounding response. "*Yes!*"

"Then without further delay, let the match begin!" the announcer called above them. "Good luck, champions. Show your Emperor and adoring Imperial enthusiasts a good time!"

The crowd clapped and the warriors below took fighting stances. For a moment, time stood still. They appeared to be sizing each other up, making strategies against their opponents. Joel's heart pounded. He couldn't imagine what it must have felt like to be down there, having to choose who was the weakest, who to attack first.

"Well, come on!" Prince Alerio bellowed, drawing the attention of everyone around them. "Someone do something!"

From the open gates came the sound of hooves and the whine of metal wheels on stone. As the wheels transitioned onto the sand, the noise changed to a soft scratching that grated on Joel's nerves. He looked on as half a dozen chariots driven by men wearing leather loin guards and not much else sped toward the competitors with drawn cutlasses in their hands. A team of horses pulled each chariot. The beasts reared and snorted, the sound of their hooves pounding off the soft ground reaching every corner of the amphitheater. Sunlight glared off the horses' bronze armor, forcing spectators and warriors alike to shield their eyes.

Hasain grunted. "The horses are armored, but the riders aren't?"

"That's right." Alerio grinned. "The horses are valuable—the mountain savages, not so much."

Joel had to bite his tongue to keep himself in check. Hasain, likewise, said nothing, but the way his face remained pinched was a clear indication of his displeasure.

Down below, the warriors moved into a defensive formation, putting their backs together. It would appear for now they would work together against these new foes. The chariots circled the men, coming closer with each cycle. Joel held his breath, noting how even the wheels of the chariots were dangerous. The hubs had been modified. Instead of blunt axle caps, each wheel sported a long, sharp barb. It was only a matter of moments before several gladiators cried out and dropped down to clutch at their slashed thighs. Joel put his hand to his mouth as he watched blood paint the white sand crimson.

One of the gladiators let out a fierce battle cry and lifted his pike. Taking aim, he hurled the weapon toward an oncoming rider as the chariot closed in. The pike shot through the air, a blur of lethal motion too fast for the rider to avoid. Joel gasped as the rider fell from the chariot, the pike driven through his stomach.

Alerio and his cronies cheered and hollered while Liro smiled savagely.

"I told you Nikodemos was a sure bet! Look at him!" Balios exclaimed.

Stavros crossed his arms over his lean upper torso. "We'll see when the chariot riders are knocked out and the alliance is broken. Perhaps your Nikodemos will have only managed to put a mark above his head."

Joel couldn't be bothered to listen to any more of their blather. The wounded driver lay on the ground, writhing and crying out in agony as blood pooled beneath him. The horse he'd been steering made for an open gate, expertly navigating any obstacles in its way. Clearly the beast had been trained in the event its rider should fall. Joel imagined someone was waiting just out of sight to collect the valuable animal and take it back to its stable. The man with the pike through his gut had already stopped moving. No one came to collect him.

One by one, the other riders fell, but not before six or seven warriors had been gashed open by cutlasses or the barbed wheels of the chariots. Any sense of comradery shared at the start of the match had vanished by this point, and Joel watched numbly as the able-bodied overwhelmed any who'd been weakened. The sound of swords clashing and cries of despair echoed off the stone walls. Hasain retched when a head rolled away from its body, and Joel slammed his eyes shut a moment too late. He'd seen the blood as it spurted from the severed stump that had been the gladiator's neck. The vision would haunt Joel forever, he was sure.

Alerio jabbed his cousin in the ribs, heckling him. "Look at your little thief, thinking he can take on the barbarian. He has a spine! I'll give him that."

Joel risked opening his eyes. Below, Stavros' pick, the Thief from Paion, went head to head with the hulking barbarian. The two warriors spun around one other in a dance with death, each taking swings and jabs with their swords. Joel could hear the swish of metal as the blades cut through the air.

Stavros smirked at Alerio. "Your barbarian may be bigger, but the thief has speed on his side."

His victorious smile was short lived, as Balios pointed out a flaw in the thief's plan. "If he keeps backing up, he's going to fall right into the pit!"

Pit?

Joel peered down into the arena and realized, with a sense of dread, that Balios was right. Along the outer edges of the field, the ground yielded, giving way to half a dozen deep, square pits. He couldn't see into them but was certain something terrible waited at the bottom. His mind conjured up images of sharpened spikes before he could push the terrible thought away.

Liro leaned forward, also inspecting the pits. "Are they merely deep holes or is there something lethal at the bottom of each?"

"Patience, exalted guest." Alerio's grin chilled Joel to the bone.

Stavros lifted both hands into the air, worry tracing his handsome face. He gritted his teeth and seemed to hold his breath. Joel didn't want to look, but he couldn't force his eyes shut either. He watched in abject horror as the thief took a step back and then another, and finally, one too many. The gladiator wheeled his arms in an attempt to catch his balance, but his efforts were in vain. The Thief from Paion toppled into the pit.

Alerio and his companions, Liro included, cried out in various states of distress or victory. Balios made some sort of snide comment about Stavros needing to pay up.

Joel slammed his eyes closed again, trying to block out the sound of the thief's tortured screams. What was down there to make him plead so? A moment later, the howl of a large cat rose up to meet Joel's ears. The fallen warrior screamed for some time before his cries grew more akin to gurgles and helpless whimpers. And then silence. Joel could feel Hasain tremble.

The fighting continued, some men tumbling into the pits while others were pushed into them. Countless more fell under competitor swords until only three men remained standing atop the blood-soaked ground. Of them, Nikodemos and the barbarian dwarfed a third nameless man. Liro raised the question of his identity, and even Alerio seemed not to know.

"He's fast, but his luck will no doubt run out any moment."

"Luck?" Liro asked. "I thought they were the victors. Is the match not over?"

Again came the smile that would have Joel scrabble away. "Wait and see."

Before any more questions could be asked, a horn blared and the master of ceremonies reappeared at the podium. "For the pleasure of our people and the challenge of our champions, we have one final surprise! Fighters, prepare yourselves, for your greatest task has yet to come!"

What more could there possibly be? Hadn't these men done enough to reclaim their status as human? Joel swallowed against his churning stomach, wishing with all he was that he could be anywhere else. He'd had more than his fill of this blood sport, though it appeared his opinion was in the minority. The crowd's excitement was a tangible force buzzing all around him. *How can these people enjoy this? I don't understand—*

An awful, bloodcurdling shriek nearly made Joel's heart stop beating. He whipped his head toward the arena gate even as every other spectator in the amphitheater did the same. A spike of cold coursed through his body, from the tips of his toes to his fingers. *What was that? What kind of beast makes such a sound? Some sort of giant, wild cat?* The warriors gripped their weapons, and with wary eyes, they too watched the distant gate. Movement from the shadowed enclave beyond the gate caught Joel's attention and he observed, paralyzed, unable to tear his gaze away.

From inside the gate, the shriek ripped through the air again, more sharply than before. A guttural growl followed. Joel's eyes widened when the unidentified creature stepped from the darkness and into the light of the arena. His heart sank. This wasn't a big cat. This was something much worse.

With a face and upper body reminiscent of a man, the creature was clearly some sort of Otherfolk, but not one Joel had ever seen before. It stood no taller than the average human, but sharp horns and large, feathered wings gave the impression it was dangerous. It had powerful legs, similar to quadrupedal animals, with the shortened thighs and hock joints over upright feet. Instead of hair, it sported a mane of long, dark feathers which caught the sunlight and glittered as it moved. The feathers trailed the length of its spine and swept down its powerful tail.

Shackles hung from the creature's arms, legs, neck, and wings, and a team of soldiers yanked on the chains and prodded it with sharpened pikes. The creature had nowhere to go and no way to lash out as they pulled it into the ring.

Each time a soldier would venture too close, the beast would hiss or growl, only to be rewarded with a sharp jab. One such blow fell low on its side, drawing blood. The creature cried out miserably and rolled onto its side, refusing to go any farther. A soldier jabbed it in the ribs, and it howled again but didn't move.

The remaining gladiators began to advance, but one of the soldiers commanded them back. As they hesitated, the master of ceremonies' voice boomed across the amphitheater. "It would seem the beast doesn't wish to comply. Should it be taught a lesson?"

Joel looked on in horror as the crowd roared. All around him, men were placing bets and exchanging coins. No one cared about the injustice of the situation. What had this poor creature done to deserve this treatment? And why was it deemed fair for the gladiators to now have to fight it?

In the arena, one of the soldiers had broken away from the others and was now on his way back with a metal poker. Joel trembled when he realized one end of the rod was red hot. The creature seemed to realize this as well and scrambled to gain its feet. It wasn't fast enough. The soldier holding the hot poker lunged, and Joel looked away.

It bleated, one of the most mournful sounds Joel had ever heard. Beside him, Hasain wheezed and fell back in his seat, visibly trying to distance himself from the horror below. Face pale and constricted, the young lord looked as though he might pass out. Joel put a hand on Hasain's shoulder, causing him to jump. The grief and terror in his eyes were nearly enough to undo Joel.

"Hasain?" he whispered. His cousin declined to respond.

The soldiers retreated back through the gate, and the bars were once again lowered, locking the three gladiators and single beast inside the arena. As if by magic, the shackles holding down the creature fell away, clanking as they hit the sand. An eerie hush fell over the crowd, and Joel could hear his heart pounding in his ears. *What now?*

Men and beast stood in a stalemate for what felt like an eternity before one of the gladiators lifted his pike and took a tentative step forward.

The creature's response was instantaneous. It dropped into a low crouch, holding out a trembling hand. "No," it cried. "Please, mercy!"

Joel retched, clapping a hand to his mouth. "It speaks."

"Of course he speaks." Hasain's terse voice reprimanded Joel as if he should have known better. The Radek lord's dark eyes were still trained on the arena. "Demharlin are people, just like humans. He may not speak much of the Imperial language, but he's no animal. He understands what they mean to do."

Demharlin? Joel thought back to one of his academic texts, *Annals of the Unknown Peoples,* which outlined the different known species of Otherfolk. The demharlin derived from old harpy, goblin, and demon bloodlines and tended to live high in the mountains or on cliff sides where they could keep an eye out for predators. Joel grimaced. Hasain must be right. The more Joel thought on it, the more sure he was.

"Why doesn't he fly?" Hasain whispered. If Joel hadn't been so close, he wouldn't have heard his cousin speak.

Joel kept his voice low. "Perhaps magic? Maybe it can't fly—"

"*He.*" Hasain corrected in no uncertain terms. "He's male."

The demharlin shrieked again, and Joel turned back to watch. The barbarian had thrown the pike but missed. Wild eyes searching desperately for an escape, the demharlin skittered away from the weapon, kicking up sand in its wake.

Joel watched as it ran to the far wall of the stadium. Using clawed hands and feet, the demharlin latched onto the brick barrier and hauled itself upward. The people seated above gasped. Some of them even leapt to their feet. Joel held his breath. The poor creature was nowhere near the top of the wall yet and very likely wouldn't make it. Already winded, it slipped, losing almost half of its progress. The warriors were now directly below, waiting like hunting hounds at the base of the wall.

The demharlin didn't accept defeat just yet. Spreading one feathered wing, it flapped hard, sending gusts of wind and sand into the gladiators' faces. The men fell back just enough for it to leap into the air in an attempt to take flight—the opposing wing hung limply at its side, refusing to work. The demharlin wailed and crashed to the ground.

Joel chanced a look at Hasain. Now they knew why it hadn't flown before.

Hasain's pale features drew tight. "They broke his wing. Those bastards. This was never a fair fight."

The three men encircled the writhing creature, and Joel prepared himself for what was sure to follow. The demharlin reared onto its haunches, dark feathers standing on end. Even now with three swords drawn on it, it pleaded. "Please, mercy."

Joel couldn't hear the words so much as feel them in his torn heart. He pressed a hand to his mouth. "He still refuses to fight. The poor creature."

"Untamable. Wild. Ferocious." Hasain's voice sounded a thousand leagues distant. "That's how people judge them to be. But what of you, cousin? Would you call the demharlin a monster?"

Joel felt his cheeks go hot. He'd told little Calisto Nemesio not so long ago that he wouldn't dare pass judgment on any creature, but hadn't he, just now? He took in a sharp breath of air. "The monsters aren't the ones in the cage. They're the ones who *make* the cage."

Hasain's dark eyes sought Joel out for only a moment before the shrieking demharlin drew their attention once more. The gladiators advanced, taking swipes at the creature, backing it against the wall. The spectators who had considered fleeing when the demharlin climbed the stone barrier now peeked their heads over the side, trying to get the best view.

When one sword hit true and gouged a deep, red wound into its arm, the creature finally fought back. Joel clapped a hand over his mouth as he watched the frightened demharlin morph from a being desperate for escape to a raging, bloodthirsty beast.

Not unlike a giant cat, the demharlin pounced on the closest man, taking him down in a whirl of fangs and claws. The unnamed gladiator managed a single, choked scream before the demharlin took hold of his head and twisted it until it had made a full circle. Joel retched again but managed not to vomit. Thankfully, he was too far away to hear the crunch of bones being broken. The demharlin threw the lifeless body aside and turned its fierce gaze onto the two remaining warriors.

The crowd wailed in unison, and the last two warriors, Nikodemos and the barbarian, hesitated for only a moment before they rushed the creature in unison. The demharlin met them head on, teeth bared and claws at the ready.

The men's swords rose and fell so fast they were but a blur, a haze of silver and crimson. The demharlin screeched in agony, a haunting sound even the roar of the crowd couldn't drown out. A moment later, Nikodemos grunted and fell onto his back, holding his stomach—or rather, trying to hold his intestines inside his slashed gut.

The demharlin let out a shriek as it too toppled to the ground, convulsing, flailing. Blood spurted every which way, from gashes on its stomach, arms, and face. The barbarian danced around the creature, avoiding the demharlin's wings and tail, seeking any opportunity, any opening, to lay a final blow. When the poor creature rolled onto its back, the warrior found what he was looking for. With one swift strike of his broadsword, he cut a clean line across its throat. Joel could hear one last gurgled cry and then only the cheers of the spectators. The monster was dead. From the seat beside Joel, Hasain let out a strangled gasp.

The demharlin lay still, eyes open and unseeing, a smudge of black feathers resting atop a pool of crimson, and blood seeped from the creature's gored throat. Hollow emptiness filled Joel's heart. Had this horror show finally come to an end? Was it over?

It seemed Hasain had seen enough. Joel glanced over just in time to see the young Radek lord sweep away. His drawn face nearly matched the color of his white mage robes. Joel began to stand, to give chase, but Hasain waved him down. The devastated look in his eyes told Joel all he needed to know. His cousin wanted no company. He needed to get away from this ongoing nightmare. Joel didn't blame him.

"We have our victor!" proclaimed the master of ceremonies.

Joel watched as the barbarian stood over the writhing form of Nikodemos the Murderer. The roar of the crowd was too loud for him to ever hope to hear their words, but the two men were indeed speaking. Nikodemos' lips moved as he stared up at the other man with wide, pleading eyes.

Across the field, the gate was lifted and a troop of soldiers marched onto the field. Nikodemos grew more frantic. He raised one bloodied, shaking hand and pointed at the barbarian's weapon. Joel could taste the bile rising in his throat. The man was asking for mercy—for an end to his suffering.

Give it. Show mercy. For the love of The Two, someone here must know the meaning of the word!

The soldiers shouted as they approached, commanding the victor to drop his sword. Joel held his breath.

Please. End his suffering.

The barbarian looked deliberately at the soldiers as he raised his weapon high into the air. With a single downward thrust, he granted mercy.

Nikodemos took one final, shuddering breath and then went still. The hands clutching his gashed stomach slipped to the ground. Numbness settled over Joel's mind and soul. He couldn't even think to look away.

The entire amphitheater was on its feet—cheering, laughing, screaming—everyone except Joel. He could only stare at the gleaming crimson sand, the mangled body of the demharlin, the corpses of the fallen gladiators. His heart ached for home, for a place where mercy wasn't uncommon and barbarians weren't the only ones to dispense it.

CHAPTER NINE

Gib groaned as he found his feet. The day's council meeting had gone just about as well as expected. He was glad to be done with it at last. Honestly, by the end of some days, he could scarcely recall which sides of the debates he supported. Gib rubbed his temples and waited for the balcony to clear so he could rejoin Marc.

The other understudies were sluggish as they left their seats, still casting wary glances at the Crowned Prince. Deegan, for his part, seemed content to ignore them. He waited until only their party remained before turning to grin at Aodan. "Is this what you have to sit through every day?"

The bodyguard shifted in his seat and stretched both arms over his head. "Usually I sit in the window down there. It'd be a good place fer a nap if not for the pissin' and whinin'."

Deegan laughed as he stood, taking a moment to stretch his own limbs. "I would have thought you'd like being up here so high so you could have a grand view of everything happening."

"What's there to see? Just a bunch of miserable old codgers hell bent on makin' everyone else miserable too." Aodan leapt to his feet so quickly it startled Gib. "You lot with me now. I gotta get outta this cage before I go mad."

Deegan and Diddy shook their heads but followed without objection. Smiling, Gib brought up the rear of the party.

As always, the stairs were packed, but the benefit of moving with the royal procession gave Gib a glimpse of what true privilege really was. People all but fell out of the way on their trek to the council room floor. Gib grinned when they came upon their destination, but they didn't wait there for long either. Aodan swept onto the council floor without hesitation, and the two princes and Gib had no choice but to follow.

The councilors still at the table quieted, and Neetra glared openly as the party made their way to the head of the room. "Is it to be common procedure for the servants and understudies to traipse through like this?" asked the High Councilor in a snide tone.

King Rishi gave a withering scowl but declined to respond. Instead, he watched as an efficient switch was made. Without a single word, the royal guardsmen who'd been standing behind the table moved as a unit, encircling Crowned Prince Deegan. The prince was ushered out of the room in near silence, no doubt to be taken back to Queen Dahlia. At the same time, Aodan took his place in the window sill behind King Rishi, beckoning Diddy and Gib to join him there.

Despite the fluidity and silence of the exchange, Neetra scowled when it was over. "Such disruptions are most inappropriate." He stacked several papers and tapped his fingers on the tabletop. When King Rishi still refused to acknowledge him, Neetra pressed on. "I can't help but think Seneschal Koal would have well-founded criticism for such behavior."

Gib winced. That was going to do it. If Neetra was looking for a reaction, his wish was all but granted.

King Rishi slammed a fist on the table so hard that quills and inkwells shuddered beneath the force of the blow. "Then perhaps you shouldn't have demanded he go to the Northern Empire!"

Neetra was on his feet in an instant. "Someone had to go! Arden is in no position to ignore a summons from the Northern Empire. Surely you must see this!"

Koal would have already put an end to the heated exchange, but when Gib looked to Marc, the dean sat frozen in his seat. Was he not going to say anything? Someone needed to stop this before it got out of hand.

King Rishi jumped up as well, his chair nearly toppling in the process. "Easy for you to say when you have nothing to lose! My Right Hand and son are both out there!"

"I would have gone!" Neetra wailed, pointing to the various councilors still present. "I will have it be known that I offered to go, but the King, in his infinite wisdom, denied me!"

King Rishi leaned across the table. "Why would I send a snake to do my bidding? You look to poison our entire country, admit it!"

Marc finally stood up and put a hand on the King's shoulder, only to have it knocked away. He opened his mouth, but his voice was lost in the commotion. Gib pressed back into the window as far as he could go and noticed Diddy doing the same. Their eyes met for a moment, sharing terror. Even Aodan poised himself, ready to leap in if the argument continued on its downward spiral.

Neetra wasn't finished yet. The flash in his dark eyes reminded Gib of a cat chasing a bird. "The King's allegiance to Arden is most reassuring, given the circumstances of how you came to part with your homeland."

The room fell silent. Neetra was striking below the belt. Why was no one reprimanding him for it? King Rishi sneered, arms trembling, but amazingly enough, he managed to stay his tongue. Gib's lungs felt as though they would burst. *Please let this be the end of it. Let Neetra think he's won for now.*

The quiet lulled on just long enough to give a false sense of security. They all should have known better.

"Of course," the High Councilor continued tersely, "I suppose you haven't much choice, have you? After all, should Arden reject you, where would you next go? Burned bridges aren't safe for crossing."

In a heartbeat, King Rishi launched himself, and Gib thought for sure this had to be the end for Neetra. But Aodan was beside the King in a flash, pulling him back. Marc, likewise, had hold of the King's opposite arm. Somehow, the two men managed to restrain him.

No one could stop him from yelling though. "You speak treason! I could have you hung for this, Neetra Adelwijn. If you weren't the brother of Koal and my Queen, I would—"

Neetra lurched back, cowardly eyes glancing around the table at the gathered councilors. "He meant to attack me! You all saw it! And even now he threatens my very life!"

"Get out!" King Rishi screamed, still struggling against his captors. "All of you, *get the hell out!*"

The councilors leapt to their feet and grabbed their belongings. Quiet as death, they all scrambled for the door with red faces. Gib thought to get to his feet and join them—surely the hall would be better than in here—but Diddy grabbed his arm and held fast.

As the last councilor departed, King Rishi slumped against his bodyguard, visibly shaking. Marc grabbed a chair and brought it to him. "Sit. Take a breath."

"And fer fuck's sake, Rishi," Aodan gasped. "Calm down. What the hell were ya thinkin'?"

King Rishi put his face in his hands and sat still. His choppy breaths were the only sound for the longest time. "I can't listen to him anymore. There's nothing I do, nothing I say, nothing I think that isn't under his constant scrutiny. He speaks against me at every opportunity, turning the councilors on me!"

Marc was grim. "He's trying to rattle you, make you doubt yourself. Don't give in to him. When Koal returns—"

"What if Koal doesn't return? No one will say it, but we're all thinking it! What if he doesn't come back? What then? Koal was always the voice of reason."

"You're already lettin' him get the upper hand. Ya need to calm yourself and look at this rationally." Aodan dropped his voice, barely a whisper against the King's earlier outburst. "Neetra knows his only strength lies in Koal's absence. That's why he's makin' a scene now. Once his brother returns, he knows he won't stand a chance of gettin' his way. Don't think the other councilors don't see it. They know what he's doin'."

King Rishi was quiet for a long time, but finally he lifted his strained voice. "Something bad is going to happen. I can feel it."

"You're a seer now?" Marc tried to smile, but Gib could tell the dean was still shaken from the shouting match. "Look, I want Koal to return as much as anyone else, but worrying like this won't help. We've had no word indicating danger."

The King shook his head. "It doesn't matter. For the first time in my life, I can't see where I'm going. I've finally lost my way, and Neetra only stands to gain from that."

Aodan folded his arms over his chest. "Horseshit. That imbecile couldn't lead the way outta a wet bag. Only fools follow fools. If they wanna go with him, let 'em."

King Rishi's smile was empty. "Even the councilors who were on my side when Koal was here are second guessing themselves now." His dark eyes flicked toward Marc, who reddened under such close scrutiny. "They need Koal's firm leadership, I suppose."

"I've never appreciated Koal's position before now," Marc admitted. "Not as well as I should have anyway. How in hell does he manage everything? I can barely make it to council meetings on time—"

"Where were you, anyway?" The King shot Marc a narrow look. "We stood there forever waiting for you."

"Today wasn't my fault, I promise! The damned door to my office keeps slipping open. I had to have Nawaz come take a look at it. I tried to be on time. Ask Gib."

Gib winced. He wished Marc hadn't mentioned the door at all. Not now.

The King sat up straight, and Aodan stiffened in his spot. A knot pulled tight in Gib's stomach as his thoughts flitted back to the conversation he and Nawaz had with Marc earlier. He hoped the dean hadn't just made more trouble for himself.

"Slipping open?" King Rishi questioned. "It's not locking properly?"

"How long has *that* been goin' on?" Aodan's calm belied the fire in his single eye.

Marc winced, a dawning expression of regret on his face. "Just the last few days. I'll get a smith to come look at the lock and be done with it."

"You have it warded, don't ya? Yer office is protected, ain't it?" The rough push of Aodan's voice made Gib shudder.

Marc's hesitation was all the answer anyone needed. The King was on his feet in an instant, and Aodan was snarling some sort of profanity Gib had never heard before. Marc recoiled but stood his ground. "I've never had reason to ward it before! I mean, what would anyone even want in there?"

Aodan's voice dropped to a growl as he stalked up to the dean. "Ya think that Princess Gudrin's birth recordings are 'no reason to ward it'?"

Marc stiffened, his crimson face contorting in rage, an emotion Gib had rarely seen on the dean's fair features before. "I never said that! The royal family's confidential records have always been a top priority of mine!"

179

Confidential records? In Marc's office? It seemed odd to Gib. Why would a princess's birthing records be stored there? Were *all* of the royal children's documents kept there?

"We have to go to your office. Now!" the King demanded. His scowl fell onto Gib as though he'd only just noticed the understudy's presence. Gib stiffened as everyone, even Diddy, turned to stare at him as well.

King Rishi narrowed his eyes. "Gibben Nemesio, were you anyone else, I'd dismiss you now, without a second thought but—Koal trusts you."

Gib held his breath, not sure if he was meant to respond or not, but the King didn't wait for an answer. He crossed the room in three long strides, never once breaking eye contact. "You were there the day the assassin tried to be rid of me, and yet I think you've not mentioned it once since the event. You can keep a secret, can't you?"

Aodan's jaw was clenched tight, red blotches covering his face and neck. His watchful eye bore into the back of King Rishi's head. "Careful now. No rash decisions."

The King waved off the bodyguard's concerns. "He's Koal's understudy. It may be revealed to him with or without my consent. At least this way I have a chance to swear him to secrecy." King Rishi redirected his focus, and Gib could barely meet the King's eyes. "If you should learn anything sensitive about my family—any of them—you will keep their best interests at heart, won't you?"

Gib had to take a ragged breath. The sound filled the room. "Of course, Highness."

The King turned his back to Gib and paced over to the door. "It's most unusual, the position you find yourself in. Don't expect to be entrusted all at once. If you should discover anything vital about us today, know I will hold you to your word." He paused, letting the full weight of the matter settle. "Should you betray us, you will be held accountable to the full extent of my law, Nemesio. You will be imprisoned, convicted, and executed as a traitor. Is that clear?"

Gib swallowed. *All of this, over birthing records?* He didn't know if he could respond. It wasn't until he felt Diddy's hand on his back that Gib could shake his head clear and answer. "Yes, Your Majesty. I understand."

King Rishi still refused to look at Gib, opting instead to brace himself against the doorframe. "Then you'll also understand that now is your last chance to leave. If for any reason you do not wish to proceed, get up and go. No one will stop you and surely we won't blame you for having the good sense to stay out of this."

Was this a test of some sort? Gib's emotions sought to undo him. Some part of him wanted to accept the King's offer and leave now. If he was none the wiser, there would be no secret to keep and no worry of accidentally revealing it, but—Diddy was his friend. If there was some way he could better serve his friend and prince then he would do it. "My loyalty is to the Crown. I would serve in whatever capacity you see fit."

Aodan remained rigid, watching Gib narrowly. Marc refused to make eye contact, and Diddy let out a long breath. A small eternity passed before the King bowed his head ever so slightly. "You may come to regret that one day. Come with us."

Everyone was on their feet and out the door at once. Just outside, King Rishi informed the royal guardsmen that he was going to Dean Marc's office and that Blessed Mage Natori needed to be sent to meet him there immediately.

Less than a bell toll later, the door of Marc's office came into view. Gib sighed with relief. At least the damned thing had stayed closed this time.

Marc reached out first and pushed against the handle. His eyebrows shot up in a fleeting look of surprise when the door didn't budge. Without missing a beat, he pulled a key from his bag and disengaged the lock.

"Seems to be working now." The King's relieved sigh beckoned Gib to feel at ease, but a sinking sense of dread blossomed instead.

It would have been easy to allow King Rishi this reassurance. Gib might not have even thought ill of Marc if he'd chosen not to clarify, but the dean was a better sort than that. Head hung low, Marc kept his fist firmly on the handle and held the door shut. "Except I didn't lock it on my way out."

Aodan made a strangled sound and pushed past the dean to take the handle. Shoulder down, he poised himself as if ready to burst through, but King Rishi held up a hand. "Wait. Hold off for a moment."

The bodyguard whipped his head around, hair catching the sunlight in a fiery halo. The fearsome look on his face didn't soften even when he glared at the King. "Oh, aye? An' wait for whoever may be in there ta jump out the window and make a run for it?"

Marc cast his eyes skyward. "There's *no one* in there! It's just the damned lock acting up—"

"It never once seemed suspicious to ya that the lock only started slippin' since ya took Koal's position? What goes on in that empty head of yers?"

Gib grimaced. Apart from when the assassin had shot the King, he couldn't recall a time he'd seen Aodan so wound up. Gib still couldn't figure out why birth records would be the cause of this much worry.

The King frowned. "Aodan, wait for Natori to arrive."

"I'm not waitin' with my thumb up my arse fer no good reason. It's now or never!" Aodan signaled toward the royal guardsmen who had accompanied the party. "With me, soldiers!" The sentinels moved to flank Aodan, longswords drawn and at the ready. In the next instant, Aodan shoved the door open and they stormed inside.

No immediate sounds could be detected, and Gib felt like he was drowning in the quiet. Beside him, Diddy's breaths were ragged.

"It's clear."

Aodan and the soldiers reappeared at the door a moment later, and everyone waiting in the hall let out a collective sigh.

Marc threw up his hands. "How about that? What did I say? It's a simple matter of the latch not catching—or catching at the wrong time."

Neither the King nor his bodyguard seemed convinced, and Gib wasn't sure he faulted them. In fact, he might have even agreed. The fact that the door had only now begun to have these problems seemed too suspicious to be coincidence.

The office wasn't big enough for their entire party, and King Rishi wasted no time in demanding the royal guardsmen wait outside. The door remained open while they examined their surroundings for signs of mischief and waited for Natori to arrive.

Aodan snorted disapproval. "How can ya know whether everythin's here or not? Ya got things strewn from floor to ceiling!"

"I know where everything is." The clipped tone in Marc's voice suggested he'd just about reached his limit.

The King waved them both to stand down. His grim features commanded respect, and the other men dutifully fell into silence. King Rishi paced, hands clasped behind his back. "When did this start exactly?"

Marc frowned as he thought. "This is day three." He turned a heated look at Aodan, who leered in response. "Considering how long Koal has been gone, you would think if someone was going to search my things they would have taken action sooner."

"Perhaps."

Gib jumped at the new voice in the room. Blessed Mage Natori stepped across the threshold without waiting for permission to enter. Sword on one hip, her authority seemed to precede her, and the soldiers didn't hinder her entrance.

"Or perhaps they were waiting for an opportune time." The mage knelt like Nawaz had earlier and inspected the lock. Her frown did little to comfort Gib.

The King groaned when she didn't immediately say anything. "Well?"

Natori stood and looked around the rest of the room. "It appears whole. I can't feel any magic traces on it. If someone has been coming in here, they must have their own key."

"Or Marc just doesn't lock the door," Aodan muttered.

Marc opened his mouth, but Natori had already turned her peculiar, violet eyes on him. "You don't lock your office? Are you not in possession of some *sensitive* materials?"

Marc sighed. "Here we go again."

"Where do you keep the birthing records?" King Rishi asked. "The documents concerning Gudrin and the others, where are they? How do you know they're safe?"

Gib remained silent but took in all that was said. Gudrin and the *others*? Who? And what information could be so sensitive it would need this much hiding and protecting?

Diddy cleared his throat. When Gib glanced up, their eyes made contact. His mouth went dry. It would be a lie to say he wasn't curious, but the larger part of him still didn't want to know the truth. What if it was a secret too enormous to keep? *You can always ask Joel later*— He winced. No. He couldn't ask Joel.

Marc produced his keys once more. "Those are kept in here." He strode over to the closet and jiggled the handle. The door didn't budge. Fixing a dark look on Aodan, he went on in a smug tone. "This door stays locked."

Gib watched, breathless, as the dean unlocked the closet and stepped aside for the others to look. Gib was vaguely aware of conversation going on around him, but his mind wandered back to that morning.

The office door had been left ajar. He'd come inside the office and thought he'd heard a noise in the closet, so he'd looked. It *hadn't* been locked. It had been left wide open.

The entire room tilted.

"Gib? Gib, are you all right?" Diddy's voice sounded far off even though the prince was standing right there. "You've gone pale. Sit down. What's wrong?"

Gib did as was directed, dropping into a chair. As his vision cleared, he became vividly aware of everyone in the room staring at him. Through chattering teeth, his voice was barely audible. "It was open this morning."

No one seemed to grasp the implication of what he was saying. The King and his bodyguard studied him with narrow looks, and Marc's wide-eyed bewilderment offered no help. Even Diddy, who had knelt beside the chair, seemed confused.

Gib swallowed and tried again. "The closet door. It was open this morning."

Overwhelming silence engulfed the room. The King stiffened. Marc's mouth dropped open. Diddy gasped, and Aodan went terrifyingly quiet.

"I came to join you for the meeting, but your office door was open and you weren't here," Gib blurted. "I was worried something may be amiss, so I came in and called for you. No one answered, but I thought I heard a noise coming from the closet so I went to investigate." He looked down at his lap, shameful heat rising to his cheeks. "I didn't mean to pry,

I only wanted to make sure you weren't hurt. The closet wasn't locked. I looked inside it. No one was in there, unless they were hiding."

Aodan rushed the door even as Marc fumbled to get the key into the lock. The King and Blessed Mage hovered close by, leaving only Diddy to tend to Gib. As soon as the door was open, Aodan squirmed inside and Marc followed at his back.

"Where are the records?" Gib had never heard Aodan sound so desperate or angry.

"Right here. This box."

Aodan re-emerged with a small crate. In one deft move, the bodyguard cleared Marc's desk, knocking everything to the floor, and set the box down. He tore the lid off before anyone could say differently and shuffled through the multitude of scrolls and parchment. "Does it look like it's been tampered with? Where are the birth records?"

"They're at the bottom, folded not rolled." Marc put his hands in his hair and gripped the raven strands between his fingers. "And I don't—I don't know. Nothing *looks* any different." He went back to the closet and peered inside, looking over every detail. "I mean, it's always cluttered in here, but everything looks the same."

King Rishi swept up to stand behind Aodan and watched, utterly focused, while the bodyguard fumbled through the papers. The muscles in Gib's neck wound tighter with each passing moment.

"Ha!" Aodan slapped a page down on the desk, then another, and one more. "They're here. All of 'em."

The King closed his eyes and hung his head back, getting his own breathing under control. He set a hand on Aodan's shoulder as if to stabilize himself, and the two of them shared a heavy look. "But it would have been foolish for someone to take the records. What if they were viewed and then left here?"

What was so wrong with these birth records? Gib chewed his bottom lip. He didn't want to jump to any conclusions, but he was beginning to wonder if the princess wasn't who the kingdom thought she was. Perhaps Queen Dahlia wasn't her mother? It didn't seem an unreasonable theory, given Hasain's parentage. Was that what this was about?

Aodan's pale face went red as he thumbed back through the documents. "The wordin' is vague. The spy would have a lot of guesswork on their hands, but if they knew enough ta look for them in the first place... An' how in hell would they have gotten in the closet in the first place?" His glare shot back over to the dean.

Marc shook his head and fell into his chair. "I don't know. It's not possible. I'm the only one with a key to that door besides Koal and you." He looked at the King. "Koal's key would be in the Northern Empire with him."

King Rishi frowned, thinking out loud. "Mine is safe. I know where it is. There's no way in hell it's been tampered with."

Natori approached the closet door. Her eyes slipped shut as she laid her hands against the wooden frame. Everyone in the room watched her, waiting with bated breath for her to speak. Finally, Natori sighed and opened her eyes. "No magic. Not even a trace. It has to be a key or a lock pick."

King Rishi wrapped his arms around himself, suddenly appearing impossibly thin. His voice was as haunted as his eyes. "Someone has a key. Who would even have access to them?"

It was a heavy implication. If there were only three known keys, possessed by the King, seneschal, and dean, then someone close to one of them had to be the culprit.

"I'm going to ward the entire room," Natori announced. She went to the hallway door and laid a hand on it. "Marc, you'll be the only one who may come and go freely until the King tells me otherwise. Everyone else will have to be given your express permission."

Marc groaned. "How in hell do I do that? I'm a healer, not a mage. Our magics are very different, you know."

Natori's dry response may have been humorous under better circumstances. "I'm aware. I'll link you to the magic. The door will recognize you, but you'll have to hold it open for anyone else. Same for the window and closet door."

"Hear that, Gib? No more crawling in through the window." If Marc's joke was meant to be funny, he failed miserably.

As if awoken from a spell, King Rishi drew up to his full height and snapped his head around to glare venomously at the dean. "Is this funny to you? Does my family mean so little that you would make light of this?"

Marc leaned back in his chair with wide eyes. "I didn't say that. You know I value the safety of your children and family." His gaze fell on Aodan briefly, whose stance grew rigid in response. "I would protect all of them, even the ones who feel they don't need protecting."

Aodan opened his mouth but was silenced by the King with one wave. He leaned across the dean's desk, face to face with him. "If any harm comes to my daughter or sons, you can bet you'll have to deal with my wrath!"

Marc was on his feet in an instant, holding the ruler's glare with his own. "Is this how little you trust me? How could you *ever* think I'd allow harm to befall them? Chhaya's bane, Rishi, you're like a brother to me! They're all my family as much as yours as far as I'm concerned and you know it!"

Natori sighed as she watched them from the doorway. "Do either of you plan on solving this problem, or are you content to tear one another apart? Surely you must have taken into consideration that this is precisely what the persons behind this act are hoping for?"

185

King Rishi and Marc froze where they stood, not unlike scolded children.

The King sighed. "She makes a valid point. Why would they tear down a wall if the foundation is already weak? They're just waiting for us to crumble."

Marc plunked back down in his seat. "Yeah, I suppose so. Sorry."

For a time, the room fell into awkward silence.

Finally, Aodan crossed his arms over his chest. "So they've shaken us. How do we proceed?"

The King heaved an exhale and dropped into the other chair. He used one hand to cover his pale face. "I don't know. We'll have to strategize in private—" His brow furrowed and he stole a look over at the youngest two in their company. "You two go."

"Father?" Diddy balked.

King Rishi silenced the prince with one stern look. "Neither of you need be troubled any more today."

"My family is worth any trouble I may encounter!"

The King locked his jaw, impatience thinly veiled behind dark eyes. Wordlessly, Gib grabbed Diddy's elbow, and Aodan took the prince's other arm. Together, they guided him toward the door.

"No one's questionin' your loyalty, Diddy. Ya know that," the bodyguard said. "This is a discussion for the King and his advisors, not a young prince and an understudy. C'mon now, out with ya."

Diddy grabbed Aodan's arm. "If there's anything I can do to help, I would."

"We know."

Once they were in the hall, Diddy lowered his voice. "Aodan, Father is under too much pressure. You must see it, too. Hasain has gone to the Northern Empire as an ambassador, Deegan is sitting in on the council meetings to fill his spot—I know I'm not a Radek, but I would do what either of them would. My only desire is to be a good son. Please—"

"Hey, enough of that." Aodan put his hands on both of Diddy's shoulders. "This isn't about names or bloodlines. You *are* a good son, Didier, and there may come a time where yer called to do somethin' dangerous or difficult. Rishi doesn't give these tasks lightly. He had no choice sendin' Hasain. And Deegan had ta grow up sooner or later. Don't mistake his hesitance to use you as a lack of love or trust. He's merely been able to keep you safe for a while longer. That's all."

Diddy wiped an errant tear from his cheek. "You will let him know I only wait for his call, won't you?"

"He knows, but I'll remind 'im if ya want. Now—" Aodan looked pointedly at the soldiers and Gib before returning his full focus to Diddy. "—do as yer king commands. Go back to the palace, check on yer mother and the young ones. And fer the love of The Two, hold yer head up like

186

the prince ya are."

Aodan returned to the office then, and Diddy and Gib, flanked by the four soldiers, began their trek down the empty corridor.

Gib cleared his throat. "I suppose I don't need to go back to the palace. I could just go to my room."

"All right," replied Diddy. "I'm sure you have studies to catch up on."

"Always." Gib searched for something else to say, wishing he could avoid the obvious, but words came pouring out of his mouth without consent. He never had been good at avoiding the truth. "Diddy, if there's anything I can do to help you, please let me know. I mean, I know there are things you can't tell me, but despite that, I would help you in whatever capacity I'm able."

Diddy twisted his hands together and cast a timid look around. "I suppose you'll have to visit the library at some point, won't you?"

Gib frowned. He wasn't sure where Diddy was going with this. "I suppose. Why?"

"Might I suggest some study material?" Diddy leaned in close and dropped his voice so low Gib had to strain to hear it. "For any confusion you may have had today, I would highly recommend *Annals of the Unknown Peoples*. The fourth segment is particularly enlightening."

A light went on in Gib's mind. *He's trying to tell me something important.*

"Th–thank you. I will check into that."

His mind was heavy as he said farewell. It would no doubt bring him strife to investigate this matter further and perhaps it wouldn't be worth the trouble—but his mind was already made up.

To the library it is.

Joel wandered the stone corridors, heart numb and stomach bunched into queasy knots. The urge to vomit came and went, churning his guts and burning the back of his throat, and visions of bloodshed and violence weighed heavily in his thoughts. A gripping, horrible fear that he'd never be able to unsee the horrors witnessed earlier paralyzed his mind. Would he be stuck in this nightmare forever?

He stopped beside a pillar, leaning against the cold marble for support. Slamming his eyes closed, Joel bade himself to relax. He needed to calm down. He needed to think clearly. He needed to find Hasain.

Immediately following the gladiator tournament, Joel had returned to the Imperial palace in search of his cousin. Hasain had left the match so abruptly and in such distress that Joel was worried. He had to find Hasain, talk to him, and ensure he was all right—only the young Radek lord was nowhere to be found. He hadn't been in his bedchamber within the suite nor was he sitting in the private garden outside. Joel had searched the library next, but Hasain wasn't there either, leaving Joel to ramble aimlessly through the palace halls.

What am I doing? Why am I even here? Tears welled beneath his closed eyelids. *I should be in Arden, with my family, with Gib. Not thousands of leagues away, in this vile empire where men are slaughtered like animals—*

"Lord Joel Adelwijn?"

Joel's eyes flew open, the soft tenor voice catching him off guard. Blinking away blurry tears, he spun around so swiftly the newcomer took one uncertain step back.

Kirk Bhadrayu's fair face pinched with concern. "I–I'm sorry. I didn't mean to impose. I was just passing through and saw you standing there— and thought I'd make myself known." His shameful green eyes shifted downward.

Joel cleared his throat, hoping the anguish in his soul wouldn't be so apparent when he spoke. "No. It's all right. You're not imposing."

Kirk lowered his voice a pitch further, barely more than a whisper. "Are you okay?"

For a moment, Joel couldn't bring himself to utter a response. Even the stiff nod he gave was difficult. "I'm searching for one of my comrades—Lord Hasain. I lost track of him when I left the amphitheater earlier."

Kirk's demeanor grew darker yet. Letting out a sigh through tightly pursed lips, the mage trainee replied in a solemn tone, "You attended the arena match?"

Joel grimaced. "I'm afraid it wasn't by choice." He hesitated, glancing around to ensure they were alone. "Emperor Lichas insisted we go. I would have preferred to sit in the garden instead." *Should I have said that?*

Kirk nodded, a silent show of his understanding. "I'm sorry you had to see it."

"Were you there today?"

"No. Thankfully my master doesn't require we partake—though some of his other trainees opt to go." A fleeting smile passed across Kirk's lips. "Like you, I prefer the serenity of the gardens over the violence of the arena. Some would call me a coward for admitting such a thing—"

"I wouldn't."

They locked eyes, and Joel felt a strange sense of comradery toward the young mage trainee. Perhaps if fate had chosen differently and they'd grown up sharing the same country, he and Kirk could have been friends. Perhaps they still could be—

No, Joel reprimanded himself for entertaining such dangerous thoughts. *Kirk is young, but he's still an Imperial. No matter how honest or forthcoming he seems, I can't fully trust him. Ever. And surely we cannot be friends. When I leave Teivel, it's almost a certainty I'll never see him again.*

A rosy colored flush settled on Kirk's high cheekbones. "I'm afraid I haven't seen Lord Hasain today. Perhaps he ventured into the royal courtyard. I often find it easy to clear my mind there. It's worth a look if you haven't yet searched there." Kirk scraped one of his sandals across the tiled floor.

"Perhaps." *I guess searching there is better than standing around looking like a lost soul.* Joel's head spun as he tried to recall how to get to the royal gardens. "I'm afraid I don't know the way. Might you point me in the correct direction?"

Kirk smiled. "I can show you there myself if you'd like."

Joel hesitated, knowing he walked a fine line. The others would see this type of interaction as troubling or as fraternizing with the enemy. But Kirk wasn't like the other Imperials! He was kind while they were cruel, modest despite the pomposity surrounding him, and genuine, *truly* sincere.

I do trust his word. Father and Hasain can call me foolish all they want, but I know Kirk isn't being false. Not after the conversation I overheard in the garden. Not after I witnessed the way those other boys treated him. He's an outcast, the same as I used to be. And I really could use someone to talk to.

Joel allowed himself to smile back as the last bit of doubt was cast from his mind. "I'd like that very much. Pleasant companionship after such brutality would be most appreciated."

Kirk bowed. "Allow me to lead the way, Lord Adelwijn."

"Joel. Just Joel, if you would."

A shy laugh filled the hall, and Kirk's blush deepened as he led the way toward the courtyard. "Forgive me, Lord—Joel. I'm not used to such requests. Master Titus is very strict. If he caught me talking in such a way, I'm certain he'd punish me."

Joel frowned. "That seems a bit extreme."

"I've been reprimanded for lesser crimes. It's just the way things are here. The Imperial highborns demand the utmost respect from their servants."

The scent of saffron and wild flowers hung in the air as they left the palace and stepped onto the cobblestone path outside. The late afternoon sun lay low in the sky, casting shadows across the grass. The rays of light bathed Joel's skin in drowsy warmth, and despite the horrors he'd witnessed earlier, he found his tense shoulders and queasy stomach beginning to relax.

"But you aren't a servant," he pointed out as they walked. "You're a trainee. Soon you will be a mage—practically royalty, judging by the way the Northern Empire holds their mages in such high regard. Why does the Archmage treat you so poorly? Why do your fellow trainees torment you if you're all destined to be mages anyway? If you're all equals?"

"Equal?" Sadness filmed Kirk's eyes as he stared at the flowering vines creeping up the palace walls. "I'll never be their equal. Not really anyway."

Joel knew he shouldn't press the matter but couldn't help himself. "Why not?"

Kirk wrapped his arms around his shoulders, as though his tunic suddenly wasn't enough to keep his fair skin warm. "Because of my past. Archmage Titus never truly wanted to take me as an underling. The only reason he did is because I'm one of the most gifted mage trainees my age. But that doesn't mean he has to like me. I'm lowborn, you see. When my mother grew ill five years ago, she was unable to work anymore, and we found ourselves tossed into the streets. Mother didn't last long there. I was ten when she made the journey across the veil. My sister had barely seen her ninth Naming Day."

Joel winced, unsure of what to say. "I'm—I'm sorry."

"Kenisha and I were taken in by a local orphanage for the next two years. It was a rough life. Too many children living together and not nearly enough food to go around, but at least we had a roof above our heads. If we'd still been on the streets during the brutal winter, I have no doubt we would have perished."

As the young trainee told his story, Joel couldn't help but think of Gib. How many times growing up had Gib and his siblings gone to bed at night with empty, aching stomachs? How many times had they cried themselves to sleep because their parents weren't there to tuck them in? He stole a glance at Kirk as they walked. *People like Gib, like his brothers and sister, like Kirk—they are stronger than any highborn I've ever known. To be thrown into such dire circumstances and somehow climb their way out—they're heroes and they don't even know it.*

"If I ever have the means," Kirk continued. "I hope to one day return to the orphanage and dispense charity of my own. If it hadn't been for the kind souls who worked tirelessly to keep the place afloat, my sister and I wouldn't have survived. I only wish more people cared about the welfare of the homeless children in this world."

Joel nodded, his heart touched by the trainee's words. "I think people would rather close their eyes and pretend such problems don't exist. I was one of those people until recent years. I was born into wealth. I grew up with private tutors, luxurious clothing, and I don't ever recall a time I went to bed hungry. I looked upon the poor in the streets—the ones without homes, dressed in rags—and yet I didn't truly *see* them. Not really. I was living a life so far removed from them that it never even dawned on me to think about what it must have been like to be in their position."

"You seem to be empathetic toward their plight now. What made you open your eyes?"

Joel blinked. *Gib.* From the moment he and Joel had been placed together as roommates, Gib had been opening Joel's eyes. He was taught that riches couldn't buy integrity, that strength of heart was a far greater weapon than any sword, and compassion could be shared, even by those who'd never received any themselves. *Gib taught me how to love myself and how to love others. He, the poor farm boy with nothing left to lose, saved me. And then I cast him aside like he meant nothing to me. I chose to come to this horrible place instead of standing by the person who loved me most.*

He swallowed down the agony building in his throat. Kirk was still awaiting an answer. "I befriended someone who'd spent his entire life poor. He told me stories, similar to yours, about worrying from day to day if there would be food on the table for his brothers and whether or not the harvest crop would be plentiful enough to ensure they survived another winter. I guess I began to see things differently after hearing his tales. Suddenly, my own problems seemed petty and insignificant."

Kirk's eyes were thoughtful when he replied. "I've lived among the highborns long enough to know that they too have plights. Perhaps of a different sort, but plights the same. Everyone—highborn or low—has secret demons they need to work around."

Joel chuckled lightly. "That we do." They walked along the tiled path for several paces before Joel pressed Kirk to tell more of his story. "So, how did you end up at the palace? How did the Imperial mages find you beyond the dome?"

"It's custom to send scouts into even the poorest districts of the city. Every year, just after Harvest, scores of Imperial mages peruse the streets, seeking children with the ability to yield magic. It's a reaping of sorts. Those with promise are whisked away to the palace."

"What if they choose not to go?"

Kirk turned a somber eye onto Joel. "They aren't given a choice. Though quite honestly, any child born into poverty would be crazy not to accept a life inside the magic dome. Their chances of survival are dramatically better without the need to worry about cold or hunger."

"But what about the families they have to leave behind? Are they ever allowed to visit their kin?"

"I'm afraid not. Once they become apprentice mages and swear their oaths, the Imperial mages become their only brethren."

Joel gave him a sideways glance. "But you still have your sister."

The sun caught Kirk's hair, casting warm light over the grains of gold among the darker brown hues. "When the mages came to take me away, I was terrified to leave Kenisha. As it was, I was nearly too old to be living at the orphanage, and I knew her time there was limited, too. I couldn't imagine her being thrown back into the streets. So I begged—quite unabashedly. I told the mages she could do any job asked of her, if only they allowed her to come to the palace. I threatened not to comply if they didn't bring her. I said everything I could think of, and in the end, Kenisha was able to go. I later found out there was a shortage of servants. I doubt they'd have let her come otherwise."

"Well, that's fortunate."

Kirk frowned. "Sometimes I wonder. Sometimes I think maybe she was better off outside the dome." They walked in silence the rest of the way.

Joel was just as impressed by the royal courtyard as he'd been the first time Adrian Titus had led the envoys through it. Joel's attempts to hold back his awe failed, and he was certain he must have looked a fool as he stood with an open mouth and wide eyes, staring at the immaculately trimmed shrubs and white marbled statues.

Kirk smiled. "Have you seen the koi pond up close?"

Joel could only shake his head, and with light laughter following in his footsteps, Kirk led him closer to the pool. Joel gazed down into the placid water, staring at the giant fish swaying beneath the surface.

"Did you know they can live to be over one hundred years old?" Kirk asked, nodding toward the water. "I read it in a book."

"That's incredible," Joel murmured. His eyes skimmed the garden, passing over the various flowers of every color and shape. "All of this is incredible, really. The beauty of this place is undeniable."

"Yes. Shame that it's all a façade." Kirk shook his head in a slow, deliberate manner. "A veil of exquisiteness to hide the corruption beneath."

A weak smile crossed Joel's lips. "Rest assured Teivel isn't the only place in the world to know corruption. It can be found anywhere. But there is also good to be found. Honest, caring people do exist."

His mind wandered to thoughts of the kind people in his life. Where would he have been now without the support of his loving parents? Without the guidance of his mentors, Dean Marc and Cenric? Without Gib's unfaltering love? So many people had helped shape his life. They'd been there, lifting him up during his hardships, never allowing him to fall. In that moment, Joel realized just how fortunate he truly was. *Without them, I'd be lost.*

"I suppose I won't ever know," Kirk replied. "My skills are far too valuable to the Empire. Even after my apprenticeship is complete, they'll make sure I'm stationed right here, inside the 'safety' of the palace for the rest of my life."

"I'm sorry." Joel didn't know what else to say. Guilt gnawing at his stomach, he turned his attention to the flowerbeds that lined the perimeter of the courtyard. Flora of all shapes and sizes blanketed the ground, their colors so vibrant and varied they reminded Joel of a rainbow. Their sweet, luscious scent infiltrated his nostrils as he stepped closer to get a better look. "I've never seen so many different flowers in one place before."

Kirk came over to stand nearby. "Careful of the purple ones." He pointed toward a patch of effervescent violet blossoms, hanging in bunches from long stems.

"Why?" Joel asked, squinting as he focused all his attention onto the flowers. "What are they?"

"Wolfsbane," replied Kirk in a grave tone. "Its petals are highly toxic. If ingested, without immediate care from a healer, it can easily be fatal."

Joel blinked and unwittingly took a step back. "Then why in the name of The Two is it allowed to grow in a *royal courtyard*?"

"My master says Emperor Sarpedon keeps it as a reminder to his foes how easily they could meet their doom, if they ever were to cross him. Wolfsbane has been grown and harvested in this very garden for centuries. The Northern Empire cultivates it for—less than desirable purposes. Assassination attempts, mainly. Some people don't wish to get blood on their hands." Kirk's smile was frigid. "There's a popular Imperial saying about 'taking a walk through the garden with your enemy.' As I'm sure you can guess, they're not taking a stroll with plans to make amends."

Joel played with the sleeve of his mage robe. "Your country is filled with such wonderful people."

Kirk actually laughed, but the broken undertone in his voice couldn't be ignored. "We're not all so bloodthirsty, I swear to you. The people I grew up with—those at the orphanage—were some of the most kind and giving people in the world. However, within the palace walls, those with power are determined to keep it, while everyone else is just as determined to steal it away. Greed has turned honorable men into animals—entire families have been torn apart—simply because they want to advance their own name. They'll do whatever it takes to gain power. The Sarpedon bloodline is the worst offender."

Joel glanced around the courtyard to ensure they were alone. "Kirk, why doesn't the Emperor age?"

The mage trainee stiffened his shoulders, casting a wary look around the vicinity. "I don't—we aren't—" Kirk sucked in a tense breath of air, and his green eyes finally met Joel's. "I'm sorry. It's forbidden to talk about."

A spike of apprehension ghosted its way up Joel's spine. What did the young trainee know that would cause such grim terror to manifest on his normally placid features? And why was the topic so taboo that Lichas Sarpedon had forbidden it from being discussed? What in the two worlds was he so adamant about hiding?

Joel gave a stiff nod and didn't interrogate further. "I wouldn't want you to get into trouble at my expense. I'm sorry. I won't press the matter."

Kirk let out the air he'd been holding. "Thank you. To be completely truthful, I don't have an answer for you anyway. I've heard rumors, of course, but to my knowledge, they are only that—rumors, gossip, tales. My master has mentioned in passing that Emperor Sarpedon is—blessed."

"Blessed?"

Kirk's voice was but a wisp of air on the breeze. "By the Blessed Son

193

of Light, the Giver of All Power."

"Well, that seems a bit far-fetched," Joel admitted. "I've heard of a deity blessing a bountiful crop or mild winter before—but never has there been proof of one extending a human's *life*." He stroked his chin. *I need to mention all this to NezReth and Father. Surely it's a tall tale, but there could be some ounce of truth within the story.* "What about Prince Alerio? He's of age to take the throne. If the Emperor never gets any older—"

"Why do you think the prince is trying so hard to marry your princess?" Kirk countered in a flat tone. "He wants a way out of Teivel. He knows he'll never get the crown so long as his sire lives."

"I'm shocked he hasn't tried to take it forcefully, given what you said about the power hungry highborns in this city."

Kirk's eyes moved around the courtyard, never resting on one particular place. "He's not stupid. He watched two older brothers attempt to do just that, and now they're dead. The Emperor tried his own sons and found them guilty of attempted murder. Ambition led them both to an early grave."

Joel swallowed down a wave of nausea. "Sarpedon had his own sons killed?"

"Without hesitation. I imagine Prince Alerio won't make the same mistake."

"No," Joel replied, focusing his gaze onto the placid water of the pond, watching the koi fish again. "He'll attempt to stake his grounds elsewhere. King Rishi will see right through him though. The King will never allow Alerio to marry his daughter, or anyone else from Arden for that matter."

Kirk nodded. "Your king seems to be a wise man."

"Not a popular opinion among your fellow Imperial citizens."

"You're right." Kirk's voice trailed off as a servant boy passed by with a pair of metal scissors and began to trim the hedges nearby. Kirk motioned for Joel to follow in the opposite direction, and once they were standing beneath the shade of an olive tree—safely out of earshot—Kirk cleared his throat and continued on. "I must admit even I'm a little wary of your great King Rishi, try as I might not to be. He's viewed as a traitor here."

"That's a matter of opinion."

Kirk winced. "I know. But you have to realize how difficult it is to think otherwise when I've been told my entire life that the King of Arden betrayed his country and even made deals with a demon to ensure his ploy saw fruition."

Joel raised an eyebrow. "Pardon? What is this about a demon?"

"Here in the Empire, it's whispered that Rishi Radek wields the power of a demon." Kirk's voice trembled as he spoke. "He made a pact with an ancient evil being to secure Arden for himself. Even now, the demon remains in his servitude, disposing of all those who would stand in his way—"

Joel held his hands up defensively. "That's a lie!" Head spinning, he tried to slow the rapid pounding in his chest. *Chhaya's bane, what in the two worlds are they teaching the people here? King Rishi, wielding a demon? I've never heard such a ridiculous fabrication in my entire life!* Joel straightened to his full height. "King Rishi is a good and honest king. My father has worked with him for years. My aunt is *married* to him. Whatever defamations the Northern Empire has been spreading are just that—*lies*. King Rishi would *never* be fool enough to make deals with a demon."

"I'm sorry," Kirk apologized, taking a step back. "I didn't mean to offend your king. It's just—it's what we've been told."

"I know," Joel replied, his own voice clipped. "I just wanted to clarify."

"Understandable." Kirk stared at the ground and said nothing more.

Awkward silence blanketed the pair of mages for some time. Joel took a deep breath and loosened his stance, suddenly feeling bad for lashing out at Kirk. *It's not his fault. The Empire has been whispering lies into his ears since birth. Can I truly blame him for believing them? Wouldn't I have done the same? Haven't I already done the same? The people of the Northern Empire have always been painted in such a negative light. Until I came here, I lumped them all together and labeled them as "evil." But there are decent people here. Isn't Kirk proof enough of that?*

Joel cleared his throat. "I apologize for my impetuous reaction. I didn't mean to lash out at you. This place seems to have brought out the worst in me."

"You're far from home. I don't blame you for being on guard. Apology accepted." Kirk sighed, his mouth curling upward, the first sign of a smile returning to his lips. "Now, about this Lord Hasain Radek of yours. We should keep looking—"

His sentence was cut short as the sound of sandals hitting stone pavers grabbed both men's attention. Joel turned to look down the path as Kirk did the same. A young girl dressed in servant garb raced toward them. Her brown hair was pulled into a bun, drawing attention to the worried frown and creased eyebrows that had overtaken her pretty, oval face.

Kirk's smile immediately fell away. "Kenisha? What's wrong?" As she approached, he reached out to take hold of her slender hands.

The girl crumbled against his chest. "I've been looking all over for you!"

"What happened?" Kirk asked, embracing her gently around the shoulders. "Are you all right?"

Tears welled in the corners of her green eyes, but she blinked them away. Stealing a suspicious glance toward Joel, she lowered her voice a pitch. "I need to talk to you, brother. Right now."

Kirk nodded. "Of course." He kept one hand on her shoulder and motioned toward Joel with the other. "Kenisha, this is Joel Adelwijn of Arden. Joel, this is my sister."

Joel offered his hand for a shake. "Lady Kenisha, it's a pleasure to meet you—"

"Lady?" Kenisha stared at his hand in bewilderment, like she'd seen a ghost. Keeping her own hands a safe distance away, she jerked her head around to frown at Kirk. "I need to talk to you somewhere private. *Alone.*"

Kirk squeezed her arm. "It's okay. You can speak freely, sister. He won't betray us."

Joel took a step back, giving the siblings more room. He could tell by Kenisha's rigid stance that her suspicions were far from eased, but it appeared she was going to trust her brother. Paling even more, she spoke in such a soft voice that Joel had to strain to hear the words. "I'm making plans to leave the palace."

Kirk's voice dropped to an anxious whisper. "*What?* Keni, no—"

"I can't stay long," she continued. "The prince will be back from the gladiator match soon. But I had to tell you about this."

"You can't just leave! Where will you go? It's not safe out there!"

"It's not safe here either, Kirk! And I won't allow that—that *vile pig* to touch me again." Rage briefly flashed behind her eyes. "Listen, one of the handmaidens I work with has family on the western border of the city. Her grandparents own an inn out there, and she says they'll hire me as a tavern wench if I mention her name."

"The western border? Don't you remember how dangerous it is out there?"

"I'll be all right," Kenisha replied. "It's not like I'll be on the street. I'll work for my room and board. You don't have to worry—"

Kirk shook his head fiercely. "You're my sister. I'll always worry. Besides, even if these strangers were willing to take you in, there's no guarantee you can even get there. You can't just go walking out of the palace gates! The guards won't let you through."

Kenisha's eyes darted around the garden. "I'm not going to use the gate. I know another way out."

"Another way?"

Her voice came out in a rushed whisper. "Over by the servant quarters, there's a passageway that leads down into the catacombs. Fabius, one of the pages, told me he's explored the system extensively. He says there's a drainage opening that comes out on the far side of the palace wall, large enough for a person to slip through."

"*That's* your plan? That sounds crazy! How do you even know if you can trust this page? You could just as easily get lost down there and never find your way out!" Kirk gripped his sister's hand again. "Don't go. I'll figure something out. Just give me a little more time."

"Time is running out. I can't stay here much longer. I can feel the stone walls closing in around me—"

"We have to stay together," Kirk pleaded with her. "You can't go beyond the dome. Not with winter on the rise. Please, reconsider."

"You can't protect me forever." Kenisha smiled sadly, squeezing his hand. "You know I appreciate everything you've done for me, right? I wouldn't be alive if it wasn't for you. When Mama died, we both should have perished with her, but *you* saw us through. *You* kept our hope alive even when mine had withered away."

Kirk's jaw trembled. "It's my job to protect you."

"No," she replied with a deep sigh. "Not anymore. I have to protect myself."

"I'll—I'll go with you when you leave."

"Absolutely not. You have a good, decent life here, Kirk. And what's even more important is you have the opportunity to better yourself. I won't let you throw that away."

As Joel observed their interaction, he realized Kenisha couldn't have been any older than Heidi. He couldn't even imagine his own sister being thrown into a situation like this and him being powerless to help her. His heart ached as he watched the siblings, knowing the terror both must have felt.

Just then, the sound of voices from beyond the hedges floated over to where they stood, signaling the approach of newcomers. Kenisha raised her head in alarm. "I have to go. I'll be in touch. When the time comes for me to leave the palace, I'll try to get word to you."

Kirk reached for her as she darted away, but his hand fell just short. "Keni, wait!"

She looked over her shoulder long enough to utter, "I love you, brother." And then Kirk was left to stare at the back of her head as she ran away.

For several moments, the mage trainee stood there, hand still extended and eyes misty with tears, but finally he dropped the arm to his side and blinked the wetness in his eyes away. His silence betrayed his anguish as he stared into the distance as if he were lost.

Joel wrung his hands, unsure if he should walk away or offer words of comfort. He elected the latter, knowing if he'd been in the same position, kind words would have been appreciated. "I'm sorry. I wish there was something I could do to help."

Kirk wrapped his arms around himself and gasped. "I feel like I failed her."

"No," Joel replied. He moved closer, reaching out to tentatively set a hand onto Kirk's shoulder. "I don't really know either of you, but only a fool could deny the love you share for each other. She knows you do your best."

"My best isn't good enough to keep her safe anymore."

Joel didn't know how to respond. All he knew was the more time he spent with Kirk, the more Joel wished they could be friends. But they couldn't, not really. His time in Teivel was running out. Soon he'd have to return to Arden. He could only hope that Kirk and his sister found happiness. After all they'd been through, didn't they deserve it?

Joel wandered in the direction of the suite, his troubled mind recounting the woes of Kirk and Kenisha Bhadrayu. He wished he could do more to help the siblings, but he couldn't even help himself. *I feel so helpless in this place.* Sighing, Joel stopped to rest against a marble column.

Before him, the sun shone through a great window facing the courtyard, bathing him in light. The shimmering rays should have felt warm, but he could glean no such comfort from any of it. As far as he was concerned, the sun may never shine again.

"If not for where we are, it would be lovely, wouldn't it?"

The breath caught in Joel's throat as he whirled around. "Hasain! Where did you come from? I've been looking all over for you!"

Hasain's pale face hung in a forlorn frown and his eyes were red. Joel couldn't recall a time his cousin had looked so frail. The Radek lord opted to look out the window as he spoke in a trembling voice. "I needed a walk to clear my mind."

Joel nodded. Reasonable. The royal garden had been a welcome relief after the gore he'd witnessed. Hasain must have desired the same reprieve. "Take care next time. I feel we shouldn't wander alone here."

"I needed to be by myself." Hasain's voice was clipped, and Joel knew better than to press further. "This place is barbaric. How could anyone fault my father for leaving?"

"I suppose they don't know any better. If this is all they're used to, they don't even know enough to dream of anything better. Likewise, they don't think to question the cruelty of their arena because it's always been a part of their lives."

Hasain gasped and tipped his head down. Joel politely ignored the strangled sob, allowing his cousin to regain the control he was typically so proud of. "They were slaughtered like animals. All of them, but especially him."

Joel knit his brows together. *Who?*

"They broke his wing and threw him in there like he was a wild beast."

Oh. The demharlin. Joel wished he could offer some form of comfort but didn't know what to say. He'd never known Hasain sympathized so readily with the Otherfolk. He was often so aloof and contemptuous toward other humans that it surprised Joel to see Hasain so devastated by the death of the demharlin.

A few moments passed while neither said anything. At long last, Joel couldn't take the silence anymore. "It was wrong for them to treat it— him—so badly. I'm sorry your heart is heavy with this burden, Hasain. You know there was nothing you could do, don't you?"

Hasain's dark eyes flicked up, and his dark orbs were just as troubled as before. "If I could—have no doubt—I would have slaughtered his captors the same way they slaughtered him."

Cold spiked like shards of ice beneath Joel's skin. He hadn't been prepared for the unmasked rage in his cousin's voice. Hasain didn't even look like himself. Fury warped his features and contorted his face into a frightening caricature of his normal self. Joel withdrew slightly. What grief could force Hasain to look so terrible?

It's this place. Joel rubbed the back of one hand absently. *He's not handling the Empire well. None of us are. How much more can we be expected to take before our spirits break?*

The echo of footfalls through the hall broke Joel's cold thoughts, and he glanced up to see who approached.

"Oh, look! We've finally managed to find the missing lords!" Prince Alerio's voice danced along the corridor.

Joel shuddered. Hasain also seemed to withdraw farther into himself.

Liro strode alongside the prince like he'd always been a part of Alerio's entourage. "We were beginning to wonder if you'd both slunk away to weep for the losers."

Alerio laughed and his followers mirrored him. He waved a hand at Liro. "Stop now. My sides hurt." He took a couple of deep breaths, managing to chase away his giggles, before standing back to his full height. "We go now to take refreshments after sitting in the hot sun. Would either of you care to join us?" The coy twist of his voice gave away his game. He was challenging them.

Hasain was dangerously quiet, and Joel found himself stepping forward to speak on both of their behalves. "Forgive us, Highness. Lord Hasain and I are not used to such blood sport. Refreshment may not set well with us just yet."

Liro lifted his face to smirk at Alerio. "I told you they'd taken ill. As pampered as they are, the sight of a bit of blood has put them off."

Laughter filled the entire length of the corridor as the prince and his courtiers enjoyed the joke. Joel could feel his face go hot but held his ground, hoping desperately Hasain would also be able to keep his composure.

Alerio flicked a wrist at them as he passed. "You Ardenians are too entertaining. I shan't know what to do with myself when you leave. I would suggest you go take your rest, my lords, so you might be able to take your meal this evening." He and the others walked on, their scornful laughter bouncing off the stone walls even after they rounded the corner and disappeared from sight.

Joel's feet were rooted in place. He shook so terribly he didn't dare try to take a single step.

Hasain sighed heavily. "I hate this place. I want to go home."

Joel couldn't say anything, but he agreed. He wished, more than anything, that he could go home as well.

Gib stood outside the library doors for what seemed like an eternity. He felt a fool for hesitating, but he couldn't shake the worry of knowing too much. If he were to find the book Diddy had suggested, would there be any going back? What if he couldn't keep whatever secrets the book revealed? On the other hand, if he never learned the truth, he might risk failing Diddy or the royal family at a crucial moment. Sighing, he pulled the door open.

The aroma of incense welcomed him into the cozy space. Unlike the rest of Academy, the library was often so quiet that the soft glow of mage orbs could lull an unsuspecting student off to slumber if they weren't careful. Gib looked first right and then left, taking in the endless rows of books stacked to the ceiling twice his height. He had no idea where to even start. Weighing his options, he decided he'd have to go to the desk and ask for help, lest he be there all night trying to find this book.

The counter stood in the middle of the room, directly in front of the doors. He couldn't see anyone there but stepped up to the desk anyway. The attendants were never very far away.

Hushed whispers bounced off the walls around him as he waited, but Gib paid the voices little mind. He was entirely focused on remembering the name of the text and finding a secluded spot to sit. Perhaps if he was lucky, he would be able to find an available seat next to one of the windows. At least that way he'd be able to keep track of the time.

"Gibben Nemesio?"

Gib startled at his full name and was surprised when he turned to look up at Kezra's elder brother, Zandi. He looked sharp in his mage robes, and his emerald eyes glimmered along with his smile. Gib inclined his head by way of greeting. The last time they'd crossed paths, Gib had been terribly rude. He couldn't imagine why the other man was offering anything more than a cold shoulder now.

"What brings you here?" Zandi asked. "I would have thought a councilor understudy such as yourself would have meeting notes to pour over. Or did one of your Academy professors assign you research?" Zandi made conversation easily enough while he rummaged through sheets of parchment paper on the unattended desk. The gentle lilt in his voice was almost hypnotic.

Gib had to focus to respond. "Independent research. I have to find a book."

Zandi found the piece of parchment he must have been looking for and began to scribble onto it with a quill. "Oh, you'll have to ask Syther about that. Unless it's magic studies, I have no idea where anything is in here."

Syther? Syther Lais? Joel's original roommate and first love? Gib's stomach went sour even as he caught sight of the librarian. *Now I remember why I try to avoid coming to the library.*

Syther and Joel had parted ways—rather unpleasantly—the season before Gib came to Silver, but Gib knew who the other man was, and the two of them had met several times over the past few years—their encounters never seeming to grow any less awkward.

Gib was greeted with an acidic scowl as the slight man slipped up behind the counter. He must have had a stool of some sort back there because, in reality, Syther was no taller than Gib. Yet from behind the counter, Syther loomed above them. His critical eyes swept up and then down, probably taking in every detail and noting any hair out of place or smudge on Gib's tunic. As cold and lofty as ever, Syther finally sighed and spoke through his nose. "What do you want?"

Fumbling closer, Gib kept his voice low. "I'm looking for a book titled *Annals of the Unknown Peoples*. Do you know where I'd find it?"

Syther knit his brow in apparent confusion, and even Zandi seemed to hesitate as he scribbled. Gib felt his breath catch. It wasn't a restricted book, was it? Surely Diddy would have known if it was.

The librarian recovered an instant later and pointed toward the right wing. "In the back, on the north wall. You'll have to climb the ladder."

Gib tried not to wince. "It's up high?"

"Alphabetically arranged." Syther smiled, but it felt more like a sneer, reminding Gib of the former Instructions Master and recordkeeper on the council, Diedrick Lyle.

Gib nodded and took a step back. He opened his mouth to offer a word of thanks, but Zandi cleared his throat then and pushed the quill and parchment toward Syther. "All right, the mage orbs along the front wall are fixed. There was a flow problem, but I've straightened it out now."

Syther took the paper. "Thanks. It was manageable without the orbs functioning during the day, but night is fast approaching. The students would have been crying if they couldn't read their texts."

A moment's hesitation gave way to quiet laughter. Zandi and Syther seemed to be privy to some joke Gib wasn't aware of. Zandi took a step back and waved to the librarian. "I'll see you around sometime." Syther smiled, and as far as Gib could tell, the gesture seemed to be genuine. A moment later, Syther had promptly turned his back, ignoring Gib entirely.

Gib nearly snorted aloud. *Well, it's nice to know some things will never change.*

"I'll show you where it is," Zandi offered in a quiet voice.

Gib blinked up at him. "Pardon?"

A smile broke across Zandi's face as though Gib had said something funny. "The book. I know where it is. I suppose I could even give you a leg up onto the ladder if you need it."

A short laugh burst from Gib's throat before he could stop it. Zandi was joking with him? Was all forgiven then, despite Gib being so foul upon their last meeting? Some of the tension left his shoulders as he grinned back at the mage. "Or you could just reach up and grab it for me, no ladders needed."

Zandi's smile flicked a little higher onto his cheeks. "From the top shelf? Even I may need a step stool for that." He laughed and swept off toward the north side of the library.

Gib raced to keep up, fully appreciating how tall Zandi was now that it took two of Gib's strides to match one of the other man's. As they approached the bookcase, Gib peered up. It still boggled his mind to think about how many books had to be crammed into this room. *Hundreds, at least. Maybe even thousands.*

Without hesitation, Zandi pulled a ladder over and braced it against the shelf. "I already see it up there. I remember the golden binding from when I was in my third year of Academy." He paused long enough to steal a glance back at Gib and blushed when he was caught. "What sort of independent study are you doing anyway?"

Gib's mind grounded to a halt while he fished for something to say. This secret-keeping nonsense was already proving to be a chore. "I'm not sure yet. A friend suggested the book." He offered his best smile in hopes it would deter further investigation. "I don't even know what it's about yet."

Zandi pulled the text from among the other books and made his way back down. His cheeks were rosy as he handed the book to Gib. "Really? Interesting read for a politician."

"Is that so?" Gib glanced down. The image of a dragon wrapped around a gathering of different fantastical characters was etched into the cover with gold powder. Interesting. What could this possibly have to do with the royal family's birthing records?

Zandi cleared his throat. "I would think you'd be more interested in histories and law studies. Do you plan to travel one day?"

Flipping open to the index, Gib shrugged and trotted over to a table near the window. "Not particularly. Why?" He ran his finger down the neat print and found a page number for section four. *The Demharlin.*

Zandi sat across from Gib, folding long arms over the table. "Well, Folk studies tend to be reserved for those who either intend to explore the wilds or trek to foreign lands. Or, on rare occasion, for those who mean to actually interact with the different peoples."

Gib could feel the heavy stare but didn't look up or respond. He couldn't think of anything to say without possibly revealing too much.

Taking in an audible gulp of air, Zandi plunged on. "When I was still young and naïve, I entertained the idea of such adventures. I find Otherfolk interesting and think humanity should seek to preserve the other species who share our world."

Gib's eyebrow quirked on its own accord. "Most people I know aren't interested in sharing the world."

"You'll make an odd politician. You don't seem at all the type to wipe out entire races of people and then ask questions later."

Though he *was* trying to read, Gib felt compelled to engage with the man who had so kindly offered to help him. "Well, being a politician was never my goal. I mean, really, I never had any intention to even leave my farm. If I hadn't been drafted, I'd still be in Willowdale."

Zandi smiled, but his eyes were wistful. "What was it like out there? Away from the city?"

"Quiet," Gib chuckled. "My neighbor once had a chicken lay an egg that hatched two chicks. That was big news for a year."

"That sounds wonderful. Here there's always talk of new laws and old laws. You never know what may be acceptable today but not tomorrow. And if you're caught in the wrong? You can be hauled away in shackles."

"Willowdale sounds quaint at first, but it's not perfect. Nothing ever happens out there. It's like a stagnant pond." He glanced around to make sure they were alone. "Change doesn't happen in the outreaches. If I were still on the farm, I'd be married now and probably already have fathered a baby or two—not because it would be what I wanted, but because it's what's expected."

"Then perhaps Willowdale isn't so different from Silver. If my father had his way, I'd be married as well." The tremble on Zandi's delicate jaw gave away his carefully disguised melancholy. "I don't—I don't wish to upset you as I did when last we met, but I have to tell you what an inspiration you are. Even if you and Joel Adelwijn aren't lovers anymore, the fact that the two of you stood united and unashamed still gives hope to so many of us who wouldn't dare."

Gib had to take a deep breath to calm his nerves. It still hurt to hear talk of him and Joel being done, but he was starting to be able to keep his head cool. When he'd collected himself, Gib let out a long sigh and replied, "We never meant to draw attention. We weren't trying to set an example. We're just people, like anyone else."

"I know. That's what made you both so perfect." Zandi wiped an eye with the back of his sleeve. "I won't press you any more. I know it must be hard to speak about such things. Just know you have supporters. There are people who still root for you."

Gib shook his head, face feeling warm. "I didn't mean to be so foul to you before, at the Rose Bouquet." He winced. "Well, I mean, I did. But only because I was already hurt and in no mood to hear what anyone had to say. It wasn't your fault—it was mine."

"I know. Kezra has said too many good things about you for me to ever suspect any different. She's not one to sugar-coat anything, so I know you're a good person."

"Not perfect though, and not a hero by any stretch of the word. I just want you to know that. If you're going to have an opinion of me, I'd have it be a fair one. I'm sorry to kill your hero, but I'm not him. I'm only me. A humble farmer. Gib from Willowdale."

Zandi smiled, still sad, but no longer looking forlorn. "Gibben Nemesio from Willowdale—a good man and a fool." He chuckled. "Kezra's right about you."

Gib laughed at what Zandi had to say for the second time today. "Fool? I suppose that sounds exactly like something she'd say about me."

"You should hear what she says about me. 'Fool' is nothing—a badge of honor even!"

Smiles were shared as they lapsed into comfortable silence. Gib refocused on the text before him, trying to make sense of why Diddy had suggested it in the first place. His confusion must have been apparent for, after a short time, Zandi took pity on him and leaned across the table. "Which Folk are you basing your 'independent study' on?"

"Uh... Demharlins?" Gib flipped the page back and forth, taking in the text on either side.

Zandi pressed the back of his hand to his mouth to hide the smile playing on his lips. "Demharlin. The word is both plural and singular. What did you need to know about them?"

Rubbing the back of his neck, Gib sighed. "I'm not sure, really. As I said, a friend suggested I study up on them."

"Huh. I see." Zandi's mouth slanted down, but even the frown was handsome on his dark, heart-shaped face. "They're indigenous to our mountains, you know. There are several documented clans throughout the Pinnacles."

Gib studied an illustration which compared two of the creatures side by side. Both had similar features, with feathered crests, wings, and tails. The only difference in the two were their overall sizes and genders. The woman stood probably a foot taller than her male counterpart.

Zandi tapped one long finger on the open page. "Their women are rare, rumored to be as few as one in thirty or more. And they only reproduce once every forty years or something like that. It's a wonder the race hasn't died out."

"I suppose that's interesting, but I don't know why my friend wanted me to study them. Do they ever come into the populated areas of Arden?"

"Not in recent history. Human cities and towns have driven them farther up into the mountains. I mean, they thrive there. Their feathers and tough hides keep them warm, but they don't have much range over the flatter places."

Gib frowned. "Their teeth and claws look nasty. Maybe it's a good thing they're not common in the lowlands. They could pose a threat."

"I suppose," Zandi shrugged. "But I don't think they'd want to fight humanity anyway. Humans tend to live on the ground and in small homes. Demharlin prefer high altitudes and open space."

"But if they're overcrowded in the mountains, what then? Would they be tempted to attack humans to gain more land?" Gib knew he was grasping at straws now. What in the two worlds did these creatures have to do with the conversation he'd witnessed earlier? Had Diddy given him the name of the wrong book?

"Oh, the Pinnacles aren't their *sole* habitat. They can live anywhere there are mountains or cliffs. Some have been sighted as far south as Tembo and across the western sea on the cliffs of Derry. I don't know that they'd be looking for more land."

"Huh." Gib continued to leaf through the book. "Maybe I'll have to borrow this. It may take a while to learn what I'm supposed to know. There's more here than I would have thought."

Zandi smiled. "I know. The demharlin are one of my favorites because they're so interesting. The other species of Folk are too, but some of them are so secretive that they're hard to observe—like the naga in Shantar. My mother is native to the land. She's told me bedtime stories of the naga since I was a baby, but most of the tales are rumors and speculation."

Gib flipped through until he found another drawing. This one was of a demharlin and a human standing side by side. The caption beneath their feet simply listed the illustration as "shifted form." What did that mean? He turned the book toward Zandi and pointed. "Is this a size comparison? What does shifted form mean?"

"Oh, the magic left behind from their demon heritage allows the demharlin to be shape shifters. They can take on the appearance of species who are similar to them, like humans or goblins. They may be able to shift to look like harpies as well. I'm not sure."

Gib's stomach sank. These creatures could disguise themselves to look human? Was *that* what Diddy was trying to tell him? Maybe there was one or more of these demharlin hunting the King or his family. Gib had thought the council was King Rishi's biggest worry, but maybe the royal family's troubles ran deeper.

"There are several species of Folk who can shift." Zandi's voice was more a background noise, but Gib nodded along to appease the other man. "It depends on their origins, really. The sirens and banshee can also shift. It has to do with those species having demon bloodlines. They all have strong natural magic—"

Gib closed the book and stood promptly. "I think I've figured out what I'm supposed to be studying. Thank you for your help."

Zandi reeled, looking around, before he stood as well. "All—all right. I guess you'll be off now?"

"It's getting late." Gib nearly winced. It hadn't been his intention to glean knowledge from Zandi only to run out on him, but he really did need to go somewhere more private to pour over all of this.

"I suppose." Zandi looked out the darkening window. "Well, good luck."

Ugh. Stop being an arse. After the way you treated him at the tavern, you need to redeem yourself. Though, truth be told, it was becoming less and less difficult to converse with Zandi. Gib floundered for something more to say. "Thank you though. Really, you were a big help."

Zandi walked just ahead of him as both men took their leave. "Eh, I like talking probably even more than you like listening. I should thank you."

A smile pulled at Gib's mouth, and a strange feeling stirred to life just under his skin. It was an unexplainable pang of warmth that left him wanting to shiver. He wasn't sure when his opinion of Zandi had changed, but it had. Gib found himself liking the mage more the more they spoke to one another. "I'd say you're decent company, especially after our rocky start."

Zandi flashed a dazzling smile over his shoulder, emerald eyes dancing in the low light. "Decent company? Is that the best you can say for me?"

"Well, I—" Gib sputtered, trying to redeem himself.

Zandi's laughter was melodic, pleasing to the ear. "It's hard to say what sort of company you are. You barely talk at all."

As they approached the desk, Gib's face burst with heat. "I talk. You just haven't been around when I'm talking!" He set the book on the counter and looked around. Syther seemed to have disappeared.

"Oh?" One of Zandi's dark brows arched coyly, and the bindi painted onto his forehead glittered in the false light. He leaned against the desk. "Well then, where would I find you while you *are* talking? I mean, if I'm ever going to determine whether you're good company or not, I would have to hear you say a little more."

Gib's insides danced in a strange mix of excitement and anxiety. This interaction with Zandi wasn't wrong, was it? He thought of Joel's icy blue eyes, and his heart twisted, though not as sharply as it once had. Is this what it was like to move on? Gib wasn't sure he liked it. *Oh, hell. It's not like I'm asking Zandi for his hand or anything! Joel told me I deserved to be happy. He even encouraged it. What will it hurt if I befriend Zandi?* When he finally responded, his voice sounded more confident than he was feeling inside. "I go to the Rose Bouquet with my friends some evenings. Usually the last one of the sennight."

"So if I showed up on one of those evenings I might chance to see you?"

Gib smiled despite his shaking nerves. "Yeah. You might."

"All right then." Zandi locked eyes with him and flashed a devious beam. "I suppose I'll see you soon. Perhaps you'll have something more to say."

"Maybe. You might even find you enjoy my company."

CHAPTER TEN

Joel licked his dry lips and glanced around the council chamber. All the envoys, foreign and local alike, were already present and called to order. He tapped his fingers on the dry piece of parchment he'd been given for note-taking and waited for the discussion to start. No matter how many times he sat in this dark, windowless chamber, he never seemed able to calm his rapid heart or frayed nerves. Had they really been in Teivel for three fortnights? He'd lost track of the days. Joel gazed over at his father and stiffened at what he saw.

Koal's mouth was drawn into a thin frown. In the dim light, the seneschal of Arden looked tired and gaunt. Joel wished he could somehow offer more support. His father was being worn too thin. Six sennights in this foreign country had taken its toll on him the most.

Emperor Sarpedon gestured toward Adrian Titus, who nodded his head once before addressing the group. "I believe we were to pick up where we last left off. Chancellor Garron, you have agreed to sign the treaty discussed at the meeting two days ago?"

The chancellor of Nales bowed his head before he spoke. "After much deliberation, Archmage, I have decided it will be in my country's best interest to sign." His stiff voice masked any emotion he may have been feeling, but Joel was sure he could feel unspoken tension leaching from the leader.

Nales was a small country and its precarious position on the Northern Empire's southern border probably left the chancellor feeling vulnerable. What could he possibly do to save his tiny country if Emperor Sarpedon decided to take it? Of course signing the treaty was in his best interest.

A scroll was sent across the table along with a quill and inkwell. Chancellor Garron's brow knitted as he pulled it closer to read it.

Adrian waved his hand, an irritated scowl flashing across his lips. "I believe you'll find the wording to your liking. The Northern Empire will be allowed to use your seaports, free of charge and with priority, while we commence our war with Derry. In return, once we have conquered the island nation, the Empire will share the spoils gained there. They're all mentioned in the treaty—limestone from the cliffs, silver ore, livestock, etcetera."

"Yes, yes. I see." Garron's hand hovered over the quill for a moment before he took it and signed his name.

Joel tried not to stare while the foreign ruler made his treaty, but morbid curiosity stole over him, and he just couldn't look away. Beside him, Hasain's breathing hitched.

As soon as Chancellor Garron set his quill down, the scroll was swept away. Adrian didn't waste even a moment before turning his sharp gaze onto Koal. The seneschal stiffened but didn't avert his eyes.

"Has Arden reconsidered our offer, Seneschal Koal?"

"I stand by my previous decision." Koal was met with cold disapproval when he offered nothing more.

The Emperor shot a stern look at the Archmage, and Adrian's shoulders noticeably stiffened under the pressure. The false light cast dramatic shadows over his eyes and mouth, aging him. "Port Ostlea would be an invaluable asset to us in our time of war. Of all the ports on the western sea, Ostlea sits closest to Derry. Would the silver and other mining ores from the island not tempt even your king?"

Koal heaved a sigh. "I'm afraid there's nothing you could offer to change Arden's mind. The war on Derry is not ours, and I won't make arrangements contrary to that. We came here to negotiate peace, not house naval forces for a foreign army."

Joel reminded himself to breathe. The stale air in the enclosed council room coupled with the heavy silence to create a stifling blanket. The Imperial councilors looked on the Ardenian envoys with cold frowns and judging eyes. Koal met the glares head on, refusing to budge even a little.

The torture lasted only a moment longer before Adrian redirected his attention to the Dhaki princes, Kadar and Rami. "His Grace has also taken the time to outline the peace agreements Shiraz has consented to." He sent a scroll across the table to them. "You'll see it has been written out in both your language and ours. You need only sign it once. This will ensure the northern trade routes from Beihai can be utilized to their full capacity. In return, the Empire will help to fortify your northwestern and eastern borders."

The interpreter relayed the message to the princes, who each took their turns signing. Koal waited for them to go quiet before clearing his throat pointedly. "Remind me, why is it that Shiraz feels the need to reinforce its shared border with Arden if we were called here to come to a peaceful resolution?"

Joel was content to frown down at the empty parchment sitting before him but caught sight of Cenric moving out of the corner of his eye. The ambassador leaned toward Koal and whispered something about remembering proper etiquette. Koal seemed entirely unmoved and didn't respond. Liro, on the other hand, scoffed and lifted his nose into the air.

Prince Kadar lifted his gleaming eyes to look at Koal. His voice was low and deliberate, as if he might have been having trouble containing his emotions. It was difficult for Joel to be sure, with the difference in languages. "Shiraz has people and lands to protect, Seneschal Koal. It was our hope to find peace with Arden as well but thus far our efforts have proven fruitless."

Koal leaned back in his seat. "It's unfortunate we haven't been able to find any middle ground, I would agree, but surely there's no need for walls to be constructed and fortified between our lands."

Rami hissed a string of harsh words, but no translation was offered. Kadar waved a hand at him, silencing his clipped words, but never took his eyes away from Koal. "If you seek peace then a wall should not bother you. We must take this opportunity to ensure nothing more will be taken from us."

Joel slammed his eyes shut and heard Hasain shift in his seat. Koal didn't respond, but it may have been due to lack of time. Almost immediately, Adrian's sly voice picked up once more. "If Port Ostlea were to be open to us, the Northern Empire would be available to lend military aid, should Arden need it."

"You have this figured out from all ends, don't you?" Koal wasn't reserved with his proclamation. "You get your trades with Shiraz and help them build a wall, you use Arden's seaport to propel your war on Derry and 'help' us in the event we go to war with Shiraz. That's a nice pedestal you've perched yourselves on."

Cenric nudged Koal's elbow. He gave the seneschal a heavy look but still kept his mouth closed. Joel's heart hammered in his chest. How could Cenric keep so calm? Everything was beginning to unravel right before their eyes.

Adrian's face pinched, his cheeks going a fiery red, but before he could say anything, Prince Alerio leaned around him to address Koal for the first time. "Such is the business of treaties and alliances."

Koal folded his arms over his chest. "Alliances are to be made where both parties benefit from them, Your Highness. And right now, I fail to see where any of these treaties benefit Arden."

The prince smiled, and with a shudder, Joel had to look away. He'd never make a good politician. He couldn't bear looking into the faces of snakes. Alerio went on as casually as if he were discussing the weather. "You could give permission for a marital alliance between our countries. That would ensure Arden's safety with the Northern Empire."

Hasain's fist clenched, crumpling his parchment into a ball.

Koal's voice was every bit as icy as Hasain was ablaze. "I will *not* be making any such alliances concerning the heirs of Arden. My King would have to give such permission—"

"But of course, your king didn't come to Teivel to discuss such things for himself." Adrian glared coolly from his seat, and Joel winced when he heard Liro laugh.

"The Radek children are just that—children—and I will not be auctioning them off no matter how high the bid." Koal's sharp voice clipped on the final word, and Joel sank down into his seat. Years of living with his father had taught Joel that this is where the discussion should be abandoned.

But Prince Alerio apparently didn't care. "*Seneschal*." The prince spit out the word as if it tasted bitter on his tongue. "What was the point in Arden coming here if no treaties were going to be made? It was the hope of His Grace to find peace."

"Again," Koal ground out, "Alliances are made when both parties benefit. I've yet to see any benefit for Arden."

Joel's heart thudded to a feeble stop. He wanted to be proud of his father for keeping to his morals, but the silence in the council chamber was frightening. Not a single word or sound was uttered for what felt like an eternity. Finally, a throat was cleared, and all eyes turned to Emperor Lichas Sarpedon.

His mouth was set in a grim line, and his eyes were cold and calculating. "It would be in Arden's best interest to align with us, Seneschal. After all, should Shiraz declare war, who will be your ally? No one."

Koal tapped his fingers, the sound resonating in the otherwise silent room. A heavy sigh escaped his lips, and he seemed to be weighing something in his mind. "With all due respect, Your Grace, Arden has seen more than one war in her time. We have managed well in the past, and I can't see any reason to change our alliances now. Even with any threat that may come from Shiraz—" Koal paused briefly to make eye contact with Prince Kadar "—I am confident in Arden's ability to defend herself. And more to the point, Shiraz has asked for help to build a wall, not their army. It would hardly seem they were making a plan for attack, unless I'm unaware of something."

Heavy quiet fell once more as the interpreter whispered to the Dhaki princes. When he was done relaying Koal's words, both Kadar and Rami withdrew in their seats, casting icy glares toward the seneschal.

Adrian was the first to move as he slid a roll of parchment across the table. "If it would please you, you may look upon the treaty once more. Consider what has been offered to you, Seneschal Koal. Perhaps you should contact your king. Does he know what decisions you are making in his stead? He might find our offer more favorable than you think—"

Koal scoffed, and his elbow was nudged by Cenric once more, a severe look in his eyes. The seneschal disregarded Cenric's good sense, however, and proceeded onward without so much as a flinch. "King Rishi's submission cannot be bought with treasures or trinkets. I assure you, he'll care for your offer as little as I do."

Adrian's right eye twitched. His jaw was locked so hard that Joel could almost hear teeth cracking under the pressure. The Archmage took a stilted breath. "It would seem the viper has built his nest then."

Joel's arm shot out on its own accord to catch Hasain before the Radek lord could stand. Koal, however, was on his feet in an instant. Joel's entire body went rigid as he prepared himself for shouting and fury.

Yet when he spoke, Koal's voice was an unnerving whisper. "All this talk of vipers, yet the only venom I've encountered here is yours. I've heard enough. I won't sit idly while your foul mouth disgraces my king." The seneschal reached across the table and snatched up the treaty. He didn't even glance down at it before shredding the parchment and flinging the tiny pieces back at the Archmage. "As far as Arden is concerned, this meeting is over. We're not making any progress here. It's time for us to leave. We're going home."

Koal turned on his heel and stormed from the room without waiting to be dismissed, and Joel and the other Ardenian envoys were forced to run to catch up with him. Joel could feel the terrible glares of a dozen angry councilors on his back as he left, but he didn't dare risk a glimpse back to confirm it.

Joel's hands trembled as he placed the last of his belongings into his rucksack. *There. I think that's everything.* He cast an extended gaze around the bedchamber, the room that had been his for the past six sennights. It was almost hard to believe that when he walked out the next morning, it would be for the last time. He was going home. *And none too soon. I've experienced more than enough Imperial culture to last a lifetime. I'll be content with never having to see this place again.*

Joel left the rucksack on his bed and ventured into the common room, where the other members of the party were collecting their items and stowing them away. Koal sat at the desk, scribbling notes onto a fresh sheet of parchment paper. Cenric hovered above him, and they spoke in hushed voices about their final report to the King.

"Why are they bothering to send King Rishi a report if we're all to be sent home tomorrow?" Joel asked as he took a seat beside Hasain on the lounge. "The message won't even get to Arden before we arrive."

Cenric didn't look up from the table but raised his voice to respond. "We're going to send it with a cockatrice. With luck, the message will reach the King late tonight so he'll be prepared for our arrival on the morn."

Hasain folded his arms across his chest. "With luck, the message will reach my father *at all*. Do you really think Sarpedon will allow us to utilize one of the Northern Empire's cockatrices after the display in the council chamber earlier?"

The quill resting in Koal's grasp stopped moving as he lifted his eyes to give Hasain a sharp look. "The Emperor has already agreed to it, Hasain. He said we're welcome to leave on our own free will."

"Forgive me for my skepticism," the young Radek lord growled. "I have placed little faith in the promises of our host."

Liro marched into the room just then, his own pack slung over one shoulder. He raised his nose into the air as his icy glare landed on Hasain. "Despite your rather uninformed opinion, our hosts have proven to be most civilized. Even after that unruly display in the council room, look at the graciousness His Grace has shown by allowing us to go home. However, the decision to leave without a treaty is, in my opinion, wrong. There's so much we would stand to gain if we allied ourselves with the Northern Empire."

Hasain's glare was as sharp as a dagger. "You've acclimated to life in Teivel with such ease, Liro, that I'd almost be willing to mistake your enthusiasm for disloyalty. If you're enjoying the Empire's 'civility' so much, why not do us all a favor and stay here?"

"How ironic," Liro smirked. "The son of the traitor speaking of disloyalty."

Joel held his breath as he watched Hasain ball his hands into fists. *Please, not this again.*

"Enough," Koal grunted, giving the young lords a withering glare. "Liro, I've made my decision. There's nothing left to discuss with Emperor Sarpedon, the Shiraz princes, or even Chancellor Garron. It's clear to me they're all determined to be pitted against us and any treaties or alliances they have offered will only stand to harm our nation while blatantly benefiting theirs. Therefore, we're returning to Arden."

"And why is the decision to leave yours alone to make, Father?" Liro countered. "We shouldn't be so hasty to abandon our mission."

Koal narrowed his eyes farther, a troubled frown distorting his aging face. He folded the parchment paper and used hot wax to seal it. "NezReth, have this sent to King Rishi immediately."

At once, the Blessed Mage emerged from the shadows, startling Joel enough to make him jump in place. He hadn't realized NezReth was even in the room. Koal handed off the message, and NezReth whisked away without a single word.

"I'm going to finish packing," Koal announced after a moment of uncomfortable silence. As he rose from the chair, his hard gaze settled onto the lounge. "No one is to wander far. Do you understand?"

Joel found himself nodding alongside Hasain. Liro rolled his eyes but kept his mouth shut. His right hand reached up to clasp something hanging from a golden chain around his neck, drawing Joel's attention. It was an opal of some sort, turquoise in color and as smooth as silk. Liro held the stone in the palm of his hand, caressing it as though it was the most precious treasure in the world.

"What is that?" Joel asked.

Liro's voice was an eerie calm. "A gift from the Archmage."

Hasain raised an eyebrow but didn't say anything. Joel couldn't keep quiet however and pressed gently, "The Archmage? Are you sure it's a good idea to be accepting random trinkets from the Northern Empire?"

Liro clamped a fist around the stone. "It's a focus stone. Archmage Titus gives them to all of his mage students."

"But you're not a student." Hasain did voice his opinion now. "You're not even an Imperial mage. Why would he decide to bestow such an item on *you*?"

Liro whirled around to glare at the two occupants sitting on the lounge. "The Archmage and I have mutual respect for one another, something you would know nothing about, bastard."

Hasain snorted. "Well, if that isn't the pot calling the kettle black."

Liro's eyes gleamed in a dangerous way, and Joel found his back pressing against the lounge in an attempt to distance himself from his brother's wrath.

Cenric tapped a firm hand on the table, efficiently stopping the argument before it had a chance to spiral downward. The ambassador cleared his throat and fixed Liro with a stern stare. "When NezReth returns, you should let him have a look at that—just to make sure it hasn't been tampered with. We can't be too careful."

Liro locked his jaw. "You fools all worry for nothing. I won't stand here and listen to this idiocy." He slipped the opal beneath the collar of his mage robe and stormed from the room.

Hasain shook his head. "I'm quite literally counting down the marks until I can remove myself from his presence."

"Good luck with that." Joel chuckled as the color slowly returned to his face. "I'm afraid you'll still have to tolerate each other when you resume your apprenticeships in the council room."

"I don't plan on sitting with the understudies much longer. Father informed me before I left that it won't be long before I'm to sit on the royal council myself. I expect that when a seat next opens, I'll be the one to take it."

"If my uncle doesn't get his way," Joel reminded. "Neetra is pushing for Liro to sit on the council as well."

An irritated sigh escaped Hasain's lips. "I'm not concerned."

"Maybe you should be. Neetra is High Councilor, after all—"

"And my father is the *King*!" Hasain countered through gritted teeth. "If he says I'm to be on the council, then I am. No one will dare question his judgment!"

Joel smartly held his tongue. Hasain's clipped voice was proof enough that the young Radek lord was upset. *And rightfully so. He knows he shouldn't count his chickens before they hatch. He may be the son of the King, but if Neetra's able to rally the council, Liro could very well steal the next available seat right out from under Hasain's nose.*

Hasain still glowered as he took to his feet. "I'm going for a walk."

Joel began to protest. "But my father said—"

"I won't be going far. I just need to—to get out of here for a little while."

Joel bit his lip but could only watch as Hasain swept to the door and disappeared into the hallway. For a moment, he debated following the young lord. Ever since the gladiator tournament, Hasain had been more withdrawn than Joel had ever before witnessed. *Not that he's generally chipper under normal circumstances. But I don't recall a time he's been so moody and unpredictable either.* Being in such a hostile environment was clearly taking its toll on him.

Joel sighed, looking to his mentor. "Do you think I should go after him?"

"No. Let him be," Cenric replied. A faint, pained smile flitted across his face. "Hasain is under an immense amount of stress. It's not easy having fingers pointed and accusations thrown at you for over a moonturn. I imagine his patience must be growing thin." The ambassador chuckled. "And we both know Hasain Radek never had much patience to begin with."

Joel tried not to grin. "You must have had quite the time when he was your understudy a year ago. Was it difficult getting him to keep his opinions to himself?"

Cenric laughed as he came over to sit on the lounge beside Joel. "On the contrary, Hasain was quite reserved. I suspect homesickness played a part. His decision not to pursue an ambassador's life came quite easily. Though there was one time he made a snide remark to Sovereign Khalfani Heru and I full-heartedly believed the ruler would have had us both carted to the middle of the desert and left stranded there beneath the Gyptian sun." Cenric wiped a tear from his eye in between fits of laughter. "Oh, the look on Hasain's face when he realized his error was priceless. I don't believe I've ever witnessed an understudy more eager to return to Arden."

"I don't know," Joel replied, staring at his feet. "I'm pretty damned excited to go home."

"Mm, I think we all are."

Joel blinked, lost in his own tumultuous thoughts. Before coming to the Northern Empire, he'd been so certain he wanted to be an envoy—he'd even sacrificed his life with Gib to pursue the dream—but the reality of an ambassadorial life was so utterly different than he ever imagined. He could barely stomach the negotiations and endless council sessions, and the changes he'd hoped to bring would likely never see fruition. He'd dreamed of peaceful talks between nations but had witnessed only shouting and slandering. Where were the trade agreements and treaties of comradery he'd wanted to help create? Why was he returning to Arden with only a broken spirit? This wasn't the way he'd pictured any of this playing out.

A hand squeezed his shoulder, drawing Joel's attention back to the present. Cenric gazed at him, concern lingering in his hazel orbs. "Is everything all right?"

Joel thought to lie but knew his mentor would know the deceit for what it was. *He knows me too well. I have to tell him what's really on my mind.* With a deep sigh, he met Cenric's eyes and admitted the truth. "I hope you won't be incredibly disappointed in me, but—I've been thinking that perhaps—perhaps I no longer wish to become an ambassador."

A deafening silence followed his confession, and for a brief moment, Joel mistook the mentor's stillness for anger. But then, a warm smile broke across Cenric's face and the hand touching Joel's shoulder gripped a bit tighter. "I know. I could tell you had a change of heart."

Joel shifted his gaze to the marble floor, guilt eating his innards and making it impossible to maintain eye contact with the older man. "I feel like I've wasted your time—that it's all been for nothing. I feel like I've disappointed you."

Cenric's eyebrows knitted. "You didn't waste anyone's time, least of all mine. This journey is *yours*, Joel. It's never been about whether or not you want to be an envoy—it's about discovering your interests, your passions, emotional growth and maturity, and deciding the kind of man you want to be when your internship comes to an end. Those are the things that matter. Those are the reasons I take an understudy every year. It's not about recruiting young men and women to serve as Ardenian envoys. I don't give a damn what my underlings go on to do, so long as they're happy, so long as they're making a difference in the world. I suppose I can rest easy tonight."

Joel's thoughts were a jumble of feelings. "What do you mean?"

"Because *you*, my friend, *will* make a difference. You'll leave a mark on the world, even if you don't believe it now. Humanity will be a better place because you're a part of it. And that's all I could ever ask for. I'm honored to be your mentor."

A wave of emotion rolled over Joel. It was a strange, confusing mix of sadness, uncertainty, and triumph that he didn't have the will or desire to decipher. *I don't even know where to go from here. I know I still want to help people. I want to be a good person. I just want to do it surrounded by my family and friends, not a thousand leagues from home.* A single tear slipped from the corner of one eye as Joel nodded once, slowly. "Thank you for placing so much faith in me, even if I keep none for myself. I don't know what I'll do with myself when we get home. I had this grand dream of being a renowned ambassador, but now that I've realized it's not the life I want, I don't know how I'm going to change the world."

"You'll figure it out," Cenric replied, giving Joel's back a pat. "No one ever said you needed to be an envoy in order to make the world a better place. Look at all the good things people like your father, Dean Marc, and your companion Gib are doing right inside Silver City! It only takes one tiny little pebble thrown into stagnant water to create a ripple that affects the entire lake."

"Yes," Joel said, wiping the moisture from his eyes. "I guess you're right."

Cenric gave one final thump on the shoulder before excusing himself, leaving Joel alone to ponder his mentor's words. Deep down, he knew Cenric was right, but still the guilt ate at his heart. *I caused so much grief by coming, and now I'll have to make amends when I go home—if it's not too late.* Joel's heart pounded in his ears. Gib would forgive him, wouldn't he?

A rustling sound from the terrace caught his attention. Joel turned toward the noise and blinked in surprise when Kirk Bhadrayu appeared in the open doorway. The mage trainee looked gaunt and frightened, skin a pasty white against his disheveled brown locks.

Joel immediately rose from the lounge and swept over to the trainee. "Kirk? What's the matter?"

"I need to talk to you," Kirk replied, chest heaving.

Joel's frown deepened. Had Kirk run the entire way there?

"I swear, it's of the utmost importance. Will you hear me out?"

"Yes, of course." Joel motioned for the other man to come inside.

Kirk stepped into the suite, the shadows cloaking his pale face but not completely disguising the terror in his eyes. "Th–thank you."

"What happened?" Joel asked. "Is this something to do with your sister?"

Kirk shook his head, and when he next spoke, it was in such a hushed voice that Joel had to lean closer to hear the trembling words. "No. This is about something else. This has to do with the well-being of you and your friends."

A horrifying wave of panic swept over Joel, crippling his mind and body. "O–oh?"

"I have reason to believe you're all in terrible danger."

Joel leaned against the stone wall for support. "Danger? What do you mean?"

Kirk's eyes shifted around the room, worry lines warping his youthful face. "Just now, I was returning a study tome to my master's library when I overheard the Archmage speaking in the next room. Normally I wouldn't have stayed to pry, but he—he was talking with the prince."

"Alerio?" Joel asked in a flat voice.

"Yes. They were going on about the Emperor's plan to deal with

Arden. I shouldn't have been listening to any of it! If Adrian knew I was eavesdropping—if he knew I was here, telling you—" Kirk gasped, unable to finish.

Joel reached out and lightly touched the boy's trembling arm. "Tell me what was said. Please, Kirk. I won't betray you. You know I won't."

Kirk nodded, taking a moment to breathe deeply and collect himself before continuing. "They—they spoke about betraying you. The prince said that since coercion with Seneschal Koal and your party has failed here in Teivel, they'll now take Arden by force. Tomorrow, when the portal opens to send you home, the Emperor has ordered it to be overrun by his army of mages and soldiers." His face grew even paler. "I–I think they mean to kill you all."

The entire room swayed. Joel gripped the wall and struggled to regain his balance. His lungs burned, but he couldn't seem to get enough air no matter how hard he gasped for it. "You need to tell my father what you just told me."

Kirk took a step back, shaking his head. "No, please. I can't—"

"Kirk, *please*. He needs to hear it. If what you say is true, then all our lives are at stake."

"He won't believe me! I'm just another Imperial to him. He has no reason to trust me!"

Joel squeezed the trainee's arm. "*I* trust you. I'll be right here with you. It will be okay."

Koal paced back and forth across the suite with his hands clasped behind his back and a terrible mask of rage painted onto his face. Those gathered in the room watched and waited. The silence was so intense Joel felt as though he were suffocating.

Finally, after what seemed like an eternity, Cenric raised his voice. "Seneschal, what do you want to do?"

Koal stopped. He stood completely still, staring with unfocused eyes through the open space leading to the terrace. His brows furrowed, and Joel could tell his father's thoughts were tumultuous and deep. What would he decide to do? Would he heed Kirk's warning?

Shadows crept into the suite as the sky above turned from gold to red to navy. Darkness had already begun to cloak the city. Night was falling. Joel swallowed as he awaited a decision from his father. *We're running out of time.*

Koal whirled around to face Kirk. His eyes speared the young trainee, and Kirk recoiled under the scrutiny. "You're absolutely *sure* you didn't mishear anything?"

"Yes, Lord Adelwijn," Kirk responded. He sat on the very edge of the lounge, shoulders rigid and hands fidgeting with the sleeves of his golden tunic. "They made no attempt to hide the scheme. There's no way I could have mistook what was said."

A sharp sigh of protest sounded from the opposite side of the room, and all eyes turned toward the noise. Apparently, Liro wasn't having any of this. He threw his hands into the air and glared at Kirk. "So we're going to just trust this *trainee's* word? We don't even know him!"

Joel narrowed his eyes. "I know him."

"Oh, *please!*" Liro spat. "How can you possibly claim to know someone you've only just met?"

Joel did his best to ignore his elder brother's putrid words. Joel took a tentative step forward, stepping into Koal's path and forcing the seneschal to halt in place. "Father, we can trust Kirk. Please, believe me."

Koal stared down the length of his nose at Joel, expression impossibly stern but searching for any trace of doubt in his son's eyes. Koal stood face to face with Joel, measuring him in silence. Joel could scarcely breathe. *Please, Father*, he begged silently. *Don't be stubborn. Heed the warning*. He winced when his father stepped around and resumed pacing. What did this mean? Had he come to a conclusion?

"NezReth," Koal called to the Blessed Mage, who lingered in the shadows near the open terrace. The mage was, no doubt, watching for Imperial spies. "If Sarpedon attempts to overwhelm the portal tomorrow, what are his odds of success? Surely Natori and the other Ardenian mages will sense something is amiss and bring the portal down before the entire Imperial army is able to march through."

NezReth didn't tear his violet eyes from the garden outside as he replied. "Once the portal is opened, I can communicate with Natori and warn her of the danger." His voice was serene in the midst of the chaos. "However, if the Northern Empire is in control of the rift, there is nothing any of us can do to close it—short of killing the mages who control the mage-spell, of course."

"That's highly improbable," Hasain muttered. "Their mages will be well protected. We'd be dead a hundred times over by the time we could find and destroy the ones commanding the portal spell."

The Blessed Mage nodded in agreement. "Lord Hasain is right. And I have not the strength to work the spell alone. None of us do. We would have to accept assistance from the Imperial mages."

Koal ran fingers through his greying hair as he paced. "Then we can't allow the portal to be opened at all. I cannot afford to put the King—or the rest of the country—in danger. We'll have to find another way home."

Liro's voice was caustic. "Or we can disregard this *boy* entirely! Why should we trust anything he says?"

"Is there any reason why we *shouldn't* trust him?" Cenric asked, rubbing his chin thoughtfully. "What would he stand to gain by fabricating a story like this?"

Kirk's cheeks flushed a deep hue of pink. "I swear on the Blessed Son, I didn't make the story up. If—if my master knew I was here now, speaking to you, I'd be arrested on the spot and tried as a traitor."

Cenric regarded the trainee from across the room. "If you stand to lose so much, why risk warning us at all? Why put your very life in jeopardy to help perfect strangers?" His questions were gentle, not demanding like Liro's had been.

Kirk glanced over at Joel before replying in a timid voice. "Just after your party first arrived in Teivel, Lord Joel Adelwijn did me a generous favor. He—he could have turned a blind eye or walked away, but he didn't. He was the first person in a very long time to treat me with kindness, for which I'll be eternally grateful. I don't want to see him—or any of you—hurt. That's why I came to warn you."

The trainee's speech struck a chord deep within Joel's soul. "Can't you all see he's telling the truth?"

Koal and Cenric exchanged glances. NezReth watched Kirk out of the corner of his eerie eyes but said nothing. Liro huffed a sigh and crossed his arms over his chest. Heart thudding rapidly in his ears, Joel held his breath, waiting for someone to speak.

It was Hasain, of all people, who finally broke the silence. "I trust Joel's judgment. If he believes this trainee, then so do I."

"Agreed," Cenric said with a nod. "And if there's even a small chance Sarpedon plans to overtake Arden, we can't allow that portal to open tomorrow." He rubbed the back of his neck, worry lines chiseling his face. "Of course, that will leave *us* in quite the predicament. How are we going to get home?"

"Yes," Liro hissed like a cornered viper. "How *are* we going to get home?"

Hasain sneered at him. "Weren't you just complaining about how you wished to stay longer?"

"None of us are staying!" Koal cut in. He whirled around, fierce eyes settling onto NezReth. "What if we leave tonight? Unannounced and under cover of darkness? We can escape Teivel before they even know what's happened."

The Blessed Mage stiffened. "That will be very difficult, Seneschal. The city is patrolled by hundreds of sentinels—not to mention scores of mages, trained to seek out potential trespassers. It would be a treacherous journey."

"But it's possible," Koal pressed. "We can make for the mountains, find a way to get word to Rishi, hide until a rescue group can be sent for us—"

Liro let out an incredulous snort. "Listen to yourself, Father. You sound delusional! All of you do!"

Koal glared over at his eldest son. "We're not going to sit here with tucked tails and wait for the Empire to come for us."

Hasain nodded in agreement. "Better to be a moving target than a sitting duck. I say we go."

"Why don't we take a vote, Seneschal?" Cenric suggested.

Liro raised his chin into the air and pointed savagely at Kirk. "I vote we turn this traitorous boy over to the Imperial authorities and go home as planned. There's no reason why Emperor Sarpedon would attack Arden."

"I can think of a few reasons," muttered Hasain.

Cenric's hazel eyes flitted around the room. "NezReth? Joel? What say you?"

"I believe Kirk," Joel replied quietly. "I think we should leave tonight."

NezReth fixed an unwavering gaze onto Koal. "I will follow whatever command you give."

Koal remained silent as he debated. Time seemed to stretch into infinity. Joel held his breath until his lungs nearly burst and he was forced to gasp for air. He hated waiting for an answer. He hated having no control over the situation. Surely his father wouldn't take up Liro's unpopular opinion, would he? Joel swallowed down a spike of fear. His father wouldn't turn Kirk into the authorities, right?

"We'll go." Koal's firm voice brought Joel back to the moment. The seneschal clasped his hands behind his back as he stared into the darkening sky beyond the terrace. "Tonight, in the marks before dawn, we'll slip away."

Everyone in the room let out a collective sigh, save Liro, who curled a lip and turned his nose upward. "This is madness."

Koal either didn't hear the remark or didn't care. He was too busy delegating tasks. "Cenric, find me that map of Teivel. Do we have an accurate diagram of the landscape outside the city? NezReth, you have past experience in these mountains. Are there any allies we can call upon if the need arises? Hasain, Joel, Liro—you three need to find any provisions you can—warm clothing, blankets, food, if possible."

Joel stared aimlessly across the suite, feeling numb. *What is going to happen to us? How can we possibly escape?* He didn't mean to despair so feverishly, but the terrible thoughts came without accord. *We could die tonight, like King Rishi warned we would. I might never see Gib again. I may never get the chance to apologize to him.*

His father's voice was a low hum. "Using the gate is out of the question. We can't overpower the guards there without them sounding the alarm." Joel glanced up and watched as Koal leaned over the table, staring intently at the map which Cenric had just spread across the tabletop.

"Do you think with enough rope we can scale the wall?" the ambassador asked, setting a hand on either side of the canvas to hold it in place.

Koal rubbed his blotched face with one large hand. "Even if we could, it's too well guarded. I had a good look at the structure when we were first brought through. Imperial sentinels man the entire length. Getting all six of us up and over unseen would be damned near impossible. We'd have a better chance of magically sprouting claws and whiskers and burrowing our way underneath the palace like moles than to successfully scale that wall."

Cenric tittered a nervous laugh. "It's reassuring to know you haven't lost your sense of humor amid our troubles, Seneschal."

Joel lost focus on the conversation at that point. His father's words struck a sudden chord. *Underneath the palace. Underneath.* Joel's gasp was loud enough to draw the attention of Koal and Cenric, but he ignored their stares altogether and whipped his head around to address Kirk.

"Two sennights ago, in the royal courtyard, I heard your sister speak of a passage through the catacombs! Do you remember?"

Kirk's eyes widened with recall. "Y–yes."

Joel crossed the room in three long strides and set a hand on Kirk's shoulder. "Can you show us the way?"

"Show us the way where?" Koal demanded. "What are you talking about?"

All eyes in the room fell onto Joel and Kirk. The trainee cringed beneath the scrutiny. "I don't know how to get there myself. Only Kenisha does."

Joel froze. "Where is she now?"

"I–I believe she's in the servant quarters."

"If we find her, can she show us to the passageway?" Joel asked.

Koal slammed a fist on the table, drawing both boys' attentions. "Dammit Joel, talk to me! What are you going on about? Passageway where?"

Joel turned to face his father, explaining in a rushed, excited voice, "Kirk's sister knows a way out. She said there's a passageway through the catacombs, beneath the palace." He licked his lips nervously. "We wouldn't have to worry about the wall at all. We can bypass it entirely this way."

Koal raised an eyebrow. "Through the catacombs?"

Kirk finally found his voice, timid as it was. "The passageway yields to a drainage canal that flows out beyond the wall. My sister told me the opening is wide enough for a person to crawl through."

Cenric stepped away from the table, a worried frown contorting his features. "Are you *sure?*"

Kirk winced, biting his lower lip. "No. I'm not entirely sure. It's what she told me."

"Da," Joel pleaded, taking a tentative step toward Koal. "We need to find his sister. This could be our only means of escape."

Liro stood in the corridor that separated the common room from the bedchambers. He leaned against the wall, openly glaring at Joel. "You're a fool, brother. Maybe *you'd* enjoy getting lost endlessly in a maze of tombs, but I would *not!*" Cruel eyes shifted toward Koal. "Father, Joel's perverted condition has clearly clouded his judgment on the matter. We can't trust him to make rational decisions."

Anger rushed to Joel's face in a hot wave. He jerked his head around to glare at Liro. "How *dare* you!"

Joel's rage was only second to Liro's scorn. The older brother flashed a smug smile. "How dare *I*? How dare *you* for asking us to put our lives in the hands of some boy you're undoubtedly polishing up to be your new shiny bauble in the Nemesio brat's absence."

"You leave Gib out of this!" Joel clenched his hands into fists, doing all he could to contain the anger threatening to boil over. "This has nothing to do with him!"

"Yes," Liro replied snidely. "Clearly you've already moved on to pursue other interests."

Never in Joel's eighteen years had he resorted to physical violence, but Liro's terrible words stabbed him so viscously in the heart and filled him with such agonizing pain that all Joel wanted to do in that moment was lunge at his older brother. *How can he say such hateful words about me? About Gib? And to assume that I'm seducing Kirk now*—Joel blinked back tears, refusing to allow his brother the satisfaction of seeing the droplets fall.

Koal slammed his hand on the tabletop again, only this time, his fury was directed at Liro. "Bad form, Liro Adelwijn! Have you not a *single* drop of integrity left? It isn't any wonder no one wants anything to do with you!"

Liro reeled like he'd taken a physical blow. His dull eyes landed on Koal and glazed over with some unreadable emotion. "Is this how you justify your lack of want for me, Father? Because we both know that isn't true."

Koal's voice was a dangerous snarl. "Your entire childhood, you lived under my roof, went to the finest schools, had the best of everything. Your mother and I doted on you tirelessly, loved you unconditionally. Any 'lack of want' you think you've perceived is no fault of mine or hers. I know my heart and your place in it, but I'll be damned if I can prove it to you! You've poisoned yourself with your hate."

Joel shuddered as he witnessed father and son glare at one another through gritted teeth and clenched hands. All the air seemed to have been removed from the room. The tension ascended from the shadows to grip Joel's heart, and he gasped, finding it difficult to breathe.

Cenric moved to stand beside the seneschal, the sound of his faint footfalls hitting the stone floor rising above the silence. Koal blinked, as though he'd just awakened from a deep trance, and broke eye contact with Liro to meet Cenric's troubled gaze.

Cenric cleared his throat. "We need to make a decision."

Conflict plagued Koal's eyes, and Joel braced himself for whatever choice might be made. He locked his jaw to prevent the pleas that sat on the tip of his tongue from escaping, but his mind couldn't be quieted. *Please, Da. You have to trust me. This is the only way we have a chance to escape. What can I do to prove to you that Kirk won't betray us?*

Joel startled when he felt a firm hand grip his shoulder and was surprised to see his father had approached while Joel had been lost in contemplation. Koal scrutinized his son closely, and Joel did his best to meet his sire's measured gaze.

"You're sure about this?" Koal asked, never taking his eyes from Joel's face. "Do you truly believe we can place our trust in this young man?"

Joel could feel the hairs on the back of his neck rise. *Is this what I think it is? Is Father giving me the final say? Does the fate of our party lie solely on me?*

He glanced around the room. Cenric gave him a nod of encouragement. NezReth stood in the shadows, his expression unreadable but not disapproving. Hasain's face was a well-guarded mask, and Liro's seething wrath couldn't be avoided. With a shuddering sigh, Joel looked over at Kirk briefly before returning to his father.

"I know we can trust him. His word is honorable."

Koal nodded, once and decisively. "All right. Let's find this sister of his and see if she can lead us to safety."

The Ardenian envoys waited in an enclave just beyond the corridor leading to the servant quarters. Kirk left them with express instructions to remain silent and out of sight and informed them he'd be back shortly.

Time crawled as tensions ran high. Liro was the first to break protocol and make underhanded remarks about their situation. Joel shushed him to little avail. Eventually Koal put a swift end to the sniveling but was quick to follow up with a lament of his own. "Where are they, Joel? This is taking too long."

"We can't leave without them, can we?" Hasain asked. "None of us knows the way, right?" He shifted a hopeful look to NezReth, but the Blessed Mage only met the gaze with vacant eyes.

No. None of them knew where they were going. They were entirely at Kirk and Kenisha's mercy.

Liro groaned. "I'm sure they're well on their way to inform the

Imperial authorities by now. We're all fools for going through with this—you lot for trusting the servant in the first place and me for not leaving all of you to your fate."

Joel whirled on one heel to glare at his brother, but once again Koal silenced Liro. Joel was left to endure his brother's smug smile.

Footsteps could be heard in the close distance and everyone, even Liro, tensed. Koal's hand shot for the hilt of his sword, and Joel could feel Hasain pooling mage energy into his hands. Joel thought to do the same, but in the moment, his mind seized. Could he take a life if it came down to that? Even if it was the life of an Imperial soldier who would take his if he didn't fight back?

Kirk and his sister rounded the corner, and Joel's tension dissipated. *Thank The Two, it's only them.*

The Imperial siblings slowed briefly, their eyes flashing from each envoy to the next. Joel's stomach sank when he realized his father hadn't stood down just yet. Koal's hand still gripped the hilt of his weapon. Likewise, Hasain hadn't retracted his magic. What were they doing? Were they *trying* to scare off their guides?

NezReth lifted his chin, eyes unfocused. "They're alone. No soldiers."

Koal responded instantly, dropping the hand that had been clutching the sword, and Hasain followed, releasing the energy back into the air. Kirk and Kenisha ventured forward after that. Both had donned cloaks, obscuring their hair and faces and making it difficult to tell exactly what they were thinking or feeling.

Kenisha's voice was a hushed whisper. "Follow me then. Stay close."

"What if someone sees us? What then?" Cenric, who'd been quiet up until then, asked.

Her response was wry and clear. "I'd suggest you run, Ambassador."

"All right. Let's be done with this." Koal's terse words suggested this conversation had met its end, and no one questioned his authority. "Lead the way."

Kenisha led them through several corridors that Joel didn't recognize. This was definitely part of the palace he'd never seen before. Everything was ensconced in shadow, and the fine ornaments which decorated the rest of the royal building were notably missing. The farther they went, the worse repair the building was in. Some of the pillars were even chipped or cracked.

"Mind the stairs," Kenisha warned as they passed through an arched doorway and came to stand at the head of an ominous stairwell. "Sometimes they're slick. Don't fall. It's a long way down."

Joel gulped as he looked onward. Indeed, it *was* a long way down. The spiraling staircase turned in an endless corkscrew down into the ground. The others were already beginning to descend into the darkness, and Joel

225

had no option other than to follow.

The farther they went, the more moisture accumulated on the smooth stone steps and the less light made its way to them. Joel pressed his hand to the wall to keep his balance and caught the faint silhouette of Hasain doing the same. A few steps farther and NezReth cleared his throat before blue light flickered out from his upturned palm. The mage orb threw off a scant amount of illumination, hopefully enough to keep them all from breaking their skulls. Cool air pricked Joel's skin. If he wasn't mistaken, the temperature continued to drop with every step he took.

Just as he was starting to wonder if the twisting stairs would ever come to an end, his feet met solid ground, and he whispered a muffled prayer. A narrow corridor stretched out before the party. In the dim light, Joel could see cobwebs hanging from the ceiling, tents of silk above their heads. The foul stench of decayed plants and mildew made him want to gag, and all around him the sound of trickling water echoed off the stone walls.

"What is this place?" Hasain asked.

Kirk shared a dark look with his sister before lifting his voice. "These are the catacombs, Lord Hasain. The great Imperial royals of the past are all laid to rest down here."

In the hazy light of the mage orb, Hasain's face went pale. Joel sucked his bottom lip into his mouth. He didn't feel so well himself. Knowing that corpses lay within the vaults lining either side of the passageway only made him all the more unsettled.

Cenric huffed a sigh. "Let's not tarry."

"Not afraid, are we?" Liro arched a brow. "Surely we're all well-schooled enough to know better than to fear the dead." He stole a glance at Kirk and Kenisha before a sly smile pulled at his mouth. "Well, perhaps not *all* of us are so well schooled."

"Enough. We're moving on." Koal's gruff command forced the conversation to a halt.

Kenisha lowered her head and crept forward without another word. The envoys fell in behind her, with NezReth near the front of the line. His summoned light was the only illumination in the passage. Joel could feel Liro and Hasain crowding in on the mage to keep the orb within their sight.

Not a single word was shared as they made their way deeper and deeper into the ground. The air continued to grow colder and stale smelling the farther they went, and Joel realized belatedly that he was gasping for breath. The thought of being so far beneath the ground coupled with their tight confines was nearly enough to unhinge his frazzled mind.

A sturdy hand squeezed his shoulder. "Deep, steady breaths, Joel. You're doing fine. It's going to be all right." The calm of Cenric's voice eased the tension, but only just so.

Joel glanced back, but in the low light, he couldn't make out his mentor's face. Did Cenric even believe his own words? Joel wasn't sure, but his desperation made him choose to believe. *We're all right. We're going to be all right.*

He had nearly convinced himself to calm down when he bumped straight into Hasain's back. Flailing to catch his balance, Joel frowned. "What's going on? Why did you stop?"

Hasain didn't offer to speak. Pointing to the front of the line, the Radek lord leaned aside to allow Joel to see for himself.

Up ahead, the path forked. Kenisha had stopped and was looking back and forth between the two halls. Koal questioned her impatiently but all she did was shake her head. "I wasn't told about this."

Koal sighed and folded his arms over his chest. "We haven't the time for delays. What are the odds of them both leading to the outside?"

"They may very well both lead outside, Seneschal." Kirk's voice shook when he spoke. "But if we take the wrong path, then who knows where we'll come out?"

"Does anyone else see the frivolity of this venture now?" Liro snarled. "We could be comfortably resting in our suite, preparing for the morrow when we would return to Arden the way we originally planned."

Koal waved his hand, dismissing his eldest son's complaint. "Too late now. Stay quiet. We have to think."

Joel held his breath, willing his pounding heart to slow. What would they do if they couldn't figure out which way to go? They were losing time standing here, but if they chose wrong and exited the catacombs in a bad place, then they had no guarantee of making it anyway. He hoped his father would come up with a solution—and fast.

Before any suggestions could be made, however, angry shouts began to echo off the walls. Joel's blood froze in his veins as he whipped his head back in the direction they'd come. Everyone fell silent as they took in the sounds of boots slapping on the damp floor, resonating all around them. The voices grew to a deafening crescendo, and one rose above the others to demand "the cowards" be found. Joel gasped and fell back a step, bumping into his mentor.

Koal let out an angry hiss. "We've been missed!"

"Which way do we go?" Hasain's choked cry sounded like that of a scared child, but Joel couldn't find fault with that. He felt much the same way.

At the head of their group, Kenisha gasped and pointed to the right. "This way! The air feels like it's moving faster from this side."

Behind them, Joel could see the faint glow of torchlight. Time was up. With a lurch, the envoys moved as one down the selected corridor. Dignity forsaken, Joel gasped for air with no concern for how loud he was being.

"More steps! Take care!" Koal called back to them.

The stairwell was short this time, but when they reached the bottom step, all of their taller members were forced to duck. The low ceiling only added to the claustrophobic feel of the tombs, and Joel dug at the neck of his robes, feeling as though he was being strangled.

"There's standing water in there!" Koal shouted. "We won't be able to see what we're stepping on!"

Kirk urged them forward. "We haven't a choice now. They're gaining on us."

Joel looked back and had to cling to the dampened wall for support. Kirk was right. The light was getting brighter. He tried to suck in a deep breath but only managed to wheeze. The soldier's angry voices clouded his mind with terror, making it difficult to think.

"We have to move on, Seneschal," Cenric insisted, his tone oddly calm despite the dire circumstances.

They were on the move again. Joel followed along blindly. Hasain pulled on Joel's arm while Cenric pushed from behind, forcing Joel to keep lurching ahead. The walls seemed to close around him as he tromped through black, ankle-deep water. He slammed his eyes shut despite the danger of it. He couldn't look. He couldn't see their tomb for what it was.

The farther they went, the less sense Joel could make of anything. Blood roared in his ears, and it took all he had just to keep up with the others. He could almost feel the Imperial soldiers at his back, breathing down his neck. They were losing their lead.

His feet slid away from one another and he fell to his knees, but Hasain dragged Joel back up almost instantaneously. Pain shot through his legs as he staggered forward, but he knew he had to keep going. *I can't die here. I won't.*

Cenric's strained voice rose behind them. "We're about to have company, Koal!"

Everyone stopped moving, and a moment later, Koal pushed past, sword already drawn as he made his way to the back of the line. "You all need to keep moving. *Now!*"

Joel bleated and reached for his father, but Hasain was already pulling on Joel's arm again. He struggled against the vice-like grip. "Stop! Let me go! He can't face them alone. He'll die. Let me go!"

The shouts of the Imperial soldiers swelled to fill the cramped corridor as they rounded the corner. Joel froze in the midst of his fight to escape, staring in abject horror. There they were—too many soldiers to count—rushing toward the envoys, with their bronze armor and drawn longswords.

He struggled against the hold again and was surprised, when this time, he broke away. Behind him, Joel could feel Hasain pooling his magic once more, and a defiant streak of hope fluttered within Joel's chest. NezReth had also turned to face the oncoming soldiers. The mage's expression was set in a grim mask, and his power crackled dangerously around the tunnel.

Again, Koal waved for them to fall back. "I said keep going! Get the hell out of here!"

"No. We're not leaving you." Joel didn't even recognize his own unwavering voice. The panic from a moment before was entirely forgotten as he flexed his mage energy. It surged to him like never before. He could do this. He hadn't been sure earlier, but now he knew without any doubt. If those heathens tried to hurt his father, they would pay dearly.

Koal frowned back at them but had no time to argue. The soldiers were closing in. The one to the front of the group shouted above the rest. "Envoys of Arden, halt! By order of His Grace, Emperor Sarpedon, you are to drop your weapons and return with us to the palace!"

Squaring his shoulders, Koal didn't budge from his spot. "Nay. Tell your emperor that our negotiations are over. We're leaving. Now."

"Stand down, Koal Adelwijn! You've lost!"

Koal gripped the base of his sword and held the weapon before him. "I'll stand down when you cut the legs clear off my body—if you aren't dead first."

The soldier's face twisted in animalistic rage as he launched forward, blade aimed at Koal's throat. The seneschal readied himself, but he didn't need to. Joel had already called a surge of power to himself and blasted it at the soldier. The blow hit true, searing into the man's chest and knocking him off his feet. Joel didn't have time to dwell on how much damage he'd done. The other soldiers were already diving forward to take their fallen comrade's spot, and Joel was pooling his magic again.

Another burst of crackling blue fire shot forth, this bolt from Hasain. A second man collapsed to the ground with a splash. "There's too many of them to take out like this!" Hasain gasped. "More are turning the corner even now."

Despair pressed dangerously on Joel's heart, but he refused to give in. He opened his mouth in the hope that brave words would come tumbling out, but NezReth beat him to it. "*Fall back! All of you!*" The Blessed Mage darted past them. Blue energy crackled and flowed down either arm as he raised them over his head.

They didn't have enough space to properly do as they were told. Joel was tripping on Hasain, who was tripping on Cenric. They had only managed to back away a few precious paces when NezReth unleashed his wrath in a bolt of blinding sparks and fury. Joel slammed his eyes shut, expecting to hear men screaming in agony—yet all he could hear was the low rumble of cracking stone. He dared to open his eyes.

The Imperial soldiers stood frozen with wide, elevated eyes. NezReth's bolt had seared a hole into the ceiling above their heads. Even now, as Joel watched, deep lines were forming at the site of impact and trickling away from the crater like water escaping a pond. Again came the rumble of crumbling rock, a low, devastating reverberation worse than any thunder Joel had ever heard. Fine, gritty sand rained down through the cracks, and then entire pieces of the ceiling began to drop.

The soldiers *did* shout then. Their voices were laced with terror as they clambered over each other in their attempts to fall back. Joel watched as chucks of mortar and stone plummeted from the ceiling. *One. Two. Three.* Joel lost count as the entire ceiling bowed under the pressure of the loose rock. A sickening feeling clenched his heart. *Oh no—*

"It's going to go!" NezReth screamed above the torrent. "Get out of here!"

Joel took another step back. The entire corridor trembled—above him, around him, beneath his feet. He felt as though he was trapped inside a box, being violently shaken with no means of escape. All around him, rocks were careening to the floor, pelting his skin and face like massive hailstones. *Oh gods, the entire ceiling is giving way!* Letting out a terrified cry, Joel tucked his head and squeezed his eyes closed. If this was the end, he didn't want to see it. *Chhaya, please, be merciful. If we're to die, let it be swift.*

The sound of falling rock drowned out all other noise. Joel held his breath, waiting for the final blow, waiting to die—but Death never came for him. The tempest passed and the angry shards of rubble falling from above subsided. He opened one eye tentatively. *Am I alive?* His heart skipped a beat. *Is anyone else alive?*

He breathed a sigh of relief when he heard his father's voice nearby. "Is everyone all right? Sound off!" Murmurs rose above the silence, music to Joel's ears as each and every member of the group called their name. It seemed their party had made it through the rockfall relatively unscathed. He stood up, brushing dust from his soaked robe, and cast a wary glance in the direction the soldiers had been. A barricade of rubble blocked the way.

Hasain gripped the wall as he climbed to his feet. "We better hope this passage leads *somewhere*, seeing as there's no way back now."

NezReth stepped closer to the mountain of stone, titling his head to the side. Joel paused too, listening for any sign of life on the far side. Nothing. He couldn't hear a damned thing.

"I do not hear them," the Blessed Mage confirmed a moment later. "But it is safe to assume that at least a handful escaped."

Koal sheathed his sword as he returned to the head of the party. "Then we need to keep going. If they don't already know about this supposed drainage opening, it won't take them long to figure it out."

Up ahead, Kirk leaned shakily against his sister, eyes wide as he stared at the fallen rubble. He whispered something into Kenisha's ear and her face pinched. Placing an arm around his shoulder, she murmured soft

230

words back to him.

Joel made his way over to them. "Are you all right?" he asked, placing a hand on Kirk's trembling shoulder. He hadn't been injured, had he? "Are you hurt?"

"N–no," the trainee replied, shaking his head. "It's just—they saw me. And Keni. They saw us both. They *have* to know we're helping you escape."

Joel flinched as he realized the implication of Kirk's words. *Daya. They can never safely return to Teivel now.*

"There's no going back," Kenisha said, her voice a whisper in the shadows.

A strangled whimper pushed its way from Kirk's chest all the way to his lips. "I don't know what we're going to do."

Joel narrowed his eyes. "I do." He swung around, scanning the dark tunnel until his eyes landed on Koal. "Father, we have to bring them with us."

Liro snorted. "Don't be ridiculous. Our 'noble' king would rather feed newborn babes to hungry wolves than allow *two* Imperials into the realm."

"Liro!" Joel gasped.

His elder brother shrugged and turned to smirk at Koal. "Am I not mistaken, Father? Am I wrong in my assumption?"

Koal let out a defeated sigh. He could barely meet Joel's pleading eyes. "Joel, Arden is no place for Imperial-born, no matter how sincere they appear to be."

"*How can you say that?*" Joel demanded. He pointed sharply at Kirk and Kenisha. "They've risked everything to help us escape! *Everything!* We can't just turn a blind eye now! What would it say about *us* if we abandon them in their time of need?"

Koal rubbed the back of his neck. "King Rishi won't approve it. You know that."

"Then you can return to Arden without me!" Joel replied, blood rushing to his face, turning his cheeks an angry scarlet. He crossed his arms over his chest and set his jaw defiantly. "Either we *all* go, or I'm staying. You can tell King Rishi why I didn't make it when he asks."

Koal's face was nearly as red as Joel's. "This isn't a time for games, Joel—"

"Oh, I'm not playing, Father. I'm very, *very* serious."

Kirk winced as the seneschal threw his hands into the air and barked a string of ill-mannered profanities. The boy leaned a little closer to Joel and spoke tentatively, "Joel, it's—it's okay. Keni and I will figure something out. You can't stay behind. You have to go home—"

"No, it's not fair." Joel shook his head sharply. "I won't be a bystander to such injustice. You're my friend. I'm going to stand by my convictions and by you."

Cenric cleared his throat. The sound echoed down the narrow passageway. "Koal, we can't stand here and argue. And we can't allow Joel to stay behind." His hazel eyes were compassionate when he turned to look at the Imperial siblings. "Allow them to accompany us to Arden. There's no harm in it."

"My father will understand," Hasain added. Joel would have hugged his cousin if they were under different circumstances. "They've helped us. It's only fair that we return the favor."

Koal let out a groan. "Fine." He fixed Joel with a withering glare. "Upon our arrival, *you* can be the one to explain this to King Rishi."

Joel opened his mouth to utter a word of gratitude, but Koal had already swung around and disappeared into the shadows of the corridor.

"Down there," Kenisha said. "That's the way out."

Joel crouched in the narrow tunnel with the rest of the party. Water had long since saturated his mage robe; the pristine white fabric was soiled grey with dirt and grime from the trek through the catacombs. Every muscle in his body ached and both knees felt as though they were on fire. During their escape from the Imperial soldiers, he'd taken a brutal fall. Pain continued to shoot through his legs, but for the time being, there was nothing to be done except grimace and bear it.

Koal leaned down and poked his head beneath the increasingly low ceiling. "I can see a drainage opening up ahead."

"It comes out on the far side of the palace wall," Kenisha explained. "From there, it'll be a quick dash into the city."

Koal looked over his shoulder at the rest of the party. "We're going to have to crawl the rest of the way. The tunnel gets even more narrow up ahead. It looks like a tight squeeze."

Joel's skin began to crawl even as Hasain asked the question everyone had to be thinking. "We'll fit through, won't we?"

Cenric's eyes danced as he turned to flash the Radek lord a sly smile. "Guess we'll find out. Would you like to go first?"

Hasain huffed under his breath. "I'll pass."

Koal was already moving forward. "Everyone be quiet and follow me. Stay close."

Seriously? Stay close? Joel mused. *As tight as these quarters are, it would take an act of The Two to become separated!*

Koal led the way. Joel found himself directly behind Kirk and didn't have to glance back to know Hasain trailed behind. Joel could hear Hasain's disgusted grunts as they were all forced to crawl through the murky, stagnant water. Joel could feel slimy vegetation between his fingers, and the rancid smell was nearly unbearable.

The party inched forward. The only sound to be heard was the dirty water sloshing around their extremities and the occasional retch of revulsion. Joel gritted his chattering teeth, feeling cold and fatigued. His knees ached almost to the point of tears, but he knew he couldn't stop. *Just keep moving forward. Almost there. Don't stop.*

Faint light reflected off the water ahead, and he belatedly realized NezReth had dismissed the mage orb. This light source was from something else. Joel's heart quickened as he leaned around Kirk's body and saw a trace of nighttime sky ahead.

He had to stop long enough for Kirk to make his exit. The trainee scrambled through the opening, leaving Joel with a clear view of the outside world. The silhouettes of marble houses and perfectly sculpted hedges collided with the horizon before him. His lungs took in a greedy breath of fresh air, the first in a long time. A tapestry of stars twinkled in the navy sky above, enticing him to make the final push to freedom. Kirk offered a hand, and with his help, Joel squirmed the rest of the way out of the tunnel.

The great wall of the palace loomed behind them, casting a black shadow across the cobblestone streets. Joel leaned against it as he waited for Hasain and Cenric to climb out of the drainage tunnel. The initial relief he'd felt after escaping the catacombs was already begining to flitter away. They were above ground again, but traversing the city was going to be twice as difficult. *We're still so far from safety.*

Koal's eyes scanned the wall. His wary stance and grim face sent chills down Joel's spine. Were sentries up there? Surely there had to be. He titled his head back and peered into the darkness but could see nothing. That didn't stop the panic from rising up to close a firm grip around Joel's neck. *We have to go. We can't stand out in the open like this.*

Almost as though Koal could hear Joel's inner monologue, the seneschal stepped away from the partition and motioned for them to follow. Moving as an efficient unit, they darted across the empty space separating the palace from the rest of the city. Joel's chest was heaving by the time they reached the first row of stone houses.

Safely within the shadows again, Koal stopped. He leaned in close so he could whisper. Kirk and Kenisha fidgeted nervously when he pointed at them. "We're counting on you two to guide us the hell out of here. You'll walk with NezReth and me at the front of the line. Joel, Hasain, you flank Cenric and stay close behind me. Liro—" The elder Adelwijn son ticked an eyebrow as he fell beneath Koal's frigid scrutiny. "You protect us from the rear."

"Of course, Father," came Liro's airy response. He clutched a hand around the focus stone gifted to him by Archmage Titus.

Kirk scraped a sandal across the ground. "We have to avoid using magic at all costs. At least until we're beyond the dome. The Imperial mages have linked part of their consciousness to the dome. Any trace of magic used while we remain inside will be detected."

"They'll be alerted to our exact position," NezReth stated in a flat voice.

Kirk nodded. "Yes. The magic defense system will also trigger once we cross the barrier, but it will be more difficult for them to track us out there beyond the inner city."

"We'll have to move fast once we cross then." Koal's hard gaze shifted back and forth among the members of the group. "All right, you heard the lad. Absolutely no magic." He drew his blade in one graceful motion and turned on his heel. "Let's go. Stay in formation, all of you."

Joel winced as he took his place in line behind his father. If they faced another Imperial patrol tonight, would luck still be on their side? Surely their good fortune was due to run out. Joel shuddered. He could feel the fear pressing on his heart, smothering any courage he might still be grasping onto. Cenric patted Joel's arm and offered a strained smile. The kind gesture helped, if only a little.

Koal led the way through twisting streets and shadowed alleys. Under different circumstances, Joel would have stopped to admire the beautiful marble columns, luscious gardens, and ivy-covered buildings, but not tonight. He could find no enjoyment in this nightmare they'd found themselves trapped within.

The sky above was a veil of stars. A full moon hung from the navy canvas like a beacon from the Gods, illuminating the land below with eerie, pale light. The city itself remained dark. No mage orbs or lanterns lined the streets and no light could be seen through any of the shuttered windows. A shiver ran up Joel's spine. It almost felt like they were the only living souls left in the world.

They'd been creeping along for several minutes with no incident when a gut-wrenching sense of dread began to form in the pit of his stomach. This all seemed too easy. Where were all the guards? The city should have been swarming with them. *They know we're trying to escape. Why aren't they here looking for us?* Joel frowned. *Unless they think we perished underground in the rockslide. It's doubtful they would just assume we're dead though. They'd need proof. So where are they?* His intuition kept screaming that something was amiss. He couldn't continue to remain silent.

The mage reached forward to tap Koal's shoulder. "Father, wait a moment!"

Koal hushed his son with a single, furious glare. "*Quiet.*"

Joel planted his feet, refusing to go on. Everyone else exchanged confused glances before they, too, drew to a halt. He lowered his voice to a feverish whisper. "Something is wrong. I can feel it—"

Koal whirled around to face him. "I know something isn't right! Are you trying to wake up the entire city?"

Joel opened his mouth to retort, but any words he might have uttered were dampened by the attack.

Like a lethal bolt of lightning, energy surged through the air, building to a horrible crescendo. Joel reacted without thinking, throwing up a magic shield around the party. A second later, red shards of magic came hurtling at them from all directions. *An ambush!*

Hasain's energy shot out to reinforce the shield, and Kirk joined them an instant later. His raw, potent magic glossed over the barrier, sewing up any weak spots within the defensive nexus like a threaded needle. The three mages braced themselves against the onslaught from the Imperial mages.

NezReth and Liro stepped forward as one, both pooling their energies and taking aim before Joel could even register what was happening. Liro's power was impressive. The Blessed Mage's was nothing short of terrifying. Together, their movements were fluid and well trained. They allotted themselves no second guesses or mistakes. As the enemies hurled smoldering red splinters toward them, Liro and NezReth countered, releasing crackling bolts of their own. Though Joel couldn't see the Imperial mages through the sizzling air, he could hear their cries of pain followed by the thud of bodies crashing to the pavement as they went down.

Koal's voice fought for dominance over the turmoil. "We can't just stand here! We have to move!" He had his sword held high and pointed at Kenisha. "Lead us." Her pale face trembled as she shook her head and launched forward.

Joel refused to give up, but it was difficult to move and keep the defensive shield from unraveling. More than once, he sensed tears in the magic where the Imperial mages were mercilessly striking it. Without ever exchanging a word, Hasain and Kirk worked with him to keep the barrier intact.

"Keep moving. They're losing ground!"

His father's voice should have been a beacon of hope, but there was nothing left in Joel to celebrate. Sore to the bones and exhausted beyond repair, he could barely keep his feet moving and mind focused.

"There're more of them coming from the east!" Liro screamed in warning from the rear of the group.

"*Get down!*" NezReth's voice rose shrill against the night, cutting through the sounds of their pounding feet. Joel didn't want to look back but couldn't help himself. He turned just in time to watch a crimson bolt swipe the side of Liro's face. His brother dropped motionless to the ground.

"Liro!"

Their procession came to an abrupt halt as Koal shoved his way through the others. Joel started to follow, but a grunt from Hasain reminded the mage to stay focused. They needed to keep the shield intact.

He watched as Koal took to one knee and examined Liro's prone form. NezReth continued his counter attack, he alone standing between the seneschal and certain doom. Joel's heart pounded. He'd never seen his brother so defenseless. *Get up. Move. Please wake up.*

The red bolts finally ceased, and the Blessed Mage turned back to the party, a fierce scowl on his face. "That's all of them for now. Reserve your energy." He knelt next to Koal and put a hand to Liro's forehead. "We have to move on."

Joel scurried over to them, bile rising up his throat. The worry lines on his father's face were almost enough to undo him. "Da?"

"He's alive." Koal's voice was hollow, on the brink of defeat. He swooped down low to take one of Liro's arms. "Hasain, help me. Get his other arm."

Hasain hesitated only a split second before he did as told, and together they hoisted Liro's limp body from the ground and held him between the two of them. A trickle of blood ran from one temple down the side of Liro's blanched face, but he was still breathing.

Shouts rang out through the night all around them, but Joel could barely hear the commotion through the pounding in his ears. The Imperial army was coming. *Oh Goddesses, help us.*

"What do we do?" Hasain asked, his voice a pitch below pure hysteria.

"Go!" Koal's heavy tone was unwavering in the midst of the chaos. "Run! Quickly! Lead us out of here!"

Kirk jumped forward. "This way."

They followed at the mage trainee's heels with no regard for keeping quiet anymore. As they wove through the maze of houses and merchant shops, their boots slammed on the cobblestone pavers, ringing out through the night. The enraged shouts of the Imperial soldiers echoed around them, coming from every direction.

Joel could hear his own ragged breaths as he ran, and agonizing pain shot from his knees down the length of his legs with every step. Behind him, with Liro's lifeless form slumped between them, Koal and Hasain struggled to keep up. Each time Joel glanced back, the distance between his father and cousin and the rest of the group continued to widen. A hopeless thought paralyzed his mind. *They're falling behind.*

"Wait!" Joel called to the rest of the group. "Stop!"

Kirk hesitated but drew to a halt within the shadows of a towering stone mansion, waiting in tense silence for the remaining members of the party to catch up.

Hasain leaned heavily against the side of the building. His chest heaved with every sharp inhale, and even now, his grip around Liro's torso was slipping. "We're never going to make it like this. Not if we have to carry him."

Joel narrowed his eyes. "We're not leaving my brother behind to die!"

Hasain's lip curled. "It's him or *all* of us!"

"No!" Joel refused to believe the words. "There has to be another way."

NezReth's eyes were shut tight in concentration. He didn't open them even when he spoke. "I can feel a great source of energy nearby."

Kirk's face lit up. Even through the darkness, Joel could see it. "It's the portal! We're close by."

The portal. Renewed hope raced through Joel's veins. He understood. If they could find the strength to activate the portal themselves, they wouldn't need to outrun the Imperial army. He swung around to face his father. "Da! If we can make it to the portal, we have a chance!"

Koal redistributed Liro's weight as he, too, leaned against the marble slab for support. "NezReth? Is it possible?"

The Blessed Mage sighed. "For us to do it alone—I–I do not know. It would be very difficult."

"What choice do we have?" Hasain asked. "It's too late to escape on foot." Light from the Imperial torches flickered in his hollow eyes.

"They're almost here!" Cenric warned, though there was no need. Everyone knew. The streets echoed with the sounds of clanging armor and boots scraping the ground as the enemy closed in.

Koal peered down the alley. "Take us there."

The group dashed forward again, but Joel hung back. "Father, go ahead of me with Liro." Koal grunted in protest, but Joel refused to budge. "If they attack from behind, I'll hold them off." Hasain lumbered on, and Koal was forced to move as well. Joel followed at their heels, throwing up a magic shield as he ran. It wouldn't hold for long, but at least it was something.

Up ahead, cloaks billowed behind the others as they ran. Joel focused his attention onto the rustling fabric. If he could forget that he was fleeing for his life, the monumental task of lifting each foot and placing it in front of the other seemed easier.

Hasain tripped, losing his grip on Liro, and Koal was forced to bear all of the unconscious man's weight.

"How much farther?" Koal called through gritted teeth.

Kirk didn't even pause. "We're almost there!"

Hasain picked himself up. His voice quivered as he took hold of Liro's arm. "I can't—can't carry him anymore—"

Koal locked eyes with Hasain. "Yes, you can. We can do this. Together now."

Hands shaking, Hasain struggled to sling the limp arm over his shoulder. "O–okay."

Joel could hear footsteps on the adjacent street. Koal and Hasain were lurching forward once again, but Joel knew he needed to give them more time. He readied a ball of magic in his palm and waited, poised for attack.

The first sentinel marched around the corner, and Joel choked back a frightened gasp. The man's eyes were like little black beads, cold and unforgiving as they glared out through the cracks in his helm. One hand grasped a sharpened broadsword, but even as the soldier raised the weapon and darted into the alley, Joel had already unleashed his magic, sending the fiery ball loose. It sailed through the static air, striking the soldier in the weakest part of his armor, near his throat.

The man howled and went down, writhing on the ground. The undeniable scent of burning flesh and hair filled the street. Joel would have gagged had he not been focused on summoning another sphere of power.

A second soldier came at Joel. This man bore a thick, metal shield. As he passed by his fallen comrade, the sentinel raised the shield to protect his chest and head. Joel aimed for his exposed legs instead, intending to disable him. The man collapsed with an anguished cry, blood spurting from his gashed thigh. Joel pooled a third crackling ball into his outstretched hand.

"Enough!"

A shiver ran up his spine as he recognized the strident voice calling from the depths of the alley. Archmage Adrian Titus, in his elegant golden robe and crimson sash, strolled into view. A dozen Imperial soldiers waited behind him. Joel took a tentative step back. *Daya, help me.*

Adrian raised a hand into the air. "Playtime is over."

Joel tightened his defensive magic, wrapping the invisible shield in layers around his body. He knew he was no match for the Archmage, but he had to stall for the others as long as was possible. He had to give NezReth a chance to conjure the portal spell.

"Where are your traitorous friends, Lord Adelwijn?" Adrian asked. He lifted his chin, and in the moonlight, Joel caught a glimpse of a sinister smirk. It was the first and only time he'd ever seen the Archmage smile.

Joel refused to answer. He narrowed his eyes into slits and readied the magic resting in his palm.

Adrian laughed, an uncanny, baleful sound that resonated off the marble walls surrounding their space. "I wouldn't try that if I were you."

Joel swallowed. "What does it matter? You're going to try to kill me either way. I won't go down without a fight, and neither will my friends."

"You can fight, but it will all be for naught. None of you can escape the might of the Northern Empire. Every last one of you will perish before daybreak. You may even cry for a swift end when you realize how painful your deaths will be." His eerie smile made Joel cringe. "It's a dirty business, slaughtering traitors, but orders are orders."

Adrian took another step, the faint aura of magic swirling around his

238

slender form. His defensive shields were sturdy. Joel couldn't hope to break through them with only one strike.

The Archmage opened his mouth to speak again but paused before he'd uttered even a single word. Confusion flicked across his face, and his steel blue eyes grew unfocused. Joel's skin prickled as he too felt the power Adrian had undoubtedly sensed. It was the same power Joel had felt the day they first came to Teivel. *It's the portal! They've reached it! NezReth is beginning the spell!*

"To the portal!" Adrian shrieked. "Don't let them escape!"

The Archmage's attention had flitted elsewhere for a precious instant, and Joel took his chance. He flung his magic with all his strength. The ball exploded against the enemy's shield, forcing Adrian and his men to step back. Joel whirled around and ran.

He ran faster and harder than ever before, barreling down the alley, hoping to put crucial distance between himself and the Imperials. He could hear Adrian screaming for the soldiers to kill Joel. Their snarling voices droned in his eardrums. *Don't look back. It will only slow you down—*

A blast of magic crashed into his mage shield, searing the back of his robe and knocking him forward. Joel hit the stone pavement face first, the air deflating from his stomach in a violent whoosh. He could feel hot, wet liquid gushing from his nose even as he scrambled to his feet.

The attack completely shattered his shield. Hastily, Joel cast another one but knew it was even weaker than the first. One more powerful strike and he was done for. *Don't give up*, he told himself. *Keep running. Just keep running.*

Koal and the others were no longer in sight. Joel wasn't sure which way to go. *No, no, no! I can't lose them!* As he staggered forward, blood began to drip from his chin. Somehow, despite the yells of the soldiers and his own wheezing gasps, Joel could hear each nauseating splatter as the crimson droplets hit his boots.

Focus. Find the portal. He extended his consciousness, reaching out with tendrils of his mind. He sought out the telltale magic he'd felt moments before—and found it. *Straight ahead. I'm nearly there.*

A dark object whizzed by his ear. *What is that?* A moment later, a second arrow skittered off the ground dangerously near his feet. Ducking low, Joel ran as fast as his legs would allow. He refused to look over his shoulder but could feel the enemy bearing down on him. He knew if he risked a glance back, the sight would undo him. He could only run for his life and pray to the heavens.

His skin prickled with growing intensity the closer he drew to the portal. He could sense the rippling waves of magic ahead and knew he had to be close. Rounding one final street corner, Joel let out a relieved cry at the sight of the courtyard—the one that had first welcomed him to the city six sennights ago. Shadows cast a dusky blanket across the lush shrubbery and flowerbeds, but he hardly noticed them in his dart toward the far side. Across the sprawling garden, Joel could see the outline of the portal, the flecked granite shimmering beneath the moon. Cenric reached out and grasped Joel's hand as he stumbled to the base of the portal.

"Are you all right?" the ambassador asked.

Joel touched a hand to his bloody face and winced. "I'll be fine."

NezReth was already drawing energy. Joel could feel the heavy magic pooling around them. The Blessed Mage focused all his attention onto the empty space beneath the archway, never once glancing away. His eyes burned with such intensity that Joel unwittingly took a step back.

Tendrils of blue flame swirled around the stone arch as NezReth worked to build his spell, but Joel knew the portal wouldn't be ready before the Imperials reached them. One glance over his shoulder confirmed the horrible thought. Scores of Imperial soldiers and mages piled into the garden, their angry cries and sharpened blades striking terror in Joel's heart.

"We have to hold them back!" Kirk yelled.

Hasain left Koal's side to take a stand beside Joel and the young Imperial trainee. "Shield the portal. We'll give NezReth the time he needs!"

Joel reached with his consciousness, drawing magic from ley lines of energy buried deep below the ground, pooling it to his hands. He extended the magic outward. It spread from his palms to encircle first himself, before stretching farther yet to encompass the entire portal in a glowing, cerulean sphere. The barrier wavered despite his best efforts to stabilize it. He could feel his energy reserves draining. Fighting off the Imperial ambushers had already burnt through so much of his power.

A moment later, Hasain and Kirk joined him, lending their magic to the cause, and Joel felt an immediate lift in his energy. Together, they threaded the shield tight, sealing all holes, creating a shell of energy that visibly pulsated beneath the glow of the moon. Not a moment later, the onslaught began.

Joel braced himself as the Imperial mages began their attack. They fired crackling bolts of magic that ricocheted off the shield and sent sparks flying every which way. Again and again, the blows came, relentless and devastating. Each time a new bolt struck, the shield quivered and cracked in response. Joel and the others moved swiftly to reseal the weakened areas, but as more enemies piled into the courtyard and joined in the attack, the task became overwhelming. Joel could see the fissures in the shield. They were forming faster than he was able to mend them. Panic sprang to life in his chest. He wanted to scream at NezReth to hurry but knew it would do no good. The Blessed Mage needed more time. But time was running out.

Joel's vision began to cloud as he felt the last of his reserves being pulled from his weary body. The siege continued, vicious and driven. The enemy knew the shield was buckling beneath their attack. They knew their opponents weakened even as they battered harder. Joel reached farther, tapping deeper into the ley lines, drawing the energy to his fingertips. The raw, untamed magic coursed through Joel's veins, but his body cried in agony as it struggled to hold the faltering shield steady. He was nearly spent.

Joel could feel the portal swelling behind him and a final rush of hope fluttered in his chest. If only he could hold out a few moments longer—

Suddenly, the tendrils of magic binding the portal spell to the granite archway began to fragment. He could feel the energy fizzling, threatening to fade completely. *No! What's happening? Why is the portal dying?*

'*It's not enough. NezReth can't do it alone!*' Kirk's lips didn't move, but his voice came from all around—inside Joel's head. The internal dialogue was so jarring Joel nearly lost his focus. '*I'm going to help him. You have to hold the shield without me!*'

Joel wanted to scream in protest, but he couldn't do anything except meet the trainee's gaze with wide, frightened eyes. Hasain and Joel couldn't possibly hold off the enemy alone. They could barely maintain the defense with three people. The Imperials would break through if Kirk abandoned them—

Again, the wispy voice shot through his mind. '*You can do this. You have to.*'

Joel gritted his teeth. The burden of responsibility was difficult to bear. He would have to hold out or *all* of them would be lost.

A hand gripped his shoulder. Cenric. "Use my strength as you would," the ambassador said. Koal had left Liro's body slumped near the archway and now stood beside Hasain, offering support as well. The seneschal kept one hand wrapped around the base of his blade, but with the other, he reached out to grasp Hasain's forearm. Though neither man possessed magic, they could still lend their strength.

Joel hesitated only a moment before tapping into Cenric's life force, guiding the energy from his body to Joel's own, using it to further fuel the spell. The shield buckled as Kirk redistributed his focus to the portal, but Hasain's power lifted a moment later to take up the slack. Together, they braced against the attack.

Out of the corner of his eye, Joel saw Kenisha kneel beside her brother, aiding him with energy. The gateway flared with renewed vigor as Kirk's magic joined with NezReth's, giving the Blessed Mage the extra burst of power he so desperately needed. The tendrils locked into place and spread to engulf the entire arch. Joel could feel the magic pooling in the center of the structure. They only needed a few more precious moments before they could pass through.

A blast of arcane energy burst against the shield, sending shards of magic careening down onto them. Joel cried out as the debris scorched his skin and hair, but he could do nothing more. Adrian Titus stood just beyond the barricade, eyes fierce and maniacal. Joel watched in horror as the Archmage summoned a second crackling globule.

"*Joel!*" Hasain screeched in warning.

Both of them scrambled to repair the damaged section of the shield, but they weren't fast enough. Adrian hurled the sphere directly at the weak spot. The explosion sent Joel sprawling to his knees. He whimpered in pain but found himself unable to stand or even move from where he'd fallen. All his energy was tied into the shield—the shield that was rapidly eroding before his eyes.

Blood drained from his face at the sight of the gaping hole in the shield where Adrian's bolt had struck. He raised a shaking hand, directing what little remained of his energy in an attempt to patch the breach, but his reaction was too sluggish.

The snap of an Imperial bowstring cut through the night. Time came to a sudden, grinding halt. Joel saw the arrow gleaming as it floated, deft as a feather, through the air. He observed Hasain's eyes widen in an abject horror that rivaled Joel's own. He felt the grip tighten on his shoulder, each fingertip pressing into his flesh like blunted needles. He could even hear his own scream as he watched, completely helpless, as the deadly weapon found its mark.

"*Da!*"

Koal let out a sharp grunt and teetered to the ground, clutching his hands around the shaft that now lay embedded in his shoulder.

Gut-wrenching terror pierced Joel's heart. *Oh gods. He's been shot. Oh gods!*

The seneschal's crumbled form lay motionless on the granite step. White panic blinded Joel. He couldn't breathe. He couldn't think. All he could do was stare at the horrible scene playing out right before his eyes.

"Focus, Joel! I can't hold the shield without you!"

Hasain's command was a fuzzy murmur at the back of Joel's mind. He couldn't hear anything above the devastating pounding in his ears. With a shaking hand, he reached for his father. *Please don't let him be dead. I promised I would keep him safe. I promised I'd see him home to Mother.* Koal's arm twitched. The movement was slight, but Joel saw it. *Oh, Daya, is he—? Yes! Yes, he's alive!*

Koal staggered to his feet. The ugly arrow still protruded from a gash in his blood-stained armor, but in the moment, all that mattered was that he lived.

"Joel!" Hasain's voice was on the edge of hysteria this time.

He'd lost all control. The shield bowed dangerously, threatening to dissipate. Joel refocused his dwindling energy, doing all he could to stabilize the barrier, but it wasn't enough. An entire section of the shield came tumbling down.

Gasping, Joel attempted to back away, but his body was so wrecked he couldn't even crawl. Hasain had slammed his eyes closed. Joel could feel Hasain trying to salvage the shield even then.

"Bring them down! Kill them!" Adrian screeched in triumph.

Joel looked through the broken section of the shield, watching helplessly as a pack of enemy soldiers stared at him down the length of their loaded crossbows. They aimed the weapons at his prone form, and Joel's blood ran cold. He knew the polished, onyx arrowheads would be the last thing he ever saw. All he could do was lie there petrified, waiting for death to take him.

I'm sorry, Gib. Please forgive me. I love you.

A shadow crossed his field of vision. He barely had a chance to register Cenric's dark form dash in front of him before the snap of half a dozen crossbow strings reached his ears. A moment later, Cenric slumped to his knees.

"*No!*" Joel cried in shock. *Oh gods. No. No. It can't be—no!*

Tears poured down his face as he took Cenric into his arms. The chaos surrounding them faded into nothingness. Cenric and Joel could have been alone in the world for all he knew.

Cenric choked, a horrible, wet sound. "I'm getting—too old for this."

"*Why?*" Joel could barely see through his tears. His anguish was second only to Cenric's. "Why did you jump in front of me? You have a family waiting for you—and now—" He broke down into incoherent sobs as his trembling hands brushed past each coarse arrow fletching protruding from the ambassador's back.

Cenric managed a weak smile, but the agony in his eyes was enough to completely undo Joel. "The world—will weep much less for the loss of one old envoy. You—must live."

Bile rose in Joel's throat as he watched blood saturate Cenric's tunic, bathing the azure fabric crimson. Somewhere in the back of Joel's consciousness, he was aware of the portal flaring to life and Hasain screaming that the shield was about to collapse.

"You can make it," Joel gasped, cradling his mentor's broken body. "We're almost home. Just hang on. I'm going to get you out of here."

Cenric shook his head. "No. It's my—my time."

"Joel! Help me!" Koal's desperate voice drew his attention. The seneschal clutched his wounded shoulder with one hand. His sword lay discarded on the stone steps as he struggled to hoist Liro up. "Help me with your brother! Now!"

A pallid fog rolled over Cenric's eyes, snuffing out the enduring shine Joel had grown so fond of. "My family—tell them—tell them I love them. Go now."

Joel gripped the ambassador's tunic, cold blood rushing over his fingertips. "No. You can't die. I won't leave you."

Again, Koal yelled for assistance. "Joel! I can't do this alone!"

"Go," Cenric rasped, a spurt of blood resting on the corner of his mouth. "Go help—your father." Somehow, the ambassador managed to get his arm between the two of them and shoved Joel back a step. "*Leave me.*"

Joel clambered to his feet, taking a blind step toward Koal. The portal raged in Joel's ears, blasting him with bitter air and shards of ice. The wave almost sent him spiraling to the ground, but somehow he managed to stumble up the granite step to join his father.

"Get his other arm," Koal shouted above the torrent. "We have to carry him through the portal."

Joel numbly took hold of Liro's arm, slinging the limp appendage over one shoulder. Taking a lumbering step, he did his best to hold his brother steady. Koal grunted as Liro's weight pressed on the arrow, still embedded in the seneschal's shoulder. Three steps farther and they were standing in front of the crackling portal.

"Go!" Hasain hissed. "I'll hold them off!"

"On three," Koal said.

Joel met his father's terrible gaze and somehow managed to nod.

"One. Two. *Three!*"

Together, father and son jumped.

Joel's strength failed him as he tumbled through the portal. He was at the mercy of the Void, weightless and falling. His mouth was open, screaming, but he couldn't hear his own voice above the crackle of lightning. And then it was over.

He collapsed in a pile of snow, the cold seeping through clothing and cutting at his exposed skin. Liro and Koal hit the ground beside him an instant later. *Cenric. He might still be alive.*

Letting out a wail, Joel attempted to crawl back toward the portal. "I have to go back for Cenric!"

Koal grabbed hold of his son's arm. "He's already gone."

"*No!*" Even as he moaned the word, he knew his father was right. A crushing despair pressed down on Joel's lungs, and he gasped, unable to breathe. *I can't—can't leave him there!* Somehow, Joel managed to roll onto his back, leaving a crimson imprint behind that painted the snow an ugly red. He retched at the sight of Cenric's blood.

Kirk and Kenisha crashed through the portal, their cloaks billowing around them. Kenisha clutched her brother's arm, and her eyes were wide with terror.

"Hasain? NezReth?" Koal demanded, wincing as he stumbled to his feet. "Where are they?"

Even as the question was fired, Joel could see the Blessed Mage standing on the far side of the portal. NezReth's eyes remained cloudy, still bound in trance by the spell. Hasain trailed him, keeping a hand on the mage's back, guiding him forward. Behind them, the shield shattered, crumbling into a million fragments of shimmering light. Hasain must have known. Without waiting another instant, he pushed NezReth forward and together they dove through the portal. A hail of arrows followed in their wake, slicing paths through the snow and coming to rest by their boots. Joel's heart thudded to a stop when he saw the Imperial soldiers rush the archway.

"Bring it down!" Hasain screeched. "They're coming through!"

NezReth swung around to face the portal, horrible anger contorting his features. His eyes burned with fury as he raised both hands above his head. Energy crackled down the lengths of his arms like rods of lightning. Joel could feel the Blessed Mage release the magic. He watched as it was hurled back toward the portal—

In a flash of blinding light, the stone arch burst in an explosion of rubble and roaring flame. The force of the impact sent every person sprawling to their knees. When the destruction passed, a mound of scorched rock was all that remained of the portal.

Grave, devastating silence fell across the courtyard. No one spoke. No one moved. Joel lay in the blood-stained snow, body trembling and mind numb. All he could do was bury his battered face against one arm and sob for the loss of his mentor.

CHAPTER ELEVEN

The candles burned low in the sitting room of the royal suite. Gib rubbed his eyes and tried to focus while the King, Aodan, and Marc discussed their options. They kept their voices stifled while the rest of the world slept.

King Rishi set the letter from Koal on his Senet board and paced by the open window. His face was drawn into a tight frown. "Why such a sudden return? The message is so vague that you know there *must* be something he's not telling us."

"Might not have been able ta say everythin' he wanted." Aodan shifted in his seat. "The Empire probably read it before it was sent out."

The King nodded. "No doubt. He must have felt it important to warn us though."

Marc sighed, his eyelids heavy. "I don't know what you expect us to do tonight. Wouldn't it be better for everyone to be well rested for the morning?"

"No." King Rishi never looked up. His repetitions back and forth across the floor were maddening. "We need to be prepared for his return. Soldiers and mages need to be posted all around the courtyard. If the Empire tries anything shady, we need to be ready for it."

"Don't you think if they were going to try something then they wouldn't have let the letter come through?"

Marc may have had a point, but Gib was beyond being able to tell what it was. He yawned behind his hand and fought to keep his eyes open. Surely they would dismiss him any time now, and he would be able to slink back to the dormitory and fall into bed. He'd lost track of the time ages ago, but he suspected it had to be closer to sunrise than sunset now.

The Blessed Mage Natori stood by one of the bookcases. Dark rings circled her eyes, but she still managed to set Gib on edge. Her hand rested atop the hilt of her sword, and he was sure she was prepared to strike, despite her apparent lethargy. "Should I rally the sentinels now? Give them their orders for first light?"

The King barely spared her a glance. "Sooner. The mark before first light."

Aodan snorted. "It's nearly the mark b'fore sunrise *now*. Better give

246

that order if yer gonna."

Natori gave a brief nod. "Right. I'll deliver the message. Aodan, you summon Roland. We'll need skilled, trustworthy warriors on hand."

"Aye, an' get my teeth kicked in fer my troubles." Aodan leapt from his seat and made for the door. He and the mage had only just stopped to remove their slippers when Natori whirled around on one heel. Gib shrank in his seat as her shrewd eyes fixed on him—no, on the window.

Behind him came the sudden crackling of energy, and without turning around Gib could see blue light flashing, reflecting off the walls of the suite. Heart in his throat, he dared to look out the window and gasped when he saw the portal in the courtyard below had fired to life. "They're back!"

The King roared a command for them all to go to the courtyard even as Natori confirmed NezReth was the one who powered the spell. Marc grabbed Gib's arm, sprinting to the door, telling him to stay close. Marc might need to mend injuries and might have to call on Gib for aid. King Rishi disappeared into an adjacent room and came back wielding a sharpened longsword.

They were out in the hall before Gib's head could stop spinning. Royal soldiers raced to keep up. He ran with the rest of them, sleep suddenly a million leagues from his mind. He'd longed for the moment when he'd be reunited with Joel, but he hadn't anticipated the raw tension roiling his guts. Something had to be wrong. Why were they here so early? Was Joel all right? What about Koal?

The slippers from the King's suite were ill suited to the slick stone of the palace floors, and Gib had to catch his balance more than once. As they tore down the corridors, he watched King Rishi and Natori lead the way. They both had their swords drawn in preparation for battle. Natori's weapon was even bathed in blue, hissing magic. Gib's breath caught at the awe of it. It was like something from a *Tale of Fae*, fierce and frightening.

He suddenly wished he carried a blade, too. Turning to see if he could spot a spare of any sort, he noted one member of their party seemed to be missing. Where was Aodan? He wasn't up by the King, and he wasn't guarding their backs either. Had he gone back to get a weapon?

"On your guard now!" King Rishi's voice filled the entire palace. "Who knows what the enemy has in mind!"

"The portal has already closed," Natori replied through arduous breaths.

Gib tried to keep his nerves in check. Had there been enough time for everyone to get through? He craned his neck, trying to see around the gate that led into the courtyard.

The gate opened and soldiers grabbed torches as they passed from the lighted hall into the dark night. Someone thrust one into Gib's hand, and he accepted it without protest.

The frigid air was unforgiving as it hit his face and snow came up well past the tops of his dainty slippers, but Gib barely noticed. The courtyard was impossibly long as they trudged across it. Gib sucked in a sharp breath. Where was the stone archway? It had been there a moment ago when the blue light had first flared, but now all that remained was a pile of rubble.

"Where is everyone? Are they all here?" the King demanded as he strode ahead of Gib.

"All but one. Two extras." Aodan's rough voice responded. He barked a command to the soldiers. "Bring the torches here to the injured. Keep those two under lock an' key. Don't let them outta yer sight!"

Gib frowned. How had Aodan gotten out here so fast? And who were the two shrouded figures cowering away from him? Gib didn't have time to think about it. Marc grabbed his shoulder and dragged him toward the envoys. "Hold up the light where I can see!"

Gib pushed the torch higher into the air and any thoughts outside that moment vanished. Koal stood lopsided, leaning against Hasain. The front of the seneschal's armor was marred crimson and his right hand had come up to stabilize an arrow shaft embedded in his left shoulder. Gib froze, recalling the uncanny similarity to the King's assassination attempt almost three years prior.

"Koal! What the hell happened?" King Rishi's voice was hoarse. His long strides carried him over to the seneschal in an instant. Sheathing his sword in one fluid movement, he helped support Koal.

Marc plowed through the snow and put both hands on the seneschal's chest. "Can you breathe?"

Koal lurched away from the touch, his curt voice labored. "I'm fine for now. Check Liro."

Fine? Damn him and his pride! Gib couldn't tell if he was scared or furious. Who did Koal think he was fooling? Having an arrow sticking out of his chest was no small matter.

Marc began to protest, but Koal put an immediate end to it. "*Liro!* He's unconscious." Red faced, Marc looked at the King. The seneschal was having none of their concern. "If the arrow hit my heart or lung, I'd already be dead. Go see to Liro."

The King nodded once and gestured for Marc to go to Liro before pointing at a royal guard. "Summon more healers. Now!"

As Gib followed, a horrible feeling began to churn in his stomach. Where was Joel? Blinking around in the darkness, he couldn't immediately find the mage and paralyzing fear blossomed in his heart. Joel had returned, hadn't he? Surely he must be here, but the dark was so thick Gib couldn't find him.

"Down here, Gib," Marc directed.

Liro lay on the ground beside the rubble of the archway. At first he appeared as bad off as Koal suggested, but when Gib lowered the torch, he could see Liro's eyes fluttering open and closed. He was trying to come out of his "sleep."

Somewhere in the background, Gib could hear the King conversing with Koal, attempting to keep him alert and talking. Natori questioned NezReth about the collapsed portal. Marc was trying to get Liro to respond to his voice. Hundreds of different things were happening, but Gib could scarcely take in any of it. His eyes were fixed on Aodan, who had crouched beside a still form everyone else seemed to have overlooked.

"J–Joel?" The young mage didn't stir, and the sight of his blood-soaked robes made Gib's head swim. He lumbered a step closer, voice rising to a screech. "*Joel?*"

Joel's eyes opened. He turned his head and looked straight through Gib. His mouth moved but all that came out was a guttural sob. Gib was at his side in an instant, on his knees in the ruined snow, trying to determine where the blood was coming from. "Marc! Marc, he needs you! He's bleeding everywhere!"

A hand closed over his and gently took the torch away. "Nay, lad. He's all right. Joel's gonna be fine."

Gib turned an incredulous stare up at Aodan. "N–no. Look at him! He's bleeding out!"

A pained look crossed the bodyguard's features and his demeanor softened. He put a bare knee down in the snow—it was beyond reasoning how the Derr wasn't freezing to death out here in just his kilt and slippers—and lowered the torch to better illuminate Joel's robes. "Calm yerself, Nemesio. It's not his blood."

The nausea was tempered by his relief. *Not Joel's blood?* Gib looked again, closer this time. The light flickered in the cold night but burned brightly enough for him to see Aodan spoke the truth. He couldn't find an actual wound or source of the bleeding. Joel's nose and lower face were smeared and beginning to bruise, but there was no way a nosebleed had caused the damage to his robes.

Gib was finally able to take a breath. "But then—whose?"

He looked around. Koal and Hasain still stood huddled together, the King at their side. Liro was beginning to respond to Marc's voice, following a finger with his eyes and clutching some trinket around his neck. NezReth leaned against Natori, pale and unstable, just inside the torch's circle of light. Sinking realization dawned. "Where's Ambassador Cenric?"

Joel sucked in a ragged breath and broke down into unintelligible sobs. *Oh.* Gib sat, dumbstruck, in the snow. He didn't know what to say or do so he simply put a hand atop Joel's head. His companion trembled under the touch but didn't try to move away.

"He fell a hero," NezReth said. Still clutching Natori's shoulders, he looked toward King Rishi. "His tomb should be decorated as a hero."

Aodan groaned as he stood. "He's dead, then? You're certain?"

"Yes." Hasain's weak voice lifted for the first time. He looked as exhausted as the others. "There wasn't enough time or manpower to bring his body back. May The Two forgive us."

The wind blew cold across the barren courtyard. Gib shuddered. It felt as if they stood on the very edge of the world.

"Chhaya, keep vigil." Koal's voice was resilient despite his injury. "For one of your children comes." Gib lowered his head and closed his eyes as he and the others joined in. "Our hearts are heavy as our brother crosses the veil today." He'd heard the death rite issued before, but it stung his throat to say the words himself. He hadn't had to utter it since his own father had been laid to rest.

The wind, still blustering gusts of ice and snow, was the only sound to betray the silence that followed.

"What happened?" King Rishi demanded at long last, breaking the quiet. Additional healers and soldiers began to pour into the courtyard as he spoke.

Koal frowned. "They made me an offer I had to refuse. When I told them we were leaving, they decided they were going to miss me and implored I stay."

One corner of the King's mouth curled upward, the first glimpse of a smile Gib had witnessed in ages. The scowl the King had sported a moment before quickly resurfaced. "You look terrible. Marc, get over here."

Liro was sitting up now, still holding whatever bauble it was he had around his neck. When Marc rose, the mage offered no resistance. Koal, on the other hand, openly balked.

"Chhaya's bane, Koal!" the dean huffed. "You've been impaled. Liro's fine. Let me look at you."

Koal groaned. "I'm not dead yet." He winced when Marc peeled back a layer of armor and fabric. "It didn't even hurt much until now."

Marc chuckled. "Adrenaline. That'll fade soon enough. Let's get you inside. I need proper light and none of us need to stand out here to catch our deaths."

"Like the lot of you in your pretty little slippers?" Koal gasped when Marc touched a tender spot.

"If I lose my toes to frostbite, I'm holding you accountable." King Rishi finally left Koal's side but froze when he seemed to notice something new. His voice went cold. "Wait. Who are our—guests?"

Following the King's gaze, Gib watched as a cluster of royal guardsmen circled the two strangers he'd hardly noticed earlier. A young man and woman, probably around the same age as he and Joel, trembled as they huddled close together. Their strange silken garments confirmed they must have come through the portal with the Ardenian envoys. Gib clenched his jaw. What were two Imperials doing here?

Koal cleared his throat. "They're friends of Joel's. He vouched for them, and I must admit, we wouldn't have made it back without their help." When King Rishi gave the seneschal a cross glare, he only squared his good shoulder and set his mouth in a firm line. "I can say no more on the matter. You'll have to question Joel. Just—do so gently."

Frowning, the King swept over, and despite knowing this had nothing to do with him, Gib couldn't help but pull away as the ruler loomed above them. Joel, however, lifted his vacant eyes. His unfocused stare passed straight through the King.

"Joel Adelwijn, explain yourself," King Rishi demanded in a firm tone.

Joel's mouth moved, but the only thing to come out was another sob. He closed his lips, swallowed audibly, and tried again. He got the same result. After another miserable attempt, all he could do was retch and weep. "I'm sorry."

King Rishi's features lost their harsh edge. Gib watched, transfixed, as the King dropped to one knee and offered a hand. "Sit up. Get out of the snow."

Joel wiped at his tears but did as he was instructed. Taking the offered hand, he managed to pull himself into a sitting position. The King tipped Joel's chin up, examining his bruising nose. "Do you need a healer?"

"N–no." Joel wavered in his spot, and Gib reached out to help stabilize him.

King Rishi also set a hand on the young mage's shoulder. "Tell me what happened."

Joel's vacant eyes flitted around the courtyard. Even in the low light, Gib could tell Joel was scared and confused. He turned his dazed expression back to the King and launched into frantic mumbling. "We weren't safe. Kirk came to warn us! If they hadn't led us, we would have died! I almost—they shot at me, but Cenric—"

Gib's head spun. What? How was he supposed to put any of that together?

The King's squint suggested he was at the same loss. He nodded, reassuring Joel, and spoke in a low, soothing tone. "Breathe, Joel. Calm yourself." While Joel tried to pull himself together, King Rishi turned to look over his shoulder at the two Imperials. "Are they the ones who helped?"

"Yes." Joel looked down at his hands and shuddered violently. Gib tried to rub some warmth into the mage's back. "I'm sorry, Unc—Highness. Father told me not to. I know it was a risk to bring them, but—but they'd have been killed!"

King Rishi's expression was bare and open. His eyes glimmered as he laid a free hand over Joel's. "You did what you felt was right. No apologies are to be made for that." Letting out a deep sigh, the ruler stood. "Come then. On your feet." He lifted Joel by his forearms, and Gib scrambled to support the mage from behind.

As soon as they were standing, a healer approached and began to examine Joel's nose. Gib stayed with Joel to make sure he didn't collapse. Attention so dedicated to Joel, Gib didn't even see Hasain make an approach.

"How's Joel? Is he all right?" Hasain asked through chattering teeth.

The King put an arm around his son's shoulders. "He'll be fine. How are you?"

"Koal saw to it that I was kept safe." Hasain's voice was uneven, and he covered his face with one hand. "I failed him in return. I thought I could keep the shield up until we got through the portal, but when Joel was in trouble, I couldn't keep the magic going. I'm not as brave or strong as you've taught me to be."

Gib winced. He couldn't imagine how bad it must have been for both Joel and Hasain to be so shaken. What had happened for Koal to be shot and Cenric killed?

"As long as you did all you could, you didn't fail." The King's steadfast voice was reassuring. "Now tell me, what do you know of these two?"

Hasain followed his father's gaze toward the Imperial youths. They huddled together, trying to ward off the cold, but their light garb did them no favors. Hasain sighed. "Kirk was one of our attendants. Joel grew to trust him over the course of our stay. The girl is his sister, Kenisha. She helped us, too."

"And this Kirk was the one to inform you of the danger?"

Hasain opened his mouth to respond, but Koal beat him to it. "He came to us in our suite." The seneschal cradled his left arm as Marc worked tirelessly in the low light. "We'd all be dead if not for his tip off, Rishi."

The other healers were swarming now, bringing torches and supplies. Gib watched as two young men helped Liro stand and led him toward the palace.

Gib patted Joel's shoulder. "Come on. Let's get inside." Joel didn't respond other than to shuffle along beside him.

Koal made slow progress in the same direction. He didn't say anything, but Gib could tell the man's injured shoulder was beginning to hurt. His voice lacked its typical eloquence as he spoke to King Rishi. "And you were right. There's definitely something wrong with Emperor Sarpedon. He looks like he's our age."

King Rishi narrowed his eyes. "He's been our age since I was a child."

"They were pushing for a marriage alliance with Gudrin." Koal winced as he walked. Marc and the King slowed their paces to stay beside him. "Prince Alerio apparently has no intent to take his father's crown."

Aodan had been quiet for quite some time until then. Rushing over to walk with them, his face pulled into a crimson sneer. "Well, he sure as hell ain't marryin' Gudrin either!"

Koal nodded. "Yes. That was one of the offers I had to refuse. Several times." The King and his bodyguard went quiet, and Gib could all but feel the rage rolling off them.

The palace gate loomed ahead. Gib was anxious to get Joel inside, but Koal came to a stop so the rest of them stopped as well. Hasain muttered something in the seneschal's ear, and he nodded gravely. He dropped his voice to a whisper. "There's one more thing. Aodan, you may want to go check in on your cousins."

Aodan's brow furrowed. "In the mountains?"

"Yes. There may have been one at the arena."

"A cousin? You're sure?"

Hasain's voice trembled. "We're sure. We all saw it."

"That could mean there's trouble in the mountains," King Rishi muttered, sounding as though he was thinking out loud rather than addressing the others.

Gib frowned. What sort of trouble? Did this have to do with the Northern Empire as well? He wanted to stay and find out more, but the healer attending to Joel was beckoning him toward the palace. Gib loosened his grip on his companion's arm but instantly Joel tightened his. Their eyes met and even though not a single word was exchanged, Gib knew he needed to follow his companion. He'd be able to ask Koal or Marc for more information later. Joel needed him now, and Gib wasn't going to let him down.

The grief welled in Joel's chest, threatening to bleed into his very soul. He retched on a wet sob and clamped his mouth shut. *No more tears. I've already cried enough.*

Five days had passed since they'd escaped the Northern Empire. Five days since they'd fallen through the portal into the snow. *Five days since Cenric—*

Joel rubbed his damp eyes with the back of his hand. A log crackled in the hearth behind him and he winced. The haunting sound roused atrocious memories and sent him careening back to the moment when he'd lost control of the shield. He hadn't been able to hold off the onslaught of Imperial magic long enough. The shield had shattered. His father had taken an arrow to the shoulder. Cenric had died. All because of him.

It's my fault. I needed to be stronger. I needed to hold on. I failed him.

Cenric's funeral had taken place earlier that morning. The bitter

253

winter air had been easier to confront than the faces of the deceased envoy's family. Seeing the tears stream down Cerys Leal's cheeks as she mourned the loss of her husband had been enough to undo Joel. His heart fissured completely when Gara and Nia broke down into inconsolable sobs. Nage Nessuno held Nia while she cried, offering his fiancé support. Cenric wouldn't be there to see her marry. He wouldn't be able to watch with prideful eyes as Gara graduated Academy. Two young girls had lost their father, and Joel knew there were no words he could offer to ease the pain.

He pulled his legs tight against his chest and closed his eyes, listening to the roar of the fire. The warmth of the Adelwijn sitting room offered no comfort as his mind continued to linger on the burial ceremony. Joel blinked back tears. Cenric couldn't even be laid to rest. They prepared a beautiful marble tomb, but his family had no chance to say their final goodbyes. There hadn't been a body to bury. Having no knowledge of what those wicked bastards in the Northern Empire had done with his remains was the worst part. Rash anger surged in Joel's blood. If they defiled Cenric's body, he'd somehow make them pay.

I should have found a way to bring his body with us. I should have gone back for him. Joel's lower lip quivered despite his best effort to keep it still. He knew he wasn't thinking rationally. There hadn't been time to go back, but even admitting the fact did nothing to lessen the guilt. *I made the call to leave the city. Everything that happened was my fault. I should have been the one to die.*

Nearly silent footsteps filtered down the corridor as someone drew near. Hastily, Joel wiped his eyes dry and pulled himself together. He didn't need anyone treading lightly around him or bestowing stares of pity. *Mother has been treating me like I'm a cracked plate. Father too.* He sniffled. Maybe they were right. Perhaps he was closer to shattering than he realized.

Koal entered the room. His left arm hung limp against his side, wrapped inside a cloth sling. When he took notice of Joel, his grim expression lightened a touch. "It's nice to see you out of your room."

"Mother insisted I sit by the fire and warm myself," Joel said.

"Not an unreasonable suggestion." Koal kept his voice neutral, leaving Joel unable to get a good feel for what his father might be thinking. His morning had no doubt been trying, too.

The seneschal had been among those to attend Cenric's funeral, along with Liro, Joel's mother, and two sisters. King Rishi and Queen Dahlia even made a brief appearance to express their condolences to the fallen hero's family. Notably absent was Joel's uncle, Neetra Adelwijn. Anger swelled inside Joel's chest. Cenric had served Arden faithfully for over two decades. For the High Councilor to not pay his respects was unacceptable.

Koal lingered near the fireplace, resting his unbound hand against the mantel. "I'd sit with you, but I have notes to finish before the afternoon session."

"The High Council is meeting today then?" Joel asked.

Koal stared into the dancing flames. "Aye."

"There will be talk of what actions need to be taken against the Northern Empire, right?"

A twinge of guilt touched Koal's face. He turned to regard Joel with somber eyes. "The subject will be breached, no doubt, but whether action against the Empire is even an option remains to be seen."

Joel uttered a gasp. "*Something* needs to be done!" he protested. "They *killed* Cenric! Are you just going to let them get away with it?"

Koal threw his good hand into the air. "What would you have me do, Joel? Go to war with the Northern Empire? Do you think that's what Cenric would have wanted? To send thousands of our soldiers to their deaths?"

Joel's lower lip quivered. "I didn't say that. I just—I want justice for Cenric."

He didn't hear his father move, but a moment later, a firm hand squeezed the back of his neck. "We all do," Koal replied. The seneschal's voice softened. "I know how close the two of you were. Cenric was a good man, an honorable man. I wouldn't have chosen anyone else to mentor my son. The lessons he taught you are invaluable. As—as long as you remember the qualities he imparted upon you, he'll always be here." Joel sniffled but couldn't bring himself to respond. He heard his father let out a deep sigh. "I have to finish those notes now, but if you'd like to speak more about this later—"

"I'll be fine, Father." Joel glared at the floor.

Koal hesitated before replying in a stilted voice, "The offer stands if you change your mind." He gave Joel's back one final pat and then departed.

Joel listened to the sound of his father's footfalls as he retreated to the study. Once again, the mage was left to wallow in his grief. He hugged his arms tighter around his legs and let out a bitter sob. *It's not fair. None of this is fair. He's dead and there's nothing anyone can do about it.*

As much as Joel didn't want to admit it, he knew his father was right. Arden couldn't go to war with the Northern Empire. Sarpedon's army dwarfed Arden's. It would be a suicidal mission. *Not to mention, I watched the Emperor sign treaties with both Chancellor Garron and the Dhaki princes. Surely Nales and Shiraz would lend their own troops to the Empire's cause if we tried to march on the nation.*

A shadow fell across the room. Someone new was making an approach from the corridor. *Who is it now?* Joel swallowed down his sorrow and glanced up.

Kirk Bhadrayu winced as though he'd stepped on a shard of broken glass. Even in the low light, Joel could see the remorse flash behind the Imperial's eyes.

"Oh, I'm sorry," Kirk said, hesitating beneath the doorframe. "I didn't know anyone was in here."

"You don't need to apologize." Joel's voice came out sounding strained and tired. "You're allowed to go wherever you'd like in the estate."

Kirk played with the long sleeves of his tunic, one of many outfits that had been gifted to him by Joel's mother. The deep jade and rich yellow fabric brought out the green in his eyes. *The Ardenian styles suit him well,* Joel thought to himself. *His accent is the only hint anyone will have that he's not native to Silver City.*

"I'm on my way to meet with Dean Marc," Kirk said.

"Moving to the dormitory then?"

The trainee nodded. "My classes have been set. Dean Marc sent word that he found a room for me. I suppose it's just as well. I don't want to impose on your family any more than I already have."

Joel shook his head. "You're not imposing. We wouldn't have made it out of Teivel alive if it wasn't for your help. Letting Kenisha and you stay here is the least we can do."

After proper questioning by the King, Kirk and his sister had been deemed trustworthy, and Koal had even offered to house them at the Adelwijn estate until the siblings found their feet. It was a nice gesture, especially by the seneschal's standards.

After learning that Kirk and Kenisha saved our lives, Mother wouldn't have had it any other way. Lady Mrifa, always the doting host, had been spoiling her new guests to no end. *Which is probably a good thing. I haven't exactly been in my right mind. Kirk must think I hate him.* Joel winced. That was far from true, of course. He owed his life to the young mage trainee.

Kirk stared into the burning hearth as though the flames held him spellbound. "Thank you, Joel. For everything. I haven't allowed myself to hope in so long—" He took a deep breath. "But now, I can. Keni too. This is a new beginning for both of us. And it's all because of you. I'll never be able to properly express my gratitude but—but I just want you to know how much your kindness means to me." He remained quiet for some time, watching the twirling fire. Then Kirk's gaze shifted to Joel, and his hushed voice could be heard above the blaze. "I hope we can still be friends."

Joel could barely meet his eyes. "Of course we can. I'm just—I—it's a difficult time—"

"I know it is." Kirk's voice was sympathetic. He took one step forward but seemed unwilling to move from his position beneath the doorframe. "And I'll have you know, the way you're feeling is perfectly justified. Don't let anyone tell you differently." He offered a weak smile. "You deserve as much space and time as you need."

"I—" Joel's words caught in his throat. "I don't mean to be so distant. It's just—it's how I grieve."

Kirk absently traced the embroidered sleeve of his tunic. "Cenric

256

seemed like an honorable man."

"He was." Joel swallowed. *Not now. No more tears.*

Silence threatened to smother out even the roaring fire.

"Well, I should be going," Kirk said at long last. "I wouldn't want to keep Dean Marc waiting."

"Good luck," Joel replied. He tried to sound spirited but knew the attempt fell flat.

"Goodbye, Joel."

Kirk departed, leaving Joel alone. The solitude was both a solace and a miserable reminder of his loss. With arms wrapped around his legs and chin resting gently on his knees, he uttered a choked sob. *Will this pain ever fade?*

Gib shoved his hands farther into the pockets of his overcoat as he walked. Snow sloshed around his boots and even more fell from the sky to settle amongst his curls. *I should have worn a hat. After sixteen winters, there's no excuse. Good thing I'm not far from where I need to be.*

Face burning from the sharp wind, he all but ran the remaining furlong. The impressive grounds of the Adelwijn estate loomed ahead, and Gib stopped only long enough to pry the icy wrought-iron gate open before slipping into the courtyard and continuing on his way. A breath later and he stood before the tall, oak door. Habit and mannerism told him to knock, though Seneschal Koal and the rest of his family had made it perfectly clear that he didn't need to.

That was before though. When Joel and I were—

Gib winced. Would Joel be here now? In his rush to be out of the cold, he'd allowed himself to forget the reason he'd been worrying himself sick for the past five days.

Memories of Joel's pale, bloodied face and terrified eyes came back to haunt Gib's mind. The vision of Joel, crumpled in the snow beside the ruined portal, unable to speak coherently or even sit up without help, was a constant wrenching in his gut. Whatever nightmare the mage had faced in the Northern Empire had scarred him deeply. Bearing witness to his terrible sobs and tear-stained cheeks had wedged a blade into Gib's heart, and he could think of nothing else but ensuring Joel was all right.

He pushed through the heavy door just as Tabitha came to answer it. A young girl trailed the loyal servant, and Gib faintly recognized her as one of the two people who had come through the portal with the Ardenian envoys. *That's right. Koal mentioned in passing that they were staying here.*

Tabitha ushered him inside. She seemed genuinely surprised to see him. "Gibben, it's been a while since you've visited."

"Duty has kept me busy," he replied, knowing how lame he must have sounded. It wasn't the truth. He'd been avoiding coming here because he felt that the privilege was no longer his. He and Joel were no more. Didn't it make sense that he not come barging in as though he lived there?

"Of course," Tabitha replied. "You did a great service by assisting Lord Marc Arrio in the seneschal's absence." She motioned toward the Imperial girl. "This is Kenisha Bhadrayu, our honored guest."

Gib bowed his head, pushing aside the twinge of distrust that flared in his chest. "Thank you for helping my friends, Lady Kenisha. Without your assistance, they never would have escaped the evils of the Northern Empire."

A dusting of pink sprinkled the young girl's oval face. "Just Kenisha, m'lord. I'm no lady, only a humble servant."

"I'm Gibben Nemesio, and I'm no lord either, just a humble understudy."

Gib's words were rewarded with a shy smile. Briefly returning the gesture, he turned his attention back to Tabitha. "I'm here for Seneschal Koal. We're to travel to the council meeting at the palace together. Can you tell him I've arrived?"

"The seneschal is in his study," Tabitha replied. "I'm sure he won't be long. You're welcome to wait in the sitting room for him. Otos just stoked the fire."

Gib sighed with relief. "Oh wonderful, my hands are freezing. Thank you, Tabitha."

The two young women giggled as they went toward the kitchen while Gib rambled through the long corridor leading to the sitting room. As he passed by the elegant staircase that led to the second story, his heart beat a little faster in his chest. Was Joel up there? Was he all right? *Should I go see? Just to make sure he's okay? No. Stop being an idiot. He hasn't made any indication he wants to see you. Give him his damned space. Do you want to chase him farther away?* Gib forced himself to keep moving.

I should have just met Koal at the palace. I shouldn't be here. He knew exactly why he'd come though. He wanted to see Joel. But only to ensure he was all right. *Is there something so wrong with that? He's been part of my life since the day I came to Silver. I can't pretend his welfare doesn't matter. I just want to hear it from him—that he's okay without me.*

The promise of fire and warmth helped lift Gib's spirits and he quickened his pace, but his mind was so full that he wasn't paying attention to where he was going. He nearly collided with a person traveling in the opposite direction.

The Imperial boy who'd come through the portal with Koal and the others jumped out of Gib's way, gasping sharply. Dressed in a green tunic and trousers, with deep brown hair and fair skin, he might have passed for an Ardenian if Gib hadn't known better. Gib fished for the boy's name.

Kris? Kurt? Kiran? No. Kirk! That's it.

"O—oh, pardon me," Kirk said, pressing his back against the wall even though the corridor had more than enough room for both of them. The Imperial boy's face contorted, and confusion clouded his wide eyes. The boy was clearly trying to place Gib's face.

So many people were in the courtyard that night. I suppose he wouldn't recognize me.

Sparing the boy further embarrassment, Gib huffed a sigh. "I'm Gibben, Seneschal Koal's understudy." He didn't mean for his voice to come out sounding so curt. Really, he had no reason to dislike Kirk, but just knowing he came from the same people who'd murdered Ambassador Cenric and nearly killed Koal left a bitter taste in Gib's mouth, and he couldn't shake the feeling.

"Seneschal Koal is in his study," Kirk whispered, giving no indication Gib's name had meant anything to him.

"Yes, I know. Thank you." Again, Gib's voice clipped without consent. *Stop it. It's not his fault Koal's injured and Joel's an emotional wreck. He helped them escape.* Gib opened his mouth to issue an apology, but Kirk scooted past and Gib lost his chance.

"Good day," the Imperial boy said. He turned his back to Gib and departed. A few moments later, Gib heard the front door open and close.

Nerves still frayed, Gib stuffed his hands into his pockets and continued to the sitting room. *Stop. Just stop. Koal has entrusted these Imperials. There's no reason to be so hostile.*

He'd already blundered into the sitting room before he realized someone occupied the couch. Hollow sapphire eyes rose to meet him, and Gib froze in place. "J—Joel."

Joel's pale face looked ghostly in the firelight, and the dark rings beneath his eyes matched the horrible bruise on his nose. The mage's shoulders were slouched, with frail arms wrapped around his legs, and the wet streaks on either cheek were proof enough that he'd been crying. Gib's soul ached, the desire to rush to Joel's side overriding any common sense he still possessed. He caught himself after only one step, however, and forced his feet to remain planted on the hard marble floor.

"Gib," Joel rasped. He wiped a sleeve across his face, but it was too late to hide the tears. "What—what are you doing here?"

Gib winced. That hadn't been the reaction he'd hoped for. A sudden thought dawned on him. When Gib had passed Kirk in the corridor, the Imperial had come from this very room. He hadn't made Joel cry, had he? *Why* had Kirk even been in there? What could he possibly have to say to Joel? Irrational jealousy sprang to life in Gib's chest so sharply it startled him. *Just stop. You're being ridiculous!* He cleared his throat. "I, uh, I'm here to see Koal. I didn't—didn't know you would be here."

"O—oh. You're here for my father." Joel sighed, and his shoulders lost a bit of their rigidity. "I didn't want you to see me like this." His hands flopped in the air, gesturing weakly at himself.

Gib snorted. "Oh hell, you've never looked better." When his comment was met with silent skepticism, he added tersely, "Well, you're still prettier than me anyway."

Joel's laugh was broken. "Stop it."

"Seriously. I especially love what you've done with your snout. The ladies at court will be jealous."

A single tear rolled down Joel's cheek, and Gib knew his joke had fallen short. Unable to stop himself, he reached a hand toward the other man. "If—if you need someone to talk to, you know I'm here for you, don't you?"

Joel glared at the floor. "I'm fine."

Gib didn't want to push Joel too far, but he called the bluff for what it was. Three steps across the cold tiles found him standing before the mage. "That's horseshit. No one would be 'fine' after what you've been through."

Joel still refused to meet Gib's gaze, and his heart sank. *He's doing it again. He's shutting me out. Dammit, it took so long to get him to open up. I can't let him barricade himself inside a shell again. He needs to talk to me!*

"You don't have to always be so stoic," Gib murmured. "It's okay to crumble. I'm here—there are people here to hold you up. People who love you." With a tentative hand, he reached out to cup the side of Joel's face. "Please don't shut me out. Let me help you."

Devastating blue eyes rose, wavering but able to hold Gib's. Joel stared at him with a measuring gaze and Gib could sense the mage's conflict. Joel parted trembling lips—surely he meant to say something profound—but a moment later, his demeanor went frigid. Joel locked his jaw and looked away.

Gib let his hand fall. The opportunity had passed. Joel's rejection stung like a deep gash in Gib's flesh, but he could do nothing else, could utter no words, to change the other man's mind.

I'll wait. He just needs time.

The study door flew open, jarring Gib from his reverie of misery. Koal walked into the room, his left arm in a sling, leaving him with only one hand to carry his rucksack. Gib jumped to assist the seneschal. The distraction helped hold the tears at bay.

CHAPTER TWELVE

"You don't have to carry that for me, you know. I'm no cripple."

Gib grinned at his mentor as he readjusted the pack slung over his shoulder. "You could have fooled me with that sling."

"Laugh it up." Koal groaned as they made their way through the palace halls. "Marc could hardly speak for laughing so hard when he discovered the King and I would have matching scars."

A chuckle escaped before Gib could reel it in. "He has a point. Opposite shoulders, but I've thought it myself."

A small smile peeked at the corner of Koal's mouth, a welcome sight after the somber mood he'd been in earlier. "I suppose. Rishi jumped at the opportunity to declare himself the 'handsome twin.' It's good to see neither of them matured since I left."

Gib didn't have the heart to tell his mentor the truth about how much Marc and King Rishi had suffered in Koal's absence. Maybe there would be a time to inform the seneschal, but today was far too soon. Koal needed to focus his attention on restoring order to the High Council and reigning in that imbecile, Neetra.

Their conversation went stale as the council room doors loomed ahead, but the silence was companionable. Gib was content to let the calm envelop him. His thoughts touched on Joel again. He recognized that the mage wanted space, but Gib also knew Joel well enough to realize he would lock his emotions inside until he burst. Surely there must be something Gib could do. *If he won't talk to me, perhaps someone else will have better luck.* Nawaz and Diddy came to mind. Joel had always been close with them. *I can't just idly watch as he suffers.*

"Oh, there you are. Back on your feet, are you?"

Gib stiffened as Neetra Adelwijn's jarring voice called down the corridor.

Koal turned to face his younger brother, and Gib could hear the seneschal utter a grunt. "You'd have seen me on my feet sooner, had you come to visit me."

Neetra waved a dismissive hand as he approached, and Gib noticed with dismay that Liro trailed the High Councilor. "I would have heard if you were on death's door. I received no such message, therefore, I

261

assumed you were recuperating."

Gib could feel himself sneering. He wished Koal realized what sort of trouble Neetra had made while the seneschal was gone. If only Koal knew how viciously his brother had goaded King Rishi or his attempts to sweet talk the members of the High Council into making unsavory decisions.

Neetra nonchalantly pushed onto another topic. "There have been whispers that you've consented to allow Nawaz and Heidi to marry. Is it true?"

The air around them went still, and Gib didn't have to look at his mentor to know he was livid. Koal's good hand balled into a fist at his side. "You were missed at Cenric's funeral."

Neetra didn't even bat an eye. "Missed? I doubt that."

"He was honored as a hero. He gave his life for Arden. The High Councilor should have been there to pay his respects."

"My time is often not my own. You know that. I had a previous engagement."

Gib gritted his teeth when he caught Liro leering. Though Gib hadn't known Cenric well, he knew enough to understand Neetra's flippant attitude was entirely unacceptable.

"So," Neetra continued. "About Nawaz and Heidi—"

Koal pressed his lips together. "This is hardly the time or place to discuss this."

"You've been avoiding this discussion for three years, brother. It's most unbecoming for a man of your position to be so noncommittal. What's your answer?"

The seneschal clenched his jaw and stole a look around the corridor. Gib imagined he might be looking for an escape route and didn't fault him. "I've told you before, Nawaz may have Heidi's hand if—and only if—he asks for it properly. I won't force my daughter into an unhappy marriage no matter how badly she may think she wants it. I've decided to grant him permission to court her, but that doesn't mean there'll be a wedding any time soon."

The victorious spark in Neetra's eyes made Gib's stomach flip. Even Liro's dull expression lifted in surprise. Koal turned his face away, conflict lacing his features.

Gib's stomach flopped like a fish out of water. Nawaz had been fretting over this very thing not long ago. He'd even begged Marc to send him to the border to avoid marriage. At the time, Gib had been unsure Koal would ever consent anyway, but clearly something had changed the seneschal's mind. Did Heidi know? Nawaz certainly didn't, and Kezra— Gib couldn't breathe. *Kezra needs to know.*

"It will be her choice to accept or not," Neetra said. "I care not who the dolt marries, but it's high time he does. My generosity can only extend so far. It's time for him to be out from under my roof."

The seneschal frowned and countered Neetra on the wisdom of pushing a marriage onto someone who wasn't ready. Gib's rational mind knew he should probably listen and try to glean more details from their exchange, but all he could think about was Kezra. He could do nothing to help Joel, but he could try to help her. He glanced around, wishing for the life of him that he could excuse himself from just this one meeting. Surely Koal would allow it if he could conjure up a good enough reason.

It wasn't meant to be. Gib could see the King and his bodyguard arriving. The meeting would be called to order shortly. There wasn't going to be a chance for Gib to ask to leave, let alone receive permission.

King Rishi's mood plummeted as he drew closer, his neutral features hardening. He cast a smoldering glare at Neetra but offered no words. Gib barely spared the King or Aodan a glance as he tried to remember if Kezra would be on duty that evening.

"You look awful, Aodan." Neetra's voice was cool, void of any care or sympathy. "You're not ill, are you?"

Gib raised his eyes from the floor and realized Neetra was right. Aodan looked like hell. With dark rings beneath his eyes and a severe, gaunt look about his face, he reminded Gib of someone who hadn't slept in days.

The bodyguard curled his nose. "Why don' ya sit with me today an' find out?"

Neetra's utter disgust would have been comical if not for the circumstances. "Repulsive! If you bring some disease into the council room and infect the rest of us, I feel you should be held accountable!"

Liro had remained quiet until now, but something in their conversation must have captured his attention. He flashed a smug smile at Koal. "You know, Father, I didn't see the Derr at Ambassador Cenric's funeral. Will he receive a tongue lashing as well or were we purposely sparing the envoy's wife from having to tolerate his presence?"

The King turned sharply, mouth open and nose curled, but Koal responded first. "Aodan answers to the King alone. Worry not about him, Liro."

Cruel contempt lingered in Liro's eyes. "I don't worry for him, believe you me. I'm simply at a loss as to how someone could look so tired while their duties remain so light."

King Rishi had had enough. "*You spoiled, petulant child!* What would you know of work? You certainly have no idea when to hold your tongue!"

If Liro was intimidated by the scolding, he didn't show it. Cool as ice, he offered a sly response. "Apologies, Highness. I only meant that perhaps your guardian should consider taking a holiday if he's overwhelmed. Maybe a trip to visit family is in store? The mountains, perhaps?"

Neetra guffawed, and the King reeled like he'd been struck across the cheek. His dark eyes speared Liro much like someone might view a troublesome insect. Aodan scowled, bristling where he stood.

Gib didn't understand the slight. Aodan was from the island of Derry. He wouldn't have any family on the mainland. And what was wrong with the mountains? Did the highborns look down on people from the mountain range? It seemed absurd to Gib, but then, Liro's viewpoints always had been skewed.

Koal leaned closer to Liro, his voice a menacing shiver on Gib's spine. "I don't know what you think you're trying to prove, but if you don't keep that unruly mouth of yours shut, then I'll do it for you."

Liro's eyes were unreadable as he bowed curtly to King Rishi. For the moment, it seemed he was done wiggling his rotten tongue. The other councilors were beginning to show up. Neetra made some small gesture to the King before dismissing himself, and both High Councilor and his understudy made their way into the council room.

Gib thought to go take his seat as well, before the hallway became congested. However, before he could take even one step, Koal's hushed voice caught his attention. "How *was* everything, Aodan? Are you all right?"

The bodyguard nodded. "Aye. It must've been a distant cousin ya saw. No one seemed to know anythin'."

Gib's brow furrowed. So Aodan *did* have family in Arden? What happened to his cousin? Gib opened his mouth to ask but thought twice when the King's stony glare landed on him. Perhaps this was one of those things he was meant to keep secret. He supposed it would be easy enough, seeing as he had no idea what was going on.

Under different circumstances, he might have pondered the conversation further, but in the moment, he was entirely preoccupied with letting Kezra know what he'd overheard regarding Nawaz and Heidi's marriage proposal. Gib went into the meeting with a heavy mind, knowing he wouldn't be able to focus on anything being said.

The cold wind whipped against Gib's face before he could pull his cloak tighter. Standing at the door outside the Galloway estate, he tried to convince himself that he'd come too far to turn back now. Neetra and Koal's conversation kept replaying through his mind. The High Councilor had spoken so casually, as if this marriage didn't stand to ruin Nawaz. Kezra hadn't been mentioned, but Gib knew the words would have cut her deep.

Gib's mind wandered to the task ahead. Kezra was sure to not take his news well, but he wanted her to find out from a friend, not from a gossiping courtier or a frenzied Nawaz. His stomach soured. Nothing about this was fair. Why should anyone be forced into marriage?

The frigid wind stung his cheeks, but dread held him back. How could he possibly hope to offer comfort regarding something he knew so little about? It wasn't as though he'd ever been in the position of having to marry and, frankly, the one romantic relationship he'd experienced was currently in shambles. He could do little more than be a willing shoulder to lean on. He owed Kezra that much. After all, she'd listened to his woes. Reluctantly, he took the cold knocker in his hand and banged the door three times.

After a moment, the door opened and Gib was met with a warm smile and kind eyes. Tamil Malin-Rai bore a striking resemblance to her elder sister, with rich brown skin, emerald eyes, and raven hair. Wrapped in a colorful sari, she ushered Gib into the house before the cold could drift inside.

Despite being the lady of the estate, Tamil answered the door herself. Gib had to admit it was a bit strange, but then again, none of the Malin-Rai children he knew seemed to fit the mold of "proper" lords and ladies. Tamil's marriage last summer had set a lot of tongues wagging. The fact that the daughter of Lord Anders Malin-Rai had snuck off to marry in secret had been nothing short of scandalous. Of course, her then-suitor, Tular Galloway, hadn't been Anders' first choice for marriage—hell, Tular wouldn't have been even his *last* choice. Regardless, the wedding had happened, and now Tamil and Tular lived here, away from Anders and away from the palace.

"Gib Nemesio, welcome," Tamil greeted.

He bowed his head. "Thank you. I'm here to see Kezra, if she's in."

"She is. I'll go fetch her."

Gib's face burned. "Oh, you don't have to—"

She smiled and his face only scorched hotter. Who else was she going to send? She didn't employ any servants.

Gib stammered. "Uh, I mean, thank you."

Her beam only grew wider as she backed away. Gib was left to stand awkwardly in the foyer as Tamil went to get her sister. He removed his dripping cloak and hung it over one arm, unsure where to put it. Cool rivulets of what was once snow drizzled down his temples and neck. With a groan, he ran his hands through his mop of curls, hoping to dislodge any remaining slush.

"Gib? What are you doing here?"

Gib spun around in time to see Zandi descend the grand staircase. Gib nearly slipped in the puddle of melted snow around his feet, and Zandi giggled in response. A strange mix of relief and dread churned in Gib's stomach. It was far too easy to be swept away by Zandi's glimmering eyes and giddy smile, but Gib couldn't share the merriment. Every time he thought he could be happy to see Kezra's brother, he inevitably thought of Joel and despair washed over him anew.

"Uh, I came to see Kezra. What—what are you doing here?"

The color in Zandi's cheeks deepened. "I often stay here to—be away from Anders." Worry knitted his brows. "Is all well? You don't appear to be in the mood for festivities."

Gib's mouth opened, but no words came out. He didn't want to share his news with anyone but Kezra. It was only fair she know first. "I'm afraid not."

Sudden terror flashed in Zandi's eyes. "It's not war, is it?"

"No, no! Nothing like that." Gib glanced down the hallway Tamil had disappeared into but saw no one. "I can't—I don't wish to tell anyone before I speak to Kezra. You do understand, right?"

Zandi nodded. "Of course." He stepped off the bottom step of the staircase and lifted a hand. "Here, at least let me take your cloak. I'll hang it for you." Before Gib could raise his voice in protest, Zandi snatched the garment away with a tsk. "This is wet! You'll catch your death out there."

"It wasn't wet when I left. Snow melts into water. You knew that, didn't you?"

"Laugh it up now. When you're lying in bed sick with influenza, you won't be able to!" Zandi hung the cloak in a nearby closet, and Gib watched as the mage performed the same spell he'd used at the festival two moonturns prior. The fabric lightened under Zandi's ministrations as the water evaporated. Gib watched in awe. He supposed magic would always amaze him.

He opened his mouth to utter thanks, but voices from the hall caught his attention. Kezra and Tamil talked to one another as they entered the room.

As soon as she spotted him, Kezra grinned deviously. "Miss me, Nemesio?"

Gib wanted to joke with her, but he just couldn't. No matter how he might try to cushion the news, it was still going to cut her to the bone. "I have to talk to you."

Kezra's smile fell away. Clearing his throat, Zandi took Tamil by the elbow and guided her away so Gib could speak privately with his friend. Gib wished he could thank the Malin-Rai lord, but Kezra was already staring at him with guarded eyes, silently demanding more information. He cursed himself for being so transparent. She clearly knew nothing good was afoot.

His heart hammered in his chest. "I, uh, I've news for you. Nothing good, I'm afraid."

Kezra stiffened where she stood. "Did you just come from council? Has this to do with that? War? Or revoking women's positions as soldiers?"

266

"I did just come from council, but this is about something I heard earlier. It has nothing to do with war or disposing your job."

A flicker of hope grazed her emerald eyes. "Then what steals your smile? Why do you look like you've seen death?"

He hated what he was about to do to her. "Nawaz." The color drained from Kezra's face, and she sunk down, sitting on the first step of the staircase. Gib realized how bad the word might have sounded and rushed to elaborate. "He's not hurt or anything. It's just—Neetra and Koal had a conversation earlier and I thought you should know about it."

Kezra took a ragged breath, and Gib couldn't be sure if she trembled in sorrow or rage. "Marriage to Heidi?"

Gib's head swam with rushing blood. "Koal has agreed. He said if Nawaz asks properly, then he may marry her."

"Then all he needs to do is refuse to ask!"

Memories of Nawaz's distress in Marc's office rose up like a wave. "He may not have a choice, Kezra. Neetra will take his title if he refuses to marry."

Kezra jumped to her feet so fast Gib nearly fell over in his haste to get out of her way. "That bastard only wants to be rid of him! Nawaz told me himself that all he's ever wanted was to be seen as a son, and Neetra won't give him even that! He doesn't want an inheritance. He doesn't want the Adelwijn name! What could Neetra hope to gain by forcing Nawaz to marry?"

Gib pressed his back to the door. "M–Marc thinks it may have something to do with Neetra wanting to set up a marriage for one of the twins. He said Neetra can't do that unless his eldest is married off first."

"Horseshit! The twins aren't even fourteen yet! What marriage is so important to Neetra?"

"I–I don't know."

Kezra crossed her arms over her chest. "It's bad form. Neetra is just looking for an excuse to get rid of him! Nawaz knows it, too, but he still clings to the hope that one day that monster will accept him! He needs to just cut his losses and forgo his title."

Gib bit the inside of his cheek. "That's a lot to ask, isn't it? I mean, could you drop *your* title so easily?"

Ice rippled across the room, and Kezra's voice was a poisonous hiss. "If it had to be done, yes. If I could revoke my name, just to be rid of Anders, I would do it in a heartbeat."

Gib knew he was asking for trouble, but he couldn't help his treacherous mouth. "You could perhaps take a new name—Nawaz's name—and be done with your father that way."

Kezra drew closer, and he pressed his back against the door so hard he could feel the brass handle prodding his flesh. "Take a new name?" Her growl made Gib shudder. "Wait for my hero to ride in and save me? *Never!*

I will not be some rich lord's useless housewife. While there is breath in my body, I will *never* depend on anyone to rescue me."

Gib didn't know what to say. He'd known she would be upset, even angry, but this blinding rage? This was new and it chilled him to the bone. "I—I'm sorry, Kezra. I only wanted you to hear the news from a friend."

Kezra fell back a step. "I'm sorry. I didn't mean to—it's not your fault."

"It's not Nawaz's fault either." Gib didn't know where his conviction came from, but as long as she was slipping back into the Kezra he knew, he'd try to reason with her. "Neetra is pushing him."

Kezra's voice darkened again. "Perhaps someone should push Neetra for once."

It wasn't a bad idea in theory, but her frigid demeanor made Gib uncomfortable. He opened his mouth to respond, but the sound of whickering horses signaled that riders were approaching. He and Kezra were at the window in an instant.

Two men dismounted outside. Gib recognized them even from a distance. Nawaz and Tular. Both frantic, they tied the pair of horses to the gate and ran toward the door.

"They know," Gib whispered. There was no way they didn't—not with this sense of urgency.

The door shot open, and Tular and Nawaz stumbled inside, bringing a rush of bitter air with them. Nawaz's panic was clear as his widened eyes scanned the room. He barely seemed to notice Gib's presence when his pained gaze flitted past.

His eyes landed on Kezra, and he reached a hand out to her. "Kez, I have to talk to you."

Kezra lingered by the staircase, her dark features torn between terror and fury, her rigid stance doing nothing to hide her heaving chest. "I've given you an answer once before."

"You know then?" Nawaz did glance at Gib now. "Koal has finally relented. It's only a matter of time before Heidi finds out—"

"That spoiled brat's temper tantrum is none of my concern!"

Nawaz advanced on her. "This isn't about Heidi, and you know it! Neetra won't settle until he's rid of me. Kezra, I need your help—"

She dove up the stairs before he could finish the sentence. Without asking permission, Nawaz pursued her. A moment later, Gib heard the sound of a door slamming and their muffled voices as they argued.

Gib swallowed the jagged lump that had formed in his throat. *I should leave. I'll be of no more help here.* He'd done all he could. He'd tried to break the news to Kezra before she could hear it from someone who wouldn't care about her feelings. Now, however, he wondered if he should have come at all. Hand on the back of his burning neck, he went to the closet where Zandi had hung his cloak.

"Tular?" Tamil's timid voice barely carried across the room. "What's wrong?"

Her husband sighed as he pulled off his hat. "Neetra's demanding Nawaz get married or be disowned."

Tamil gasped. "Oh no."

Gib slung the cloak around his shoulders and turned away from the closet just in time to see Zandi slink into the room.

"Are you leaving?" the mage asked.

Gib nodded. "Yuh." *Really? Yuh?* He frowned and cleared his throat. "I don't see any reason to stay. There isn't going to be anything else I can do for either of them."

"You're a good friend, Gib," Zandi replied. "She's maybe never said it, and probably never will say it, but you're dear to her. There are so few people who accept her for herself, but you've never questioned her or made her feel inadequate. She loves that about you."

Gib laughed before he could stop himself. It seemed a joke to him that anyone could call Kezra's quality into question. "Inadequate? Kezra is the fiercest warrior I know!"

Zandi's smile, even while sad, was dazzling. "You don't even know why you're so wonderful, do you?"

Gib backed away, his stomach churning. What was this fluttering in his belly? Why was Zandi able to do this to him even though he longed for Joel in the worst way? Was it wrong? Should he feel terrible about his conflicted feelings? Thoughts of Joel rejecting him earlier and the face of the Imperial boy evoked sudden, rash anger in Gib's mind. He shook his head, trying to clear his jumbled thoughts.

Zandi must have taken the gesture for dismissal. His eyes widened. "Oh no, I didn't mean—I'm sorry if I was too forward. I only meant that Kezra is lucky to have a friend like you."

"It's all right. I don't mean to be aloof. My mind is over-full right now, with so much going on."

Zandi nodded and kept his distance, and for some reason, that only bothered Gib all the more. He imagined Zandi must have nice, soft hands, a firm embrace— *Stop. Stop this! You're confused.*

"I, uh, I should go now."

Zandi inclined his head. His cheeks were red, Gib was sure of it, but the mage maintained his composure well. "Safe travels."

Gib reached for the door handle but hesitated when the slam of the upstairs door echoed through the home. Kezra's voice carried down the staircase. Gib couldn't recall a time he'd heard her sound so distraught. "I will not be a chained animal! I didn't complete my training and take a job as a sentinel just to marry and be a housewife!" She thundered down the stairs, Nawaz on her heels.

"He'll disown me!" Nawaz protested. "I won't cage you! Please, just marry me!"

Red-faced, Kezra stormed away from him. "I said no. If you don't stand up to him then there's nothing I can do for you."

Before she could slip away, Nawaz caught her arm. "Kezra, *please!*"

Gib knew what was going to happen an instant before it did. He winced, watching Kezra as she spun around, hand raised, and slammed a clenched fist against Nawaz's nose. Nawaz's head rocked back from the force of the impact, and the sickening crack of knuckle on flesh made Gib shudder.

Tamil cried out in shock, and Kezra put a hand over her own mouth, as though she was horrified by her actions. Then, as the color drained from her face, she whirled and fled the room. Both Zandi and Tamil swept after her.

Nawaz didn't move. He stood rooted in place, cradling his nose as blood began to trickle through his fingers. Tular grunted something about getting a rag and disappeared into the other room, leaving Gib alone with the defeated lord.

"She as much as said she loved me, you know."

Gib's brow furrowed. He had no doubt of Kezra's affection for Nawaz. In fact, he was sure anyone who really knew anything about them had no doubt either.

"But she won't marry me," Nawaz continued. His voice was lifeless. "What good is love without conviction?"

"She may just need time," Gib offered quietly. "She's determined to make her own way. Marriage wasn't ever part of her plan, I don't think."

Nawaz's voice cracked. "I don't have time. She's made her choice. She's seen to it that I can't go forward with her."

Gib's heart pounded as he watched Nawaz heave his shoulders and glare at the floor with blurry eyes. When Tular returned with a damp cloth, Gib silently let himself out. He could say nothing more and could offer no further comfort.

Nawaz's words burned him like a brand. What good *was* love without conviction? Even if Joel still loved him, there was no sign they would ever be more than they were right now. It was a difficult time, but Joel had barely spared a word for Gib and had outright turned down all his affections and offerings of support. Perhaps Joel's mind was already set, and if it was—like Nawaz—Gib could do nothing to change it.

His heart ached as he wove through the streets. Some of his grief was for Kezra and Nawaz, surely, but another, greater part was reserved for himself. He and Joel were done. Gib just needed to accept it. He couldn't go forward with Joel.

Joel leaned against a pillar, the cold marble pressing against the back of his formal mage robes. The sounds of the celebration rose around him, parading through the open space and bouncing off the vaulted ceiling high above. Light from the golden chandeliers shone down, illuminating the ballroom and chasing every last shadow from the floor. But not the shadows enclosing his heart.

Joel's eyes moved across the room, taking in the sights of the wedding reception. Two long banquet tables had been constructed for the occasion on either side of the ballroom, each of them able to sit fifty or more people. They both brimmed with food and drink—from roasted quail, blackened pork, winterberry pie, and various breads, cheeses, and wine, the variety was enough to impress even the most privileged highborns. Joel curled his nose as the savory smells reached him. He hadn't the appetite to indulge— not today or any day since his return to Arden three sennights prior.

His gaze skimmed the dais at the front of the room where the wedding party sat at a smaller table covered in lace cloth. Nawaz Arrio looked handsome in his brocaded doublet and ruffled sleeves, but his mood was as dark as the brass buttons trailing from his neck to belt were shiny. He could have been attending a funeral service if his frown was any indication.

Nawaz raised a goblet with trembling hands and took a hurried drink. Joel sighed as he watched. *He looks as miserable as I feel.*

Sitting beside Nawaz, Heidi's beaming smile and elated laughter were a sharp contrast to her husband's forlorn demeanor. In her chiffon gown, sparkling with pearls and fine glass beads, she was a lovely sight to behold. A silver circlet sat atop her head, shining with sapphires that matched her blue eyes too perfectly to be coincidence, and when she raised a dainty hand to touch Nawaz's shoulder, flowing lace sleeves cascaded down her sides like the wings of a swan.

Heidi squeezed her husband's hand before turning to converse with her cousins, Neetra's twin children, Inan and Inez Adelwijn, who sat to her immediate right. If Nawaz noticed her affections, he chose not to respond, opting instead to stare into his half-empty goblet as though he was transfixed by the wine inside. Joel frowned. Heidi seemed clueless of Nawaz's agony.

The wedding ceremony earlier had gone about as well as could be asked. Nearly two hundred guests packed themselves inside the Temple of the Sun to watch Nawaz and Heidi say their vows to one another. Despite Heidi's apparent glee, the ritual had been somber and hasty. A priest blessed the pair and braided, golden rings were exchanged, and then the entire procession trudged through the snow to the palace, where the newlyweds were now being honored in the same ballroom where Gib and Joel had stopped the assassin almost three years prior.

Joel's stomach clenched when his gaze fell upon his former

companion. Gib sat near the head of one of the lengthy banquet tables, with Tayver and Calisto flanking either side. The three brothers conversed among themselves as they ate. As the mage watched, Tayver quirked his brows and grinned devilishly at the other two. He must have said something funny because even Gib's face lit up. Joel wrapped his arms around his frail shoulders and looked away. He couldn't bear to watch any longer. Gib's handsome smile and boundless eyes would surely undo him.

They'd been avoiding each other since the afternoon when Gib had come to the Adelwijn estate. Joel had been mourning the death of his mentor and pushed Gib away when he'd offered companionship. *I pushed him away a second time. Even if I do miss him now, it's too late—* Joel shut his eyes, willing the tears to stay where they were. *I was careless with his emotions. I shut him out. I rejected him. He has every right to never speak to me again.* His bottom lip trembled as he dared take one final glance at Gib. *It's too late to reconcile now, isn't it?*

The clang of silverware tapping a wine glass ripped Joel from his dark thoughts. He glanced up in time to see Hasain stand, drawing attention to himself. The ballroom grew quiet as the young lord raised his chalice into the air and turned to face the dais.

"Lords and ladies, friends and family, I would like to take a moment to make a toast." Hasain flashed a haughty smile to the newlyweds, and Joel cringed at the pain he saw in Nawaz's eyes. "To my good friend Nawaz Arrio and his beautiful bride, Heidi, may your marriage be long and fruitful, and may The Two bless you and keep you happy."

If Hasain expected Nawaz to respond, he was surely left disappointed. Clenching his jaw, Nawaz only nodded once, solemnly and without any trace of comradery. Heidi raised her own goblet, seemingly oblivious, and thanked Hasain for his kind words.

Raw anger sprung to life in Joel's chest as he recalled the conversation between Koal and Hasain he'd overheard while still in Teivel. Hasain had shamelessly pushed for the marriage with no concern for Nawaz's feelings. Even now, the Radek lord's behavior spoke volumes about his true intent. In the back of Joel's mind, he wondered where Kezra Malin-Rai was today. Did she share Nawaz's heartbreak?

Music drifted to where Joel stood, and all around him, people left their seats to dance. On the dais, he watched his own mother and father rise from the table. Koal took his wife's hand and together they walked onto the open floor. Joel almost smiled when he heard Mrifa's laughter. It was a small comfort to know she was happy again. Koal's absence had been difficult on her.

Joel raised a brow when he noticed the King himself was making his way to the dais. People on the ballroom floor moved aside for him, watching with curious glances of their own. The royal family was present—after all, Queen Dahlia was the aunt of the bride—but so far, they'd remained inconspicuous, choosing to sit near the far end of the banquet table as to not draw the attention of the newlyweds' guests.

As King Rishi stepped onto the raised platform, Heidi broke down into giddy titters. Joel watched as the King gave a small bow to her and extended one hand. They exchanged words, though Joel couldn't hear what was said over the din. A moment later, Heidi left her seat and joined the King. Together, they swept onto the floor, Heidi gushing at the attention everyone paid her. Joel shook his head. He supposed he'd never hear the end of this. *Heidi will never forget that the King of Arden asked her for a dance. And she won't let anyone else forget either.*

His gaze returned to the dais, where Nawaz still slouched in his seat and stared with vapid eyes into the crowd. With a deep sigh, Joel made his way to the table. He knew Nawaz wasn't in the mood for merriment, but perhaps Joel could offer some small amount of comfort if only because, to an extent, he understood the pain Nawaz was going through.

Joel cleared his throat as he neared. "Hey."

Nawaz glanced up, blinking in confusion, as if he hadn't noticed Joel's approach until he'd spoken. For a moment, Joel feared the other man might not reply at all, but finally, Nawaz sighed and croaked out a simple, "Hey yourself."

Well, at least I got him to talk. That's a start. Joel set a hand on the table, absently stroking the decorative lace cloth covering the fine cherry. "How are you?" He winced after he said it.

Nawaz's lifeless stare spoke more than words ever could.

With a sigh, Joel dropped all pretenses of false gaiety. "I know none of this is how you planned. I'm sorry."

Nawaz grunted, setting down his chalice with an uneven clunk. "Life doesn't always go as planned."

"I can attest to that."

Joel hadn't meant for the words to roll off his tongue with such bitterness. He knew he was supposed to be offering support to his friend, but in that moment, all he could think about was his failed romance with Gib. *This wasn't part of our plan. We were supposed to be companions forever. How did we ever become so broken?*

"Why haven't you spoken to him?" asked Nawaz.

The sudden question startled Joel. "W–who?"

Nawaz's crystal eyes speared him. "You know who."

Joel had to place a hand upon the table to keep from turning around and looking for Gib. "It wasn't meant to be. I pushed him away. I'm sure he wants nothing to do with me now."

"Horseshit," Nawaz spat. "Both of you are being pig-headed. One of you needs to break the silence. I'm serious, Joel."

Heidi's laughter reached the dais then, and both men turned to watch as King Rishi placed a light kiss on the back of the young bride's hand.

Heidi gushed, her powdered cheeks flushing with color.

Nawaz slumped lower in his chair, his mood utterly somber again. "Don't stop fighting for what you want. Don't let him walk away or you'll regret it forever. You'll wind up a fool like me." He watched Heidi bitterly out of the corner of his eye.

"You know this isn't her fault, right?" Joel asked in a gentle tone, grateful to be handed the opening to direct the conversation toward something other than his own failed relationship.

Nawaz rubbed at his temples but didn't immediately respond.

"I know you're not excited about this marriage. I don't even fault you for being upset," Joel continued. "But Heidi *is* my sister. Please, if you can't love her, at least—at least be kind. She's not to blame."

Inez, who'd remained quiet until that moment, leaned around Heidi's empty seat to place a hand on Nawaz's forearm. "You're right," she said, voice vicious. "*Neetra* is to blame." Beside Inez, her twin brother, Inan, nodded mutely in agreement.

All four of them turned to glare at the High Councilor, who lounged at the very far end of the long table, sipping from a chalice and looking rather proud of himself. Inez was right. This *was* all Neetra's fault. He'd pushed for his stepson to marry Heidi, just like he'd pushed the King to send envoys to the Northern Empire. If not for Neetra, Nawaz would still be happy. Cenric would still be alive. There wouldn't have been any reason to leave Gib. Lives wouldn't have been shattered beyond repair. Raw anger seeped into Joel's veins as he watched his uncle take another swig of wine. He wished someone would smack the smirk right off Neetra's face.

"I suppose congratulations are in order."

Joel turned in time to see Liro saunter onto the platform, a drink in hand. Nawaz drew back in disgust.

Liro's haughty leer was even more despicable than Neetra's. He raised his goblet in a mocking gesture and glared down the length of his nose at Nawaz. "Just look at the lofty position you've fallen into. Living free of charge beneath my father's roof, marrying a girl far above your own deplorable social class—great feats, considering you faced disownment only two sennights ago." Liro laughed. It was an ugly, sinister sound.

Any other time, Joel would have expected Nawaz to defend himself, but now the young lord only sighed in defeat, a true testament to just how broken his spirit had become. Joel could barely stand to look at his deflated eyes. *I have to stand up for Nawaz. He would do the same for me.*

Joel turned on his heel to face his older brother. "This is a time for celebration. If you aren't here to wish Nawaz and Heidi well, I suggest you leave now."

Liro's sneer only grew wider. "But I *am* here to give well wishes, just like everyone else, although—" He paused, casting a look around the room. "I couldn't help but notice Nawaz's good friend, Kezra Malin-Rai, is absent. Funny, that. I figured such a loyal friend as she would be first in line to bless your marriage."

Inan audibly gasped, and Inez was quick to squeeze Nawaz's arm, offering a small measure of comfort. She kept her smoldering eyes fixed on Liro, but her words were meant for Nawaz. "Don't listen to him. He's just trying to cause trouble. He's only jealous because his own prospects are so few. Surely there's no woman in all of Arden who can tolerate his presence."

Liro turned a fierce scowl on her. "Watch your clever mouth, you little bitch!" He stepped closer, leaning precariously over the table. "My uncle would do well to marry *you* off next. Perhaps a husband would help rein in that despicable tongue of yours."

Inez clenched her hands into fists and started to stand, but Inan set a hand on her shoulder and shook his head. "Inez, don't."

Nawaz gripped his chalice so tightly Joel wouldn't have been shocked to see it break in two. The young lord's eyes glinted dangerously as he measured Liro. "It's fortunate for you, Liro, that my bride wouldn't enjoy the sight of her eldest brother's blood spilled across the ballroom floor."

Liro's own eyes went wide before narrowing into angry slits. "*What* did you say?"

Nawaz smiled, but it held not a trace of warmth. All benevolence he possessed had long since withered away. "If I had it my way, I'd cut your tongue from your mouth before you could even raise your voice in protest."

The uncomfortable silence that followed was almost harder to endure than the young lord's candid threat. Joel held his breath, staring back and forth between his brother and Nawaz, preparing to intervene if one or the other suddenly leapt across the table. They glowered at each other, Liro seething, and Nawaz so still it sent an eerie chill rushing up Joel's spine.

Heidi's lilted voice rose above the lull. She was making her way back to the table, though she'd stopped to talk with Neetra's servant and the man who had all but raised Nawaz and the twins, Bailey.

Nawaz never took his eyes away from Liro, though he surely must have known his wife was approaching. "Leave," he whispered, the word falling from his mouth like the hiss of a serpent. "Now."

Heidi and Bailey were right behind them, still conversing, but within earshot. Joel's stance went rigid, and he even contemplated turning around and leading Heidi away from the confrontation. She didn't need to witness a brawl at her own wedding celebration.

Liro finally seemed to notice them too. Locking his jaw, he bowed mockingly and turned a cold gaze onto Heidi. "I'll take my leave now." He stormed away without saying anything more.

Heidi looked around the somber table. "Is everything—all right?"

Nawaz sighed and his shoulders sagged once again. "Everything's fine. Come sit down."

Heidi hesitated at first, but after a gentle prod from Bailey, she made her way back to her chair.

More guests were beginning to approach the dais now, so Joel said his farewells. As he turned to leave, however, Nawaz leaned across the table and caught his arm. "Remember what I said. Talk to him."

Joel gave a breathless nod and turned his back to the dais. *Nawaz is right. I can't live inside these walls of stone forever.* He scanned the room, seeking out Gib.

He caught a glimpse of his companion, standing on the far side of the ballroom. Gib looked lovely in his fawn-colored jerkin and white tunic. His curls were almost long enough to graze the tops of his shoulders now. Strands of gold mingled with the darker shades of brown beneath the light of the chandeliers, matching his chestnut eyes as though The Two Themselves had planned it that way.

Joel's stomach twisted. *Gods, I miss him.*

He took a step but stopped short as Marc and Lady Beatrice made their way through the crowd and promptly engaged Gib in conversation. Joel planted his feet on the red velvet carpet. He didn't want to intrude. *I'll just wait until they're done speaking.*

"Hello, Lord Joel Adelwijn."

The tenor voice, despite being soft, caught Joel off guard. His gaze fell away from Gib.

Kirk Bhadrayu stood before him, dressed in a flowing white robe and a blue sash that wrapped around the slender trunk of his body. His eyes retained warmth, though the smile that flitted across his lips was hesitant. Joel couldn't fault Kirk for that. The last time they'd exchanged words, Kirk's best attempt at a friendly interaction had been met with cold resignation.

Joel inclined his head in greeting. "Lord Joel Adelwijn? I wasn't aware we were on such formal standings."

A more genuine smile spread across Kirk's face. "Apologies. I didn't want to be rude."

"You look well." Joel nodded toward the young man's attire. "I see you've been fitted for your student mage robes. The Ardenian colors suit you."

Kirk looked briefly down at his garment. "Do you really think so? Kenisha told me I look like a barbarian."

A chuckle burst free from Joel's throat before he could think to stop it. "A barbarian?"

"Indeed." Kirk grinned sheepishly. "Though she looks like a love-struck fool. Look at her over there! I can hardly stand to watch!" He motioned across the ballroom.

Joel followed his gaze and was surprised to see Kirk's sister howling with laughter as she danced with a young man. "Huh. I do believe that's Weapons Master Roland's son."

"She's been hanging off his arm all afternoon." Kirk scoffed, crossing his arms over his chest. "I've never in my entire life seen her so smitten."

A sly grin crept upon Joel's mouth. He leaned a little closer to Kirk and conspired jokingly, "You best stay watchful or you might be attending a *second* wedding ceremony this year."

"Ha ha. You're hilarious."

"On rare occasions, perhaps."

Kirk glanced away from the dancing long enough to make timid eye contact with Joel. The trainee's fair cheeks flushed pink. "It's nice to see your smile again."

Joel could feel his own face growing warm. He played with one of his sleeves to spare himself from having to meet Kirk's gaze. "To be honest, I'd nearly forgotten how to." He let out a deep sigh. "Thank you."

"No, thank you. Your country is delightful. I'm so grateful to be in Arden."

"*Our* country," Joel reminded him. "You're a part of it now, too."

The song ended and many of the dancers on the floor took a reprieve. Kenisha trotted back to the banquet table with her suitor, her lips moving rapidly as she engaged him in cheery conversation. Joel had to admit, he'd never seen her in such high spirits either.

"I suppose I should go meet her 'friend,'" Kirk muttered under his breath.

Again, Joel was surprised by how easy the laughter fell from his lips. "For what it's worth, Roland Korbin's son is okay. I mean, I don't really know him, but I don't think he'd take advantage of her or anything."

"I believe you, but she's my sister, and—"

"You feel the need to protect her." Joel smiled and nodded. "I know. I'm the same way with Heidi and Carmen."

Kirk bowed. "Farewell. Please tell your sister that I wish her and Nawaz Arrio all the best."

"I will. Goodbye."

Joel watched Kirk slip into the crowd, a warm, pleasant sensation spreading from Joel's belly to his chest. *I'd almost forgotten what it's like to smile, to laugh—to have a friend I can talk to. I forgot how much I missed it all.*

Marc's boisterous laughter cut through the air, catching Joel's ear. The dean and Lady Beatrice now stood at the foot of the dais, conversing with Koal, who'd also taken a break from dancing.

Gib.

Joel looked to the place where he'd last spotted the understudy. Gib was no longer there. Frowning, Joel scanned the entire room. Still there was no sign of his former companion. He even walked the entire length of each banquet table. Nothing. Where had Gib gone? He hadn't left, had he?

Weaving through the ballroom toward the grand entranceway, Joel continued his search.

"*Hello?* Gib?"

Gib blinked. He'd been so transfixed watching Joel as the mage went to the front of the ballroom and began to speak to Nawaz that he'd missed almost everything Tayver had just said. Forcing himself to tear his eyes away from the dais, Gib cranked his neck around and met his brother's critical glare. "Sorry, what was that?"

With an exasperated huff, Tayver rolled his eyes. "I was asking what you thought about the dress."

"Dress?"

The younger brother groaned. "*Heidi's* dress! You know, the one I helped design?"

Gib winced. "Oh, right. It's great, Tay." When that earned him only a baleful scowl, he sighed and issued an apology. "I'm sorry. My head's been full all day. Really, you did a great job on the gown. I should have told you so earlier."

Tayver leaned back in his chair, cocking one eyebrow. His gaze flickered past Gib, and even without looking, Gib knew his brother was watching Joel as the mage spoke to those sitting on the dais. "You should go talk to him."

Gib stiffened. He really didn't want to have this conversation right now. "I already tried. He shut me out."

"Then try again. I mean, it's obvious you aren't ready to give up on him."

"It doesn't matter what I want. I can only push so much. He clearly wants nothing more to do with me."

Tayver's voice grew softer. "You might not get another chance. Stop being stubborn and go say whatever is on your mind, because it's clear that you have something you want to tell him."

Gib bit his lip and stole another forlorn glance at Joel. Heidi was making her way back to her seat, and Nawaz had reached across the table to clasp Joel's arm as the two exchanged goodbyes. Gib sighed. "*Fine.* I'll be back."

Tayver gave him a hearty thump on the back. "That's the spirit. Let me know how it goes."

Gib swatted at his brother, but Tayver was crafty enough to escape the blow. Mustering up what little courage he could find, Gib slipped from his chair and started to weave through the crowd. He didn't make a straight line for the dais. Instead, he meandered slowly, giving plenty of time to start doubting himself. Would Joel be receptive to talking? Would he feel the same way? Or would he become angry or even hostile?

Gib stopped in his tracks, wringing his hands together as he stared at the tiled floor. *Maybe this is a bad idea. I promised to give him space. I promised myself I'd try to move on. I can't keep doing this*— Gib locked his jaw. He and Joel had been companions for nearly three years. He couldn't walk away just yet. *One more attempt. One more try. If he doesn't let me in now, this is it. This has to stop.* With renewed determination, he lifted his chin.

"Gibben!" Marc's jovial voice cut through the crowd.

The dean and his wife, Beatrice, came to a stop before him. Marc wore a black overcoat while the lady donned a flowy, velvet dress. Dressed in matching colors, they looked the perfect couple.

Marc reached out to pat Gib's arm. "Enjoying yourself?"

"Yes," Gib replied. "I can hardly believe all this was thrown together in less than two sennights."

"Aye. The power of the pocketbook." Marc grinned, staring past Gib in the direction of the dais. "My nephew cleans up well, doesn't he?"

Gib chuckled. "Surprisingly, yes." He gave a little bow to Lady Beatrice, his former Ardenian Law professor. "How are you feeling? When is the baby due to arrive?"

Beatrice set one hand on her *very* round belly. Her smile was tight. "Any time now. I'd feel much better if there weren't reports of an influenza outbreak in the Northern provinces. Hopefully it stays far away from Silver City."

Marc rubbed his wife's shoulders. "Stop worrying so much! Your constant fretting isn't good for the baby, you know."

"I'm fretting *because* we have a little one on the way. I'd like to not have to worry about the baby falling ill."

"On the bright side," Gib offered, clearing his throat. "If the influenza does reach Silver, you can take comfort in knowing that you're married to one of the most capable Healers in the entire city."

Beatrice smiled up at her husband. "I suppose he's capable enough— when he's not busy being a clown."

An infectious beam spread across Marc's face. He gave Gib a wink. "She likes my roguish charm. That's why she married me. Don't let her convince you otherwise."

Beatrice slapped his chest lightly. "I married you because you wouldn't stop asking. Eventually I had to do something to get you to shut up." She narrowed her eyes at her husband. "You really *are* a clown though."

Still chortling, Marc motioned toward the dais. "Speaking of clowns, we should go see Nawaz before your feet start to swell again."

"Yes, all right." Beatrice snickered. "I wouldn't want to ask you to carry me home or anything."

Marc and Beatrice said goodbye and walked away. Gib watched them depart, shaking his head. Like Koal and Lady Mrifa, the dean and his wife seemed to be in one of those rare, fairytale relationships that always seemed to be perfect. Gib knew it wasn't true—no relationship was without its share of hardships, but he couldn't help be a little envious.

I used to think I'd fallen into such a romance. Joel and I were perfect for so long. I can hardly comprehend how broken we've become.

Sighing, Gib turned to look upon his former love—and froze.

Joel hadn't moved from his position near the dais, but he was no longer alone. The Imperial boy who'd come through the portal with the envoys, Kirk, stood beside him. Even as Gib watched, Joel leaned closer to the boy and grinned. Gib's skin crawled at the sight of Kirk's blush. Were they—were they flirting? His hands clenched into fists at his side.

Gentle laughter drifted to where he stood. Joel was laughing with the Imperial now. *Laughing!* He hadn't even spared a genuine smile for Gib, yet here he was, being open with this boy he barely knew.

The anger rushed upon him so fast Gib wasn't sure where it even came from. It manifested out of nowhere and gripped his body with such precision that he was left teetering where he stood. Gib turned on one heel and fled. He couldn't process all the feelings swirling in his head, and he sure as hell couldn't face Joel or anyone else right now. Perhaps if he ran fast enough, he could escape the raw emotions attempting to latch onto his heart. He staggered up the grand staircase and through the door. No one seemed to notice his departure—least of all Joel, who was still entirely enamored by the Imperial boy.

Gib wandered without a destination through the corridors surrounding the ballroom. As he trudged forward, his mind went from a burning inferno of rage to a numb, desolate void. The farther he walked, the more overwhelmed he became by deep, incessant sorrow. The grief swelled in his chest, rising to his lungs, throat, and eyes, threatening to spill over. When the stairwell leading to the gallery far above came into view, he could do nothing more than slump against the bottom rung and stare into the gloom.

Gib clutched his head with both hands, at a loss. He'd been only a dozen paces away from Joel. He could have shouted to him from across the floor. He almost could have reached out and touched him. He'd known what he wanted to say and had been prepared to fight for what he wanted—and then—

Joel looked so happy, smiling and laughing with the Imperial boy. He clearly doesn't need me to rescue him. It was foolish to assume he ever did. He's moving on without me, and I'm an idiot to keep holding onto the idea that we still have a future together. Gib's eyes slammed shut as he tried to contain the tears brimming beneath his lids.

He wasn't sure how long he sat there. Whether it was only a few seconds or an entire mark, he couldn't know. Time seemed to have come to a grinding halt. All he knew was that he couldn't return to the ballroom. He couldn't face the sight of Joel laughing and enjoying himself with his new friend. Not when Gib himself felt so utterly hopeless.

"Gib?" a tentative voice called from beyond the stairwell.

Gib wiped his face with the back of his sleeve. "Who is it?" If he hadn't been so caught up in his grief, he would have recognized the soft, lilting voice.

It was Zandi who stepped around the corner. Concern etched the young mage's long face, contorting his features but unable to fully mask his beauty.

Gib cleared his throat and tried to blink away the tears before the other man could see them. "What are you doing here?"

Zandi looked over his shoulder briefly. "I was just sitting at the banquet table, bored out of my mind, and then I saw you leave rather hastily and wanted to make sure everything was all right."

"You were in the ballroom? I didn't see you. I didn't even know you'd been invited to the wedding."

A nervous chuckle escaped Zandi's lips as he reached up to toy with a strand of his raven-colored hair. "Heidi and I shared two whole classes together in Academy. I guess that was enough to warrant an invitation to her wedding."

Gib found himself smiling despite his lousy mood. "I think she invited people she'd never even met before."

"Would you believe she even extended an invitation to Kezra?"

Gib winced. "Not the smartest idea, I'd reckon."

Kezra, of course, hadn't made an appearance—not that Gib could fault her for it. He was certain it would have been too painful to look upon Nawaz and know the young lord was no longer hers. Gib let out a shaky sigh. Is that how it would be for Joel and him, too? Would he be forced to watch Joel from afar and know there was no way to share in his joy or tears?

Zandi crept closer. "Do you mind if I join you? You look like you could use some company."

"Do I?" Gib croaked, forcing a weak smile.

Zandi's face pinched as he nodded and took a seat next to Gib. "Why are you out here alone? Did something happen? Did someone—upset you?"

Gib dared to meet the other man's eyes. He could tell Zandi was searching for answers. Whether or not he suspected the truth, Gib didn't know. He shifted his gaze downward, choosing to stare vacantly at his upturned palms sitting in his lap. Habit told him to dismiss the question, but he just couldn't bring himself to be on the defensive. Not this time.

"Nothing's gone the way I thought it would," Gib blurted. He focused on his hands, studying each line and blemish, certain that if he stared long enough, he would be able to dedicate all of it to memory. "When Joel got back from the Northern Empire, I was stupid enough to believe we could just pick right up where we left off and everything would be fine. It was the dream of a fool." He choked on a mirthless laugh. "I'm a fool."

Beside him, Zandi tensed, and at first, Gib thought the mage wouldn't reply at all. But after a bout of prolonged silence, soft words floated through the gloom. "You're no fool. If Joel Adelwijn dismissed someone as loyal and caring as you, then it's his loss. *He's* the fool."

Gib shook his head, still glaring at his own hands. He didn't want this to happen. He didn't want to feel such rash anger toward his former companion. Joel didn't deserve it. He'd never been anything but supportive. Gib's fingers began to tremble as he stared at them. "I don't know what the future holds anymore. I used to have a path. But now—now I'm hopelessly lost. I'm just blundering around, waiting for someone to set me on course again."

He gasped when Zandi reached out and took hold of his hands. The mage's touch was warm and his melodic voice drifted through the shadows, soothing Gib's broken soul. "No one can choose a path for you, Gib. That decision is yours alone to make." Gib could feel Zandi's heavy gaze but didn't dare look up. "It's up to you to decide what you want."

Gib blinked. *What I want—what do I want?* His mind was so muddled by a million different feelings he didn't even know anymore. All he knew was he was tired—tired of fighting for nothing, tired of hoping in vain, and tired of running from every potential chance at finding happiness again.

He let out a shuddering sigh when Zandi squeezed his hands. He could feel the other man's hot, jagged breaths on the side of his face and noticed belatedly that Zandi had scooted closer. Still, Gib couldn't raise his eyes to meet those of the mage.

"You have to choose your path, but that doesn't mean you have to walk it alone." Zandi's voice was like a wisp of air rustling through newly blossomed leaves. "You have so many people who care about you, who would risk life and limb if it meant seeing you happy again. Seneschal Koal, Dean Marc, Prince Didier, Tarquin, Nage, Kezra, me—" Gib did glance up then, and it was Zandi who lowered his face in an attempt to hide his painted cheeks.

"You—care that much about me?"

"Isn't it obvious?" Zandi's thick lashes fluttered as he raised his head to make slow, deliberate eye contact with Gib. "I never wanted to come between you and Joel. But I've always admired you, Gib. And when Joel left, I thought maybe—maybe there was a small chance for me. Talk about being a fool."

Gib's head spun. He didn't know what to say or do. Never in his life had he been so conflicted. "I—" He took a deep breath and tried again. "I don't dislike you, Zandi. The opposite might even be true. It's just—what Joel and I had—it's going to take me time to move on. It's still an open wound. I don't want to lead you on with false hope. You deserve better than a companion still grieving his last love."

"I understand. Some wounds may never truly heal. We just have to—try to forget."

Even in the dim light of the corridor, Gib could see the mage's terrible, broken smile, and for the first time, Gib found himself wondering what kind of pain Zandi had suffered for him to be so understanding in this moment. Had he experienced the same, gut-wrenching heartbreak Gib now faced? Were they more alike than Gib realized?

Joel is happy with his new life. I deserve to be happy, too. Zandi has been nothing but supportive through this entire ordeal with the Northern Empire. He's been there for me, even when I was miserable to him in return. He clearly cares about me. Is it so wrong of me to care for him in return?

Zandi began to pull his hand away, but Gib found himself latching onto it as though it was his last lifeline. "Wait," he said through trembling lips. "Perhaps—perhaps if we take things slow—" He fumbled over his own disordered words, and Zandi's imploring gaze was doing no favors. "I can't promise anything. I'm just me—Gibben Nemesio, a humble understudy—but if you can overlook my many faults, if you'll have me—"

"Of course I will have you." Zandi's eyes went wide, as if the mere suggestion was unspeakable. "However much time you need, you'll have it. We can take things as slow as you want, Gib. I just—I just want you in my life."

Gib opened his mouth, trying to respond, but the cocktail of emotions rolling in his stomach was too much. He couldn't speak.

Zandi reached up with one hand, his smile impossibly beautiful, and stroked Gib's cheek like it was the most precious thing in the two worlds. "Hey," Zandi whispered. "Everything's going to be okay. I know it is."

He leaned closer yet and instead of running again, Gib turned and met Zandi's piercing, emerald eyes head on.

Gib smiled, still sad, but determined to push past it. "I know it will be." Gib set all the hurt free as he pressed his mouth to Zandi's, losing himself in a gentle kiss. It was time to move on. It was time to heal.

A tear slipped down Joel's cheek as he backed away before the two young men in the hall could see him. The hope he'd been foolish enough to believe in deflated in a single breath, crumbling like the stones of the archway. All that remained in its wake was pain—horrible, aching pain.

He'd followed Zandi after noticing the young man leaving the ballroom, and when Gib and Zandi began to speak, Joel had lingered in the shadows. He had seen the way they looked at each other and the way Gib's eyes lit up when Zandi sat down. Joel had seen the kiss—

He clutched his chest, unbearable agony seizing his heart. The truth was a burning pyre under his flesh, slowly boiling him from the inside out and leaving his soul a shriveled, blackened husk. He gasped on a strangled whimper and staggered back toward the ballroom. *Stop crying. You did this. You went to the Northern Empire and left him here alone. You pushed him away. You even told him to move on with his life—and now he has.*

Joel could barely see through the tears clouding his vision. He was too late. Gib's heart already belonged to another.

CHAPTER THIRTEEN

Joel set a hand against his mouth and yawned loudly. His eyes kept fluttering shut no matter how hard he focused his attention on the oak door in front of him. Bright, morning sunlight flooded the corridor, streaming trails of gold through the large bay windows of the academy. Holding back another yawn, Joel blinked several times in rapid succession, hoping the exercise would help rouse his drowsy mind.

It wasn't truly that early, but over the past three moonturns, he'd grown accustomed to lounging about in bed until well after morning meal. *I've made a horrid habit out of sleeping in past the ninth bell toll every day. Serves me right for staggering around like the walking dead when I'm asked to be up with the sun.*

He'd been waiting outside Marc's office for what felt like the entire morning, but in reality, Joel knew it only seemed that way because his eyelids were still heavy and he'd been in such a rush to leave the estate that he hadn't the time to scarf down breakfast. *I don't know why I thought that was a good idea. Tabitha all but begged me to sit and eat. Here there are countless waifs starving on the street, and my family servant can't even force feed me fresh eggs and bacon.* On cue, Joel's stomach gurgled. He groaned. Whatever Marc needed to talk to him about better be important.

He pulled the note from within a hidden pocket inside his robe and turned it over in his hands. Nawaz had delivered the message the previous night, saying Marc wanted to see Joel. Something about discussing his future. Perhaps it was possible Marc was going to offer a job of some sort.

Of course, Joel had a sneaking suspicion this meeting had been conceived not by the dean, but by Joel's father. Koal had informed Joel on more than one occasion that moping around the house was doing him no favors. If Joel hadn't been so busy trying to contemplate a way to avoid being put to work, he probably would have agreed. He *was* moping. He *knew* he was moping. But he just couldn't bring himself to look forward to anything of late. Even a prospective job offering from Marc did nothing to inspire joy.

What's wrong with me? We've been back from the Northern Empire for over three moonturns now. Joel sighed and leaned heavily against the doorframe. *Everyone else has gotten on with their lives. Maybe Father is right. Maybe I do just need a good kick in the arse. At least if I get a job, it might keep me from thinking about Cenric's death. Or Gib—*

Joel winced. There it was again. The dark storm cloud that followed him everywhere. *Daya, he's moved on! Why can't I do the same?*

The door opened behind him, and Joel was forced to stand straight or topple to the floor. He spun around in time to see Marc poke his head through the gap.

"Oh, good, you're here," the dean said, his voice disgustingly chipper for such an early mark.

Joel let out a testy sigh. "I've *been* here."

Marc waved a hand, beckoning Joel inside. "Sorry. I was catching up on paperwork. I still have three additional piles to sort through, but that'll have to wait until after I spend my morning treating influenza patients at the Healer's Pavilion and then drag my arse over to the palace for the council meeting. It's going to be a *long* day, especially if Beatrice needs help with the baby when and if I ever manage to escape work." Marc grinned. "It's nice to see you dressed proper and out before midday. I'm sure your father must be proud now that you've made an attempt to rejoin the civilized world."

So this meeting *was* Koal's idea. Joel crossed his arms over his chest and took a seat. "Father says I need to get out more. He even convinced Hasain and Diddy to invite me to go riding with them this afternoon. I'm going to assume he also played a part in all of this too, right? Why else would you send for me?"

Marc flopped into the chair behind his desk. Pressing his palms onto the desk, he leaned across the table and met Joel's rebellious stare without hesitation. "Why do *you* think you've been summoned here?"

Joel imagined he must look like a spoiled brat, sitting with his arms crossed and chin raised into the air. He let out a long sigh and hung his head. "You have some kind of job to offer me."

Marc remained silent for some time, the only sound in the room the rhythmic strumming of the dean's fingers on the desktop. Finally, he sat back in his chair and mimicked Joel by folding his own arms over his chest. "I know you've been grieving and I don't fault you for it, but Joel, it's been three moonturns. Life has to go on."

The air became so thick Joel couldn't even swallow. "Life doesn't go on for everyone. It didn't go on for Cenric."

"You're right. It didn't." Marc tilted his head, staring out the office window. "It's tragic, what happened to Ambassador Leal, but that doesn't mean your own life needs to come to a grinding halt. Is that what Cenric would have wanted? For you to wither away in solitude?" With a sigh, Marc shifted his gaze back to Joel. "Life is precious. If I've learned anything after all my years as a Healer, it's that. Don't waste this gift, Joel. Don't waste the opportunity to live."

Joel swallowed down the lump that had formed at the base of his throat. "The night of our escape—the night Cenric died—I told him I didn't want to be an ambassador anymore. I had made it into this huge dream. I was going to help change the world and bring peace to Arden—but in the Northern Empire, I realized it wasn't actually what I wanted. I wasn't any good at politics and I missed home terribly. My plan fell through, and now I don't know what I want to do."

"You have the potential to do anything you put your mind to. Cenric saw that potential in you. Hell, we *all* see it."

"Cenric said no matter what I went on to do, I would change the world." Joel blinked away tears. "But I can't see it. All I see is a failure. I've done nothing but ruin lives. If I'd chosen differently, Cenric might be alive. Gib wouldn't hate me. Father wouldn't have been injured—"

Marc raised both hands into the air. "Stop. Just stop. None of that is your fault, and you're certainly *not* a failure." Tense silence enveloped the room. Marc let out a huff and leaned forward in his chair, forcing Joel to meet his stare. "Besides, if you were as incompetent as you seem to think you are, I wouldn't have summoned you here, asking for your help."

Joel kept his mouth clamped shut, but his crystal eyes implored the dean for more.

Sighing, Marc pressed on. "I'm not sure if you've heard or not, but there's a real shortage of mage trainers at Academy right now."

"Father might have said something in passing."

"Right, so—" Marc twiddled his thumbs. "How would you feel about teaching?"

Joel sat back in the chair. "*Me?* You can't be serious. I've barely completed my own training."

"Well, it would only be the first year students for now," Marc insisted. "And you wouldn't be teaching alone. Kirk Bhadrayu would be—"

Joel's head shot up. "Kirk? What about him?"

A smile touched upon Marc's face. "He'd be teaching with you. The two of you would be leading the first years together."

"But Kirk's a trainee."

Marc issued an incredulous snort. "An *Imperial* trainee. Might as well be a senior mage by Arden's standards. I don't know what they're teaching their gifted children in the Northern Empire, but Kirk's knowledge and skill both exceed what we're capable of here in Arden. With a little more time, I feel he'll become an exceptionally powerful mage. And in the meantime, he's agreed to share all he knows with our students and trained mages alike."

"If he's so powerful, why are you asking me to teach with him? *He* might be fully capable, but I've only *just* earned my title."

"This is true," Marc replied, nodding in agreement. "But Kirk is young, too. Not to mention, he's foreign. He hardly knows anything about our culture or laws. He'll need someone there to assist him. Who better to offer guidance than you?" The twinkle in Marc's dark eyes couldn't be ignored. "Besides, he asked for you by name. He wants you to help him teach the students."

Joel blinked. *Kirk asked for me? Why?* His eyes wandered around the office as he mulled over all Marc had said. *I guess he doesn't really know anyone else here. We made a connection in the Northern Empire. We're acquaintances—maybe even friends.* Heat rose to bathe Joel's cheeks, though he wasn't sure why. *Yes, we're friends.*

"What say you?" Marc asked. "You spoke about wanting to make a difference in the world. Well, you can. Right now. By doing this, you'll help ensure Arden's young mages are trained to their highest capabilities. We could really use your help, Joel."

Joel had never really given thought to teaching. The idea of it hadn't ever crossed his mind. Would he be any good at it? He had no life experience or great wisdom to offer these youngsters, and he surely wasn't a striking image of success. He had no claim to fame, other than being son of the seneschal, and seemed only to stir up controversy wherever he went. Why would Marc ask this of someone so underqualified?

Cenric believed in me, Joel reminded himself. *Maybe I just need to believe in me now, too.*

Newfound determination swelled in his chest as he raised his eyes to make contact with the dean. "All right," Joel said. "I'll do it."

Joel had barely made it out the door when Kirk found him.

"Joel!" the young man called. His white mage robe fluttered around his boots as he hurried down the corridor.

Joel's head was still spinning from the conversation he'd shared with Marc and the task to which he was now assigned, so the sight of the Imperial trainee caught him off guard. "H–hello." Taking his hand off the door handle of the dean's office, Joel moved forward, meeting the young trainee halfway down the hall.

As Kirk drew to a stop, he seemed to remember himself. His high cheekbones flushed with color as he gave a swift bow. "I, um, I was hoping to catch you here. Did you—did you speak with Dean Marc?" Kirk stared with hopeful eyes.

Joel inclined his head. "I did."

"Did he ask you about—about—" Kirk stuttered over the question, and Joel could tell the young man was embarrassed for being so forthcoming a moment before.

"He did," Joel replied cryptically.

Kirk waited with bated breath. "O–oh?"

A smile crept across Joel's face as he finally elaborated. "And I decided to accept the teaching position. It looks as though we're going to be partners."

Kirk's mouth jumped into an elated grin. "Oh, I'm so happy you've accepted! I have to admit, I was a little worried that you wouldn't."

Rubbing the back of his neck, Joel grimaced. "I almost didn't."

Kirk nodded as though he understood. "How have you been? It feels like it's been an eternity since we last spoke."

"That's my fault. I've been—moping." Joel twisted his hands together as he glanced around the corridor, busying himself so he didn't have to meet Kirk's florescent eyes. "I've been avoiding everyone in my life. I hope you can forgive me."

Kirk's mouth fell open. "There's nothing to forgive. Joel, you've been through a lot. I know that."

"No," Joel replied, shaking his head as he spoke. "That doesn't excuse my behavior. I've been acting like a sullen brat for moonturns now. It's high time I snap out of it." Wrapping his arms around his shoulders, he pressed onto a lighter topic. "So, you really think we're cut out for this mage training job?"

Kirk leaned against the corridor wall. "Between the two of us, I believe we can do it. Dean Marc can really use all the help he can get. Academy is very short on available mage trainers right now, and someone has to be here for the young ones just discovering their magical abilities."

Joel sighed. "There's a lack of available trainers because so many of Arden's skilled mages are on active border duty. You can thank the High Council for that."

"Politicians—they're the same no matter what country you live in."

They shared a quiet round of laughter, and Joel found his dark mood lifting for the first time in moonturns. *Now that the news has had time to sink in, I'm actually looking forward to working with Kirk. I think there's a lot I can learn from him.*

Kirk's smile was honest and genuine, much like his soul. "I've missed talking with you, Joel."

"Well, now that we're to work together, it's not like I can avoid you anymore." Joel winked deviously.

The Imperial mage cackled and gave Joel's arm a light swat.

Gib frowned down at his boots, wishing there was a way to *not* track mud all through the palace halls. He was grateful for the melting of winter's snow but less than enthusiastic about the muck left in its wake. His only comfort came with the knowledge that his boots weren't the only ones to mar the pristine marble tiles.

"The servants will be working overtime to get these floors back in shape," Koal remarked. Sometimes Gib had to wonder if his mentor could actually hear what he was thinking. "You should have seen what it was like out by the stables. I almost lost my boot."

Gib nodded. "Yeah. It's dangerous to wander off the path in this weather. Some of the mud holes are deeper than I am tall. I'd fall in and disappear." The seneschal and student shared a round of hearty laughter as they tromped down the corridor.

In the distance, the council chamber came into view, and the thin silhouette of King Rishi stood at its door—or rather, leaned against it. As always, Aodan was at his side and a plethora of royal guardsmen stood nearby. It was uncanny how motionless they always remained despite the chaos in the busy hall.

Koal's brow furrowed as he drew closer. "Have you forgotten how to stand? Or do you need help holding that door shut?"

King Rishi groaned. "I should've just rescheduled this damned meeting—or made you take the lead in my stead."

"And to think, you almost made it through the sick season unscathed. The influenza doesn't suit you." Koal smiled wryly.

"Aye," Aodan snorted. "It doesn't suit anyone else who has ta put up with him either."

Influenza? Gib thought it had run its course. There certainly hadn't been more than a handful of new cases since the last of the snow melted. When he glanced up from the dirty floors and got his first decent look at the King, Gib startled a little and blurted without thinking, "Daya, Highness, you look terrible!"

King Rishi turned a flat, somber gaze onto Gib even as both Koal and Aodan began to chuckle. The ruler's golden skin had gone pale and lost its luster, and dark rings around his eyes made them look dull. Despite his haggard appearance, the King arched a brow and replied in a testy voice, "Thank you for your honesty, Nemesio. For future reference, flattery is more welcomed."

Gib squirmed, feeling the heat pool in his cheeks. "Sorry. I just thought the illness had passed already. Don't you have healers to make sure you don't get sick?"

"My healer went and fathered a baby in his old age and promptly lost his mind!"

Gib grinned but managed not to laugh at Dean Marc's expense. Fatherhood surely wasn't easy for anyone, but Marc seemed extra scattered lately. Gib had noticed his lack of response during recent council meetings and how he was perpetually late for them—later than normal, that was.

"You probably could sit this one out if you need to," Koal said. "I can bring you the notes later."

King Rishi smiled, still every bit a devilish wolf whether he was ill or not. "And miss the opportunity to share the influenza with Neetra or the other councilors? That would be bad form."

Marc's booming laughter rippled down the corridor as he arrived. "Just stay the hell away from me and all will be well." He scurried toward them with a sheepish grin. "Bea's told me in no uncertain terms that if I get the baby sick I'm to be sleeping in my office until she's grown."

Aodan snorted again. "By the time she's grown, you'll be sleepin' in yer tomb."

Gib couldn't help but laugh along with the King and Koal. Marc rolled his eyes but didn't seem to take any real offense. He drew to a stop next to King Rishi, but his attention turned elsewhere. Gib only then realized Liro had been trailing the dean the entire time. All traces of laughter ceased as everyone else seemed to notice Liro's presence as well.

Marc craned his head toward Liro and muttered, "I, uh, hope your headache clears up soon. Sorry I couldn't do more."

Liro nodded once and thanked him, his voice as curt as ever. The eldest Adelwijn son stiffened to his full height and took a step back but didn't excuse himself entirely. Gib wondered what Liro could possibly want in order to stay so close, not only to the King, but also to his father. Trying not to openly sneer, Gib turned his back and waited for permission to enter the council room.

King Rishi curled his lip. "I smell shit."

"What?" Koal grimaced and looked down at his boots. "I was at the stables earlier but—"

"Well *there* you all are!" Neetra's shrill voice screeched down the hall.

Gib shuddered. He couldn't bring himself to glance up but could hear the High Councilor's footfalls fast approaching.

The King smiled cryptically at Koal. "Oops. My mistake. Just an asshole."

Koal pursed his lips, refusing to laugh. Marc, on the other hand, burst into a fit of hoarse chortling.

By the time Neetra reached them, his face was red. Stuffing his fists onto his narrow hips, the High Councilor's voice shook as he lectured them. "What are you all doing out here? Are we going to get this meeting underway today? We can't very well start without our King and seneschal present."

"Stop whining." King Rishi groaned and waved at Neetra like someone might swat at a pesky insect. "I was waiting for Marc. Now that he's here, we're ready."

"Oh, right!" Marc startled as if awoken from a dream and reached into his pocket. When he pulled his hand out, a small vial rested in his palm. With a nod, he handed it to King Rishi. "Best to just down it in one go. It'll settle your stomach and bring down any fever you may have."

The King frowned as he pulled the stopper from the bottle. "*You* didn't make it, did you?"

"Sure. I took the time to brew it special, just for you. Hurry up and drink the damned thing so we can get in there."

King Rishi groaned, put the remedy to his lips, and tipped his head back. One swallow had him coughing and sputtering. "What the *hell* is in this? It tastes awful!"

Koal threw his hands in the air while Marc folded his arms over his chest, a grin stretching his face wide. "Do you need me to hold your skirt for you, m'lady?"

Gib coughed to cover a laugh.

A sneer pulled at King Rishi's mouth as he tried his best to finish the medicine. The second attempt was only slightly better than the first. His face screwed into a grimace as he swallowed and stoppered the bottle. "No. That'll have to do. I can't drink any more of it."

"If you don't take it all, it won't be as effective—"

"I wanted something to settle my stomach, not make me *vomit!*" When Marc attempted to protest further, King Rishi simply tucked the vial into a pocket and nodded toward the council room door. "Shall we?"

Neetra made some snide remark about how he'd better not get sick and that the King was inconsiderate for bringing the illness into the council room. Gib wished he could block out the High Councilor's sniveling.

As they filed in, Liro stopped so suddenly Gib almost collided with him. Licking his lips, Liro turned to face King Rishi, regarding him with shrewd eyes. "Fresh air is often the best medicine. If his Highness does not feel well, perhaps it would be best for him to simply take a walk in the garden." Liro smiled, bowed low, and then turned and trotted toward his seat.

Gib squinted even as he watched the King frown. Take a walk in the garden? What in hell was that supposed to mean?

Koal skewered Marc with a heavy look. "What did you treat him for at the Healer's Pavilion?"

"The usual," Marc replied, still watching Liro's back as he climbed the balcony stairs and finally disappeared from view. "He had a headache and came for relief—though I had trouble locating the source of his ailment today. I do hope he feels better. There wasn't much I could do."

No more words were shared as Gib headed for his own chair. In the balcony, Liro was already seated and silent, little more than a dark smudge in the corner. Diddy and Hasain were also present, the former giving Gib a bright smile.

He grinned back at Diddy. "Are you two pretending to be twins today?"

Diddy chuckled and gestured down at his and Hasain's matching outfits. "We're going riding as soon as the council meeting is over."

"Kinda wet for that, don't you think? Might muck up your pretty riding gear."

"I know, but it'll be so nice to get out of the palace, and Joel needs the reprieve—" Diddy's eyes went wide as he seemed to realize what he'd said a moment too late. "I, uh, that is—"

And just like that, Gib's whole day went downhill. Was it insane that his heart was still such a treacherous thing? How could the mention of a simple name still cause so much hurt? Hot shame welled under his cheeks every time his heart pined for Joel, especially now. Despite taking things slow, his new relationship with Zandi was progressing, and it surely wasn't fair to be hung up on Joel while pursuing the young Malin-Rai lord.

Gib couldn't force himself to smile, but he shrugged off the concern to the best of his ability. "No, no. It's fine. I'm sure he could use the break."

Diddy's dark eyes glimmered with sorrow. An apology died on his lips when Neetra lifted his voice to call the meeting to order. Truthfully, Gib had never been happier to hear the High Councilor speak. Gib didn't want to think about his past anymore. He wanted to listen to the boring council meeting and pretend like his life wasn't in shambles. He wanted to forget about Joel Adelwijn.

The meeting dragged on much like any other. Gib listened and took notes of the various points of interest he had questions on. He felt a little bad when King Rishi's condition only worsened, forcing the ruler to leave early. Hasain and Diddy shared a quiet chuckle at their father's expense but settled back into silence when Liro hissed a warning to be quiet. And so it went until they were released well after midday meal had been served and cleaned up.

"I wonder if the kitchen will have anything to give me," Gib mused out loud.

"Surely the palace kitchen will have something," Diddy replied. He tapped Hasain's shoulder. "You could ask Rya."

Hasain stuck his nose into the air. "If I go in the kitchen, she'll put me to work. Besides, we have to collect Joel and get the horses if we're going to get any riding done before nightfall."

Gib waved them both off. "Eh, it's not any real trouble anyway. Go, both of you. Try to stay out of the mud." They each gave him an incredulous look before departing.

He watched them until they disappeared from view and then slumped against the wall, waiting for Koal. Looking down at his boots, Gib tried desperately not to think of Joel. Three moonturns with Zandi was still not enough to erase the memory of his first love. Falling for Joel had been so easy. Coaxing the same feelings for someone new was proving to be more difficult than Gib would have ever imagined. Zandi was gracious, even forgiving, but Gib had a hard time excusing his own behavior. It wasn't fair to lead Zandi on if love was never going to blossom on its own. He sighed. *Where is Koal?*

As always, his mentor was one of the last to leave the chamber. Today was worse, of course, because King Rishi wasn't there to answer any questions, leaving the seneschal to handle the entire work load. Koal finally emerged from the crowd after what felt like entire marks later. Marc was at the seneschal's heels. Both men looked as tired as Gib felt.

Rubbing his face, Marc gave Koal a thump on the shoulder. "I'm gonna take off. I've got paperwork at the office I'm behind on. See you tomorrow?"

"Yeah. I'll see you then." Koal turned to Gib. "What about you? You have classes to study for or anything?"

Truthfully, there was always something Gib could be studying for. Tarquin had been taking notes for both of them for so long it had become their "normal." There must be exams coming up but, in the moment, all Gib could really think about was his growling stomach and not letting his mind idle for too long. "I've got to find food."

Koal chuckled. "Tell me about it. Come with me to drop off these notes to the King, and I'll help you scrounge up something."

That sounded like a good plan. It had been a while since he and his mentor shared a quiet moment together. Since the brush with the Northern Empire, Koal had been busy with his duties, and since Gib didn't spend much time at the Adelwijn estate anymore, the two of them only ever saw one another for business matters.

They strolled toward the royal suite side by side and, once again, Koal apparently read Gib's mind. "It feels like it's been ages since I've seen you outside of council. You should come over for dinner some night."

Gib sucked in a sharp breath. How much did Koal know? Surely Joel had informed his family that he and Gib were no longer companions, hadn't he? It would just be too awkward to sit at the same table and try to pretend like nothing had changed. His tongue felt like a stone inside his mouth. "I've been busy."

Their footsteps echoed down the empty corridor as Koal took his time responding. "We all have been busy, but—we're quite fond of you, Gib. You've been missed. Mrifa and the girls talk about you. And Otos and Tabitha. Even Nawaz."

Gib rubbed his arms and stared at the floor as he walked upon one marble tile after the next. "I'm not sure everyone's as fond of me as you think." They entered the hall of royal portraits, and Gib couldn't help but feel scrutinized with so many unblinking, motionless eyes fixed upon him as he passed through.

"Joel's had a rough time," Koal finally replied. Gib glanced up in time to see the seneschal's face flush cherry red. "It nearly knocked me on my arse to find he'd pulled away from you, of all people. I wouldn't tell you to wait for him, by any means, but you don't have to disappear either."

Gib's heart squeezed painfully. He'd been refusing to think about Lady Mrifa and the girls, or even about Tabitha and Otos. If he didn't think about them then he didn't have to admit how much he missed them. But now, in the face of the truth, he realized how foolish he'd been. Selfish too. It was plain bad form to punish them for what he and Joel were going through.

"Dinner would be nice sometime."

Koal didn't look at him but replied with a nod. "Good. I'll tell Mrifa. I'm sure she'll go out and buy the whole market in preparation."

Gib laughed and they fell into companionable silence.

As they closed in on the royal suite, another set of footfalls echoed through the hall, moving toward them from the opposite direction. Gib raised his head to see who it was just as Koal called out a greeting.

"Aodan! What are you doing out here? Getting away from his whining?"

The bodyguard stopped long enough to reply, and Gib noted his lack of smile. "Naw. I'm goin' ta get Marc. His fever's only gettin' worse."

Koal shook his head. "Marc *told* him to drink the whole remedy."

"Stubborn as a mule." Aodan did grin at that, but only for a moment. "Did the meetin' just get over then?"

"Aye. If you hurry you might even catch Marc before he gets past the gates."

Aodan nodded and took off at a double pace.

Gib watched him disappear around the bend in the corridor. "It's a shame the King grew ill this late in the season. Now he seems to be getting the worst of it."

Koal chuckled. "He was too stubborn to get sick when everyone else was. This is his punishment. C'mon. Let's get this over with."

They were summoned into the royal suite by the Queen herself. Gib had already changed into a pair of slippers before he realized King Rishi was nowhere to be seen.

Koal also seemed to take note. Standing up, he glanced around the room. "Where is he?"

Dahlia gestured with a delicate hand toward a door Gib could only guess led farther into the family's private quarters. "He's inside. Was Marc close by? He needs to come quickly." The pained restraint in her voice set Gib's nerves on edge.

Any good humor Koal had displayed before then seeped away. The seneschal took his sister's elbow. "Take me to him. Let's see how bad this is."

Gib was nervous to follow at first, having never been past the front room, but he did without hesitation when Koal gestured for him. They walked through to a second, larger room Gib could only think of as a private living area. By the bay windows there was a table and chairs large enough for a family to sit and eat. Another Senet game table, less ornate than the one in the receiving room, was positioned on the far wall, along with various knick-knacks and items Gib couldn't name. Still, the King was missing.

"This way." The Queen didn't hesitate in the slightest to take them through yet another door and into a bed chamber. Gib hung back awkwardly by the threshold. This felt too personal. He wasn't sure the King would appreciate his being there.

As soon as he caught a glimpse of King Rishi's haggard form, however, Gib doubted very much that anyone was going to be concerned about whether or not Gib was there. Koal seemed likewise anxious and went straight for the ruler. "Chhaya's bane. What the hell happened to you?"

The King sat in a plush chair near the rear of the room and had his head resting against its tall back. His eyes slid open only when Koal called to him. "What are you doing here? Aodan sent for Marc."

"Well, you got me." Koal knelt before the ailing king. "And Marc will be here soon. You look awful."

"Really? I feel great." King Rishi winced and dropped his head back once more.

Gib swallowed. Even from his place in the doorway, he could see the sweat gathered along King Rishi's temples and forehead. His skin was even more flushed than earlier, and his entire body appeared limp and frail.

"Have you had any water lately?" Koal asked.

"I can't keep it down."

Dahlia hovered by her husband's shoulder, stroking his hair. "Do you know of anyone else being hit this hard by the influenza?" Her bottom lip trembled.

"Not that I know of," Koal replied. "My house was fortunate enough to be passed over. Roland had it a while back and was off his feet for two days, but I don't know that it was this bad."

Gib's ears detected noise. Behind him, he could hear the outer suite door open and close and muted voices conversing. Aodan had returned. It seemed an eternity before Marc and the bodyguard made their way down the hall.

"It can't be as bad as all of that," Marc was saying. "The influenza this year was fairly mild compared to past bouts." His voice dwindled when he stood directly behind Gib.

"Aye, ya say that now, but look at 'im," Aodan replied as he came into view. "He wouldn't let me come get ya at first, but when he nearly passed out, we threw 'im in the chair and didn't give 'im a choice."

"Yeah, I see." Marc slipped past Gib without a word of acknowledgement. He went to stand beside Koal and dropped his voice to a more passive tone. "Rishi? How're you doing?"

Gib's chest heaved while he waited for a response. It took entirely too long for the King to open his eyes. "How do I look like I'm doing?"

Marc smiled but it was entirely devoid of humor. "Yeah, I'm gonna take a look at you. We might need to take some stronger action than just simple remedies. This doesn't look so good."

"Shut up and do what you're going to do."

"All right. I'll try not to jostle you around too much." Marc rolled back his sleeves and put a hand across King Rishi's forehead. The frown that came to rest on his mouth was most unsettling. "Strange. You're not very hot considering how much you're sweating. Do you feel warm?"

The King winced and tried to pull away from Marc's hand. "My stomach is on fire. And my mouth. Like I ate a hot pepper."

Marc refused to relent in his examination, plucking open the buttons on the King's high collar. His fingers touched the ruler's throat, pausing there for several moments before moving his hand up toward King Rishi's jawline. "Huh. When did that start?"

Gib shuddered as he listened to the King take sharp, ragged breaths. Was he in pain? Would Marc be able to help him?

Aodan passed by in such haste that he knocked his arm on Gib's shoulder. The rise in the bodyguard's voice indicated his distress. "He mentioned it when we left the council room. What the hell's goin' on?"

"I don't know yet. That's not a typical symptom of the flu though."

Aodan crouched beside the King, and from the opposite side of the chair, Dahlia continued to rake her fingers through her husband's greying hair. Her dark eyes welled up with tears, but she fought valiantly to keep her voice calm. "You'll figure out what illness it is though, won't you?"

"I'm working on it, Dahlia, I promise." Marc didn't sound very confident, and Gib had to grab onto the door frame to keep his feet under him. He watched as Marc pressed both palms flat over the sides of the King's neck and closed his eyes in concentration, searching for the source of King Rishi's pain with Healing magic.

Time stood still while Gib held his breath, waiting alongside the others for Marc to come to some kind of conclusion. Silence cloaked the room, insufferable and indomitable. And then at once, a sharp gasp pushed its way through Marc's open mouth. The sound was as painful as an arrow to Gib's chest. The dean retracted his hands from King Rishi's neck like he'd been scalded and fell back.

"What? What is it?" Aodan demanded.

Marc fumbled for words. "I, uh, I can't—Rishi, what have you eaten today?"

The King drew a few shallow breaths before responding. "Breakfast. But it didn't stay down."

"Why? What's going on?" Koal asked, worry lining his pale face.

Marc shook his head, eyes wide and mouth trembling. "This isn't—it's not influenza. It's wolfsbane. He's been poisoned."

It felt as though the floor opened beneath Gib and he'd been swallowed whole. He couldn't catch his balance and couldn't hear for the rushing of blood in his temples. Poison? What was wolfsbane? Was it serious?

The reactions around him led Gib only to the worst conclusions. King Rishi stiffened and knit his brows, Dahlia burst into tears, and Aodan dropped onto his backside, hands shooting up to cradle his head. Koal reeled as if he'd been physically attacked while Marc floundered for more to say. When he couldn't sputter out even a single word, the dean went back to silently evaluating the King's condition.

"What else have you eaten or drunk?" Koal asked as he began to pace around the tight quarters of the bedchamber. "Rishi, we have to find out where this came from or someone else could ingest it. Did you have a cup at all today?"

The King looked around, but his eyes remained unfocused. "Not my own. Gudrin drank from my cup, and she was fine when last I saw her."

Koal froze. "When was that?"

"Not two marks ago," Dahlia replied, retching on a sob. "He was already falling ill when that happened. Gudrin is fine. She's with Bailey."

Aodan lifted his crimson face. "An' we all ate and drank from the same plates an' pitchers this mornin'. What the hell else was there?"

Marc desperately pawed at the King's neck and shoulders, perhaps trying to find the source of the poison. The entire room seemed to be spiraling into a panic, so it was odd when King Rishi's voice was the only one to hold any reason. He turned a bleary gaze on Marc. "How far along is it? Can you fix this?"

The frenzy from a moment before died on the spot. Gib felt as though he were gripped in a vice as he waited. No one moved or dared speak. Only Marc made any sound at all. Taking his friend by the hand, he began to weep. "N–no. Your organs are already shutting down. I can't fix this."

The King's eyes went wide, and for just a moment, Gib could see terror plainly written across the ruler's face. He masked it an instant later, withdrawing into himself as he leaned back in the chair and closed his eyes. Dahlia's pitiful crying made Gib wish he could cover his ears and not listen. Even Aodan, typically so stoic, gave up. He lay on the floor next to his king's chair and sobbed.

Koal's large hands rubbed at his temples as he paced. "None of this makes any sense! You're sure it was the influenza when you checked him yesterday, aren't you?"

Marc kept his head low, still holding the King's limp hand. "Yes. Early onset. Nothing to be done except drinking and resting."

"Wolfsbane acts too quickly for this to have happened prior to today," Koal said. "And no one else is showing symptoms. Where the hell did the poison come from?"

Gib had to strain to hear the King's labored voice. "It's poison even to the touch. It could have been on my clothes or gear."

"Bailey would have gotten sick too when he laid out your clothes. And you've been in close contact with your family and councilors today. No one else has fallen ill." Koal stormed over to the wall and slammed a fist off the stone. "There has to be something else!"

King Rishi's eyes slipped shut again. "There isn't anything else. Call NezReth and Natori. They can check the room. Don't touch anything."

Gib drew away from the wall and wrapped his arms around himself. He wanted to run out of the suite and pretend he hadn't seen anything. Perhaps he'd wake up momentarily and realize this was all a horrific nightmare. He took a deep breath and held it, waiting. Hoping. Nothing changed. He didn't wake up, and the King didn't look any better.

Suddenly Aodan issued a sharp gasp. "Wait," he rasped, scrambling to his feet. "The remedy! It's the only damned thing he's had that we didn't!" Aodan fished through the King's pockets without asking permission and after several agonizing moments of searching, produced the small vial.

Koal snatched it immediately and pulled out the stopper. Several shouts rang in unison before he silenced them all with one withering glare. Lifting the flask to his face, he took a short sniff and shuddered. Closing it tightly, his shoulders sagged. "This is it. I'm sure of it."

"Impossible!" Marc floundered, his face a sickly white. "I picked the vial up from the Healer's Pavilion myself. I checked to make sure it was the correct remedy! It was with me the entire time! There's no way it could have been tampered with!"

Koal rushed toward the door. "I'll get NezReth and Natori. Maybe there's something they can do. They're the strongest mages I've ever met—"

"Koal." The King's voice was barely more than a whisper, yet it enveloped everyone in the room. "It's too late for that. Marc said so."

Aodan was on his feet as well. "Aye. Marc's also the one who fed ya *poison*! We have ta try somethin'."

Marc wept harder, but the King waved his hand once, effectively silencing his bodyguard. "This was an act of betrayal, Aodan. Marc's been framed."

"Why?" Dahlia implored. She leaned her face against the top of King

Rishi's head, crying into his hair. "Why would someone frame Marc and kill Rishi?"

Koal shook his head. "Why wouldn't they? They found an opportunity to take out the King of Arden *and* one of his biggest supporters." He put his hands on his hips. "Who saw Marc give you that remedy?"

The King didn't offer to respond, so Aodan did. "Neetra. Liro. All of us. Anyone else who might have been in the hall. Guards." He sat heavily on the arm of the chair next to the ailing king, looking utterly lost.

Koal scowled. "Whoever did this wanted to make sure it was well seen. There's no way in hell Marc's going to come out of this unscathed."

Gib shuddered at Koal's words but knew he spoke the truth. Too many people had been present. He dared to raise his own meek voice. "How are we going to prove Marc didn't do it? I mean, we can't let him take the fall."

Pained, unbelieving laughter burst from Aodan's throat. "Rishi's *dyin'* an' yer worried about *Marc?*" His shoulders heaved, and he put his face down in his hands. Dahlia reached over and began to rub small circles on the bodyguard's trembling back.

Three long strides found Koal at their side. "This is a hard time for everyone, but Gib's right. We have to figure this out. The council can't lose two votes for—"

"Is *that* what yer worried for? *Votes?*" When Aodan looked up, fierce light glinted in his single, bloodshot eye. "He's *dyin'*! He's yer friend, yer king, and all ya have any worry for is the council vote?"

Gib sucked his bottom lip into his mouth, the undeniable truth tasting bitter on his tongue. Even in the wake of tragedy, they had to concern themselves with the welfare of Arden. No one spoke for so long Gib thought his heart might hammer right out of his chest.

The King's dry rasp brought them all back. "Bird." He managed to lift one shaking hand and set it on Aodan's knee. "It's all right. No man lives forever. Arden has to be cared for." He licked his lips, brows knitting tightly. "How much time, Marc? How long before this is done?"

Marc's entire body shook. "I don't—two marks? Three? One? Not long." He broke down, sitting on the floor at his friend's feet, crying. "I'm sorry, Rishi. I'm so sorry."

King Rishi flicked his hand, irritation pulling at his features briefly before his strength abandoned him once more. "No time. Whoever did this is clever. You won't catch them before I'm dead."

The proclamation sank like a stone dropped in a well. Marc shuddered and wept harder but didn't try to defend himself. Koal put a hand on the dean's shoulder. "What the hell are we supposed to do?"

"I'll go," Marc choked in between sobs. "I did this. I'll go."

The King frowned. "No. You have Beatrice and Callidora to care for."

Koal laughed incredulously. Gib had never before heard the seneschal's voice sound so crushed. "Then what would you have us do, Rishi?"

The King's face twisted, conflict clouding his dark eyes. "Lie to everyone. Tell them I killed myself." Dahlia let out a mournful whimper, and Aodan nearly fell from his seat.

"N–no," Koal said, shaking his head in protest. "No one'll ever believe it anyway."

King Rishi locked eyes with the seneschal. "Then you'll have to make them believe. You'll have to make it look like I killed myself."

Koal trembled in his place. "How would you even have us do that?"

"I don't know. Toss me from the balcony! Hang me from the rafters! Just do it!"

Aodan staggered back from the chair, eye wide and fists tugging at his red hair. "Have ya lost yer mind? Do ya hear what yer askin'?" He paused and lowered his voice. "Ya can make this go away, Rishi. All ya have ta do is open the box—"

Koal and Marc both turned uncomfortable gazes onto the King. The ruler himself stiffened in the chair and gave a firm shake of his head. "*No.* It's not an option. You know that."

Gib's heart thudded in his ears. What box? Was there a cure of some sort hidden away? He wanted to ask in the worst way but didn't dare interrupt.

Koal stood again, one hand over his mouth. He spoke as much to himself as anyone else. "Impossible. There's no way. You ask too much. I won't take your legacy away from you. Even at the cost of sending Marc into the unknown. I won't make you out to be a coward in your last moments."

King Rishi reached one hand toward Koal. It shook while he held it aloft, and he had no choice but to drop it to his lap a moment later. As Gib watched, he realized just how weak the King really was. How much time did he have left?

"You do as I say. This is an order. You are my Right Hand, Koal, and you will do as your King commands—"

"You don't get to tell me what to do anymore!" Koal lurched forward, only stopping when he loomed above King Rishi, face to face. Gripping both armrests of the chair, the seneschal leaned closer yet. "You stubborn, miserable, son of a bitch, you don't get to order me around! Not like this! I *won't* smear your name! *I won't do it!*"

Gib would have thought it impossible, but the King found his voice despite being so frail. "There's no time to argue this. By nightfall, I'll be dead. You can either save Marc, his family, and Arden, or spare my image and throw the rest away."

Silence rose up to meet the King's strenuous breathing. No one spoke. Koal took a teetering step back and turned to lean his forehead against the wall. Gib could only watch and hold his breath, waiting.

Finally Koal lifted his reddened face and, with a defeated sigh, met King Rishi's somber eyes. "I hated you from the moment you came through the portal. Loud. Arrogant. Sly. There was nothing about you I trusted. I hated that King Eitan approved of you. I thought him a fool. And yet—when Arden needed you most, you stepped in like it was your birthright. You've done nothing but serve her as if she were your own homeland. You commanded respect and earned the love of the people. You made me see you as a brother. But even now, with damned near your final breath, you've vexed me yet again. How can you ask me to do this to you?"

Agony gripped Gib's soul as he watched Koal rake the back of his hand across his eyes. Never before had Gib witnessed the seneschal in such a state of despair. Never before had he seen Koal Adelwijn cry.

The King blinked away tears of his own as he rested his head against the velvet-covered chair. "I was afraid of you. And jealous. So very jealous. Eitan had no son, yet you were his first choice. I couldn't comprehend what power you must have had to win him over so fully. I was sure you'd never accept me and terrified I'd never be as good as you. I taunted you so you wouldn't know how envious I was of you. No one's acceptance in all of Arden has meant more than yours, Koal. I ask you to do this because I would do it for you. This is how it has to be. Please. Please, just do it."

A long moment passed before Koal nodded, pressing fingers over his glistening eyelids. He laughed feebly, defeated. "All right, you stubborn arse. I'll do it, but *only* if my tomb is engraved as your favorite servant."

Weak laughter spilled from King Rishi's parched lips. He promptly grabbed for his ribs. "Ow. Stop."

"I'd always thought watching you die would be more gratifying than this."

King Rishi smiled and, despite his ashen hue and failing body, he looked like himself. "I hate you, too."

Gib wrung his hands together, glancing around the room, from one person to the next. *Now what do we do? What happens next?*

They rode fast and hard to the palace gates. Joel's mind swam with dread at the possibilities of what could be so wrong. One moment he'd been riding with Hasain and Diddy, and in the next, a page had flown up beside them, frantically demanding they return to the palace. The King had sent word for his sons to be brought to him, and Joel was pulled along with them.

Once inside the gates, Diddy's faithful servant, Gideon, met them to take their horses. Diddy asked briefly what the problem was, but Gideon answered that he didn't know. They swept through the palace without a single delay. In fact, Joel noted, the halls seemed to be barren.

Outside the suite, Joel thought to excuse himself for he hadn't been invited, but when his father opened the door, all three boys were ushered inside. One look at the seneschal's drawn face and red eyes had them silent and waiting with bated breath.

Koal didn't mince his words. "You've been called here to be delivered a blow. I don't want to give this message any more than you'll want to hear it, but there's nothing to be done for that now. Come with me." He turned and swept through the inner room of the suite, and Joel followed at the heels of Hasain and Diddy. They didn't stop until they reached the entrance to the King's private bedchamber. The cedar door stood closed, and Joel found himself not wanting to know what lay beyond.

The color had drained from both Hasain's and Diddy's faces. The former cleared his throat, voice shaking. "Koal? Is Father in?"

Koal set a hand on the brass handle. He wouldn't meet their eyes. "Yes." Without knocking or announcing his arrival, the seneschal opened the door and let them in.

Heart already racing, Joel craned his head and peered inside. He started shuffling forward but stopped dead in his tracks when he saw King Rishi's slight form sprawled upon the bed. The ruler looked like nothing more than a wisp, with closed eyes and greying hair falling loose from his woven braid. Joel couldn't remember a time he'd seen the King look so frail. *Daya, what's wrong with him?*

Hasain rushed to the bedside, grief distorting his features. "Father?"

King Rishi's bleary eyes opened entirely too slowly, and he had a difficult time focusing on his son's stricken face. The corners of his mouth flicked up for the briefest of moments before he had to close his eyes again and rest. "Hasain. Where are your brothers?"

"I'm here, Father." Diddy's voice was small as he also approached the bedside. They both reached to touch him.

"Deegan will be brought in shortly," Koal said. He stood beside the only window, and Joel sucked in a sharp breath of air when he noticed Gib shadowed the seneschal. Heart hammering within Joel's chest, he chose to stare at the intricate carpet beneath his boots. Everything else in the room felt as though it was off limits.

"What's happened to him?" Hasain asked through gasps for air. "Why is he so ill?"

"Poison." Aodan sat to one side of the King while Dahlia sat at the other. Both of their faces were tear trailed and worn. "Someone plotted against him. They've won this time."

Hasain dropped to his knees, weeping into the blanket as he sought his father's hand. Diddy sat on the foot of the bed, eyes searching but not seeing. "Poison? Is—is he—?"

King Rishi uttered a shallow sigh. "I'm dying."

Both sons gasped and began to weep. Joel put a hand to his throat. *This can't be happening.*

The King pressed on in a labored, slow tone. "Some bastard bested me. It was bound to happen sooner or later—"

"What?" Hasain bleated. "Where are NezReth and Natori? They can help you!"

"No. Marc's seen to it that I'm not in pain, but there's nothing more to do."

From his seat beyond the foot of the bed, Marc made some sort of indiscernible noise. Joel hadn't even noticed the dean when first entering the room.

Dropping his head, Hasain wailed into the quilted bedspread. King Rishi managed to lift a hand and placed it atop the young lord's head. "Don't, Hasain. Don't cry for me. I'm old and have had a good life. Don't mourn my death."

Tears streamed down Diddy's face. "Don't ask the impossible of us, Da. What'll we do without you?"

King Rishi's face lifted into a smile for a fleeting moment, as though he were enjoying a peaceful dream. "You're both grown. You'll need to watch out for Deegan and Gudrin. Keep our family whole."

Joel bit the inside of his cheek until he tasted blood. He refused to break down here. He'd already been crying for so long, and right now his cousins and aunt needed his support. He needed to be strong for their sake. Sparing a glance at Gib, Joel saw the understudy had a hand on Marc's shoulder, offering silent comfort of his own.

"There's not a lot of time. Hasain, I have to give you something." The King sounded more and more tired with each passing moment. Like sand wisping through an hourglass, his life was slipping away. "It's an unfair burden, my son, but I have no choice. I'm sorry."

Koal took up a small box and brought it to Hasain. Joel noted the concentration in his father's eyes as he held out the chest, and as soon as Hasain took it, Koal retracted his hands and backed away. Joel couldn't fathom why his father would be so unnerved by such a simple thing as a box but supposed the weight of the moment might be to blame.

The King's eyes fluttered open, looking straight through Hasain. "Don't open it now. I wrote a letter some time ago when I knew you were the one I'd give the box to. I've explained why I chose you, but—I can never ask enough for your forgiveness. Only know I have no choice. Please know that." King Rishi's desperation made Joel wish he could offer reassurance, despite not knowing what was happening.

Hasain must have felt the same way. A trace of confusion flashed behind his dark eyes, but a moment later he took his father's hand and squeezed it. "I believe you, Da. There's nothing you could ask of me that I wouldn't do for you. Worry not about this box or what's inside."

King Rishi blinked. "I love you." His fragile gaze passed over Diddy as well. "Both of you—all of you children—more than I can say. Deegan will be king, but he'll need guidance and protection. You mustn't let the crown ever come between you. Just like this box, the crown is an empty promise. It delivers more pain than favor. Your family is the only thing you ever really have in this world."

Joel wiped at his treacherous eyes. All around him, people wept. His aunt, Marc, Aodan, both Hasain and Diddy—even his father had to keep rubbing tears from his cheeks. The only person who'd managed to maintain his calm was Gib. He stood on the other side of the window, hands clasped in front of him, with a dazed look about him. Was this what it had been like when his father had died? It had been so long since Joel had spoken to Gib that he supposed he'd never be able to ask him.

Gib looked directly at Joel for no longer than a heartbeat before gazing back toward the window, and his heart twisted for an entirely different reason. There'd been a time when he could have mourned King Rishi's passing with Gib, but no longer. Now he'd have to cry for yet another loss on his own.

A lone knock cut through the stifling air, and Joel twisted his head in the direction of the common room. "Someone's here."

Koal was on his feet and out the door before anyone could say another word.

Dahlia brushed back a strand of her husband's unruly hair. "That may be Deegan, my love."

"Good. I'm so damned tired." The King's words were vapid, completely devoid of life.

Dahlia's quiet resignation didn't settle well with Joel. She'd given up. They'd all given up. Where had this poison come from? What did they plan to do to catch the person responsible? Why weren't there guards out there, right now, searching?

Koal's muted voice carried through the hall. "In here, Deegan."

The youngest prince was ushered inside. Deegan blinked, looking from one person to the next. Much as Joel had, once he spotted the King, the Crowned Prince couldn't tear his eyes away. "F–Father?"

King Rishi had just turned toward his youngest son's voice when there came a deafening crash from the hallway, followed by racing footsteps and the sound of Koal and Bailey shouting in unison, "*Gudrin, no!*"

It was too late. The door flew all the way open, knocking into Joel, and Gudrin raced through. Joel instinctively tried to grab her, but she was too fast and much too agile. She'd always been like a little cat, darting and twisting with almost super-human agility. In a glimmer of blue dress and dark hair, she whipped past Joel and only came to a stop when she stood beside Deegan. Her victorious grin fell away in an instant.

Koal and Bailey both crashed through the door a moment later, but the damage had already been done. Gudrin's eyes were fixed on the King. Her bottom lip trembled as she took a tentative step forward. "Pa–Papa?"

King Rishi tried to lift himself up onto his elbows, but he couldn't. "No," he rasped, his face stricken with grief. "She wasn't supposed to see."

Aodan leapt from his seat and rushed at the young princess, but Gudrin saw him coming. Letting out a shriek, she made a mad scramble for the King. "*No! Papa!*" She launched for the bed and, even in his shock, Joel had to wonder how the little girl could jump so far.

Aodan reached her an instant later, lifting her from the bed. "No, Gudrin. Papa's sick. You'll hurt him!"

Gudrin grabbed hold of the blanket, refusing to let go. She screamed unlike anything Joel had ever heard before and shredded the heavy blanket with her bare fingers—or something. He squinted. That couldn't be right. For just a moment, Joel had sworn he'd seen *claws* on the ends of each stubby digit.

Aodan snarled something at the flailing princess, and Joel just about fell on his backside when Gudrin growled back—not the growl of a small child, but that of a wild cat or other vicious creature. Her eyes were wide and terrified as she tried to break free from Aodan's grip. "Let go! What's wrong with him? Papa!"

"Calm down!" Aodan said, leveling the princess with a fearsome scowl. "Calm yerself an' I'll let you go to 'im. But ya can't be climbin' all over 'im, Gudrin. He's sick."

Gudrin went limp at that, any growls or snarls giving way to whimpering cries. Joel's heart slowed just a little. As the princess softened, so did Aodan. He went from restraining her to cradling her in his arms. Together they wept as he took her to the bedside and allowed her to see her father. Gudrin nuzzled against his side and the King rested his cheek atop her head and whispered sweet words to her.

Deegan joined his sister, standing beside the bed. He reached out and placed a hand on King Rishi's arm, and at last, tears began to cascade down his cheeks. Dahlia swept over and wrapped her arms around Deegan's shoulders, crying with him. Behind them, Hasain and Diddy leaned on one another as they wept. Marc sat at the back of the room, his head in his hands, and Gib continued to pat the dean's back.

Joel clenched his jaw, caught between sorrow for the loss of their king and the apprehension of what had just taken place with Gudrin. His eyes darted around the room, wondering if anyone else had noticed the frightening behavior but found no answers, only tears and heartache.

"All right." Koal's voice cut through the silent suite. "The only others we're waiting on are the Blessed Mages and Roland Korbin, and then I'm going to explain everything. No questions until I've said my peace. Not everyone who's here was meant to see this, but secrecy is going to be a must if we're to succeed." His heavy gaze fell onto first Gib and then Joel. "I'm afraid I haven't good news and our time is short, so listen well and keep your mouths shut."

The bright sun shining through the temple windows was a lie Gib could feel in his core. He could find no warmth, no comfort. Not today. All around him stood people. Some were strangers. Some he only barely knew. Others were people who'd become his second family over the past three and a half years. Hearts heavy, they all waited together to say their final goodbyes to King Rishi Radek.

Three nights prior, Gib had watched in horror as the King fell victim to his treacherous opposition. He'd been poisoned, and this time Gib hadn't been in the right place at the right time to prevent the assassination. No one had.

The people in the kingdom knew none of this, however. Even as King Rishi took his final breaths, he made Koal promise to see to it that Marc wasn't prosecuted. The world couldn't know it was the Healer's vial, laced with deadly wolfsbane, that had poisoned the King. Gib's stomach rolled. The ugly rumors of how the King had hung himself in his bedchamber made him want to retch. King Rishi had been brave, even in the end, but no one here would ever know. They couldn't know the truth, or Marc's life would also be jeopardized.

Gib folded his hands in front of himself and watched as countless people shuffled through the temple, an endless procession of foreign dignitaries, Ardenian officials, highborns, and courtiers. Each stopped at the foot of the grand, marble tomb where the deceased king had been laid out and dressed in fine clothing. In death, King Rishi looked peaceful. His hair was woven into a loose braid with a golden crown perched atop it. With clasped hands resting on his still chest and sealed eyelids, Gib could almost convince himself the King merely slumbered.

The Queen and the immediate royal family stood to the side of the tomb, as was custom. After each guest said their final goodbyes to King Rishi, condolences were given to family. Gib watched with wet eyes as Dahlia, her bodyguard Aodan, and the royal children struggled to keep their composure. Crowned Prince Deegan stayed by his mother's side while little Gudrin clung to Aodan, grasping the bodyguard's hand. Diddy stood behind her, gently rubbing his sister's shoulders and somehow managing to keep his own tears at bay. Gib was so caught up watching he barely realized Hasain had approached.

Eyes bloodshot and olive skin an unnatural pallid hue, the young lord glared at the procession line. "Look at them all," Hasain said, the tremble in his voice betraying his anguish. "Saying their goodbyes as if they knew him. Of all the men who've passed through the temple thus far, I could name only a small handful. I hate this. He would have hated it, too."

Gib nodded his agreement. He could almost hear the King's disapproving snort. "My pa's funeral was so small it was over in a mark. It was just my siblings and a few neighbors. Nothing as grand as this."

"It'd be better if only our family and loved ones were here. Father wouldn't have cared for all of these politicians looking at him. They're only here to discuss what will happen tomorrow anyway."

"Tomorrow?" Gib hadn't bothered to think that far ahead yet.

Hasain wiped his face with a sleeve. "They'll seal him away today. Tomorrow, who knows what will become of Arden. The council will meet to decide who will rule in his stead." His bottom lip trembled, but he covered it with his hand. Gib pretended not to notice.

"Rule in his stead? Until Prince Deegan is old enough to take the crown?"

"Yes. They'll vote in a steward."

Gib's heart thudded to a stop. "Wh—who would qualify for that? Will Koal—?"

"The seneschal would be the first choice." Dark despair lined Hasain's voice. "But the High Councilor would be another option. Father had no surviving brothers."

Gib had to concentrate to stop his knees from knocking together. *The High Councilor? Neetra? He can't run Arden.* "What about you? Aren't you old enough to take the crown? Even if it's only until—"

A broken, desperate laugh cut through the air. "Allow the *bastard* son to take the crown? The temples would collapse." Hasain shook his head. "No. Kieran and I don't exist to them."

Gib's brow creased. Kieran? Who the hell was Kieran?

He had no opportunity to question Hasain, for Nawaz had approached without making a sound and was giving Hasain a hearty clasp on the shoulder. Heidi was by her new husband's side, her powdered face buried in a kerchief.

"Oh, Hasain," she gasped through sniffles. "I'm so sorry. I can't believe he's gone."

Hasain inclined his head, nodding stiffly. "Thank you. Both of you." His eyes flicked from Heidi to Nawaz, and it seemed he was having a difficult time meeting his best friend's stare. Was that guilt flashing behind Hasain's dark eyes? Through the grief, it was hard for Gib to tell.

The four of them waited in silence; the only sounds to be heard were the shuffling of feet and the buzz of whispers echoing off the stone walls. Gib stared at his boots so he didn't have to meet Hasain's pained eyes or witness Heidi's damp cheeks. Likewise, he was frightened to look upon the tomb again. Another glimpse of the King's lifeless, sallow form might be enough to do him in completely.

He couldn't escape it for long though. When the chamber at last began to clear, Gib found himself swept into the procession and edging slowly toward the open tomb. His mouth went dry at the prospect of having to say goodbye to King Rishi. He wasn't ready. He'd probably *never* be ready.

Up ahead, Neetra and Liro were taking their turns to pay their respects. As expected, each gave the least they could, opting only to bow to the dead king and spare no words for the mighty ruler who'd brought so much good to the land. Gib knew he was powerless to do anything, but the sight of Liro's smug expression made his temper flame. How could he be so heartless?

"Take strength, Aunt," Liro said as he stopped before Dahlia. "Despite the teachings of the Blessed Son of Light, perhaps one so clever as Rishi Radek will find a way out of eternal damnation."

The Queen squared her shoulders and lifted her chin. Gib had to wonder where she found the strength to remain courageous in the face of such adversity. "*King* Rishi Radek. And you will never convince me that any soul desperate enough to end their own life would then be condemned for eternity. Perhaps your Blessed Son of Light isn't the best example to be followed, nephew."

Gib was sure he witnessed a tinge of pink blossom on Liro's cheeks as he bowed to Dahlia. Surely he'd leave without stirring up further trouble—but no. Instead of walking away, Liro turned next to Aodan, and Gib could hear Liro's artful voice, muted as it was, all the way from where Gib stood. "With no king left to guard, you may consider packing your bags, Derr."

The color drained from Aodan's face. For once, the bodyguard's untamable fury seemed to have abandoned him. Clenching his jaw, he looked away from Liro and tightened his grip on Princess Gudrin's hand. Liro curled his mouth into a sinister smile and finally took his leave.

A moment later, Gudrin began to cry, the desperate sobs tearing at Gib's heart. Dahlia and Aodan held her tight and whispered comforting words, but the young girl had reached her capacity. Everyone had. Diddy and Deegan wept with the others.

Hasain breathed a deep sigh, tears pooling in the corner of each slanted eye. "We'll await tomorrow and see what happens. Drastic measures may have to be taken."

Gib watched the young lord make his way up to the tomb. He didn't know exactly what Hasain meant, but he thought he understood. As Gib waited for his turn to bid farewell to the King, a feeling of duty sprung to life deep inside his core. He didn't know what he was going to say to King Rishi, but in his heart, he made a promise—a promise to do all he could to keep Arden whole.

CHAPTER FOURTEEN

Gib held onto the wall as he made his way toward the council room, taking care to go slowly so his heart didn't fail from overuse. This was it. Today the High Council would choose a steward to rule Arden.

His mind attempted to whirl away from him, to entomb him in panic, but he locked his jaw and firmly refused to despair. Koal was the seneschal of Arden, the dead king's Right Hand since well before Gib had even been born. Why wouldn't Koal be chosen to be steward? He was the only logical choice.

But Neetra was cunning. The High Councilor had many supporters. If anyone were to give Koal a run for his money, it would be his younger brother.

Gib's jaw was clenched so tightly it began to ache. Letting out a whoosh of air, he attempted to loosen his stance. He couldn't worry over this now. In just a moment he'd be inside the council room, where Arden's fate would be decided. He needed to stay focused and have a clear mind.

Turning the last bend in the hall, a new anguish washed over him. The grand oak doors leading to the council chamber were closed, and Hasain and Diddy stood beside them, looking confused and worried. Gib knew something was amiss. They'd never bothered to wait for him outside the chamber before.

Hasain paced back and forth with his arms wrapped tightly around himself. Diddy remained as still as a statue, with one hand pressed over his mouth and eyes staring vacantly. When he took notice of Gib, the prince snapped out of his trance.

"Gib!" Diddy called as he came within earshot. "Where's Koal? Has he told you to join him inside today?"

Gib furrowed his brow. "I haven't seen him yet. Join him inside? I always sit in on the council meetings. You know that."

Hasain drew to a halt and spun around. His hair and clothing were in utter disarray. "Not today, Nemesio. Neetra has commanded no understudies be present."

"What?" Gib asked, mouth falling open. "How can he do that? It's not—does he have that authority?"

"Today he does."

The three young men turned toward the new voice.

Koal strode down the corridor, his face set in a hard grimace. He kept one hand on the hilt of his broadsword while the other swung freely at his side. Red cape billowing in his wake and steel blue eyes narrowed into fierce slits, the seneschal had never looked more intimidating. Marc trailed close behind, the usual twinkle in his dark eyes and crooked smile nowhere to be seen.

Gib took an unwilling step back. "You look like you're going to war, not council."

Koal's dismal gaze speared the understudy. "Today it *is* war."

"If anyone has prayers, say them now," Marc added gravely.

As Koal passed, he extended a hand and clasped Hasain's shoulder. "You know what's to be done should our worst fears come to realization. Be sure to stay here."

"Yes." Hasain glanced around the empty corridor. "The others will come along as they can. We'll be ready."

Gib's mind piqued with curiosity, wondering what they were speaking about, but he held his tongue. Now wasn't the time for questions. If he'd learned anything while being Koal's understudy, it was that secrets couldn't be forced to light. If they needed him, they would ask.

Koal and Marc left without a word of goodbye. The bang of the heavy doors slamming shut echoed down the hall until unnerving silence was all that remained. With nothing else to do, Hasain, Diddy, and Gib sat on the marble floor and waited.

Perhaps a mark later, Gib looked up when he heard light footfalls. Joel and Nawaz trotted toward them, confusion etched across each of their faces. At the sight of Joel's flowing robes, Gib blinked and his heart twisted against his will. It'd been so long since he'd seen the mage. Why did it feel like Gib was looking upon a near stranger?

"What are you guys doin' here?" Nawaz asked. The young lord had donned his healer's jerkin, and he could have been on his way to the pavilion if not for the crossbow strapped over one shoulder. The sight of the weapon caused Gib's blood to run cold. What use would there be for it inside the palace?

Joel's eyes scanned the corridor, looking from one face to the next yet avoiding any prolonged gaze directed at Gib. "Why aren't you all inside?"

"We've been banned," Hasain choked, on the verge of tears. "The other understudies already wandered off."

Joel and Nawaz exchanged glances before moving to flank Hasain.

Nawaz shook his head. "It's already starting. Neetra won't be happy until he has Arden under his thumb."

"We must hold onto hope," Diddy insisted. "The councilmen aren't imbeciles. They *have* to vote for Uncle Koal!"

"Not imbeciles," Joel said. "But they are misled. Anything could happen in there."

Nawaz set his hand atop the butt of his crossbow. "We're prepared."

Gib bit his tongue. *Prepared for what?*

More time passed before Kezra stormed through the corridor. Since she was still clad in her sentinel tunic and breeches, her sword was slightly less unsettling when she came to a stop before them. With one cool scan, she chose to ignore Nawaz and instead turned her attention to Hasain. "What's this then? Why is everyone outside?"

Something dark flashed in Hasain's eyes as he launched himself to his feet to greet her. As he explained their plight yet again, Gib couldn't help but glance over at Nawaz. The young lord kept his red face inclined, yet every time Kezra spoke, his eyes would dart toward her. Gib took a deep breath. He understood. Gods, he understood. His own gaze kept treacherously returning to Joel.

Kezra leaned against the cold wall. "So, we wait for the fate of Arden to be decided?"

"What else can we do?" Hasain offered his hand, but she hardly even acknowledged it. When he realized she had no intention of taking hold, he went back to his place. "Would you sit with me?"

Kezra folded her arms. "I'll stand."

Once more during their wait, newcomers joined them. Weapons Master Roland and Tular Galloway approached, side by side. The master's face was set in a stone mask, but Gib was still glad to see him. Somehow, it was comforting to have an authority figure present.

Roland cast shrewd, calculating eyes around the ragtag group. "The bastard's already changed the rules, I see. Fantastic." With a grunt of displeasure, he leaned against the wall and fell quiet.

Silence descended once more. Gib rested his forehead on his knees and closed his eyes. Worry still churned his stomach, making dozing impossible, but when Kezra sat beside him and drew his attention, Gib had no idea how much time had passed. Had he been sitting there a bell toll or whole marks?

Kezra sighed, her breath a wisp of air in the stagnant hall. "You're to be a witness too, then?"

Gib's eyebrows knitted. He still had no inkling what everyone was speaking about or why they were all gathered in the corridor. "Witness?"

Kezra gave a stiff nod and lowered her voice to a whisper. "Yes, for the Queen Mother's—"

The deafening bang of the council room doors flying open made both

313

Gib and Kezra jump. They scrambled to their feet an instant later when councilors began to pour out of the chamber.

"What's happened?" Hasain asked, his voice a high, panicked squeal. "What's going on?"

No one stopped to speak to him or even acknowledge his presence. Gib craned his neck, trying to see inside the dim room. Blood rushed through his ears, and he could feel the tight pounding of his heart within his chest. Had they come to a decision? Was Arden's fate decided?

General Morathi's voice carried over the crowd. "Congratulations are in order, High Councilor."

The bottom of Gib's stomach dropped. Morathi was shaking hands with Anders Malin-Rai.

"High Councilor?" Kezra gasped.

Gib cringed and turned in time to see her back away, emerald eyes wide and lips trembling.

"*How?*" She shook her head in disbelief.

Gib didn't know what to say. If Anders had been promoted to High Councilor, then where was Neetra?

Morathi made his exit, and Anders turned cold, dark eyes on the lot of them still standing in the corridor. His frown flipped into a cruel, wicked smile when he noticed his daughter among those gathered.

"Daughter, have you come to congratulate me as well?"

His voice slithered through Gib's ears, making him shudder. Anders advanced, and Kezra backed away until she met the wall and had no room left. Still feral and afraid, she reminded Gib of a caged animal.

"How?" Kezra continued to shake her head. "How did *you* become High Councilor?"

Anders smiled. "Good old-fashioned work ethic, my gem." The sugar-sweet lilt in his voice was darkly reminiscent of Zandi's, and it made Gib want to vomit. "If you had any idea how to be a real woman, you'd understand work ethic and the rewards it grants."

Kezra pulled her mouth into a wild snarl. "What gives you the authority to judge how a woman should behave?"

Anders' smile slipped away as he strode closer, trapping Kezra against the wall. Gib thought to call for help, but everyone else was so absorbed in watching the council room doors they didn't even seem to notice what was happening right in front of them. Anders extended one hand, touching her neck. He spoke to his daughter in a low, husky tone. "With the new authority granted me, I could surely show you how to be a proper woman."

Gib felt his stomach clench, fighting to retch. Was this how Kezra's father had always treated her? No one should ever have to tolerate this—

A shriek erupted from Kezra's mouth as she slapped Anders' hand away. Everyone remaining in the hall stopped and turned to stare. The spell was broken. They were visible again.

314

"You don't get to touch me!" Kezra's wail pierced the frozen air. With teeth bared and fire in her eyes, she reached out and shoved Anders, sending him lurching back. *"Never again!"*

The silence was suffocating. No matter how hard Gib sucked air into his lungs, he couldn't catch his breath. The commotion had drawn the attention of Nawaz and Roland. Both men were on their way, crossing the room in long strides, their sights set on the new High Councilor.

Anders seemed to sense his time was up. Straightening his robes, he coolly addressed his daughter. "You'll learn your place one day. If I have to beat it into you myself, you'll learn." He turned and fled with a clenched jaw and nose high in the air.

Kezra's hands balled into fists. "I'll be your undoing, Anders Malin-Rai. You can count on it!" Her words chased after him, but in the chaos, it was anyone's guess as to whether he heard.

Nawaz reached out a tentative hand as he came within arm's length. "Are you all right?"

Kezra slapped the hand away and turned her back on him. With a red face, Nawaz tromped over to stand beside Joel on the opposing wall. Gib wrung his own hands together, wanting to offer words of solace but not daring to speak.

Harsh words shot through the open door, and Gib turned away from Kezra in time to see Koal and Marc bustle out from the depths of the council room. Koal's head was twisted around as he argued with someone still too far inside the chamber for Gib to see.

"Is this your final word on it then? You've both signed the scroll. If you wish to contest the decisions, now is the time." A cold chill settled in Gib's heart. He knew that voice. He'd recognize Liro Adelwijn's airy hiss anywhere.

Koal rounded on his son as if meaning to strike him, but Liro didn't so much as flinch. "You have my signature and Arden has my loyalty. You and that bastard have my answer!"

Liro's eyes were fierce and glad. "Be careful, Seneschal. You claim loyalty to Arden yet insult her new steward. I'm sure you're aware such a thing is viewed as treason."

Koal clenched his hands into fists. "Neetra may be steward, but my devotion is to Arden alone. I support her *king*."

"Arden has no king."

No one in the hall moved. No one even dared breathe. The silence was tangible, encompassing, and terrible.

Koal took a single step forward, looking down on his elder son with cold, unfeeling eyes. "For now. And I promise you, Liro Adelwijn, should I ever find out who is responsible for that, I'll deliver swift justice myself. No one, for any reason, shall be spared my wrath on that day."

Liro's smug demeanor faltered. For just a moment, Gib could see rage, perhaps even terror, flash behind the young lord's cold eyes. Liro had himself under absolute control an instant later, leaving Gib to doubt whether he'd actually witnessed the display of emotion at all.

"Why was *he* allowed in there?" Hasain asked as he pushed his way to the front of the crowd. "Understudies weren't granted entrance today!"

Liro cocked his head to the side and turned an arrogant smile onto Hasain. "Oh, haven't you heard? I'm not an understudy, bastard. I've been elected onto the High Council."

Hasain stumbled back a step, his face white as a sheet. "H–how?"

"It would seem the tables have turned, Radek." Liro's savage voice lashed Hasain. "Does it infuriate you to know I've claimed my rightful place while you still try to ignore yours? Does the knowledge that you *never were* my equal make you feel slighted in some way?"

Koal lurched forward, and Gib was certain that if Roland and Marc hadn't immediately stepped in to catch the seneschal's arms, he would have struck Liro this time.

Hasain didn't even seem to notice. Shaking his head, he turned a stunned, blank expression onto the newly elected councilor. "Your promotion doesn't infuriate me. It terrifies me. Arden will falter and fail in treacherous hands such as yours."

Liro's cold mask cracked yet again. "How dare you—"

Neetra's shrill call from within the council chamber drew Liro's attention, and he pursed his lips, momentarily caught between venting his wrath and following the commands of the apparent steward.

"That's right, Liro," Marc taunted with dead eyes. "Run. Your master beckons."

With a final growl, Liro turned on his heel and slunk away.

Gib watched the lord's back as he disappeared into the gloom of the council chamber. What would happen now? Was Neetra really in control of the country? Had Liro truly been voted onto the High Council?

Koal's hard stare fell across the hall. "Follow me, all of you. There's no time to explain."

No one said a word as they followed behind the seneschal. Gib wanted to question someone—anyone—but his jumbled mind couldn't think of anything to say, so he lowered his head and ran to keep up with the group.

"Koal, what happened in there?" Nawaz's voice rose above their thundering footsteps.

Koal didn't pause or stop. "Neetra is steward. Anders is High Councilor. They tried to have me removed as seneschal, but they failed by one vote."

"How did Liro get voted on?" Hasain's hands trembled as he walked just ahead of Gib. "Weren't there objections?"

"Oh, there were objections," Marc replied. "But not enough. This whole thing was planned. There's no way in hell it wasn't."

Diddy's words tumbled from his mouth as if he couldn't catch his breath. "There must be something we can do! This is treason!"

"No proof." Koal didn't even glance back as they ascended to the second floor, and Gib realized where they were heading. The hall of royal portraits loomed before them. "And at this point," the seneschal continued in a terse voice, "I don't even know who to appeal to. The numbers are quickly shifting from our favor."

"What about the Radek line?" Hasain asked. "And the rest of us? What about our family?"

They lurched to such a sudden stop that Gib collided into Nawaz's back, grazing the wooden crossbow slung over his shoulder. In lighter times, it would have been comical, but now it barely warranted more than a shared glance between them.

Koal put his hands on either of Hasain's shoulders and looked him squarely in the eye. "You know I served your father and his reign. I will sooner die than allow your family—any of them—to be hurt or tossed aside. That's why we have to hurry now." Koal's eyes skimmed the group, lingering on Kezra. "Are we *sure* everyone here is an ally?"

Gib took Kezra's rigid hand on reflex. "Anders Malin-Rai's children are their own. Kezra is our friend."

Koal must have been satisfied with the answer given. He nodded and swept off, leaving them all running to catch up. They were nearly to the royal suite before Gib realized he was still grasping Kezra's hand. She stared at the floor with a dark face, but her firm grip led him to believe his presence wasn't unwanted.

Blessed Mage Natori lingered beneath the tall doorframe of the royal suite and quickly ushered the entire group inside. Battle-ready with sword drawn and a strange, blue mage orb hovering above, she looked fierce and formidable.

Natori waved each of them through the threshold, but Gib hesitated for just a moment. *Our boots. We're supposed to remove our boots.* No one did, and in the next instant, he was being pushed along and had no choice but to move forward.

Inside the suite, the other Blessed Mage, NezReth, stood beside Bailey. The servant leaned over a candlelit table, never glancing up as his quill scratched maddeningly at an open sheet of parchment.

NezReth's uncanny violet eyes didn't blink even once as he observed the group. "Our worst case scenario has been realized then?"

Koal shook his head. "Not quite. I've retained my position as seneschal, but the rest is a wash. We need to do this now."

Gib fumbled as Roland grabbed hold of his arm. "Someone get Gib a sword!"

What is going on? Gib's head swam as the Weapons Master drew his own weapon and pointed for Gib and Kezra to join him beside Natori at the front door. Koal vanished deeper into the suite before returning with a heavy broadsword. The seneschal thrust the weapon at Gib, and he grimaced, feeling the tension in his shoulders. The blade was too long for him. Typical.

"It'll have to do," Koal said, giving Gib a thump on the arm before spinning around. "Joel, Nawaz, to the balcony window. Hasain, you too, just in case."

Gib watched in bewilderment as Nawaz nocked a bolt into his bow, and blue fire burst to life in the palms of Hasain's and Joel's hands as they pooled their mage energy.

Gib couldn't take it anymore. "What are we doing, exactly?"

"Saving someone from being exiled," Hasain replied without even sparing Gib a glance.

It was all too much. An excess of questions tumbled around Gib's mind as he tried to make sense of it all. *Exiled? Who? Why does everyone have a weapon? Are we expecting an attack?* Fed up, Gib groaned and raised his question once more. "I know I'm not supposed to ask, but will someone *please* tell me what the hell is going on?"

"A wedding, Master Nemesio," replied a gentle voice.

Queen Mother Dahlia stepped into the room without any of her usual grace or charm, her beautiful face drawn into a mockery of itself and large, brown eyes heavy with exhaustion. Little Princess Gudrin clung to one of her arms while Crowned Prince Deegan trailed just behind her.

"I'm not much fit to be a bride today," Dahlia continued in a pained tone. "But I doubt my brother will allow me to wait."

"You know this will be one of Neetra's first orders," Koal said, his own voice labored by regret. "It has to be done now."

Bailey's quill scribbled furiously. "He has to be knighted first. He can't marry the Queen Mother unless he's of noble descent. Hurry."

A commotion arose from the other room as Marc and Diddy scrambled out with Aodan in tow. The bodyguard reminded Gib of a wild-man, with disheveled red hair and single eye wide with unease. Marc and Diddy all but shoved Aodan into position between Dahlia and Koal.

"Knight him, Koal." NezReth's breathy words were barely louder than a whisper. "And then move aside so I can marry them. Time is likely running short."

Koal drew his sword in one swift motion and turned to face Aodan. "Kneel."

Aodan did as he was told, visibly shaking. Gudrin left her mother's side to set one, small hand on the bodyguard's back. Deegan did the same, offering silent support.

Placing the tip of his blade first on Aodan's left shoulder and then the right, Koal proceeded with the ceremony. "For the protection of

Arden and her people, by the power vested in me, Lord Seneschal Koal Adelwijn, I proclaim you Master Aodan Galloway, knight of Arden. Arise."

Dahlia and Aodan were as grave as they'd been the day before at the King's funeral when NezReth stepped in front of them with an open text resting in the palms of his hands. No professions of love were declared while the Blessed Mage read the wedding rites aloud. Bride and groom stood stone-faced, staring at NezReth with vacant eyes. When asked if they agreed to be wed, each responded with a simple yes and aye, respectively. No rings were given nor were pleasantries exchanged. Gloom filled every corner of the room. Gib could almost taste it on the air.

NezReth closed the ancient text so sharply a cloud of dust spewed forth from within the yellowed pages. "By the power vested in me, I declare you husband and wife."

It was over. The Queen Mother and her bodyguard were married.

Bailey wasted no time. He cleared his throat, motioning down at the drying parchment papers. "You're all to be witnesses. You'll have to sign both documents."

Gib hadn't even processed everything that had just happened when Roland jerked his head around and issued a cautionary grunt. "There's noise in the hall! We're about to have guests!"

Bailey made an undignified noise as he called for the witnesses to come forward. "Don't knock over the inkwell. Bride and groom, sign your names! Aodan, sign this one as well—Koal, you too, but not the marriage license. Family cannot bear witness. All right, everyone gather around. Step forward and sign both documents now. *Hurry!*"

In a rush of bodies, they all clambered over to the table. Gib fumbled as he picked up the quill and etched his name onto both sheets of parchment. He handed the writing utensil to Hasain next and scrambled aside, watching as everyone else took their turn.

Just as Bailey had finished scratching his own name in place, Natori hissed a warning from the doorway. "*Now!* They're here!"

Gripping the oversized sword, Gib staggered his stance, body tense and mind sharp, ready to fight if need be. The sound of clanking armor and marching boots filled his ears. He held his breath, waiting.

Half a dozen soldiers rounded the corner, clad in head-to-toe armor and swords swaying on their hips. Liro led the procession, his long strides haughty and confident. A single mage orb floated above his right shoulder, the hazy blue light illuminating the corridor and reflecting off the newly elected councilor's gleaming eyes.

"Lower your weapons!" Liro demanded as he came to a stop in front of the royal suite. The sentinels waited behind him with hands resting on hilts. "By order of the Steward of Arden, I command you to do as I say!"

Natori sneered, but she and Roland exchanged a heavy look before lowering their blades. Gib and Kezra did the same, following the example

319

given them.

Liro's smile was arrogant. "Good. Now part and let us through. I have orders to collect one Aodan Galloway."

Gudrin and Deegan both wailed from behind Dahlia, and on reflex, Diddy and Tular stepped up to flank Aodan. The bodyguard fell back a pace and watched, poised as if to flee, as Liro slithered through the crowded room. The newest member of the High Council held a scroll in hand. He waved it as shrewd eyes locked onto his target. "Ah, there you are, Derr. I have been sent to see you home. It would seem you've finally managed to outstay your welcome."

Aodan shook his head but words failed him. When Liro came even closer, the bodyguard cast a wild glance toward the balcony. Gib held his breath. *Don't jump. Don't do it. You'll break your neck.*

Venom dripped from Liro's fangs like a viper. "Is the caged bird contemplating escape?"

"What the hell is the meaning of this?" Koal demanded. The seneschal's unwavering presence brought sanity back to the situation. "Why are you here?"

Liro held the scroll out, waving it beneath his father's nose. "To deport the foreigner, of course. Perhaps you'd like to read the decree yourself?"

"*No!*" Gudrin let out a yelp and tore away from the Queen Mother. The little girl launched herself into Aodan's arms, clinging to him for dear life.

Koal barely spared a moment for the display. His stanch eyes were fixed onto his eldest son. "As seneschal of Arden, I tell you there is no foreigner among us. Aodan Galloway is a knighted noble, and his marriage to Queen Mother Dahlia Adelwijn affords him permanent residency in Arden."

Conflict flickered behind Liro's eyes as he paused and looked around the room. "That's not—that's—*impossible!*"

Bailey, still fanning the damp ink on the parchment, glared at the young lord from his position behind the table. "Oh, but I'm afraid it's *not* impossible. See for yourself, young Master, and then go tell that tyrant, Neetra Adelwijn, that he's too late!"

Gib watched as Liro floundered, mouth agape. When the councilor turned to look at the sentinels who'd accompanied him, they wouldn't meet his terrible gaze. Red faced, Liro drew his mouth into a thin line. He knew he was beaten. A smile crossed Gib's lips. This victory—small as it was—was a victory nonetheless.

"You may take your leave now, Councilor Liro." Koal's stance was rigid, one hand still hovering over the hilt of his sword and expression unreadable.

Liro scowled, baring white teeth. Raising one hand, he pointed furiously at Aodan. "Don't think this is the end! We're watching you, monster!" Aodan remained colorless, but he clutched Princess Gudrin tightly and dared meet the manic eyes of his oppressor. Liro snarled all the louder. "And we're watching *all* of your little monster bastards as well. How long can a bird stay caged without spreading its wings?"

Gib watched in bewilderment, beginning to think Liro truly had lost his mind. *What is he ranting about? Why is he talking like that?*

"Enough rambling from mad men," Koal growled. "Leave already."

Balling his hands, Liro strode toward the door without a further word. His silence was enough of an indicator of his bruised pride, and Gib couldn't help but smile wider. It felt good to have something to celebrate again—

Liro's cold stare bore into Gib, and he realized an instant later that he might have embraced the conquest too soon.

"So this is the vacant grin of a peasant." Liro sneered down at Gib as he passed by. "I suppose your utter lack of education can be blamed for that, but this—" The councilor licked his thumb and rubbed it across Gib's cheek before he could even think to balk. "Look, the dirt is so ingrained it won't even wash off. What game do you play at, thinking you'll ever be equal to the likes of me?"

"Enough sulking! Be gone!" Koal's savage reprimand boomed off the walls and made everyone jump. Gib would have shied away too, if not for the emptiness serving to ground him.

Liro rolled his eyes and headed for the door, but Gib's hand shot out on its own accord and grabbed the councilor's forearm, preventing him from taking another step. Words were falling from Gib's mouth before he could tell himself to stop. "I would never dream of being your equal, Liro. There's nothing about you I wish to become. You may appear flawless on the outside, but that pristine façade hides the ugly truth. Inside, you're ugly and dead."

Liro yanked his arm away. "How dare you speak to me that way, you filthy little—"

"Time's up. Last warning." Koal crossed the room in three long paces. "Need I escort *you* from the room, Councilor?"

Liro's mouth dropped open, but he made no sound. Scarlet rage stole over his face before he turned on his heel and stalked away, the royal sentinels marching twice as fast to catch up. The sound of receding footsteps echoed down the corridor until it faded entirely.

Gib set a hand against the doorframe to steady himself. Despite Kezra at his side and Koal's hand gripping his shoulder, he felt like his knees might give out. Distantly, he lifted his arm to wipe the grimy spot on his cheek where Liro had touched it.

"Are you all right?" Koal's placid voice helped bring Gib back to the present.

He shuddered when, for a moment, he thought perhaps everyone would be watching him, but it came as a great relief to find almost no one paid him any attention at all.

The royal family had collapsed on itself, and quiet tears were being shared as they embraced one another. Aodan looked like hell. Still blanched from his close encounter, he leaned heavily between Diddy and Tular, and Gib was certain if either young man moved, the bodyguard would have toppled to the floor. Gudrin cried into Deegan's side while Queen Mother Dahlia rubbed the little girl's shoulders, doing all she could to comfort the princess with soft murmurs. Their desperation was difficult for Gib to watch, but at least the family hadn't been torn apart by Neetra's tyranny. Not yet, anyway.

"Would you like Natori and me to accompany you?" NezReth asked as Koal took the newly scribed documents from Bailey's hand.

"If you would," replied Koal, taking care not to crumple the parchment. "Marc and Roland are going to escort me as well."

The Blessed Mage folded his arms. "With so many of us present, no one will be able to deny the documents were delivered."

"Indeed. I'm going to stay and watch them as they're recorded. Knighting and marrying Aodan won't do us any good if the documentation is 'lost' or tampered with." Tired eyes scanned the room before Koal lifted his voice to address everyone present. "All of you young ones, any who aren't staying, feel free to take your leave now. So long as you've signed both scrolls, you're dismissed."

Kezra's elbow nudged Gib in the ribs. "I'm going to leave now."

Gib had to trot to keep up as she slipped through the door in a rush. "I'll walk with you."

They weren't ten steps outside the suite before they heard a commotion as the others scrambled into the corridor. Glancing over his shoulder, Gib saw Nawaz running to close the gap between them. Joel lingered near the doorway, hands at his throat as his disconcerted eyes watched his cousin.

"Kezra." Nawaz somehow managed to keep his voice neutral, but his face was beet red. When she didn't acknowledge him or slow her pace, the young lord raised a yell. "Kezra!" Gib pressed his back to the wall as Nawaz sprinted past. Reaching out, he grabbed for Kezra's arm, but she twisted away, barely breaking stride. Nawaz let out an exasperated sigh. "At least look at me!"

Kezra whirled around so fast Gib winced, sure she was going to punch her scorned lover again. The blow never came. She clenched her hands, but they remained at her side as she turned feral eyes onto Nawaz. "*What?*"

"Are you just going to pretend I don't exist?" Nawaz asked, chest heaving. "Damn it, Kezra, I had no choice!" His voice was labored and

322

bursting with hurt. "You refused me and I had to marry! Won't you at least speak to me?"

Kezra's dark face contorted. "How's your *wife?*"

Nawaz locked his jaw. Even from a distance Gib could see the indignation and despair carved onto his face. "Pregnant, if you really must know."

His devastated, broken voice struck Gib hard in the chest, and Kezra's eyes went wide. She took one teetering step backward. "You—you lie. Tell me it's a lie."

Nawaz hung his head. "We were going to announce it sooner, but then everything with King Rishi happened and there just hasn't been a good time. I–I wanted to tell you in person." Tears glistened in his hollow eyes when he next raised his gaze. "I'm sorry, love. I'm so sorry."

He reached for her again, this time toward her face, but Kezra rejected the touch. Shaking her head in disbelief, she turned and fled.

Nawaz didn't give chase. Instead, he leaned against the stone corridor and buried his face in his hands. The sounds of wracked sobbing echoed down the corridor, the only noise to be heard in the entire palace. Sucking in a deep breath, Gib began to cross over to his friend, unsure what words could possibly be said to comfort him but determined to lend support. Nawaz had been there for Gib in his time of need, after all.

Gib stopped short when he noticed Joel had crept over and placed a hand on Nawaz's shoulder. One glance down the hall confirmed Hasain was also on the way, mouth twisted into a grimace as his guild-laden eyes studied his friend. Gib silently backed away. Joel and Hasain knew the young lord better than anyone. If they couldn't bring solace to Nawaz's shattered soul, then what hope did Gib have? Head down, he departed, wanting nothing more than to return to Academy and leave this entire mess behind.

"Gib!"

Joel had to raise his voice to be heard above the rolling thunder. Lightning flashed across the sky, illuminating black clouds, heavy with rain, and a tepid breeze rushed through the palace courtyard, the powerful gusts blowing Joel's hair about his face.

The bottom of his robe brushed the cobblestones as he trudged forward, never taking his eyes off Gib's back. The events of the day were a whirlwind in Joel's mind. With the election of Neetra Adelwijn as Arden's new steward, the country's worst fears had been realized. Liro's promotion onto the High Council came as a double blow. Everything King Rishi had worked so hard to accomplish was now at risk of crumbling, including the

King's own family.

"Gib, wait!" Joel called again. He'd been trailing his former companion since leaving the royal suite. Assured by Hasain that he'd see Nawaz home safely, Joel had run to catch up with Gib. They needed to talk. "Gibben Nemesio, *stop!*"

Ahead, Gib slowed his pace but didn't stop or turn to face Joel. The mage quickened his steps, closing the remaining distance between them in a matter of seconds. As he came within arm's length, Gib lurched to a dead halt and twisted his head around.

"Please," Joel said, sides heaving as he gasped for air. "Please talk to me."

A single, icy raindrop fell from the sky, splattering onto the tip of his nose and cascading down his cheek. Only a moment later, a deafening crash of thunder tore through the night, announcing the impending storm. The sky above opened, and sheets of rain began to pelt the palace courtyard.

Neither Gib nor Joel moved. Within the blink of an eye, their clothing soaked through and clung to their bodies like a second layer of skin. Lightning flashed in the distance, giving Joel a clear view of the twisted grimace contorting Gib's handsome face.

"Is this how you want it to be?" Joel screamed above the gale. "Fighting, barely speaking to each other? Like Nawaz and Kezra? Is that how you'd have us be, Gib? Strangers? Enemies?"

Gib's strained voice fought to be heard over the roaring wind. "This is what you wanted! I *tried* to be there for you, but you drove me away! You told me to live my life!"

"I didn't mean for us to never speak again!" Joel wiped a strand of drenched hair out of his face, absently noting Gib's crown of chestnut curls were plastered atop his head. "I can't go on like this. I can't keep pretending like we never met!"

Water cascaded down the small creases in Gib's face, dripping from his nose and chin. "It's too late, Joel. I've moved on. I can't—can't keep doing this with you. We had our chance and it didn't work out."

Joel's stomach heaved as bitter bile rose to tickle the back of his throat. So it was true. The kiss between Zandi Malin-Rai and Gib hadn't just been a casual gesture. Gib really was pursuing someone new.

Another clap of thunder crackled through the night sky, and Joel cringed. Rain lashed his face, tempering the jealousy manifesting in his chest. "I'm not asking to be your companion. I just want you in my life. As friends or any other way you'd have me. Just—" He reached out, latching onto Gib's soaked sleeve. "Just please, don't walk away again. I–I need you. We need each other, now more than ever before."

Gib glared at the ground. A river of rainwater flowed beneath their boots, forming white peaks as the wind whipped it across the courtyard.

When Gib looked up, his teeth were chattering. "With everything that's happened as of late, I just wish we could talk, like we used to."

Raking numb fingers through his dripping hair, Joel nodded. "A talk would be nice—somewhere dry, preferably." He peered through the downpour, into the darkness beyond the alabaster fountains and shriveled shrubbery. "Come to the estate with me. We can be out of the rain and have some privacy."

An eternity passed before Gib replied in a hushed tone, barely audible above the tempest. "All right. Lead the way."

When they arrived at the Adelwijn estate, Mrifa herself let them inside. "Where's your father?" she asked, moving aside so they could enter the foyer.

Joel turned to close the door, struggling against the might of the gusting wind. "He's still at the palace. Mother, I have to tell you something. Neetra has been made—"

"I know." Mrifa set a hand on his forearm. "Word spread quickly about your uncle's promotion. Tabitha overheard the news while she was at market and rushed home to tell us." She pursed her lips. "What of Dahlia and Aodan? Your father was worried Neetra might try something foul."

"They're married," Joel replied at once. "Gib and I were witnesses to it. They'd barely signed the documents before Liro came and tried to banish Aodan from the country!"

"Liro?" Mrifa's eye widened. "Why Liro?"

Joel's chest tightened. He was doing all he could to remain composed, but he could feel the deep, agonizing hopelessness seeping into his veins. He hung his head. "Liro's been promoted. He's on the High Council now."

Mrifa's hand shot to her mouth, stifling a gasp. "Oh no."

"What's going to happen to Arden?" Joel asked, his voice quivering. "With Neetra and Liro in power and the King dead, I just don't know how Father is going to keep everything from falling apart."

Mrifa reached up and set her hands against Joel's cheeks, gripping his face the way she might comfort a small child. "You don't worry about that right now. Go sit by the fire and warm yourselves, both of you. I'm going to brew you a pot of tea."

Mrifa ruffled Gib's hair and spared him an affectionate smile as she hurried off in the direction of the kitchen. Joel blinked, watching the interaction. It was his fault Gib never visited the rest of the Adelwijn family anymore. He was the reason Mrifa and the girls hadn't seen Gib in two moonturns. *I have to try to fix this. If not for my sake, then for the sake of my family.*

They love Gib as much as I do. He's a part of our family, whether he knows it or not.

Joel motioned with one hand for Gib to follow. "Come on. Let's go sit by the fire and talk."

Half a mark and one quick mage spell later, they sat in front of the hearth with dry clothes and warmed blood. Otos had entered briefly to stoke the fire. Now the flames roared high, nearly drowning out the sound of rain thwacking the terracotta roof above.

Joel had been holding his hands out, close to the fireplace, to warm his fingertips. He withdrew them and set them in his lap. Out of the corner of his eye, he saw his former companion doing the same. Drowsy heat beckoned Joel to relax, but his melancholy thoughts couldn't be quelled.

Everything had happened so fast. Four mornings ago, he'd been sitting in Marc's office, making plans to start his life over, and now King Rishi was dead and Joel's wicked uncle was in control of the High Council and probably all of Arden. And then, to be rushed into the royal suite and asked to bear witness to Dahlia and Aodan's marriage—Joel blinked. It all seemed so incredulous. Was anything in his life real anymore, or had he been existing in one unending nightmare since returning from Shantar?

"It's strange to be back here." Gib's *very* real voice cut through the room, as sharp as a needle.

The young man stared straight ahead, firelight flickering in his chestnut eyes. Perfectly placed stoicism masked any emotions he might be feeling, frustrating Joel to no end. There had been a time when they'd both known one another's thoughts even before words could be spoken. Now Joel couldn't even fathom a guess as to what Gib might be contemplating. *How did we drift so far apart?*

"It's strange to have you back here," Joel replied quietly. "It seems like so much time has passed since we last sat in this room together, but it really hasn't been all that long if you think about it."

Gib sighed, pulling his hands tight against his chest and holding them there, clenched together. "I'd almost forgotten how welcoming it feels when I walk through the front door."

Joel turned to stare at the other man. "You're *always* welcome here, Gib. Regardless of anything concerning you and me. Mother and Father think of you as a son. They love you. You know that, right?"

Gib nodded, still refusing to meet Joel's imploring gaze. "I know. I love them, too. It's just—it's hard—" His voice shook. "I hate this. I hate this wall between us."

"I know." Joel wrapped his arms around his frail shoulders, the warmth of the fire not enough to ward off the chill creeping down his spine. "I never wanted this to happen. I never intended for us to be strangers. I—" Tears stung his eyes as he took a gasping breath. "I miss you horribly, Gib. You—you're my best friend. You know me better than anyone else in the world."

"I've missed you, too." Gib toyed with a loose curl absently. "And I'd rather have you in my life as a friend than not at all."

"I feel the same," Joel said, staring into the swelling flames. "Now, more than ever, we need to stick together. All of us do. Dark times lie ahead, but in numbers we can find strength. The friendships we've forged have never been more important than they are right now."

Gib shifted in his seat and turned to look at Joel. "What do you suppose will happen? With Neetra being in control?"

For a long time Joel remained quiet. He didn't know. How could he? He wished to The Two that he'd been born with the ability to glimpse the future, but foresight had never been one of his gifts. There was no real way of knowing what lay ahead. His gut feeling was one of dark foreboding, too terrible to think of, let alone speak aloud. Nothing good could ever come of Neetra being elected steward.

He sighed. "Who knows what fate has in store for us? All we can really do is hope for the best and prepare for the worst." Joel offered a rigid smile but knew the gesture fell flat. In the moment, he couldn't have pretended to be confident even if his life depended on it. How could he, with so much at stake?

A severe frown crossed Gib's mouth. "King Rishi is dead and your uncle has Arden under his thumb, right where he's always wanted it. It's hard to imagine things getting any worse than they already are."

Joel opened his mouth to respond but was cut short by the squeal of hinges as the front door flew open. A burst of wind surged through the hall, tempting the flames inside the hearth to dance higher yet. Footsteps rushed from deeper within the house, and a moment later, Joel could hear his mother's alarmed voice rise in the foyer. "Koal, what is it? What's happened?"

The heavy door slammed shut. Joel felt his body go taut even as Gib sat up straighter on the lounge. Their eyes met briefly, and seeing the terror painted across Gib's face, Joel's blood ran cold. Putting a hand to his mouth, Joel stared into the shadowed corridor, listening and waiting, all the while knowing something was terribly, *terribly* wrong.

"What happened? *Koal?*" Mrifa's soft tone had gone shrill.

The seneschal's troubled voice drifted down the corridor like a breath of winter air. "Neetra just declared war. Arden will march on Shiraz."

The music and merriment of the Rose Bouquet was lost on Gib. He sat at a table far to the back of the tavern, a drink in hand, and watched as people danced around the open space beneath the stage. On the raised platform, a quartet of musicians played crisp, jolly music. The melancholy whine of the fiddle and rhythmic beating of hand drums mingled in Gib's ears like they'd been created to be together. The sound should have brought peace to his weary soul, but he could find none tonight.

News of the impending war had spread through the city like wildfire. Some people reacted with fear and hysteria. Others were making sure to live each moment to its fullest. Life at the tavern seemed to carry on as normal, though perhaps it was only that way because the ale clouded people's judgments and made it easier to forget war was upon them.

On the dance floor, Nia Leal held Nage as if he were the only person in the world as he swept her around in his arms. Gib traced the top of his mug and tried not to envy his friend. He was happy for Nage and truly hoped the soldier had found happiness. Hopefully Nage and Nia would never have to second guess their love. With any luck, distance and war wouldn't break them, leaving them shattered and devastated, as it had done to him and Joel.

Tarquin cleared his throat from across the table. He'd been quiet all evening. "Where did Zandi get off to?" He wasn't really curious, Gib could tell by the tone, but it wasn't in Tarquin's nature to endure grim silence.

"Over at the bar, with his librarian friend." Gib nodded vaguely but felt no more detail was needed. After all, neither of them really wanted to be having this conversation. He could tell by the uncomfortable shift of Tarquin's weight and the slant of his mouth that he was thinking heavily on something. This war may well be his end before they ever marched.

At long last, Tarquin leaned across the table. "It never seemed real before, you know? When I signed up to be a sentinel trainee, I never thought I'd actually be faced with war. Father says we all let our guard down. We grew too accustomed to King Rishi's peaceful rule."

Gib grimaced, wishing he felt more inclined to indulge his friend's worries. "I suppose so. I wonder how all the councilors feel about voting in Neetra now that he's declared *war*."

Tarquin pulled back, his face pinching with offense. "I have no proof one way or the other, but I seriously doubt my father's vote was for Neetra."

Gib rubbed his face. He hadn't meant for his words to sound so snide. "Damn it. I'm sorry. That's not what I meant. I'm just—my head's full right now. You understand, don't you?"

The blotchy crimson on Tarquin's face began to drain. He slumped back in his seat and sighed. "Yeah. I guess. We're all on edge, aren't we? It won't be long before we march for Shiraz." Tarquin drummed his fingers on the tabletop and gazed around the tavern. He opened his mouth to say more, but at that moment, his attention was captured. The young lord went red all over again as his troubled eyes locked onto something past Gib's head. Muttering about refilling his mug, Tarquin quickly scooted out of the chair and trudged away.

Gib turned to call after him but stopped short when Kezra dumped herself into the seat Tarquin had just vacated. Her eyes were red, her cheeks wet, and her tankard empty.

Gib blinked, raising his eyebrows in shock. "Kezra? Are you all right?"

She shook her head at first, unable to speak. When she finally opened her mouth, her bottom lip quivered and she had to wipe at her puffy eyes. "You ever worry you chose wrong? What if—what if you said or did something and now it's too late to go back?" Her raw voice tugged at Gib's heart.

Gib took a deep breath. His mind drifted back to the sight of Nawaz crumpled over in the palace hall, mourning the same loss Kezra was now. When Gib tried to think of something to say to her, anything that might be of use, he kept coming back to himself and Joel. Was this all there was in life? Did he really have to sit here and tell her no, she wouldn't ever actually get over Nawaz, but she might get to the point where they could pretend to be friends again? Was it even worth it to pretend?

"We all make mistakes," Gib heard himself whisper. "And not everything in life goes according to plan. I guess we just have to figure out how to live with it."

The words weren't as heartfelt and supportive as he'd have liked them to be. Some part of him really did want to hug her and tell her everything would look better tomorrow. But he wouldn't do it. Not to Kezra. Even a gentle lie was no good for a friend such as her.

Kezra huffed a wry chuckle. "With Neetra in charge, I guess we probably won't have to live with it too long, eh, Gib?" She wiped her nose with the back of a sleeve. "I suppose at least I can look forward to that. Nawaz will be safe here. He can keep his nobility and have his family. I'll go and do what I've told myself I wanted to do since I was old enough to hold a wooden blade. He'll have Neetra's favor, and I'll no longer be a source of shame for Anders. Everyone wins."

Gib smiled—a sad, defeated beam, but a smile nonetheless. It seemed the wrong sort of thing to laugh at, yet here he was, lifting his mug and chuckling along. "Here's to whatever comes. May we meet it head on, with bravery."

Though her own drink was empty, Kezra inclined her head and joined him. Their tankards clanked as they met. "May we embrace the nightfall as warriors. And with any luck, live to see a new dawn."

FINAL WORD

Arden stands on the edge of the sword. Neetra Adelwijn has taken rule as steward and declared war on Shiraz. The Radek bloodline has kept its secrets so far, but with the King dead and family broken, they may not be able to hold onto their power—and what lies inside one little box could seal the fate of not only the Radeks, but the entire country. What terrors await Gib, Joel, Kezra, and their friends when they march to war? ***Battle Dawn: Book Three of the Chronicles of Arden***, is coming in fall 2015!

If you would like to receive notifications regarding upcoming releases, please sign up for Shiriluna Nott's mailing list below. We only send updates when a new book is released.

If you enjoyed *Nightfall*, please consider leaving a review on Amazon.com. It would be very much appreciated.

Please sign up for the mailing list;
http://www.shirilunanott.com/mailinglist.html

Shiriluna's Goodreads page;
https://www.goodreads.com/author/show/9757614.Shiriluna_Nott

'Like' us on Facebook;
Shiriluna Nott's Author Page;
https://www.facebook.com/authorshirilunanott
and
SaJa H.'s Author Page
https://www.facebook.com/pages/SaJa-H/794070493991829

Follow us on Twitter;
@ShirilunaNott and @SaJaH_ofArden

Official Website
http://www.shirilunanott.com

Made in the USA
San Bernardino, CA
09 February 2018